IT MIGHT BE YOU

Jennifer Gracen

ZEBRA BOOKS
KENSINGTON PUBLISHING CORP.
http://www.kensingtonbooks.com

ZEBRA BOOKS are published by

Kensington Publishing Corp.
119 West 40th Street
New York, NY 10018

All Kensington titles, imprints, and distributed lines are available at special quantity discounts for bulk purchases for sales promotion, premiums, fund-raising, educational, or institutional use.

Special book excerpts or customized printings can also be created to fit specific needs. For details, write or phone the office of the Kensington Sales Manager: Attn.: Sales Department. Kensington Publishing Corp., 119 West 40th Street, New York, NY 10018. Phone: 1-800-221-2647.

Zebra and the Z logo Reg. U.S. Pat. & TM Off.

First Printing: March 2018
ISBN-13: 978-1-4201-4530-4
ISBN-10: 1-4201-4530-4

eISBN-13: 978-1-4201-4531-1
eISBN-10: 1-4201-4531-2

10 9 8 7 6 5 4 3 2 1

Printed in the United States of America

IT MIGHT BE YOU

Books by Jennifer Gracen

The Harrisons

It Might Be You
Between You and Me
'Tis the Season
Someone Like You
More Than You Know

and novella

Happily Ever After

*To all the readers who took
the journey and read this series,
thank you so much for loving the Harrisons.*

This one's for you.

ACKNOWLEDGMENTS

Writing this seems to get harder every time. This book ends the Harrisons series, and that's bittersweet. It's been an amazing, life-changing ride for me. So, so, so grateful.

Thank you times a gazillion to my amazing editor, Esi Sogah, who took a chance on me and opened the door. I'm forever in your debt. I've enjoyed working with you on this series more than I can say. So take these last sloppy hugs and go on witcha.

Thank you to my agent, Stephany Evans of Ayesha Pande Literary, who believes in me and my work, fights for me, and stands by me. So very glad you're in my corner.

Thank you to everyone at Kensington Publishing who has been involved with this series—copy editing, art department, publicity, marketing—but special thanks go to my fantastic publicist, Jane Nutter; Norma Perez-Hernandez, a bolt of light and energy; lovely Lauren Jernigan; and gentleman Ross Plotkin. I really appreciate everything you've done.

To my immediate family—my mom, Linda; my dad, Rob; my brother, Jamie; Natasha, Kyle, Teri, Stevie, and of course my sons, Josh and Danny—saying "thanks!" just doesn't cut it. But thanks. I love you the mostest.

My friends are the most incredible, eclectic collection of wonderful souls in the universe. I'm richer for knowing each and every one of you. Both local and online, I wouldn't get through without your friendship, support, cheering on, and love. You brighten my days. Thank you all from the bottom of my big, goopy heart.

Thank you to my beta reader, Nika Rhone. Your enthusiasm for my work and solid feedback helped me more than you can imagine. Big hug, lady. Thank you to Jeannie Moon and Patty Blount for being writing sisters who get it, and who I can trust . . . that's priceless. Thank you to The Quillies, my writing tribe from all over, rolled up in an FB group. You're fabulously talented, insightful, dirty, funny, smart, caring, and a safe place to land. Thank you to Amy Weaver, Janelle Jensen, and Karen DeLabar for being true sisters of the heart. I love you all so much.

Thank you to Team Gracen on FB; Dani Barclay, Michelle Forde, and everyone at Barclay Publicity; Cissy Hartley and everyone at WriterSpace.

Last but NEVER least, endless and heartfelt thanks to my readers. None of this would happen without you. Thank you for taking time out of your busy lives to escape into my work. I'm so honored and grateful that you do.

Chapter One

Nick Martell pulled up in front of his parents' house and cut the ignition. The engine on his sleek black Ford Mustang GT quieted, leaving him in silence to gather his thoughts.

He had so much to tell his family, he didn't know where to start. A gentle breeze blew, making the long leaves of the palm trees overhead sway against the soft blue of the evening sky. He let his head fall back against the seat and drew a few long, deep breaths as he looked at the house.

His mom had planted new flowers in the bigger pot by the front door, a bright hot pink. Nick grinned; it was her favorite color and always reminded him of her. He'd grown up in a modest three-bedroom home on a quiet street in a decent suburb, only five miles from the center of Miami. His father had been on the Miami police force for twenty-five years before retiring, devoted to the job and to his family. Nick had worshipped his dad as a kid, and aspired to be like him as a young adult, which was ultimately why he'd become a cop himself five years before. Five years of hard work . . . and now, some payoff. He figured his dad would be pretty proud of him tonight, and the elation of that made Nick's grin widen.

Lew Martell met Maria Sanchez when Nick was three

years old. Lew married Maria when Nick was four, and legally adopted Nick as his own when he was five. Though they didn't share blood, as far as Nick was concerned, Lew was his father in every way, and he knew to the core of his soul that Lew felt the same way. Even after a few years and two little sisters, he'd never been made to feel anything other than one hundred percent part of a family.

Now, as he walked up the front steps and unlocked the door to his parents' house, it was his father he couldn't wait to see the most. He knew his mom would be proud, but his dad would burst with it.

"Hello?" Nick called out as he stepped into the living room. The spicy aroma of his mother's cooking wafted in the air, enticing and comforting him at the same time.

"Ah!" His mother came in, rushing to hug him. She leaned back to look up into his face and held his cheeks. "You look good, *mijo*! You need a shave, but your eyes are smiling."

"I'm twenty-nine, Ma," he grumbled, teasing back. "You ever gonna stop telling me when I need to clean up?"

"No."

"I don't shave on my days off. I take a break. I've told you this."

She shrugged and made a disdainful face that clearly expressed her thoughts.

He just chuckled. Her dry sass was one of the things he loved most about her.

"So what's the big news?" she asked, her features brightening again. "And I'm glad you asked for a family dinner to share it, so I get to see you."

Nick rolled his eyes. He faithfully came for a family dinner every other Sunday. "Like you don't see me. I come by!"

"Not enough."

He groaned and nudged her gently with his elbow. "Admit it—you're just happy to have an excuse to cook something special."

"You said you had really big news, so yeah . . . I *might've* made one of your very favorites."

Nick inhaled deeply, trying to figure out what she'd made by what he smelled. A slow smile spread across his face. "Ahhh. You made *carne frita con cebolla* for me, didn't you?"

"Yes." Maria smiled and it lit up her pretty face. "Anyway, it'd been a while since I made it, so why not?"

He was six feet tall, and she was a petite five-foot-two, so he bent to kiss her cheek. "You're too good to me."

"Don't you forget it." She was clearly pleased that she'd pleased him. "So c'mon in. Your dad's out in the yard and your sisters are in their rooms. I'll get them out."

"Actually . . ." Nick rubbed the back of his neck. "You know what? Maybe it'd be good to just talk to you and Dad first. Part of the news is great, but part is . . . a little . . . well, they might not fully understand. So maybe you'll help me figure out a way to tell them that won't . . . upset them. I dunno."

Maria stilled at that, scrutinizing her son for a few seconds before saying, "I'll get your father."

Five minutes later, Maria and Lew sat together on the couch as Nick pulled over the armchair to sit directly opposite them. He took a deep breath, then ran his hands through his thick hair and over his scruffy jaw before starting.

"The best news first," he said, unable to keep from smiling. "I got the promotion. I'm going to be an investigator."

Lew let out a loud whoop and jumped to his feet. Maria's eyes shone with tears of pride. Nick laughed as his father pulled him up for a tight hug, warmed by delight.

Lew clapped him hard on the back, grasped him by the shoulders, then pulled back to look into Nick's eyes as he said, "Goddamn, I'm so proud of you, son. I mean, I wanted this for you, but I know *you* wanted this for you. You worked hard, showed your mettle. You've been a damn good officer, but you're just too smart not to . . . well, this is the right thing for you." He clapped his son's arms again, beaming with pride. "Good for you, Nick. Well done. Congratulations!"

"Thanks, Dad." Nick's throat felt thick, and he swallowed down the lump that had risen there. He'd known his dad would be proud, but this felt incredible.

"Mijo . . ." Maria stood and lifted her hands to cradle his face. "I'm so, so proud."

"Thanks, Ma." Nick knew she was happy, but also a little scared for him. That she knew being an investigator still meant dangerous work. That being the wife of a cop, and now the mother of a cop, meant she didn't sleep well every night. When her arms wrapped around his waist and squeezed tight, he hugged her back until she was the one to let go.

"When do you start?" Lew asked.

Nick took another deep breath as he released his mother. "Well . . . that's the other thing I need to tell you all about. Sit down. There's more. It's totally different, not about work."

All three of them sat, and as soon as they did, Nick launched into it. "A few years ago, I wanna say three years ago? They had a bone marrow donor drive at the station. Because Jim Connelly's nephew needed a donor."

Lew nodded. "Sure, I've heard of those. It's easy as pie, just a swab in your cheek, right?"

"Right," Nick said. "So I did it, and truthfully, I never thought about it again. But I guess they keep your name on the national and international bone marrow registry after that, because, well . . . I got a call two weeks ago. It seems I'm a match for a kid who needs a bone marrow transplant. He's got non-Hodgkin's lymphoma. Twelve years old."

Maria's eyes flew wide as Lew's brows furrowed.

"Really," Lew said.

"That's amazing," Maria murmured.

"Yeah. So . . ." Nick blew out a breath. "How do I nutshell this? First the registry contacted me to tell me the news. I agreed to being tested further, went in, gave blood and all that. Earlier this week, they called to tell me that yes, I'm a strong, viable match. I agreed to go through with it right then." He saw the worry creeping into his mother's face as he talked. "Ma, I talked for a while with a rep from the registry. I learned a lot. It's barely going to hurt. It's outpatient surgery. So please stop looking so worried, okay?"

"You're my son," she said. "And you're talking about a major medical procedure. I'm going to worry no matter what you say."

"That's your right," he said, tossing her a wink to try to lighten her up. "So here's where it gets a little unusual. Apparently, most donors and patients never meet or have contact, confidentiality rights and all. But the day after I confirmed I'd do it, the registry rep called me again. Said the father of the kid really wanted to talk to me, if I'd allow it. I figured sure, why not? I mean, I was going to do it no matter what. As soon as I heard I could help someone, there was no question in my mind I'd go through with it."

"Of course," Maria said. "That's who you are."

"So did you talk to the father?" Lew asked.

"Yeah. On Friday morning." Nick shifted in his seat, stretching out his legs to roll one ankle, then the other. "The guy couldn't be nicer, and I could hear the worry there and it really moved me. His son's just a kid. They're desperate. And long story short, I'm going."

"Where are you going?" Lew and Maria said at the same time, then looked at each other with a quick laugh.

"New York. Turns out the kid's father is some mega-rich businessman—I'm talking billionaire, like *crazy* money. Probably how he got around the whole 'getting to talk to the donor' thing. He wanted to talk to me to . . . well, offer incentive, I guess. He wanted me to understand that insurance should pay for everything that's medical, but beyond that, he wants to pay. Even offered to cover whatever pay I lose at work for taking time off. Bottom line is, he didn't want me to be worried about the expenses if it would make me decide not to go there and do it."

Nick shrugged, rolled his head to stretch out the muscles there. Something about the way his mother looked had him slightly tense. "I assured him that I was going to do it no matter what. And yeah, I took him up on the hotel. Because if I have to go back and forth to New York a few times, or stay there for longer than I thought? Might add up, I don't know."

"Nick . . ." Maria's voice sounded breathless all of a sudden. "You're going to New York?"

"Yeah, Ma. I leave the day after tomorrow." Nick watched her as he spoke; she really seemed off. He hated for her to worry about him. "On Friday, when I got the promotion, it was amazing, but terrible timing. I'd just talked to the father that morning! So I explained what happened, and that I feel I need to do this. Work was great about it. Better than I thought they'd be, actually."

He ran his hands absently over his knees. "I'm taking an unpaid leave for two weeks. If I have to go a few more times, they're fine with it. And the time I need off for the surgery and recovery *will* be paid leave. They were fully supportive. After it's all done, and I'm back to one hundred percent, I'll start the new job."

"New York," Maria repeated. "Billionaires, you said?"

"Uh-huh. Why?" Nick stared harder now. She looked upset. No, it was more than that. She looked . . . spooked. "Ma, you used to live in New York. You know I'm not going to, like, a war zone or something."

"Are they from Long Island?" she asked.

Lew flinched, his head swiveling to look at his wife as his eyes flew wide.

Nick's gut started humming and clenched, like right before something bad went down on the street. "What's going on?" he asked, looking from one to the other. "You're both acting weird."

"The boy," she said. "The billionaire father. What's his name, do you know?"

"Yeah, of course I know. I told you, I talked to him," Nick said. "The kid's name is Myles. His father's name is Charles." Trying to joke to break the sudden heavy vibe in the room, he added in a mock snooty voice, "Get this for big-money pretentious: his full name is Charles Roger Harrison *the third,* thank you very much."

Maria gasped sharply, her eyes rolled back in her head, and she fainted, slumping against her husband.

"I'm okay," Maria said weakly. "Stop hovering." She tried to sit up.

"No, stop!" Lew held her shoulders, keeping her down as he sat beside her on the couch. "You just fainted dead away—you need to lie still for a few minutes."

"Do what he says, Ma." Nick knelt on the carpeted floor next to her, studying her face. She was still a little pale. "You scared the shit out of us."

"Sorry," she whispered. Her eyes locked on her husband's, and Nick saw they were filled with . . . fear.

Nick took her hand and caressed the top of it. It was cold. Usually her skin was so warm, like she had a fire burning in her core. "You're fine, Ma. You're okay—we got you."

She just kept staring at Lew. He was telegraphing back to her with his own troubled gaze. Nick's gut wasn't just humming now, but blazing.

"What's going on?" He looked from one parent to the other.

"I have to tell him," Maria whispered to Lew.

"Totally your decision," he said, and took her other hand.

"Tell me what?" Nick released the hand he held. "Come on. Whatever it is, please . . . you're both starting to freak me out a little here."

Maria's dark eyes got glassy. She closed them, but the tears escaped and slid down her cheeks.

"It'll be all right," Lew told her gently. "I'm here. He loves you. Tell him."

A strangled sob burst from her mouth, and she clapped her free hand over it. More tears fell. Lew kissed her other hand, which he didn't release.

A chill prickled over Nick's skin. He'd never seen his parents like this. He moved back and again sat in his chair, but brought it closer until he sat right at her side to stare down at her. "Whatever it is, he's right. I love you. So go on—I'm listening."

Her eyes opened and focused on him, liquid with emotion. "I just pray you'll forgive me. Try to understand. . . ."

Nick didn't say anything. He clasped his hands on his knees and waited, trying to ignore the churning of his stomach.

"I . . . I lied to you, *mijo*," Maria finally said. "I know who your biological father is. I've always known who he is, and where he is."

Nick felt like she'd slammed him in the chest with a sledgehammer. The air left his lungs with a hiss. He just stared at her as his heart skipped a beat, then took off like a shot.

"The only two people I ever told were your *abuela* and . . . your father." She glanced to Lew, whose eyes never left his wife's face. "I couldn't marry him, start a life with him, with any secrets between us. I told him a month before we got married. And he didn't leave me; he supported my decision and kept my secret. He's the best man I've ever known in my life."

Lew's jaw clenched and a muscle jumped, but all he did was lift her hand to his lips and kiss the back of it.

Nick cleared his throat hard, trying to dislodge the boulder that had formed there. Maria turned, trying to lie on her side to better face her son.

"When I was twenty," she said, "I worked during the day and went to community college at night. I used to work as a waitress, but then my cousin got me in as a housekeeper for a very rich family. Better pay. So even though I lived in Queens with my family, I took the bus out to Long Island every day." She swiped at her wet cheeks. "I was young, naïve. . . . Well, I had a short affair with someone, and I got pregnant. But I quickly realized I meant nothing to him. And what was worse, much worse . . . I'd come to understand he was a horrible man. So I quit the job and left, without ever telling him I was pregnant. I didn't want him to know."

She sniffled hard, but the tears kept coming, rolling down her face. "I'd seen how awful he was to his own young son. He was downright cruel to him, and I didn't want him to do that to my baby. And I knew if I told him I was pregnant, he'd either make me get rid of it, or try to take it away from me . . . so I ran. I told Mama, and she sent me down to Florida to live with Titi until the baby came. By the time you arrived, Mama was here. She gave up her job, her whole life in New York—my other sister and my brothers—to come down here to live with us . . . you and me." A sentimental smile flickered. "You were her first grandchild, after all."

The blood roared in Nick's ears and his heart pounded, but he sat very still. After a long beat, he managed to choke out, "Who was the man? Tell me his name."

Maria gulped, sniffled hard, but met his eyes directly. "His name was Charles Harrison. The second. So this boy you're a match for? I guess he's Charles's grandson . . . and your nephew."

Lew shook his head in slow astonishment. "Jesus, what are the odds of something like this happening? I mean . . ."

Nick felt the blood drain from his face and sat back. A strange whirring noise took over his head, something like a tornado. He gripped the arms of the chair, trying to stop the sudden sense of falling. Maybe he was going to pass out too.

"Charles Harrison had four children," Maria went on quietly. "The oldest was Charles the third. You said you spoke to him? Well, he's your half brother."

Nick nodded. His head felt fuzzy, and he closed his eyes,

trying to process the words. Jesus fucking Christ, he'd had a conversation with some stranger in New York, and it turned out the guy was his half brother? He could barely breathe.

"You have four half siblings," Maria continued. "First two brothers—Charles, then Dane. Then a sister, Tess, and then the youngest son, Pierce. He was only eight years old when I worked there." Maria sniffed back the tears and sat up a little more. "Charles was *horrible* to him. He either ignored the poor boy, or picked on him, absolutely went after him. The mother had left a few years before. The other kids were older than him, early teens, so it wasn't as hard for them. But that boy . . ." Maria shook her head. "So alone. So sad. The nannies were raising him, not his own father. And then I watched him start to get angrier. He'd fight back, lash out. . . . He changed. For the worse." She sniffed hard, wiped at her face. "And I didn't want my own child to turn into him. To have that kind of life. So—"

"Were you ever going to tell me this?" Nick asked roughly. His voice felt like gravel in his throat. "I mean . . . *ever*?"

She looked at him and her eyes filled anew. "I was hoping I wouldn't have to."

Nick swore fiercely under his breath.

"She was scared," Lew said. "You have to understand—"

"No, I don't." Nick rubbed his now clammy palms on his shorts, but his eyes locked on his mother. "You're scared of the guy, fine. But *me*? Why wouldn't you tell me this? Didn't I have a right to know the truth?"

"If you ever had kids," Maria whispered, "I was going to tell you then. So you'd have a medical history."

His stomach twisted. "Ah. But *I* didn't deserve that same courtesy?"

"*Mijo*," she whispered weakly. "Please . . ."

"Please what?" Nick felt his blood surging, his temper starting to strain. "Please don't be mad? I think I have every fucking right to be mad right now, no?"

"Nick," Lew said, stern and low. "Watch how you speak to your mother."

"I'm speaking to both of you! You lied to me too," Nick spat. "You have no moral high ground here, so just step off."

Lew's jaw clenched. "I understand you're shocked. But it was your mother's decision to make. *Her* choice. I went along with it because I love and respect my wife. And by the way, I love you too. You *are* my son, in every way that counts, and we all know that."

Nick sprung to his feet and started to pace the small living room. The whirring in his head got louder as the blood rushed by his ears. He ran his hands through his hair, trying to calm himself.

This was . . . he couldn't absorb this. They'd lied to him about his whole damn life.

When he was eleven, a middle school project about genealogy had raised questions about his biological father, whom Maria had never talked about. She'd sat her son down and explained that she'd gotten pregnant via a one-night stand when she was twenty. Said she'd gotten drunk at a party and made a foolish choice—but she was adamant that Nick knew she never thought of it as a mistake. That she took responsibility for her choice, that Nick had been a gift from God to her, and most of all, that she never regretted her decision to keep her baby.

Maria had told her young son that she'd never even known the man's last name, which was why she hadn't put one on his original birth certificate. All she could tell Nick was he was white, probably some basic Anglo-Saxon mix, and he'd never known she was pregnant. When she met and fell in love with Lew, it had been another gift from God to her, and they'd built a family together, made a good life for their three kids.

Young Nick had been surprised, but hadn't given the news much thought. It did explain why Nick always felt there was something that was just . . . off. He'd heard some of his aunts whispering once when he was six years old, something about Maria being an unwed mother and his white father, and he'd assumed it was about Lew. . . .

Apparently not. Maybe his gut instincts had been strong even then. So even at the young age of eleven, Nick had been glad to know the truth about his conception because it helped some things make sense, things he'd felt that, before, he just couldn't make sense of or verbalize. When he heard relatives whisper about his mom once in a while, he'd, knowing the truth, felt a protective sting for her. Then he'd pushed it into the recesses of his mind and gone on with his life. It hadn't altered who he was. He had a dad who loved him. His mom had kept him and loved him. That's all that mattered.

Now Nick looked at his dad, and his mom . . . and betrayal broke over him like a tidal wave, crushing him with its ferocity. He could barely breathe. Honor and truth were driving forces in his life. Few things held more weight with him than honesty.

They knew that about him. Yet they'd known the truth all along and purposely kept it from him. He was almost thirty years old. Would they have ever told him the truth? Even now, he didn't know, and that made something dark and hot snake through his chest.

"You have to listen to her," Lew said. "To both of us."

Nick stopped pacing and crossed his arms over his chest as he glared at them.

"Charles was smooth," Maria said, "and he was a ruthless man. I knew he was that way in business, but he sweet-talked me and I didn't know any better. Until I saw how he treated that boy. It always made me so . . . uncomfortable."

"But you slept with him anyway," Nick ground out. "Spare me the pity party."

"You watch your mouth!" Lew shouted, springing to his feet.

Maria shot out a hand to grip her husband's arm. "Yes,"

she said to Nick. "Yes, I did. I was naïve. He was charming to me. Handsome, powerful, and very persuasive. I was young, flattered that someone like that would pay attention to someone like me."

"Don't make her do this," Lew growled at Nick, his fair cheeks splashed with high color.

"I'm okay," she said, but her wide eyes, filled with sadness and anxiety, said otherwise. "He deserves to know all of it. I can take it, and so can he."

"Damn right. So. Serious question." Nick pinned her with his eyes. "Why didn't you get an abortion? You were young, had no money. Why keep me?"

Maria's mouth dropped open in shock, but she recovered quickly. "For me, there was no choice. You were my baby, so I wanted you. That was it." She brushed her hair back from her face and he saw her hands were shaking. "I was willing to do whatever I had to, to make sure you had a good life. But a *normal* life. I didn't want Charles Harrison's money, or all the strings that would come with it. I didn't want him anywhere near you."

"You don't know how it might have been," Nick said. "You assumed."

Maria's dark eyes flashed. "Go Google Pierce Harrison sometime, the boy I'm talking about. He's a grown man now, older than you. You'll see what I saved you from. He turned into a hell-raiser. A spoiled, entitled bad boy—the whole stereotype. Got in trouble a lot. He was a professional football player in England, and he quit suddenly in the middle of a scandal. His life was a mess. I'd bet this house that his antics are a direct result of growing up the way he did . . . mistreated by his father. So I'm not sorry for leaving and saving you from that kind of life."

"Saving me from what, a rich man's life?" Nick snorted out a laugh. "Oh, please."

"You don't have to defend yourself," Lew said to her.

"Yes, she does," Nick snarled. "She absolutely does." He'd always known he had been adopted by Lew, and that somewhere out there was the man who'd helped actually create him. It had rarely bothered him. The few times it had, he'd dealt with it and hadn't let it take over his head and heart. But now, he felt like the world had teetered sideways and he didn't know which end was up. There was a name. A face. A history. A whole other family out there.

"I'm asking you," Maria said carefully, "not to go to New York. I think it'd be a disaster. I'm asking you not to meet or get involved with these people."

At that, Nick's eyes rounded. "*These people*, as you say, are my blood relatives."

"But they're not your family," Lew said. "We are. We know you, we love you, and we're trying to protect you."

"I'm a grown man who's quick on my feet, strong, smart, and licensed to carry a weapon," Nick said. "I don't need protecting from *anyone*, thank you very much."

"Yes, you do," Maria said. "You've never dealt with someone like Charles Harrison before. The older one, not the younger one. If that man finds out you exist, and that you're his son? He'll try to take over your life."

Nick snorted out a laugh. "Yeah, right."

"You don't know!" she cried, lurching to her feet. Lew's hand shot out to grab her arm and steady her. "People like that, with that kind of money and power? You have no idea what—"

"I deal with murderers, drug dealers, violent criminals, addicts who go fucking crazy, every day," Nick said. "Every single day. You think some pansy-ass white-bread billionaire scares me in the slightest?"

Maria shook her head. "You don't understand."

"I guess not. And right this moment, I don't need to. I'm outta here." Nick turned and headed for the door.

"Don't go!" she yelled, her voice breaking. "Please!"

He whirled around to face her. Her fear was palpable, and his heart squeezed at the look of terror on her face, but he was more furious than he could ever remember being. "What."

"Don't go there. I'm asking you not to go there," she begged.

His mouth twisted as he seethed, "You're asking me not to help save a kid's life to keep your secret? You've got to be fucking kidding me."

She jolted as if he'd slapped her.

"That's not what she's asking you to do," Lew said, "and you know it."

"It's what it sounds like to me."

"Then you don't know your mother if you think she'd ask you to—"

"I *don't* know who she is right now—you're right!" Nick shouted. His heart thumped wildly as he turned to his mom. "You lied to me my whole life."

Her mouth quavered and her eyes filled with fresh tears, but she stood her ground. "I lied to you to protect you. I'll never apologize for that. I just . . . should've told you sooner. That, I apologize for."

Nick's jaw clenched so tightly, his teeth ground together. "I've never felt so betrayed in my entire life. It's a fucking knife in my heart."

The tears rolled down her face. "I know," she whispered. "I'm so sorry, *mijo*. And again, I'm still begging you not to go to New York."

"That's ridiculous," Nick said, his frustration growing. "It's not like I'm going to walk in there and a neon sign's gonna go off—'long lost family member here!'"

"They'll know," she said, her voice dropping, somber. "You . . . you're so much like him. You walk in there, they're going to take one look at you and know who you are. I know it."

"*You* are the neon sign," Lew added.

Nick flinched as if he'd been slapped. "I look like him?"

"Very much so." Her voice was a ragged whisper. "Yes, you have my coloring, but his features. You're tall and lean like him. You have his frame . . . the shape of your eyes, your nose, your square jaw . . . even your hands, your long fingers. . . ."

Nick's breath caught and stuck in his chest. Somewhere in his mind, as a little boy, he'd decided his more Caucasian features were like those of Lew's Irish family. But of course, once in a while, he'd wondered if he looked like his biological father. Now, to know he *did* look like someone, much less bore a strong resemblance, undid him to the core.

"Please don't go to them," she pleaded quietly, eyes wide. "Please. It can't end well. I just don't want you to get hurt."

"I'm not going there for a goddamn family reunion," Nick seethed. "I'm going to try to help keep a sick kid from dying."

"I know. I hate to hear a child is sick. But—"

"But nothing," Nick said. "I'm not going to punish that boy for *your* sins."

Now it was Maria who flinched as if he'd hit her, gasping. She took a step back.

"That's it." Lew strode purposefully to Nick and got right in his face. "I know you're in shock, and I know you're mad. You have every right to be."

"Gee, thanks for your permission," Nick snarled. "*Dad.*"

"You wanna come at me, fine," Lew said. "But I won't have you continually insulting your mother. That's unacceptable."

"What's unacceptable is that you two kept this from me all this time," Nick said. His chest was still tight, like the air in the room was vanishing.

"You need to try and calm down," Lew said, "so we can all talk rationally about this."

"I'm sure you have questions," Maria said. "I'll try to answer whatever I can."

"And why should I believe anything that you say?" Nick asked. His blood rushed through his body and his heart beat wildly. "It's not like you just kept this from me when I was a kid who might not understand. You lied to me *my whole life*. Both of you! I . . . I can't look at either one of you." He turned away and walked straight to the door, out of the house, right to his car, even as his mother desperately called his name from the front porch. Without a look back, he slammed the car door shut with all his might, started up the engine with a roar, and sped away.

Chapter Two

Every day, when Amanda Kozlov drove past the slightly imposing gates with the sign marked PRIVATE PROPERTY, up the long driveway to the front of the elegant, contemporary estate, she had to steel her heart a bit before going inside. Charles Harrison III, his wife, Lisette, and their four children lived in such a magnificent mansion, and were such a loving family, it was hard to think of it as a sad place. But these days, it was.

For fourteen months, she'd been a private nurse for their younger son, Myles. She went to the mansion five days a week to attend to his needs. She knew she wasn't supposed to get attached to her patients, but she adored him. Now twelve, he was just starting to shed his boyishness for tweendom, but his sweet blue eyes and vibrant nature still shone with childlike optimism despite his harrowing situation. He'd been fighting valiantly for almost a year and a half now.

She parked her six-year-old Honda Civic at the far space in the wide driveway and grabbed her bag from the passenger seat. It was a gray, overcast morning, and a harsh gust of wind lifted her hair from her shoulders and flung it into her face. With a grunt of annoyance, she rummaged through her bag for an elastic. Quickly, she pulled her long, dark blond hair back and secured it into a ponytail.

The early April air was still cold, with no hint of spring yet, and carried the salty scent of the nearby Long Island Sound. The Harrison property boasted a grand front yard and a wide, grassy backyard that sloped down directly onto a strip of sand and the water. On clear days, Connecticut was easily visible across the calm waters of the Sound.

This job had taken up most of her life. Amanda had never been with a home care patient for so long before Myles Harrison, and the boy had a hold on her heart. It wasn't as if she had a family of her own, or a boyfriend. She hadn't gone on any dates since she'd ended her last relationship ten months ago. Dating wasn't even on her radar these days; the truth was, it'd been both a comfort and a necessity to drown in her work.

She knew she was lucky to have a job in such a lovely town, in a lovely home, with a genuinely lovely family. Sandy Point was one of the wealthiest communities in New York state, and the Harrison family—not just Charles and his clan, but his father, sister, and two brothers—was one of the wealthiest, most powerful families in the country. But all the money and power in the world wasn't helping young Myles Harrison beat non-Hodgkin's lymphoma. So far, he'd held his own, but it had dug its terrifying claws into him and wouldn't let go.

Amanda had been by his side as he'd gone through chemo and radiation, which unfortunately hadn't worked. All of the Harrisons, from the older patriarch to the baby cousins, had been tested as viable bone marrow donors, to no avail. Not one of the clan had been a match. Desperate, Charles had recently taken the step of going to the national bone marrow registry. And then a miracle had happened: a viable match had been found, just a week ago. All Amanda knew was the donor lived in Florida, had agreed to the procedure, and would be flying to New York shortly to start pre-testing.

It was overwhelming, the hope that surged through her. If this worked, it would save Myles's life. But if it didn't work . . . Amanda's heart skipped a beat and she swatted the thought away, a willful mental karate kick. To think of the alternative was just too devastating.

Head down against the wind, she rang the front doorbell and glanced at her watch. She was always on time, and it soothed her to see it was 12:57 PM. Her daily shift was every afternoon/evening, from one to nine. As she waited, she thought of them.

The Harrisons weren't just courteous; they were generous. They paid her exceedingly well, which she suspected they did to keep her in their employ. They liked and trusted her. From a purely business standpoint, that was a smart move, and she knew Charles Harrison III was an excellent businessman. Amanda guessed he was willing to do whatever necessary to keep her with them for as long as they needed her. And if that meant paying top dollar, even on the days she did practically nothing, that's what he'd decided to do.

She was grateful for the maximum wages, but she honestly took pleasure in caring for Myles. He was such a great kid, sweet and funny, and she liked the whole family too, which often wasn't the case. They all showed her their gratitude and expressed their appreciation on a regular basis, more than any of her other patients ever had. That alone made them more than worth her time and efforts, and she was glad to be part of the team.

There were two other private nurses. Christine was there every weekday from 7 AM to 1 PM, and Alisha came on the weekends if Myles wasn't feeling well. Amanda had wondered more than once if it was necessary, having private nurses there almost around the clock. But Charles and Lisette were worried out of their minds about their son and certainly had the funds, so they could do this, and why not? Their other kids needed them too: Ava, the oldest, was fifteen; Thomas was thirteen and a half; and little Charlotte was only five and a half. Myles and his two older siblings had been the products of Charles's first marriage, while Charlotte was his and Lisette's child.

Vanessa, Myles's biological mother, lived in L.A. She came to visit once a month for two or three days, but apparently just couldn't handle her son being so critically ill. She wasn't around much; it was Lisette who'd stepped in and been the rock that boy needed. She was the one who now opened the heavy front door to let Amanda in, offering a small grin.

"Hi, it's good to see you," Lisette said, giving Amanda a light kiss on the cheek in greeting as always. She tried to smile, but Amanda noticed it didn't reach her dark eyes. Lisette's hands fluttered, fidgeting with the end of her thick, dark braid. "Myles is in his room. He's tired today, and moody. . . . I think maybe he's nervous about what's coming, now that we found a donor. I'm not sure. I'm just glad you're here."

Amanda knew Lisette well enough by now to be able to hear what she hadn't said. *He's tired and moody* plus *I'm glad you're here* equaled *I'm worried because he seems off today*.

"I'll go right upstairs," Amanda said.

"Thank you. I'll bring you a drink. Would you like water, coffee, tea . . . ?"

"Water would be fine, thanks." Amanda took a few steps across the polished hardwood floor of the foyer, headed for the grand spiral staircase. As she made her way up the stairs, she thought about what she might say to Myles to calm his fears and reassure him.

She sighed deeply. Nothing was guaranteed, and she knew that. A bone marrow transplant was no walk through the park, but this was Myles's best shot at beating his illness.

* * *

Later that night, after a relaxing bubble bath, Amanda got into her softest pajamas, the turquoise fleece a comfort, and put on her fleece socks to shuffle around her small apartment. Her roommate wasn't home, for which she was grateful. She liked Gretchen just fine; she just liked having the place to herself more. They were both nurses, but Gretchen worked in maternity, doing the night shifts. With such different schedules, they rarely saw each other. Amanda usually got home about an hour before Gretchen left.

Now she poured herself a glass of Rioja and headed for bed. She didn't have the mental focus to read tonight; she'd scroll on Facebook for a while instead. Her bed was cozy as she sat up in the dark, the light from her phone harshly bright in the darkness. A few sips in and ten minutes later, her phone dinged—the group text thread with her two best friends since the seventh grade.

My kids are driving me batshit crazy tonight, Steph said. NEED. WINE.

Amanda laughed, took a quick selfie of herself holding her half-full glass, and sent it. Here you go, mama. I'm a step ahead of you.

One glass won't do it, Steph wrote. I need the whole bottle.

Amanda laughed again. That bad?

Their father thought it'd be fun to take them out for ice cream, Steph texted. At 7:00 at night. Dumbass. They're all sugared up, they'll never go to sleep.

Amanda checked the time. It was ten-thirty. *Jesus, they must be really wired.*

I gave up. I told Todd he could put them to bed, since he did this. I'm hiding in the bathroom. I locked the door.

Amanda couldn't help but giggle. I'll smuggle you the wine through the window.

I wish you could!!! Steph wrote back.

I'm here, I'm here, came Roni's text at last. Not ignoring y'all. On a date.

What? Spill! Amanda wrote back quickly. Roni, a lawyer who dealt with international finance, lived in New York City. Steph had married her college sweetheart at twenty-five; she lived with her husband and two kids in Connecticut. Amanda hadn't gone on even one date since breaking up with Justin. She and Steph lived vicariously through Roni's busy dating life. Another Tinder guy?

Nope, Roni wrote. Worse. Blind date through a coworker. Why am I here?

To amuse us and keep us entertained, Steph wrote.

He just went to the bathroom, Roni texted. Is it bad that I don't really care if he comes back or not?

Going that well, huh? Amanda wrote.

Is he nice, at least? Steph asked.

Yes. Very nice. To the point of boring, Roni texted. I'm falling asleep in my soup. But he's cute, so I'll need to kiss him to know if I'll see him again. Could go either way.

You're ruthless, Amanda wrote.

I prefer to think of it as pragmatic, Roni answered.

The three of them talked for a few more minutes before signing off. Amanda didn't even realize she'd finished her wine. She was cozy as could be in her bed, but made herself get up to brush her teeth. When she flopped back into bed, she realized she felt a little better. She smiled to herself as she burrowed further beneath the covers.

Wine helped, for sure. Her friends helped, always. Steph, with her suburban stay-at-home-mom life, and Roni, with her fast-paced, high-stress lawyer life. Steph loved being home with her kids. Roni loved the high stakes of her career. Amanda . . . well, her life was pretty quiet these days. Which was fine, even though she'd boxed herself into a routine. And what was worse, for now, she didn't really care to change things up. Myles Harrison was about to get a whole lot sicker before he got better, and the anguish of that would be all she'd be able to handle for a while. Her own fault for getting so emotionally attached to her patient.

It was safer to be alone. Safer to come home and know her days, and have no surprises, and just push through. Being safe was boring sometimes, but she didn't like to think about the alternative too much. She'd done exciting and ended up hurt. She'd taken a few risks before and they had left her reeling. Safe was better. Excitement and contentment . . . were for other people.

Chapter Three

As the plane began its descent into JFK Airport, Nick felt his stomach clench. He had no idea what lay ahead in the next few weeks. Agreeing to be someone's bone marrow donor was a hell of a thing on its own—much less taking a leave from work, staying in a different state, being poked and prodded and God only knew what else by doctors, and dealing with a group of strangers who were desperate for him to be the miracle they'd been praying for.

Add to all that the bizarre fact that he was related to these people and they had no idea. How the hell was he supposed to bring that up?

When he'd peeled away from his parents' house, he'd gone right to his favorite bar and called his best friend. He and Darin Peterson had met on their first day at the police training academy and been tight from that day one; there was no one else he trusted more. Darin had talked him down as they shared some beers, then driven him home when he'd exceeded his limit. The next morning, he'd gotten on the Internet and dug up everything he could on the Harrison family. His research and investigative skills had never felt so crucial.

He needn't have worried. There was a *lot* of information

readily available. This wasn't just any family—they were like the goddamn Rockefellers, for Christ sake. There was extensive material on all of them; he spent hours making notes and soaking it all up. When he pulled up younger photos of Charles Harrison II, his bio dad, his breath got stuck in his lungs. His mom had been right; the resemblance was strong and undeniable.

His mom. Thinking of her now made his stomach do that miserable little flip again. God, he was so pissed at her. Her and his dad both. They'd both tried to call several times, sent texts and emails, but he hadn't answered. All he'd done was shoot them one quick text right before he boarded the plane in Miami, letting them know he was leaving and would be in touch when he was ready.

The betrayal and rage Nick felt was so deep, so over-whelming, he hadn't even processed it yet. So he did what he had to, same as any time he went out on the street at work: he shoved all those feelings into a box in his head and sealed it up. He had too much to deal with as it was; his parents would have to wait. He wasn't ready to talk to them right now. He'd inherited his mother's temper, that was for sure. He needed time and space to cool off.

The plane touched down gently onto the tarmac, and he glanced out the window. For mid-April, it didn't look like springtime yet; everything looked gray and brown. Dead grass, naked trees, and concrete, all made even more gloomy by the overcast sky. Florida was gorgeous, always with everything in bloom, green grass and colorful flowers every-where. . . . He sighed. Maybe New York City was something to write home about, but so far, on first glance, he was unim-pressed.

He moved slowly as he disembarked, not in a hurry to face these Harrison people. He knew he'd have to tell them sooner or later who he was . . . but since he was still having a hard time wrapping his head around it, he was at a loss. He felt off his game. He was always so sure, and that confidence worked well for him as a cop. But this . . . he'd never dealt with anything like this. His whole sense of identity had been thrown for a loop. He had no idea what to do, how to handle it. So he'd just stay quiet, observe them all—watch, listen, and learn as if he were working undercover. At least that he knew how to do.

Nick was one of the last people off the plane. His long legs carried him through the terminal, but he didn't even feel aware of his surroundings. He shifted his duffel bag over his shoulder and kept following the signs toward the baggage claim.

Nick waited by the baggage carousel for almost fifteen minutes before his bag finally appeared. He pulled it off, shifted his duffel on his shoulder, and wheeled his suitcase along as he headed toward the exits. Charles Harrison had told him that someone would be waiting there for him, a driver to take him to his hotel. Charles had made all the arrangements, covering every base. If Nick allowed himself, he could almost think of it as a vacation . . . if vacations involved hospitals, needles, and sick kids.

Sure enough, a stocky, tough-looking man in a dark suit stood front and center, holding a sign that simply read MARTELL. Nick went to him and said, "I think you're looking for me. I'm Nick Martell."

"Okay, great," the man said. His eyes were almost as silver as his crew-cut hair. "You have ID to show me, though?"

Nick wanted to scoff at the suggestion, then remembered who he was dealing with. The super-wealthy and powerful Harrison family clearly didn't mess around. This guy was like a tank; Nick bet he was former Army or even Marines, just based on his vibe. He pulled out his wallet and flipped it open, showing not just his driver's license, but his badge. He watched as the guy's steely gaze glanced over both.

"Nice to meet you, Officer Martell," the man said. He extended his free hand for a handshake. "Name's Bruck. I'm Charles Harrison's driver. He's waiting outside in the car. He figured you two could talk as I drive you to your hotel, since it's a good forty-minute ride from here."

"I see." Nick knew Charles must be anxious to meet him, considering he was there to try to help save his son's life, so he didn't read too much into it. "Call me Nick, though, okay?"

"Yes, sir."

"And for God's sake, don't 'sir' me." Nick slanted him a sideways look. "First of all, I'm probably half your age. Second . . . I'm like you, not them."

Bruck only nodded. "I'll take your luggage." He reached down to grasp the handle of Nick's suitcase from his hand.

But Nick held tight and said, "No, dude, I can do that."

Bruck raised one thick brow and said, "Make you a deal. I won't call you 'sir,' and you won't call me 'dude.' Okay?"

Nick laughed, relaxing a bit for the first time all day. "Sure."

Bruck started walking and Nick followed, pulling the wheeled case along.

"You were in the service, weren't you?" Nick guessed, unable to help himself.

"Army," Bruck said. "Fifteen years."

"I can tell."

Bruck only nodded, but Nick caught the spark of esteem in his eyes.

"So now you're a driver. You his muscle too?" Nick asked casually.

"Sometimes." Bruck didn't give him more than that, but Nick didn't need any more. This guy was probably armed, and his broad build hinted at sure physical strength. "How long you been a cop?" Bruck asked. His New York accent wasn't heavy like the stereotypes Nick had heard in movies, but it was definitely noticeable.

"Five years. Just got promoted, actually," Nick found himself saying. "I'm moving up to investigator."

"Good for you," Bruck said, and Nick thought he heard real respect in his voice.

They went through sliding glass doors and made their way through the people on the sidewalk. Every building was gray; the sky was gray. . . . Nick didn't like it. He already missed the sunshine and the bright colors. *Ain't in Kansas anymore, Toto*, he thought, grinning ruefully.

Then he noticed the black Escalade parked a few feet away. He watched Bruck go to it, and frowned. Private cars weren't usually allowed to stay parked curbside at airports for more than a minute. He knew NYC security and law enforcement were pretty tight by reputation. So how the hell had Bruck done that? *Big money, that's how*, a voice whispered in his head. *You're entering a different world now, remember? Buckle up.*

Bruck opened the trunk and took the suitcase handle from Nick's hand. As he hauled it into the back, Nick pulled his duffel bag over his shoulder and put it inside. Then he took a deep breath, went to the passenger door, and opened it.

"Hello." The dark-haired man sitting in the backseat wore an expensive suit, was a little older than him, and reeked of power and prestige. But he leaned in, offering a friendly smile and a firm handshake. "So good to meet you, Mr. Martell. I trust your flight was fine?"

Nick only nodded. He peered harder into the shadows of the backseat.

"Glad to hear it," the man said, still smiling amiably. He leaned back just a bit, a shaft of sunlight lighting his face. "Well, I can't thank you enough for coming. I'm Charles Harrison. Come on, hop in."

Nick's throat thickened as he stared. He knew that Charles Harrison III was seventeen years his senior; his thick dark waves were peppered with silver and his eyes were bright blue, with deep laugh lines crinkling the corners. They had the same nose, the same square jaw. . . . Seeing this man in person had him suddenly choked up. He hadn't expected to react so viscerally. It was the damnedest thing.

Nick cleared his throat as he climbed into the backseat, closed the door, turned to his big brother, and finally managed to say, "Good to meet you too. Call me Nick."

Chapter Four

The conversation on the way to the hotel Charles had chosen was pretty one-sided: it revolved around Nick. Charles was genuinely curious about him, asking about his family, his background, his career. The irony wasn't lost on Nick. He knew Charles wanted to know about him just because he'd appeared from nowhere like an angel of mercy to possibly help his son. But Nick was uncomfortable. He was wary of how much to reveal. . . . It was a goddamn tricky situation, and he was the only one who knew why.

Charles had been about sixteen or seventeen when Nick's mother worked in the house. Would he remember her? Nick wondered. He might. Or, like so many wealthy kids, the household staff might have been invisible to him, so maybe he wouldn't remember her. Nick didn't know which option was better.

He'd decided to keep himself at an emotional distance, coming at the situation as if it were a case to be investigated. But he was just as curious as Charles—hell, more so, by a mile. He was the one with a million questions . . . but how to ask them without seeming suspect?

"Almost there, sir," Bruck said from the driver's seat.

"Thanks for the heads-up," Charles replied. "Appreciate it."

Nick had already noticed that Charles talked to and treated Bruck well, that there was obvious mutual respect between them. The way a man treated his employees said a lot about his character; Nick found himself relieved that his newfound oldest brother seemed—so far, anyway—to be a decent guy.

Nick looked out the window as Bruck turned off the parkway, noting they were entering a town called Great Neck. There were lots of trees, though they were all still bare, and it seemed pretty busy. So far, he wasn't sure what he'd expected Long Island to be like, but it seemed like any other suburban area. Maybe nicer, in fact. He'd read up on the town he was staying in when he was situated in his hotel room.

"If I mentioned this already, forgive me," Charles said. "I chose a hotel that had upscale suites, because I want you to be comfortable for as long as you're here, and I honestly have no idea how long that will be. I've also placed a hold on the room for future visits. This may take a couple of trips. I have no idea."

Nick just listened. It was interesting hearing what a powerful man could do, both with his funds and his generosity, if he wanted.

"The hotel's in the heart of a fairly busy town, so you're within walking distance of plenty of restaurants, shops, lots of things. Rented you a car. The hospital is in the next town, about three miles away. Hope that's agreeable to you."

"It's more than agreeable," Nick said. "It makes sense, and it's more than generous. Thanks for that."

"I want you comfortable here, and not to worry about expenses in the slightest. I didn't want you to have to be concerned about a thing. It's the very least I can do. In fact . . ." He reached into his inside blazer pocket and pulled out his wallet, then took a gold card from it and held it out to Nick. "This is a company corporate card. I want you to have it for as long as you're here. Use it for everything. When you go out for meals, gas up the car—"

Nick just glanced at the card held between Charles's fingers. "Not necessary. But thanks."

"I insist," Charles said, his gaze not wavering. "You were willing to come here, willing to miss work and disrupt your life . . . and I can't tell you how thankful I am for that. So this"—he waved the credit card once—"is something I can do for you."

"I was willing to come do this," Nick said, "once the registry people called and explained what was at stake. Before I ever talked to you, before you offered the hotel and everything. You know that."

Charles nodded. "And I appreciate that."

"I have a job," Nick said. "Insurance will cover the medical. While I'm here, I can pay my own way."

"May I be blunt?" Charles said plainly. "You're a police officer."

Nick grinned, fighting the urge to laugh at what he was sure might follow. "Go right ahead."

"Safe to say you don't make six figures, am I right?" Charles asked.

Nick gave one short nod. "So?"

"You're obviously a proud man, and being one myself, I respect that. But the expenses attached to this may go higher than you're counting on," Charles said. "Like I told you on the phone, if your insurance won't cover all of it, I will. End of story. But when you add to that your living expenses, for as long as you're going to be here, over several visits . . ." He exhaled a long breath. "It'll add up. Just let me cover it."

"I don't like the feeling of being bought," Nick said, with more of an edge to his voice than he'd intended.

"You said you'd already decided to do this on your own," Charles pointed out. "So I'm not buying you. I'm just trying to help. Because I can." His intense gaze held Nick's. "I'm sure by now you've read an article or two about me, and you know I can."

"Won't deny that. But you don't know me," Nick said. "I'm only here for a week or two this trip."

"And you're not planning to eat for a week or two?" Charles quipped.

Nick chuckled. "It's just . . . what if I took that card and rang up hundreds of thousands of dollars, knowing it's likely on there?"

"You won't do that."

"How do you know?"

"I know that now."

"Oh, you talked to me for twenty minutes, and you know me now?" Nick snorted derisively. "You're a big-time CEO, but you have a side gig as a mind reader?"

"COO," Charles corrected. "My father's the CEO—still a shark, and sharp as a tack."

At the offhand mention of Charles II, Nick stilled. *Their* father.

Mistaking Nick's sudden stillness for compliance, Charles took off his glasses and rubbed the lenses with a microfiber cloth. "Why do you think I wanted to meet you right away, talk to you first? It's midday on a Wednesday. I run a size-able company. You don't think I'm busy?" Charles put his glasses back on with a seemingly casual motion, but pinned him with a cunning look. "I'm pretty good at reading people. So yes, after talking to you face-to-face for twenty minutes, I'm pretty certain that you wouldn't do something like run up a corporate card on bullshit or take advantage of my generosity."

Nick didn't want to admit he was impressed, but he was. Charles was a formidable man. He was polished, obviously bright, and he had impeccable manners . . . and was currently radiating power like a goddamn forcefield.

"Besides . . ." Charles flicked a nonchalant glance away, out the window. "If someone *did* pull anything, do you really think . . ." His eyes shot back to lock on Nick's. ". . . that there wouldn't be repercussions? I don't take betrayal of my trust lightly. Someone who would take advantage of my good nature . . . would pay for it."

Nick grinned. The wolf had bared his fangs, and he wasn't intimidated. The opposite, in fact: he felt a surge of respect. In his research on the family, he'd read about how Charles Harrison III was a smart, tough businessman, a born leader. Well-liked, highly respected, but well known as a shrewd negotiator with sharp insight, and not someone to be trifled with. It was fascinating to watch how Charles subtly but surely let those qualities reveal themselves. Charles wielded power well—he was a quiet man who carried a big stick. Nick had to admire that. But he also had to make some things clear.

"I *am* an honorable man," Nick said. "Honor is every-thing to me. I also expect decency of anyone I deal with. So we've got that in common too. You've got no worries."

Charles's nod was an almost imperceptible tip of his chin. "I sensed that."

"I'm not here for a free ride. I'm not here to bilk the billion-aire who needs my help. I never would've known you were rich if you hadn't insisted on contacting me."

"My point precisely. You'd already agreed to it. Clearly you're a good man."

"I'm here to see if my bone marrow can help your son get better. That's it. We're clear on that?"

"As crystal. And I thank you for that."

Nick eyed the card Charles still held. "Feels wrong."

"I'm trying to *help*."

"Do it your way or else, though. Right?"

"No, of course not." Charles raked a hand through his thick hair. Nick wondered how much of the silver he saw in the dark strands had been brought on by stress over his son's illness. "Nick, you're helping us. I may seem pushy, and you know what, sometimes I am. My wife tells me so all the time, just before she knocks me back into place." Nick noted how Charles's sharp gaze seemed to soften at the thought of her. This guy clearly was crazy about his wife. "But I just want to help you in return for what you've agreed to do, and show my gratitude." He sighed. "I do respect your position, but try to understand mine. I just want to—"

"I know. I get it. We're talking in circles now." Nick sighed too. Looked like the stubborn gene was also something he shared with this imposing man. "Look, you already set up my hotel room. I'm sure that's on your tab, right?"

"Yes."

"And you rented a car too, you said?"

"It's waiting at the hotel for you—concierge will have the keys." The corner of Charles's mouth quirked. "Hope you don't mind fast rides."

Nick's brows shot up. "Why? What'd you do?"

Charles couldn't hold back the grin. "I might have picked something fun for a guy like you to tool around in. Just try not to get a speeding ticket."

Nick snorted out a laugh. "You're so trying to buy me."

"No!" But Charles laughed too. "Hey, you want me to send the Porsche back and get you a sensible Nissan Sentra, I'll be more than happy to do so."

Nick laughed fully now. "Jesus. What guy in their right mind says no to a Porsche? You play dirty."

Charles merely grinned and shrugged.

"Look. I appreciate the hotel, and the car sounds like fun," Nick said. "But I can carry my weight with the rest, all right?"

Charles shook his head. "Indulge me. Take the card. If you don't use it at all, that's fine. But if you actually find you need it for something, I'll know you have it."

"Charles, listen—"

"Please." Charles's voice was soft but firm. "Let me do this." His eyes flashed, a glimmer of frustration that Nick knew wasn't aimed at him. "It's the only thing I can do, and

I . . . I need to feel like I'm doing something. So please. Just take it. Humor me."

Nick sighed. He felt for the guy. All his money and power, ultimately, wasn't going to save his son's life. For a man like Charles Harrison III, to feel helpless must have been one of the most alien, harrowing things he'd ever felt in his privileged life. And he did seem like a decent guy. With a curt nod, Nick took the card and, without even looking at it, shoved it into the pocket of his jeans.

"Thank you," Charles murmured.

"I'm probably not going to use it even once," Nick said.

"That's fine." Charles scrubbed a hand over his jaw, then rubbed the back of his neck wearily. "Though I'd rather you use it to have breakfast in bed every morning, a meal out whenever you feel like it, and room service whenever you want. It's twenty-four-seven at the hotel, I checked. And there's a minibar in your room too, so . . ."

Nick's brows lifted at that. "Maybe I'll use it once or twice, then."

"Do it," Charles urged, a grin breaking through.

"I was kidding."

"I wasn't."

"We're here," Bruck told them.

Nick glanced out the window. It was a little busier here than he'd thought it would be. People were out and about, the streets were lined with stores and restaurants, and cars went by steadily. Bruck pulled up to a corner property, a modern façade whose banners announced THE PARKER HOTEL. Daffodils and crocuses lined the driveway and entrance. At least he wasn't staying in a lousy hotel.

"When's your first appointment with Dr. Greenberg?" Charles asked. "If you don't mind my asking."

"I don't mind," Nick said. "Look, this is about your kid. You want to be involved in every step I take with this thing, that's fine with me. If it were the other way around, I'd probably be climbing the walls with worry."

A muscle twitched under Charles's eye as he murmured, "You have no idea."

"So yeah, ask anything, any time. I have an appointment tomorrow afternoon at two. I have no idea what it's about. I think it's just asking me a million startup questions, taking some blood. . . . I have no clue."

"Do you want someone to go with you?" Charles asked. "I can be there if you want. Or my wife, Lisette. I know I'm biased, but she's one of the nicest people you'll ever meet in your life. Or—"

"You're serious."

"Yeah, sure. If you want company, just let me know. I have a pretty big family," Charles said.

"So I heard," Nick mumbled.

"I can meet you at the hospital if you—"

"Not necessary. But thanks. Tell you what, I'll call you after and tell you whatever you want to know, fill you in on whatever happens, okay?"

"Sure." Charles flashed a grin, then got out of the SUV. Nick did the same. Bruck was already slamming the trunk door shut, Nick's bags in his strong hands.

"I can do that," Nick said.

"Already got 'em," Bruck said, heading for the entrance without a look back.

"Guy's a tank," Nick said under his breath.

"I wouldn't mess with him," Charles whispered back, winking.

Something fluttered through Nick's chest. This guy, this powerful stranger, was joking with him and he . . . Nick liked him. Respected him. It felt weird to feel any kind of kinship with him, but he did. Maybe he was making it up in his head because he knew the truth about their connection? But damn . . . Charles was a good guy.

"I have one request," Charles said as they walked side by side to the wide glass front doors. "It may seem too much, and I understand if you say no."

Nick chuckled. "Just ask."

"We're having a family dinner tonight at my home," Charles said. "We don't often have both of my brothers and my sister over at the same time, but the whole clan will be there tonight. It's something of a celebration because a match was found. So I was wondering if you'd join us." He held the door open for Nick.

As he walked through, Nick's heart skipped a beat and his stomach went woozy. Jesus. Shit. Meeting them all at the same time? He didn't know if he was ready to handle that. "Um . . ."

"I know it may seem strange. But all of this is a little surreal, isn't it?"

"You have no idea," Nick murmured.

"So. Yes, there's a lot of us. My wife and I have four kids, as I think I mentioned when we first talked. My middle brother is married, but no kids. My sister is married and has three kids, and my youngest brother and his wife have two kids. So that's what, seventeen of us all together? But the food will be great because it always is, and my pain-in-the-ass father won't be there, so everyone will be pretty relaxed, and my two brothers are a hell of a lot more fun than I am. . . ."

Nick could barely breathe.

Then Charles rubbed his jaw, an unusual sign of ambivalence. "The thing is, Myles would like to meet you himself. If that's all right with you. I didn't know if that was a good thing or not, to be honest. I mean . . ."

Nick drew a deep breath. His heart was pounding. But he was no coward. And besides, he'd get to meet them all at once and draw his own conclusions. What kept tugging at him was wanting to meet Myles. If the kid was his nephew, and the transplant didn't work, and he was dying . . . he wanted to know him.

Curiosity won out. He decided to jump in, right then. "Why not. I'll go."

"Yeah? Great! Okay. Bruck will come back to pick you up at—"

"No way. You said there's a Porsche waiting for me?" Nick scoffed. "I'll drive myself, thank you very much. Give me your address for my GPS."

"Ha! Absolutely!" Charles looked delighted. "Dinner's at six. Bring nothing but yourself."

"Do I have to dress up or anything?" Nick eyed Charles's carefully tailored suit.

"Hell no," Charles said, laughing. "Civilian attire only. But be warned—there'll be nine kids there, from ages fifteen to two. Hope you can handle that."

Nick grinned, but it faded as something hit him. "In all seriousness, if your son wants to meet me, then I'm honored to meet him."

Charles's eyes rounded and he nodded slowly. "Awfully good of you to say."

"But you know . . . the thing is, I'm not guaranteed to . . ." Nick sighed. "What if I'm not . . . what if I came all this way and I can't help him? To get his hopes up and then . . ."

Charles's square jaw set tightly. "We can't think that way. We have to be positive."

"Yeah, well, I'm a cop. I deal in reality, not wishful thinking."

"The power of positive thinking is stronger than you might believe."

A pang hit Nick's heart. His mom often said things like that to him. Thinking of her now, out of nowhere, made him ache. He mentally shook it off. "Charles . . . you seem like a good man, really. I hope like hell I can help your son, and you're being great about everything. I just don't want you guys to be disappointed if . . ." Nick didn't realize how deeply he meant that until the words tumbled out of his mouth.

"Everything will be fine," Charles said firmly, as if it were a command. Standing side by side, they were the same exact height, and Charles peered harder at Nick for a long beat. "You know, there's something very . . . familiar about you. I feel like we've met before or something. I know that sounds weird, and I can't explain it." He stared a moment longer, then shrugged. "Maybe it's just the intensity of the situation. Or maybe you're a match for Myles because you're some long-lost cousin five times removed, who the hell knows?" Rolling his eyes at himself, Charles chuckled and turned to finish crossing the marbled lobby. "I trust you already, Nick. That's what my gut says. In any case, it's been a pleasure meeting you. Come, I'll make sure everything's fine with check-in before I leave you be."

Speechless, shaken, Nick swallowed back the lump in his throat and walked with Charles to the front desk. Lew's warning words rang in his ears: *YOU are the neon sign.*

Well, tonight, with the entire Harrison family there? He'd see just how true that may or may not be. He was too curious to turn down the chance to find out.

Chapter Five

Nick was nicely surprised by the hotel suite. Modern and luxurious, it suited him fine. There was a sitting room with a light brown suede sofa and glass coffee table, a flat-screen TV on one wall, a mini-fridge and wet bar in the corner by the windows, and an oak writing desk with a comfortable chair. He set his laptop up there and turned it on, eager to do more homework on his surroundings and the Harrisons.

He'd decided just to tell them the truth. Charles was too vulnerable and too decent for Nick to hide this from him. The guy was clearly wrung out about his son, and had extended courteous generosity to Nick without hesitation. He didn't want to repay that by holding back the truth for too long and having it misconstrued.

But going into the lion's den tonight had his nerves tingling, and the best way to counteract that was to be as prepared as possible. Since he had no idea what to expect once he told them all the truth about who he was, he at least wanted to stockpile more information on each sibling, and the old man himself.

Nick didn't want anything from the Harrisons. He sure as hell didn't want anything from his bio dad; even Charles himself had called the old man a shark. Nick was just there to help the kid. Being up-front from the start was the only way to try to prove his intentions were good.

But it'd still probably blow the roof off the place.

He dragged his suitcase and duffel bag into the bedroom. "Not too shabby," he murmured as he took in the modern, swanky décor. The lamps on both nightstands offered low light, and the king-sized bed had a dark oak headboard, draped in cream and burgundy sheets with several large pillows. He wanted nothing more than to sink into the bed, but he had a personal rule about his clothes—once he went through an airport and on a plane, the clothes had to be discarded as soon as possible. Germ city. A shower would be good too. But adrenaline was surging through him; now that he was actually on Long Island and had met one of his half siblings, he was wired. What he really wanted was to go for a workout. He went to the nightstand to look at the pamphlets. "Yes!" he said, happy to see there was a gym on the main floor of the four-floor hotel.

Fifteen minutes later, he was jogging on the treadmill. After the workout, he'd shower, relax, watch something mindless on TV . . . then head to Charles's house for dinner.

He wondered what his other half siblings were like. So far, he had to admit, he liked Charles. And Charles had dryly alluded to the fact that the other two brothers were more fun than he was. Nick knew the basics by heart already. Dane, the middle brother, didn't work for the family company but had struck out and made his own sizable fortune. He owned twenty hotels across North America and was married to a singer who worked in one of his two Manhattan hotels. Pierce was the former pro soccer player who now was invested in New York's professional soccer team, married with two kids. Maybe they were more "fun" than Charles because they weren't running an international conglomerate? Maybe it was simply because they didn't have a critically ill child on their hands? Who knew. Nick would soon find out.

As for the one sister, Tess, she was a powerhouse of her own. Stunningly beautiful, she wasn't some empty-headed socialite; she ran the Harrison family's massive non-profit organization, and hobnobbed with all sorts of celebrities and esteemed people at the tops of their fields as a means to help get funds for the many charities she supported. She was married and had kids too, three of them.

As far as Nick was concerned, his new siblings were all fairly impressive . . . at least on paper. He just hoped they weren't assholes in person.

And those four siblings all looked so much alike, it was uncanny. Dark, unruly hair, fair skinned, tall, with the same bright blue eyes. Apparently, they'd gotten the tall gene from the Harrison side, but their faces from their mother's side—they were practically clones of the former B-list movie star. And like many old-money families, their ethnic background seemed to be a strong English and German mix. It helped explain why, as a kid, Nick could think of himself as possibly Irish, like Lew's family. Now he snorted. Wait until these people got a load of their Latino half brother.

As much as he wanted to get back on the Internet and do extra digging, he needed to burn off the adrenaline more. He ran for forty-five minutes before turning to the weight machines. Maybe if he exhausted his body, it'd help ease his mind.

But an hour later, after he'd returned to his room, showered, and collapsed onto the plush bed, his mind was still churning away.

How the hell was he supposed to tell them what he'd only found out himself a few days ago? He hadn't wanted to believe his own mother, so why should they believe him?

They likely *wouldn't*. He knew that, and was expecting pushback when he dropped the bomb. But the only reason he was even there in the first place was because he was a match for Myles. Wasn't that kind of proof enough? Sure, he'd go through further testing if they wanted more irrefutable proof of Maria's story, and frankly, he should. The story was an unbelievable one.

But as much as Maria's confession had thrown his world into chaos, Nick knew one thing beyond the shadow of a doubt: she'd told him the truth. Yes, she'd lied to him about it his whole life, but he knew his mother was an honest, ethical person in all other aspects. She had nothing to gain and everything to lose by telling him the truth now, and she'd done it anyway. He was furious, but he did believe her.

His new siblings . . . well, they probably wouldn't. But he had to tell them anyway. He kept seeing the genuine appreciation in Charles's eyes when they'd parted ways in the hotel lobby, and knew he didn't want to lie to that man. Hell, even if he did, Charles had warned him flat out, in his subtle, urbane way, that he wasn't a man to be crossed . . . and Nick believed that. The Harrisons had power that he didn't. All he had was the truth.

The drive from the hotel in Great Neck to Sandy Point, where Charles and his family lived, was only fifteen minutes. Nick wished it'd been longer. The sleek white Porsche was downright orgasmic to drive, and he wanted to really let her fly. Tomorrow, after his workout and before the doctor appointment, he'd find a parkway and go for a drive. That was all there was to it; it had to be done.

As the GPS told him where to turn and he made his way into Charles's neighborhood, he whistled low. It was all private streets, gates, and huge mansions. Lots of old trees, and lots of land. This part of the town was big-time, old-world money.

Nick was grateful that the GPS kept telling him where to turn, because the tremendous estates didn't have house numbers. When he turned onto Charles's road, there wasn't

even a post with street names. Just a sign that said PRIVATE
PROPERTY and a huge iron gate. Nick glanced up, saw the
camera aimed at the entrance, and gave it a jaunty wave.
The gates immediately opened. Nice to know he'd made
the list.

A long dirt path beneath a canopy of trees opened up
to . . . holy shit, a full-out mansion. It looked like it belonged
in a movie. A giant brick mansion, majestic and imposing.
There were several cars in the large space Nick supposed
they thought of as a driveway, and he pulled into the farthest
spot. There was a Mercedes SUV, a BMW minivan, a Range
Rover Evoque, an Escalade, a sweet silver BMW i8 . . . and
a Toyota Corolla and an older Honda Civic. They stood out;
Nick figured they belonged to people who worked there.
Because hell yes, a place like this had a household staff.

He cut the engine and stepped out of the car, walking
slowly as he took in his surroundings. Many trees, stylized
landscaping, early spring flowers . . . lots of land for a private home. A gust of wind brought the scent of water nearby,
and Nick remembered Charles's property was right on the
Long Island Sound. Stiller water than an ocean, the smell on
the breeze that ruffled his close-cropped hair was strong. He
was grateful for the dark gray leather jacket he'd thought to
bring; this New York spring weather wasn't what he was
used to. He'd been chilled since he'd gotten there. He hadn't
known what to wear to this gathering, so he'd settled on a
plain white button-down and jeans. Now he zipped up the
jacket and shoved his hands into the pockets as the wind
blew and he walked closer, then up the grand front steps. He
drew a few deep breaths before ringing the doorbell. *Here
we go . . .*

The ornately carved wooden door opened to reveal a
short woman in a wine-colored tunic and black leggings.
Her long, dark hair was pulled back in a ponytail that trailed
halfway down her back. She wore no makeup, but she didn't
need it; her olive skin was flawless and her big, dark eyes

were gorgeous. Nick surmised she wasn't one of his siblings. "Are you Nick?" she asked kindly.

"I am," he answered. "Guess that means I'm in the right place."

"Oh, you are, you are," she assured him, taking him by the elbow and pulling him inside. "I'm Lisette Harrison," she said. "Charles's wife, and Myles's stepmother. I'm so thrilled to meet you in person. Thank you for coming tonight. Thank you for coming at all. We're just so grateful."

"Pleasure to meet you, ma'am." He shook her hand and smiled down at her. His instincts immediately told him this was a gentle soul standing before him. And though she was poised, even refined, he could just tell she was more like him than them—as in, she hadn't been raised with money and came from a normal background.

He remembered now: Charles had pulled the biggest cliché in the billionaire handbook: he'd fallen in love with his kids' nanny. This gorgeous, elegant lady had been the nanny? Though Nick knew full well a first impression was only on the surface, his gut told him this woman was down to earth and kind. Add to that she was so pretty, Nick could understand how Charles had fallen for her. She took his jacket from him and brought him further inside.

Nick had to admit, their home was striking. The furnishings and décor were elegant and understated, yet somehow still dripped with wealth. But the mansion felt like a home, not a museum. It was . . . welcoming. He suspected, as Lisette made small talk, that it was likely her doing.

"The rest of the family is in the living room," she said as they left the foyer and entered the front room, referring to the loud cacophony of voices that floated from down the long hallway. "But you should go see Myles first. He's upstairs in his room."

Nick's brows furrowed. "Not with the family? Is he . . . ?"

"He's all right," she said quickly, and reached to fidget with a long lock of hair from her ponytail. "But with all his younger cousins here, it's just . . . well, kids carry colds and a lot of germs, and his immune system is pretty shot. We're trying to keep him as strong and healthy as we can before the transplant." Her small fingers twisted the lock of hair tighter. "Which, of course, we're hoping will happen, but—"

"Listen." He stopped her with a soft hand on her forearm, and she blinked up at him. "Like I told your husband, I hope this works too. My first doctor's appointment is tomorrow. We'll see what they say and take it from there, right? That's all we can do right now. But I'm in. And I'll do whatever they need me to do."

Her wide brown eyes got glassy. "Thank you so much for your kindness."

Ah, hell. This woman could tear the guts out of anyone. He tried to smile. "I haven't done anything yet."

"You're here. And you're being incredibly magnanimous to a family that you don't even know. That's enough." She sniffed back her tears willfully. "I'm a very emotional person. I cry easily. Don't be scared."

Nick chuckled. "I don't scare easily. No worries."

"Well, you're a police officer, so I would imagine that's true. Good thing." She gestured to the grand staircase. "Charles is with Myles now. Myles is waiting for you. He's excited. Why don't we go up so you can see him before dinner?"

Nick read between the lines: go see Myles before being exposed to everyone's germs. "Whatever you want."

They went up the wide spiral staircase as Nick glanced around. His heart rate was definitely up, and his nerves jangled like live wires. He was in his newfound brother's home, about to meet his entire family. It was hard to wrap his head around that. But most important of all, he was about to meet the kid who mattered most. The reason he'd even found the unknown connection at all . . . this poor, sick twelve-year-old kid. Nick braced himself, not knowing what to expect.

He followed Lisette halfway down the plushly carpeted hall before she stopped and knocked on a door.

"Come on in," Charles called from the other side.

Lisette opened the door and peeked her head inside. "Myles. He's here. You ready, sweetheart?"

Nick ran a quick hand through his hair, took a deep breath, and followed Lisette into the room.

The room was spacious, with pale blue walls, a huge flat-screen TV on the wall, and a large bay window that looked out to the massive backyard and the Long Island Sound beyond it. And in the full-size bed was a pale, skinny boy with his father's big blue eyes. His head was covered with a Yankees cap, and he smiled up at Nick like he was a celebrity or something. "Hi," he said shyly, sitting up straighter against the pillows propped behind him.

"Hey there." Nick stepped farther inside. His heart felt like it was lodged in his throat, but he stayed cool on the outside. "You must be Myles."

"The being-in-bed part gives me away, right?" the boy quipped, the smile never leaving his face.

Nick shrugged and joked back, "Well, it was your mom who gave it away, really, when she, y'know . . . said your *name* and all."

Myles's smile went wider.

"Good to see you again, Nick." Charles rose from the bedside chair and went to shake his hand. The expensive suit was gone, replaced by a black pullover sweater and khakis. "You found it here okay? GPS didn't steer you wrong?"

"No problem," Nick said.

"How'd the car handle?" Charles asked, a twinkle in his eyes.

Nick snorted. "Like a dream. Your attempt at bribery is well appreciated."

Charles laughed at that, then reached a hand out to grasp Lisette's and pull her into his side. She immediately wrapped her arms around his waist and he dropped a quick kiss on her forehead. This was a tight, loving couple. Nick was glad to see that. A lot of times, a sick relative could tear a couple apart.

"Excuse me," said a female voice. Nick's head swiveled. He'd been so focused on the boy in the bed, he hadn't realized someone else was there. A gorgeous woman, with dark honey hair, sky-blue eyes, and a sweet smile. Dressed in light blue scrubs, she approached him from the corner of the room, holding things. Nick blinked. She was beautiful . . . but a beautiful blonde. Couldn't be a Harrison, then. Who was she?

"Sorry, but I have to ask you to use these before you get closer to him." She held a white surgical mask in one hand and a bottle of antiseptic hand sanitizer in the other. She offered another smile as she opened the plastic bottle cap.

Something pinged deep in his chest as he looked at her. What the . . . it was like the air around him went wavy, even crackled with something like electricity. Finally, he blinked and cleared his throat. "Um, sure. Whatever you say."

"Well, you traveled today, right?" she said. "So many germs in air travel . . ."

"Right. Of course. Sure." He took the mask from her, and when their fingers brushed, he felt a jolt shoot up his arm. He almost shivered from it. *Get a grip, dude.* "I showered when I got to the hotel, though. Hope that helps?" He looked into her eyes.

"It does. But still." She met his gaze and a light blush colored her cheeks. Maybe he hadn't been the only one who'd felt that jolt. He couldn't stop staring at her. What the hell was that about?

"This is Amanda," Lisette said, jarring him from his momentary daze. "She's one of Myles's private nurses. She's amazing." Lisette dropped her voice to a stage whisper. "She's also his favorite on the whole team, but don't tell anyone."

Amanda smiled at the compliment, winked down at

Myles, then squirted some gel into Nick's open palm. He rubbed his hands together, making sure to cover all his skin, but his eyes were glued to Amanda. He'd dated many women. He'd seen tons of gorgeous women . . . but never had one given him such a deep, visceral smack of an instant reaction. Holy shit.

He didn't believe in love at first sight. But a . . . click, some kind of recognition, at first sight? Yeah, maybe. Nick felt *something*, he couldn't deny it. It was bizarre. . . .

Then he almost grunted at himself out loud. This whole situation was messing with his head. He was losing his damn mind. He had to pull himself together.

"I'm Nick Martell," he said to her, finding his voice just before he pulled on the mask. "Pleasure to meet you."

"Nice to meet you too, Mr. Martell." Amanda's voice revealed a bit of an accent. Purest Noo Yawk. He loved it.

"Please, call me Nick."

"Well, Nick, everyone's been anxious to meet you since they got the news," she said. "It's amazing that you're a match, and that you were found. What a gift . . ." She reached up to adjust the mask over his nose and chin. Their eyes met again, and his heart gave a little kick in his chest. "Much less that you were willing and actually came here to do this."

"Everyone keeps saying that," he murmured. "Like I wouldn't have done this?"

"A lot of people might not have," she said, stepping back.

"Why not?" he asked, his voice a bit muffled from the mask.

"Because it's gonna hurt," Myles said from the bed. They all turned to look at him. His eyes were glued to Nick. "You know that, and you came anyway."

"That's right." Nick moved to the boy's side, but shot a glance at Amanda. "Can I sit on the edge of the bed? These are clean clothes, not from the airport."

"Then sure," she said.

Nick sat carefully on the edge of the mattress. "So, Myles . . . I don't know if they told you anything about me?"

"Not really," he said. "I know you're from Miami, Florida, and that you're a possible bone marrow donor because your whatever pretty much matched mine, and the odds of that are really small. I mean, they tested every single member of my family, and none of them were a match. But they found you, on the registry. Which is great." Myles quirked a wry grin. "I mean, I hate to tell you this, Obi-Wan, but you might be my only hope."

Nick swallowed hard. This kid, with the sallow skin, stuck in bed, had a sharp mind, a dry sense of humor that belied his young age, and the sweetest eyes. This kid was his *nephew*, for God's sake. "I'm glad they found me. Look . . . I'm going to do whatever they need me to do. And you and me, we're going to give this our best shot."

"And it's going to hurt you." Myles sighed. "I've been sick for a while already. I know what it's like to feel like total crap. To be poked and prodded and . . . you probably don't. So I feel bad about that. That you're going to have to feel bad to help me."

Jesus, this kid was only twelve? Nick stared hard, willing him to listen. "Hey. Myles. I don't care. I can take it."

Myles just looked at him.

"Let me tell you a little more about me." Nick cleared his throat, remembering he had an audience of three standing behind him . . . one of whom would find out before the night was through that they were siblings. He chose his words carefully. "I'm physically strong. I work out a lot, because it's important that I stay fit. Because I'm a police officer. So that means I'm not afraid of danger, I'm strong, and I always try to do what's right. Those are all good qualities for a bone marrow donor, if you ask me."

Myles nodded, taking that all in. "So you're a police-man, huh?"

"Yes, sir. Five years now."

"Cool. Do you have a gun?"

"Not with me," Nick said. "I left it home. I'm not on duty, kid."

"Have you ever been shot?"

"Nope." He added with a shrug, "Stabbed once, but it was minor, thankfully."

"That must've hurt."

"Sure, it did. But look at me—I'm fine, aren't I?"

Myles nodded slowly, studying him with fresh eyes. "I didn't know you were a cop. That's really cool."

Nick breathed a small sigh of relief. He was glad to see Myles thought positively about his being a policeman.

"So . . . if you're a cop," Myles said, "you must be pretty tough, then."

"Well, I like to think so," Nick said, only half kidding. "So what I'm trying to tell you is . . . don't worry about if it's gonna hurt, whatever they're going to do to me. Really, from what they say, it shouldn't be bad at all. I can take it. And if it'll help you get better, I don't mind. Okay?"

"Okay." Myles grinned softly. "Thanks. Thank you for coming. It's so cool to get to meet you in person. I know not everyone wants to meet the person they're donating to. They get weirded out."

A lump formed in Nick's throat. "Nah, not me. And you're welcome." He cleared his throat harder. "So the way I see it, we only have one problem, kid."

Myles's grin turned to a frown. "What's that?"

Nick flicked his chin in the direction of Myles's baseball cap. "Yankees? Seriously? I'm a big Marlins fan. You sure we can hang out?"

Everyone in the room laughed.

"You're in New York now," Charles mock warned. "Watch yourself, Nick."

Nick blew out a fake breath of exasperation and rolled his eyes before shooting Myles a wink and a grin.

"Do you have any kids of your own?" Myles asked him.

"Me? No. Been kinda married to my job. Maybe one day. Why?"

"I was wondering if you ever play video games," Myles said.

"Sure, I do." Nick shot a glance at the Xbox controller on the nightstand. "Wanna play sometime?"

"Yeah, sure!" The boy's face lit up. "I have every game you could want. What do you like to play?"

"Why don't we let you two talk," Lisette said, moving toward the door. "I have to see about dinner. It should be ready by now."

"Come on down in about ten minutes," Charles said to Nick. "Sound good?"

"Sure, whatever you want." He flicked a glance to Myles, then Amanda. "Um . . . but . . . ?"

"We eat up here," Myles said, "when there's company. Too many germs. They visit me in shifts, with masks and all."

"Oh." Nick felt bad for the kid, being sequestered away from his whole family, but figured by now he was used to it. His eyes lingered on Amanda.

"We'll be fine," she said, as if reading his thoughts.

Jesus, she was pretty. And her voice felt like . . . comfort. Warmth. Nick was drawn to her, an actual tangible pull. He wanted to touch her hair, her cheek. . . .

What. The. Actual. Fuck. What was going *on* with him?

Thankfully, Charles spoke. "Thank you, Amanda. Myles, see you real soon, okay? And I know your uncles and aunts will come back up to see you again. Nick, see you in a few." He and Lisette left the room.

Nick turned back to look at Myles. "So tell me what games you like to play, and I'll see if I know any of 'em. If I don't, you can teach me."

"Tonight?" Myles asked.

"Yeah, maybe. Or another day. I'll come back, if you want. You want me to?"

"Like . . . you'll come just to hang out with me?"

Nick nodded as something heavy snaked through his chest. *You're my nephew. And you could die if this doesn't work. I want to know you while I can.* "Is that cool? I'm here for about two weeks, and it's not like my days are filled with plans. I don't know anyone in New York. So playing video games with you sounds good to me. If it's okay with your parents, that is, and if you wanted."

"That'd be awesome!" Myles said, brightening. "My sisters don't like video games, and I'm tired of Thomas— that's my big brother—beating me all the time."

Amanda laughed. "You give him a run for his money. He doesn't win every time."

"Yeah, but when he wins, he's a sore winner," Myles grumbled.

Amanda nodded as she said, "Got a point there."

Nick looked to her and asked, "You're here every day?"

"Weekdays," she said. "From one to nine. He has a night nurse, a morning nurse, and a weekend nurse when he's not feeling well. But I'm here every day no matter what, just to keep an eye on him."

He gazed into her eyes, the color of a soft spring sky. "Good to know."

Fifteen minutes later, Nick walked down the stairs. The echoes of many voices traveled from down the hallway. Bracing himself, he went toward the sounds. All the Harrisons were in there. His blood relatives. It was a surreal, daunting thought. He took a deep breath, trying to calm the pounding of his heart, then entered what turned out to be a tremendous dining room.

A long table, set for twenty, filled the space. Nick quickly scanned the scene. Lots of windows, expensive furnishings— there was a crystal chandelier, for fuck's sake—and so many people. The young kids were noisy, and the adults were seated, except for a blonde woman who stood fussing over a bib on a baby boy in a high chair. Charles sat at the far head of the table, Lisette to his right. Three dark-haired kids flanked her, and Nick surmised they were Charles's kids. To Charles's left was . . . guy had curly hair, sitting next to a flaming redhead, so that had to be Dane and his singer wife. And then yup, there was Tess; Nick recognized her right away. She was striking. There were three very young children between her and a broad, bearded blond guy. Jesus, her husband was big. On the other side of the table was . . . of course, that had to be Pierce, and two tiny boys between him and the blonde woman. It was a rowdy scene and a lot to take in.

Even more so because he was related to most of the people in this room.

Nick's head swam and his heart kept pounding. He shoved his clammy hands into his pockets and took a few steps inside.

"Hey, there he is," Charles said with a smile, and a hush fell over the room. Seventeen pairs of eyes pinned him.

Nick tried to grin, but it felt fake on his face. "Hello."

"Everyone, this is Nick Martell," Charles announced.

"Hi!" Tess's older daughter squeaked and waved at him. He grinned at her. "Hi."

But Tess gasped audibly. She stared at him, hard, and slowly rose to her feet. Christ, she was tall, and her wide blue eyes were like icy lasers spearing him.

A chill prickled over Nick's skin, and Maria's words echoed in his head. *You're so much like him. You walk in there, they're going to take one look at you and know who you are.* Jesus, had she been right?

"Babe?" the big blond guy asked, watching her with furrowed brow.

"You're . . . who are you?" Tess demanded of Nick, her voice edgy.

"I'm the possible bone marrow donor for Myles," he said.

"No." She gazed intently, as if she'd seen a ghost.

"Charles," she stammered, her eyes never leaving Nick's face. "*Look at him.*"

"Tess," Charles said, "what's this about?"

She kept staring at him. Nick just stared back at her.

You are the neon sign.

"Dane," she gasped out. "Pierce. Come on, really look at him! He's . . . he's related to us somehow."

A hush fell over the room, as if even the babies sensed something big was happening. Nick glanced at his brothers. They looked clueless. He didn't move.

"Tess," Charles started to say with a laugh. "What are you—"

"He looks just like *Dad*," she said. "Give Dad black hair and a deep tan, take him back to his twenties, and I'd swear I was looking right at him."

Nick blew out a slow, long breath and met her gaze directly. "So I've heard."

Tess blinked and her lips parted in shock.

"Excuse me?" Charles said, his eyes narrowing as they now locked on Nick.

"Whaaaat?" Pierce's eyes flew wide.

"You've got to be kidding me," Dane blurted.

"So I'm right!" Tess said. "Oh, my God." She looked from him to her brothers, glancing wildly from one to the next. "How could you look at him and *not* know he's a Harrison somehow? Am I the only one who ever looked at old family photo albums?"

Charles stared hard at Nick for a long beat. Nick watched, seeing how his eyes widened when it hit him. "Holy shit," he breathed. "I see it now. *Holy shit!*" His hands flew up to hold his head, rake through his hair.

"Um . . . we should talk," Nick suggested. He looked around the room, at one stunned face after another, and tried to breathe. "It's, uh, nice to meet you all . . . but yeah. Charles, Tess, Dane, Pierce . . . we should go in another room and talk."

Dane shot to his feet, eyes blazing. "Tess is *right*?"

"Seems that way," Nick said. His heart felt like it was going to jump out of his chest, *Alien* style. But he didn't move a muscle, fought to keep cool.

Pierce huffed out a laugh. "This . . . this is gonna be epic, then." He got to his feet at the same time Charles did. "I can't wait to hear this."

Everyone in the room was staring at Nick like he'd just dropped out of the sky from another planet. He wanted to laugh, and crawl out of his skin, and get the hell out of there, and ask a million questions, all at the same time. But all he said was, "I only found out myself a few days ago. It's been an interesting week."

"How?" Charles shouted. The room went dead silent in the face of his outburst.

But all it did was snap Nick to attention. "Do you really want to do this here?" he asked quietly, his eyes doing a quick scan of the children's confused faces.

"Go in the den," Lisette said urgently to Charles. "All five of you. We've got this. Abby, Julia, Logan, and I will give the kids dinner. You guys just go."

"I'm not going anywhere," Charles growled, "until I have a name."

"Charles," Lisette begged.

"Who?" Charles shouted at Nick. "Tell me right now."

Nick noticed the way Charles's stare had turned wild and somewhat lethal, so he said mildly, "When you were kids, do you remember a housekeeper that worked in your home named Maria Sanchez?"

Tess gasped and her mouth dropped open. Dane's head whipped around to gape at Charles, who visibly paled.

"I don't," Pierce said. "But clearly that name rings a bell for you three?"

"I was sixteen when she worked for us," Charles stammered. He was clearly stunned, eyes wide behind his glasses.

"She was only there a short time, but of course I remember her. She was very shy, sweet. Only a few years older than me."

"You had a little crush on her," Dane said quietly to Charles.

"Yeah, well . . ." Nick licked his dry lips. "Apparently, so did your father."

Chapter Six

Charles led the way down the hall to another room, holding the door open for them all. Pierce, Dane, and Tess all filed inside. Nick went last, all his senses fired up. His blood pulsed in his veins, his hands were a little clammy, and his breaths were shallow. He hadn't felt like this since his last undercover op was about to end.

They were in a den now, with comfortable couches and plush armchairs, a wide love seat by the bay window. Lots of big windows in this house. Nick knew they must let in lots of natural light during the day, but the sky was growing darker now, a deep navy mixed in with the cloud cover. Charles closed the door behind him as the others stood together, staring at Nick like he was a scientific specimen.

"Everyone sit," Charles said.

"I'm more comfortable standing," Nick said plainly.

Charles got close, right in his face, and glared at him. "You came to my home, came near me and my son, my children . . . knowing this—this—what you know. I told you I trusted you!"

"Yes," Nick said. "But calm yourself. I'm not here to hurt anyone. I'm here to *help* someone, remember?"

Charles blinked, but didn't move. The mixture of cold fury and wild disbelief in his gaze was fascinating to Nick.

"Why don't we hear what he has to say," Pierce suggested, "before we think of beating him up, huh?"

At that, Nick looked away from Charles to Pierce. The youngest sibling was . . . flippant. Not outraged or boiling over, like the other three. Surprised, but not ready to spring into action. More curious, or even amused. Interesting.

Charles, however, looked downright lethal. "What do you want from us?"

Nick's eyes snapped back to his as he spat low, "Not a damn thing."

"Stand down, Charles," Pierce said. "Let him *talk*."

Nick and Charles stood toe to toe, eyes locked, jaws clenched.

"What do you know?" Tess asked calmly. "What can you tell us?"

"Why doesn't he start with exactly how he's related to us?" Dane asked.

At that, Nick drew a long breath and stepped back from Charles. He looked from one face to the next. They all were so alike. He didn't look like them. He wasn't like them at all. This whole thing was crazy. "Apparently, I'm the accidental result of a brief secret affair between my mother, Maria Sanchez, and your father, Charles Harrison the second. So . . ." He huffed out a breath. "That makes me your half brother."

Tess slowly sank to sit on the couch, eyes wide. Dane's mouth formed a little O of shock. Pierce nodded slowly, then almost grinned as he said, "Well, I'll be damned."

Charles didn't move, but still stared at Nick. "When were you born?"

"March 28, 1989." Nick added, "In Miami. You want to check?"

"Oh, believe me, I will," Charles vowed.

"Go right ahead. You should. God knows I've been

doing research on all of you since my mom dropped the bomb on me."

"Have you now," Charles said. Anger radiated off him in palpable waves.

"Of course I have. Just like you would if someone turned your world upside down with news like this," Nick said, unblinking. He looked to the others. "I didn't know. I never knew. She only told me last week, and she didn't want to even then."

"Why did she, then?" Charles asked, almost a challenge.

"Because when I told my parents I'd been tagged as a match for Myles, and spoken to *you*," he said pointedly to Charles, "when I told them your name, she passed out. Literally, she fainted when she heard your name. She knew she had to tell me the truth then, and she did."

The room was silent. The air was alive and thick, crackling with electricity, like a summer lightning storm.

"Your father seduced my mother when she was working for him," Nick said. "I think they were only involved for a couple of months. But my mother took off when she realized she was pregnant. Quit the job, left New York, and went to stay with her family in Miami. She was only twenty years old. She hid and kept me away from here—and, knowing my uncles and aunts, took the shame and the stigma—rather than tell the truth. You get that?"

He watched as the four of them absorbed his words.

"She never told your father. She didn't want anyone to know. She never told anyone the truth except my grandmother and my . . ." He paused. "My father. The man who married my mom and adopted me when I was five. He *is* my father. But on my original birth certificate? She was so determined no one ever find out the truth, she left the father's name blank. Go look it up for yourself."

"Your adoptive father's name is Martell?" Dane asked.

"No. My *father's* name is Martell." A burst of proud defensiveness surged through Nick. "Funny thing. He's white too. Coincidence." The side of his mouth curved a drop as he added, "But I bet when you look at me, you just see a Latino."

"I looked at you," Tess said quietly, "and all I saw was my father."

Nick paused to glance at her. She was pale, with spots of high color on her cheeks. Hell, this was a shock to all of them. He wasn't totally thoughtless. But he had to tread carefully, not let any emotion get the best of him. He was calling on every bit of academy training he had to keep his head in the game and stay cool.

But the way Charles kept glaring at him, with such open challenge, had his back up. "Pretty astute sister you've got there," Nick said to Charles. "You looked right at me, sat next to me for an hour, and didn't see it. My mother warned me if I came here, someone would look at me and know right away." He arched a brow at Charles, unable to hold back. "Wasn't you, though."

Charles's jaw set so hard a muscle jumped. "I told you to your face you seemed familiar. I fucking joked you could be a long-lost cousin. You think this is funny? You're amused by my not figuring it out?"

"Nothing about this is amusing," Nick said. "Believe me, I'm not laughing. Everything I thought I knew about my life just got turned on its head."

"When was this, again?" Dane asked. "That she told you?"

"Went to dinner at my parents' on Sunday to tell them I'd be going to New York and why. That's when I found out. Got on the plane yesterday morning and came here." He scrubbed a hand over his jaw. "Been a hell of a week."

"And we're just supposed to believe you," Charles said in a hard tone.

Nick shrugged. "Well . . . I *am* the bone marrow match. That's how any of this even came to light. It's the only reason my mother finally told me—and she begged me not to come here, by the way. Didn't want me having anything to do with any of you." He rubbed the back of his neck, trying to ease the tension while he paused to let that tidbit sink in with the four of them. "Your sister knew I was a Harrison the second she saw me. You tell me if you're supposed to believe me or not."

"Jesus fucking Christ," Dane breathed, taking a seat beside Tess. "He's telling the truth. He's our brother. Jesus."

Pierce, on the other hand, moved to Charles's side and put a hand on his shoulder. "Stand. Down."

But Charles kept watching Nick. "You should have told me," he said.

"I was trying to figure out how to tell you," Nick said, his temper straining. "I was trying to be delicate about it, believe it or not. I was going to try to talk to you after dinner. I wasn't going to draw this out. But . . . how the hell do you tell someone something like this? Much less *four* of you?"

"Makes sense to me," Pierce said. He tugged on Charles's arm. "Let's all sit down. Talk about this."

"There's not much else to talk about," Nick said. "Actually, I think I'm going to leave now." Everything in him itched for escape. The way Charles kept glaring at him, he knew he'd end up losing his temper, and he didn't want to do that.

"So just drop the bomb and run?" Charles said, almost a sneer. "Yeah. Delicate."

Nick grit his teeth and stepped close. "You're not the one whose world just got blown apart. That'd be me."

"I'm sure this has been a tremendous shock for you," Tess said, clearly trying to placate and soothe.

"Understatement of the decade," Nick said.

Charles kept watching him. "I'm still waiting for the other shoe to drop here."

"What?" It hit him suddenly, and though he was outraged, he laughed. "You're standing there worried I'm here to shake you down for money, aren't you?"

"Are you?" Charles asked flatly.

"Fuck you," Nick spat. Yup, he was done. "You go to hell."

"Charles, dammit, shut up," Pierce said. "You're not even giving him a chance to—"

"To what?" Charles asked. "Blackmail the family?"

"Are you serious?" Nick shouted. "Blackmail you? How? For what?"

"Keeping the family's secret. Getting what you think is rightfully yours," Charles listed. "Maybe some payback for your mother for all her years of—"

"Let's get something straight, right fucking now." Nick's cool was gone. Muscles tight, blood racing, he got so close he could feel Charles's breath. He glared right into his big brother's blue eyes. "First of all, don't you ever talk about my mother again. *Ever.* And second, remember something here: I don't need you," he snarled, low and deliberate. "You need me."

Charles blinked, and his features froze.

Nick flung out his words like razor blades. "I'm a cop. Which means I *uphold* the law, I don't break it. I don't want your money. I don't give a shit about your family's reputation. I don't want to be part of your family. I *have* a family. So, again, you go straight to hell, you pompous asshole."

Charles's face darkened. Nick could see his pulse pounding in his neck.

Tess sprang to her feet and cried, "This is going so wrong."

"I'm only here to help Myles," Nick said. "Which I was going to do as soon as the registry called because I'm a decent human, not because you called and offered to pay my expenses. But then, when my mother told me who I really am? I realized I'm trying to help my *nephew.* He's my god-damn nephew. Believe it or not, that means something to me."

Charles took a jerky step back, as if Nick had pushed him.

"So fuck you and your blackmail theories," Nick seethed. His heart thumped, but any prior nervousness was gone, the uncertainty replaced by searing-hot, indignant anger. "I'm here to do what I can, stay out of everyone's way, and then I'm leaving. Going right back to my life, a thousand miles away, thank God. And it's a pretty good life, thank you very much. So don't worry, your half–Puerto Rican blue-collar sibling won't dirty your doorstep, much less the family name. I want nothing from you." His blood raced through him, his heartbeat pulsed in his ears. "Hell, right now I don't even want to look at you. I'm out of here."

He turned to leave, but Charles grabbed his arm. Nick shook it off with a forceful sweep and pointed a finger in his face. "Don't fucking touch me."

Pierce quickly stepped forward, between them. "Guys. No." Dane shot to his feet as Tess gasped hard.

Charles held up his hands. "I jumped to conclusions," he said. "Don't leave yet. Hear me out."

Every muscle in Nick's body was coiled now, poised to strike. His fists were clenched tight, and his breath came a little hard as his heart raced, the adrenaline shooting through him. All the emotions he'd been trying to hold back over the last few days had burst through like a tidal wave, swallowing him whole.

"I didn't mean to offend you," Charles started to say.

Nick barked out a caustic laugh. "The hell you didn't."

"You looked me in the eye as we talked for an hour," Charles said fiercely. "As I invited you to my home, to meet my family. And you didn't even *hint* that you knew we're related. That makes me wary."

"How was I supposed to casually drop that into conversation, Charles?" Nick asked, feeling wild. "Seriously. Tell me."

Charles paused, then blew out an exasperated huff of air. "I don't know."

"Yeah, well, I didn't either."

Pierce stepped forward to Nick, almost edging Charles aside. "Hey. Nick."

Still breathing a little hard, Nick looked at him.

"You're damn lucky you didn't grow up knowing the old man," Pierce said. "Whatever you read about him? It was worse. I'd say your mother did right by you."

A wave of feeling whooshed through Nick. "You believe me? And her?"

"Why wouldn't I?" Pierce said. "All the things you said make sense to me. Look, you're a match for Myles. You look like the old man. Doesn't take a rocket scientist to put two and two together." He held out a hand. "I'm Pierce. I used to be the youngest. Guess that's you now. Nice to meet you."

Nick eyed him for a long beat . . . then shook his hand.

"Charles has spent his life defending the good name and legacy of the Harrisons," Pierce said. "It's his default mode. I, on the other hand, spent most of my life thumbing my nose at 'em. Come sit by me, man. But don't leave just yet. Okay?"

Nick shook his head and had to grin. "I have to tell you . . . I wanted to meet you the most."

"Why?" Pierce asked. "Because I'm the most screwed up of the four of us?" He offered a jaunty grin. "If you looked me up online, I'm sure that was fun reading."

"Because you're kind of the reason my mother left," Nick said quietly. Standing there, staring at Pierce, now that he was a real person and not just a name and photos . . . he tried to picture him as a scared little boy. And he tried to choose his words carefully. "She said your father was horrible to you. That it was hard to watch, and she . . . felt sorry for you. And she was scared, because she didn't want that for her child. That's why she left, and why she never told him about me. She was afraid he'd either make her get rid of it, or take the baby away and . . . treat her baby like he treated you."

Nick watched the blood drain from Pierce's face. He stood very still, even as the other siblings all gaped at Nick. Then, slowly, Pierce nodded and said, "Your mother definitely worked at the house, then. I'm sorry I don't remember her. But it sounds like she knew exactly what was going on."

"I don't mean that to be hurtful, what I just said." Nick cringed a little. "I'm sorry if it sounds shitty. I mean . . ."

"It's the truth, man. She was right, for what it's worth." Pierce's voice was gruff. "He was the worst father ever. At least, he was to me. He was better to these three, but that's . . . bottom line is, he was a ruthless bastard then, and he still is today. I haven't spoken to him in about seven years. I shut him out of my life completely."

"Sorry to hear it," Nick grumbled.

"Don't be," Pierce said. "Best thing I ever did for myself."

Nick stared. Man, did he want to hear more about this. It proved his mother's instincts to flee had been right. What a piece of work Charles Harrison II must have been . . . must still be today.

"Nick." Tess stepped forward and tentatively raised her hand to him. "I'd like a do-over, please. I'm . . . your sister. I'm Tess."

"Do-over, huh?" He shook her hand. "Hi, Tess."

"You shocked me," she said. "I'm sorry if I was . . ."

"It's okay. Totally understandable," he said. He mentally shook himself. She was trying to be nice, dammit. "I'm not an only child, by the way," he found himself saying. "I have two younger sisters, Olivia and Erica. Technically, they're my half sisters, but I've never thought of them that way. Just . . . telling you guys. I don't know why."

Tess smiled at him. "That's nice to know. Thank you for sharing that with us."

Dane watched from where he stood.

"You don't know what to make of me," Nick said to him.

"Nope," Dane said. "Not yet. Too soon."

"That's honest. I like honest."

"From the man who lied to me since minute one," Charles said.

Nick shook his head, laughed low. "Bye." He turned and headed to the door.

"Wait!" Tess cried.

"Nope," Nick said. "I don't need that shit. We're done for tonight."

"We need some time to absorb this," Dane said.

"Yeah, well, guess what? So do I." Nick opened the door and walked through.

Pierce followed him. "Stay for dinner."

"No thanks."

"Nick. Give us a chance."

Nick stopped walking to face him. "I'm just here to do the thing. That's it."

"I believe you."

"They don't."

"They'll catch up. This was a hell of a shock."

Nick huffed out a breath.

"I was the outsider here for most of my life," Pierce said quietly. "I know you don't understand, but I kind of know how you must feel right now. I'm trying to tell you I'm open. I'm . . . I'm friendly territory, all right?"

Nick eyed him warily, but nodded.

Pierce nodded back and sighed. "So . . . the old man doesn't know, huh?"

At that, Nick bristled. "Fuck no. I don't even . . . I'm not ready to go there right now. I just wanted to tell Charles first, because of Myles. Then he invited me to dinner. I figured I'd have the opportunity to tell you four together, and take it from there. That seemed like the right way to go. Now . . ." He shook his head in disgust. "I don't know. I don't know anything."

"It's okay." Pierce slowly raised a hand and put it on his shoulder. He was two inches taller than Nick, and the laugh lines around his blue eyes deepened as he grinned. "I've never had a little brother before. This could be cool."

Nick had to laugh. "You're all in. Just like that."

"Yup." He peered hard into his eyes. "Way I see it, you're here to help Myles. You stepped up, even knowing what you know. That's what matters most. The rest . . . will work itself out one way or another. Give it some time."

Charles, Dane, and Tess emerged from the den. Nick took one glance at them and said to Pierce, "Tell Myles I said good-bye."

"Nick," Tess tried. "Please, wait . . ."

But he walked down the hall. He'd seen Lisette put his jacket in the front hall closet when he arrived. He found it, grabbed it, and opened the heavy front door to leave. Then he remembered something.

As Charles, Dane, Tess, and Pierce stood together, all watching him, he pulled his wallet from his jeans pocket. He plucked out the gold card Charles had given him and speared Charles with his eyes. Then he snapped the card in half with his strong fingers, flung the pieces onto the marble floor, and turned and walked out, closing the door hard behind him.

He'd almost reached the car when he heard a woman's voice calling his name. Shit, it was Tess. She ran to him, her long curly hair streaming behind her in the wind.

"I'm done," he said. "Nothing more to say right now, Tess."

"Please come back inside," she said. "Meet the whole family. It's not often we're all in one place. And we came to celebrate *you*. Your being here. You're the miracle this entire family prayed for, don't you understand?"

His head was pounding. The adrenaline had moved to his head, doing a conga beat at his temples. "I'm no miracle." He got into the car and drove away.

Chapter Seven

The first thing Nick did the next morning was return the Porsche to Charles's rental service. He then rented a different Porsche for himself, black as night and on his own dime, thank you very much. He'd found out there were long stretches of parkway on Long Island, and he had a feeling he'd need to go on plenty of long rides over the next two weeks. Why not have a sweet ride to tool around in?

He did take a long scenic drive with the new car, trying to clear his head. For over an hour, he sped along the quiet Northern State Parkway, all the way to the end, somewhere in the next county, and then back again. He needed the movement, the sense of escape. He never turned on any music, which wasn't like him. But he was trying to process all the events of the night before. They had him in a tailspin.

His four half siblings were interesting, that was for sure. Each so different, but with threads of commonality he recognized right away. Pride. Intelligence. Stubbornness. Generosity. Dry humor. Intense loyalty.

He even saw flickers of things he recognized in himself. A real argument for nature versus nurture.

Not that he'd admit it to anyone out loud.

His mother had sent a text, as she had every morning

since he'd stormed out of their house. His father was laying off, knowing when Nick was stewing over something, he needed time and space to cool down. His mom was too worried to do that. Nick knew that, and while he felt bad for shutting her out, he was still processing her betrayal. She should've told him much sooner.

You should have told me. Charles hadn't just looked furious when he'd growled that at Nick, but . . . hurt, too. Nick knew the feeling all too well. There were no winners here. Well, maybe—hopefully—one winner. Myles. That kid was what mattered the most in this mess of a situation. By the end of the drive, Nick was determined to focus on him. His siblings knew the truth now. He had no desire to go anywhere near his biological father from everything he'd heard. All Nick cared about, from here on in, was doing his part to help Myles get well.

And, surprisingly, Amanda had gotten into his head. His dreams had been a jumble of restless chaos, but the one about finding her in the shower of his hotel room was as clear as if he'd watched it on a TV show, even now, hours later. He'd woken up rock hard, feeling edgy. Only a few minutes in her presence, and she'd burrowed into his subconscious enough for a steamy cameo in his dreams. He wanted to see her again, find out more about her. At least that much was straightforward.

When he got back to the hotel, he went to the gym and had a short workout, then went to his room to shower. By the time he looked at his phone again, there were several texts and missed calls. Texts from his mom, Darin checking in, and a hello from his sister Erica—that one he answered. He adored his sisters. Erica was now twenty-two and Olivia was about to turn twenty. They weren't babies anymore. But they'd always be his baby sisters, and God help the men who looked their way. Even though he wasn't talking to his parents yet, he'd never shut out his sisters, so he texted her a quick hi to say he was fine and they'd chat soon. Darin, he could answer that in a bit.

The text from Charles made him laugh out loud. You didn't have to return the car.

Nick guessed the rental place had contacted him. Let him stew. The hell with him.

One voice mail, from a local number he didn't recognize. He listened.

"Hi, Nick. This is Lisette Harrison. Charles gave me your number, I hope that's okay. I'm only calling because Myles said you'd mentioned you'd be back to play video games with him. He thinks you're coming over sometime today. Would you just let me know if you are or not, so I can tell him? I'd appreciate it. Thank you."

Ah, shit. Nick sighed, his mind working as he got dressed. He didn't want to set foot in that house again, but he didn't want to let Myles down a thousand times more. And it wasn't like he had any plans for the evening. When he finished getting ready, he returned Lisette's call.

"I can't talk long," he said, trying to be polite. He wasn't mad at Lisette; there was no reason to be curt with her. "I have my appointment at the hospital in less than an hour and want to get going."

"I appreciate your getting back to me at all," Lisette said. "You're not obligated to entertain Myles. You're not obligated to do anything."

It almost made him wince, the way Lisette was walking on eggshells around him out of gratitude and a hint of desperation. "Well, I did tell him I'd hang out with him if he wanted, and if it was okay with his parents. I should've checked with you before saying something like that. I apologize."

"No, don't apologize! It's fine with me!"

"And your husband?"

Lisette paused. "Myles being happy is what matters most right now."

"I'd never do anything to hurt your son," Nick promised. "I hope you know that. I know I must be public enemy number one over there right now, but—"

"You're not," she said. "Please don't think that. Besides . . . I'm here. Amanda's here. Charles can't complain. There's nothing to worry about."

The mention of Amanda gave Nick a little lift. Seeing her again would be a fantastic bonus. "I have no idea how long my appointment at the hospital will take," he said. "Why don't I give you a call whenever it's done? Maybe I'll come by tonight, after dinner. Just for an hour or so, whatever he's up to. Is that good for you?"

"Whatever works for you is fine," Lisette said. "Myles will be thrilled. He likes you, you know."

Nick drew a breath as he made sure he had everything: wallet, keys, sunglasses against the glary gray sky. "Does he know? Did Charles tell him?"

"Not yet," Lisette said. "He, um . . . he's not going to tell Myles you're his uncle until he's one hundred percent sure that you are. Surely you can understand that."

"I do," Nick said, but something hot seared through him anyway. Charles still didn't want to believe him. "He wants further testing, I assume?"

"You'd have to discuss that with him."

"Of course. Sorry."

"No, I . . . it's a . . . well, it's an incredible thing, isn't it? All of it."

"Yup." Nick shoved his wallet in his jeans. "I have to go. I'll call you when I'm done."

"Good luck," she said. "I hope it goes well."

"Me too."

By the time Nick got to the mansion, it was seven o'clock. He so did not want to be there. But at least there wouldn't be seventeen Harrisons on the other side of the door tonight, only six, four of whom were kids. He rang the bell, ignoring the tight feeling in his stomach.

It was a girl who answered. A teenager with long, sleek dark hair and bright blue eyes that swept over him in an open assessment.

"Hi," Nick said. "I'm here to see Myles."

"I know who you are," she said. "I was in the dining room last night. I'm Ava. Apparently, I'm your niece."

Nick's mouth went dry. Charles's oldest child was a beauty, and he could tell just from her shrewd gaze she was smart and strong like her dad. "You overheard, huh?"

"Hard not to. After you left, they were all flipping out. They talked about it for a long time. You got my dad all fired up." She moved aside. "Come on in."

He stepped into the foyer and removed his jacket. "I should leave this down here, right? I was at the hospital all afternoon, then went and got some dinner. . . . I don't know the rules."

"It's nice of you to think of that. Yes to the jacket. Leave your shoes here too." Ava pointed to the corner, but kept staring at him. "You're really my uncle?"

"I think so," Nick hedged, remembering Lisette's words. Charles didn't want to tell his kids yet—that wasn't Nick's call to make. He wasn't going to cause more trouble.

"What do you mean, 'you think so'?" Ava demanded. "Either you are or you aren't. Right?"

"Ava." Charles's voice rang out sharply. He appeared from the hallway. His eyes flickered briefly to Nick before going back to his daughter. "Mind your business."

"If he's my uncle, isn't that kind of my business?" she said.

Nick stood in silence. He wasn't touching this.

Charles sighed as he met his daughter's demanding gaze. "We have to run a test to make sure."

"Were you going to run that by me?" Nick asked. "Just curious."

Charles arched a brow. "If you're opposed, maybe there's a reason for that?"

Nick swallowed back the reply he wanted to let fly, minding the girl. He grinned instead. "Nothing to hide. You want me to take a test, that's fine. But you could've, oh, I don't know . . . *asked*. Some people would call that courtesy."

Charles pushed his glasses up on the bridge of his nose as his eyes met Nick's. "Consider this my asking, then."

"I don't know why you don't just believe him," Ava said. "I went and looked at those old pictures last night. Aunt Tess was right—he does look just like Grandpa when he was young. If Grandpa was Puerto Rican, that is."

"*Ava*." The word flew out of Charles like a shot.

Nick laughed. He looked kindly at her and said, "Don't sweat it. I am—you're right. Well, actually, I'm half. But obviously I have my mother's coloring."

"I don't care about 'half' anything," Ava declared. "Charlotte is my half sister, and I don't think of her that way. She's just my little sister. Blood is blood. So if you're my uncle, you're not my half uncle. That's stupid."

Nick nodded slowly, taking in this fiery girl. "I have two younger half sisters, and I think of them exactly the same way. I like you, kid."

She grinned.

"Ava," Charles said. "I'm here to take Nick up to see your brother. Did you finish all your homework?"

"About three hours ago," she said, rolling her eyes.

"Good. Why don't you go do your thing for now, all right?"

"Trying to get rid of me, Dad? So subtle." She looked back up at Nick and said, "It was nice to meet you. And . . . thank you for being here. To help Myles. It means a lot. Like, a *lot*."

"Nice to meet you too, Ava," Nick said. As soon as she

walked away, Nick said to Charles, "She gives you a run for it, huh?"

"You have no idea." Charles rubbed the back of his neck in mild frustration before looking him over. "How'd it go at the hospital today?"

"Okay, I guess." Nick gave Charles a brief overview: he'd given blood, found out he would be further tested for signs of infectious disease, and answered extensive questions about his health history. "The truth is . . . I have no idea how to answer all of it. Because I don't know any history on my father's side. I told them that. That they should contact you. So, if you could provide them with those answers, that'd be helpful."

"Are you willing to come by tomorrow afternoon?" Charles asked with a cool stare. "I'll have someone come here. We'll get the testing done right away."

"If you want. But not for nothing, I already had the inside of my cheek swabbed when I signed up to be a bone marrow donor. That's why I'm here at all," Nick pointed out. "Remember?"

Charles's mouth opened, then closed. Then he said, "Okay. That's true."

"So my end's done. The hospital has all my medical info on file. I'll give them permission to release it to you. It's on you to get your pops swabbed. Not my problem."

"No? You're a cop. I'd think having hard evidence would be paramount to someone like you. I'd think you'd be just as invested in finding out the truth as I am."

Nick wanted to snarl at him. But he reined it in. "In this case, *you're* the one chomping at the bit for overnight proof. You're a powerful man. Get it done."

Charles's face darkened. "Fine. I will. But if I need a fresh swab from you?"

"I'll do it." Nick felt his blood pulsing now, his annoyance turning red hot. He wanted to know the truth without a doubt too, but he wasn't going to let this man push him around. It made him want to push back. "So. Did you even tell dear old Dad yet?"

"No." Charles's square jaw, so like his own, set tightly. "Let's get the test done first. One step at a time."

Nick snorted. "Whatever."

"It's interesting to me—you don't seem to be in a hurry to tell him the big news," Charles noted. "Or to talk to him at all."

"He sounds like a first-class prick," Nick said. "Why would I?"

Charles blinked, obviously taken aback. "Because you say he's your father."

"No, he's not," Nick said. "He's *yours*. Lew Martell is my father. Charles Harrison the second was my sperm donor. Who, it seems, used my mother and made her scared enough of his power to leave the state and hide my existence from him. Not exactly looking to have a family reunion with him, you know?"

Charles rubbed his chin, then his jaw, seeming to contemplate what Nick had said. "My father will find out, of course. You know that."

Nick shrugged.

"You have no interest in meeting him?" Charles asked. "None at all? You're not even a *little* curious?"

Nick ran his hands through his hair and looked around. They were alone, but he dropped his voice low anyway, knowing others were in the house. "Your father, from most accounts, is a real bastard. I don't need or want him in my life. Do I want to set eyes on him at least once? Sure. Out of mere curiosity. But that's about it. I'm not looking to hug it out or anything. I'm not looking for anything at all."

Charles just stared at him, incredulous.

Nick shook his head and headed to the stairs. "I'm going up now. Your son's waiting for me. I won't stay too long— don't worry."

"I don't mind," Charles said as he walked past him. "Stay as long as he wants you to. It was good of you to come here."

"I didn't do it for you."

"You didn't have to take the car back, you know," Charles said to his back.

At that, Nick stopped halfway up the staircase to slide a look over his shoulder. "Yeah, actually, I sure as hell did."

Charles snorted, and the corner of his mouth twitched. "You're stubborn, proud, and fierce, aren't you?" he said. "With a temper usually set to a low simmer. Probably lethal when it breaks loose, right?"

"Try me and find out," Nick said calmly. It wasn't a threat, merely a statement.

But Charles's mouth curved more, into a full-out wry grin. "I don't know about your mother's family, but I have to tell you . . . those are all Harrison traits. Like, Being a Harrison 101. The more I watch you, the more I listen to you, the more I see it. It's fascinating, actually. You ever hear of nature versus nurture?"

Yeah, he had. "I thought you didn't believe me."

"I never said I didn't. I just want unequivocal proof," Charles said. "For the record? I do think you're a Harrison. Like you've pointed out, you came up as the match, and damned if you don't look like our father. But I don't like that you lied to me. Right to my face. That's what makes me not trust you."

"I didn't lie, actually. I just didn't tell you the whole truth right away. But you know what? I already explained why I did that. If you refuse to understand, that's your problem," Nick said. "Besides, you don't have to trust me. I'm just here to donate, do this thing, and then I'll go back to my life and you'll all go back to yours. Done deal."

Charles smirked and crossed his arms over his broad chest. "Really?" He studied him shrewdly. "You're going to spend a few weeks here—could be more, who knows—with your newfound siblings, nephews, nieces . . . get to know everyone . . . going to go through some possibly tough stuff, medically . . . and then you're going to just go back to your old life, like none of this happened? Like we all don't exist? Okay." He shrugged, his brows rising. "It's stone cold, but hey—so's your biological father. Maybe you have more in common than we know."

Nick shot him a withering look. "You're the one who made it clear you don't trust me, big brother. Right now, that goes both ways."

Amanda answered the soft knock on Myles's door. She opened it to see Nick Martell standing there, and her breath hitched. God, he was so gorgeous. Not just good-looking, but *hot*. Sexy as hell. Something about him hinted of sin. From the first minute she'd laid eyes on him, she'd felt a buzz in her blood just thinking about him.

She'd hoped she would see him again soon, known she probably would because of Myles . . . but when Lisette had mentioned he would be coming by tonight, Amanda had felt a surge of excitement that was almost irrational. She'd met him *once*, for Pete's sake, and spent about twenty minutes in his presence. Now, one look at him and the urge to lick his skin was overwhelming. God. This wildly physical reaction to him was insane.

"Hi." Their eyes met and she felt a bucket of butterflies unload in her stomach. Yup, it happened again. Pure chemistry. She wondered if maybe he felt it too, even a lick of it.

"Hey." He smiled down at her. He was easily at least six inches taller. "Nice to see you."

"Come on in. He fell asleep an hour ago," Amanda said, moving to let him inside. "But he might wake up soon. He naps a lot."

"Poor kid," Nick mumbled, his eyes lingering on Myles

before moving back to her. "Should I come back another time?"

"No, stay. Really, he'll probably be up soon. His naps are usually about an hour, and he wakes up on his own."

"Okay . . ." Nick closed the door behind him. "Guess it's just you and me for a bit, then. Hope you don't mind."

Her heart actually fluttered. "Not at all." She went to grab a surgical mask from the box and the hand sanitizer, trying not to feel so breathless from the thought of being alone with him, the appeal of his deep voice, or the way his warm brown eyes seemed to drink her in.

He stood still by the door, staring at Myles as he slept. She let her eyes run over him, quickly taking in every sexy inch. His inky black hair was cropped very short in back and on the sides, just a little longer on top. . . . Her fingers itched to play in it. Warm brown eyes and long, dark eyelashes—why did men always get the gorgeous long lashes? she wondered. Not fair. Straight, narrow nose and a strong, square jaw, with full lips just made for kissing . . . she felt a burn zip through her at the thought of what he could likely do with that sensual mouth. And that body, good Lord. He was so clearly muscled; the long-sleeved navy T-shirt he wore was tight over the bulges in his biceps, taut across his broad chest and shoulders, defining all his hard angles. His jeans hung on narrow hips, over long legs and what appeared to be a perfect ass. . . .

She cleared her throat. She had to keep talking, or she'd likely just ogle this tall slice of walking testosterone until she embarrassed herself. "Myles was really looking forward to hanging out with you."

"Was he?" Nick asked. "That's . . . well, I was going to say that's cool, but maybe it isn't. I don't know."

"Why not?" Amanda asked as she came at him with the hand sanitizer.

He held out his palms to her. "You're a nurse. You tell me."

She frowned as she squirted the gel. "Not getting you."

"He shouldn't be getting attached to me, or me to him," Nick said, rubbing his hands together. "Right?"

"Ah. Well. Easier said than done." She watched as he adjusted the mask over his nose and mouth. Pity to cover those gorgeously pouty lips. "Truth? I'm attached as hell. I adore him. So you're talking to someone who's already broken a cardinal rule."

"How long have you been with him?"

"Fourteen months."

Nick whistled low. "How can you *not* get invested? C'mon. You'd have to have no heart." His dark eyes flickered to Myles, empathy clear in his troubled gaze. "I can't even imagine what he's already been through . . ."

"You don't want to know," she murmured. "But he's so brave. Such a fighter. With such a wonderful spirit and a heart of gold."

"Tell me about him." Nick's eyes held hers. "Tell me what he's like."

They sat in the two cushioned chairs by the window and talked quietly for a while. Nick asked many questions about Myles, and she answered the ones about his illness and his treatments as best she could. Some of the ones about his personality, and what he liked to do, fine. But when she gently suggested maybe he should be asking the family the more personal things instead of her, he clammed up. After a minute, he tentatively explained that he couldn't right now because they didn't trust him.

Amanda frowned at him. "Um . . . why not? If you don't mind my asking. That's just a strange thing to say, that they don't trust you. They don't know you yet."

"Well . . ." He scrubbed a hand over his hair and sighed. "Turns out I'm a match for Myles because I'm his uncle. I'm a Harrison by blood. I didn't know myself until a few days ago, and I had to tell them last night. They didn't take it very well."

Her mouth dropped open.

"And to top it all off," Nick said, "Charles thinks I might be lying and saying this to blackmail the family for hush money. Which is offensive as hell, I don't mind telling you. So . . . yeah. That's the story, unreal as it is."

She gaped at him, looking him over as if with new eyes. "You . . . you're really . . . ?"

With a weary nod, he quickly recounted the tale his mother had told him last week.

Amanda was dumbfounded. She just sat there for a minute, staring as her mind processed Nick's words. It sounded like something off a reality TV show, not something that happened to actual normal people. Not that the Harrisons were normal, exactly. "They must have flipped out," she finally breathed, trying to imagine stoic, proper Charles Harrison III finding out this guy was his long-lost half brother.

"You could say that." Nick half-grinned, but it was a rueful grin, no joy there.

"Holy crap." She shook her head as if to clear it. "I'm sorry. I don't mean to . . . I mean, it's just—"

"I know. You're fine."

"This is a lot to take in." She peered closely at him. "Are *you* okay?"

His eyes rounded as they fixed on her. She watched his throat work as he swallowed. His voice was soft and low when he spoke. "You know . . . you're the first person to ask me that. Thank you."

A wave of feeling flooded her, something like warmth. Empathy, she figured. But it was warm and insistent, the natural caregiver in her rising to the surface without conscious thought. That was her, trying to care for everyone, always. It wasn't even an impulse; it was how she was wired, something deep in her DNA.

Before she could say anything more, Nick leaned in, elbows on his knees. "Amanda . . . right now, when I want to ask about Myles, it's just easier to talk to you. You're, like, the only objective person I've met here so far. You're not part of the family. You're not looking at me thinking I want something sinister. Like I'm the enemy." Something flashed in his dark eyes, and her heart panged again like it had a minute before.

He was tall and strong, self-assured, bright, and dripping masculinity. But over the mask, stark white against the warm gold of his skin, she saw something in his eyes that struck her as . . . vulnerable. What a situation he'd been tossed into. She felt for him.

He seemed like a good man. Hell, he'd come all this way to help Myles, and she knew very well plenty of people tapped to be bone marrow donors were scared of the physical risks and said no. But he'd come, and was obviously willing, and now to be set against a whole family of powerful people skeptical over his motives . . . it was probably daunting as hell, even for someone as sturdy as he clearly was. Another pang of sympathy fluttered through her. She wanted to take his hand, but squelched that impulse. She barely knew him. But . . .

"Look . . . um . . ." She licked her dry lips. Was she about to overstep her bounds? Possibly. But the look on his face . . . she trusted him, even if the Harrisons didn't. She couldn't explain why. Her intuition told her she could. "If you're going to come hang out with Nick sometimes, I'm probably going to be here when you do, because I'm here with him every day. So . . . of course I work for the Harrisons, but you can . . . think of me as neutral territory. I want you to be comfortable around Myles. And me. Okay?"

His thick, dark brows furrowed as his eyes narrowed to study her. "Really?"

"Yeah. So don't worry about any of that drama when you're here with Myles and me." She gave a small grin as she added, "I'm Switzerland."

He chuckled, his eyes crinkling. "Aha. So . . . Swiss Miss, that's you. Got it."

She laughed too. "I don't know about that nickname, but yeah."

His eyes warmed as they held hers. "That's very kind of you. Thanks."

"Sure. I just . . ." She blew out a breath. "Wow, that's some story."

"It sure is. And I don't even know the half of it. I need to talk to my mother more . . ." He looked away, apparently caught up in thought. Then those warm, dark eyes sought hers again. "You know what? Maybe we should nix the Swiss Miss thing. I don't want you to get in trouble for talking to me."

"Why would I? That's ridiculous." She shook her head. "They're really good people, Charles and Lisette. I don't know the others as well, but they've all come to visit Myles enough times that I know they're good people too. This is a big, loving family. They've banded around Myles like few families I've seen, and it's got nothing to do with their wealth. They all look out for each other. They care."

"And I'm an outsider storming the castle," he murmured.

She didn't know what to say to that. For her to speculate wasn't only pointless, it wasn't her place. So she said, "Well, when you're in here, just playing video games with the kiddo? There'll be no storming going on. Just . . . kindness. Right?"

The way he looked at her seemed to swallow her up. She almost felt a bit woozy from the intensity of his gaze. But he said, "Right. That's all I'm trying to do. Thank you for trusting me on that."

"Well, with what I know now, if Myles is your nephew . . . it makes sense you'd want to get to know him, beyond the basics of a donor meeting the patient. And I think it's really sweet. For whatever it's worth."

"It's worth something."

They stared into each other's eyes, a tangible pull between them. Something buzzed through her, a new searing shot of fizzy heat. She wanted to tear that mask off his face and look at him fully. It was a crime for a face that handsome to be half hidden, and she felt denied. She wanted to climb into his lap. Her attraction was undeniable, some crazy chemistry at work . . .

"Amanda?" Myles mumbled weakly from the bed.

She shot to her feet and went right to him. "Hey, sleepy-head. How're you feeling?"

"Thirsty," he rasped.

"Hang on." She went to the small table along the wall, which was set up with all her needs. The box of surgical masks, the bottle of hand sanitizer, the plastic container of wet wipes, latex gloves and sucking candies and bottles of pills and . . . she grabbed an unopened bottle of red Gatorade, poured some into a plastic cup, and brought it to him. She helped him to sit up more comfortably. The two armchairs by the window were a bit recessed, not in line of vision with the bed. So she told him, "Someone's here to see you, mister."

Myles's eyes flew wide. "He came back?" His head craned around her to look toward the chairs.

"Hey, buddy." Nick was there, standing behind Amanda. She could feel his presence behind her, it was so strong.

"Hey, Nick!" Myles chugged down the rest of the drink. "Ready to play?"

"Absolutely, man. What are we playing?"

"*Plants versus Zombies GW2*," Myles said with a big smile.

"I . . . have no idea what that is," Nick admitted with a laugh. "You'll have to show me how to play. And I'd say be patient while I learn, but I bet you'll have fun kicking my butt, so it's cool."

Myles smiled brightly.

"Tell you what," Amanda said. "I'll set it up for you so

you can get started, but first . . ." She handed Myles a stick of lip balm from his nightstand, which he put on his cracked lips dutifully. "Are you hungry?"

"Not really."

"You need to eat something to keep your strength up," she said.

Myles shrugged.

"We could order a pizza," Nick suggested. "My treat."

Amanda opened her mouth to say something, but Myles said, "I could eat a slice. If you want."

"I want," Nick said. He'd eaten in the hospital cafeteria, wanting to get his blood sugar back up after giving several vials of blood. But he could always eat. He looked to Amanda. "How do we do that here?"

"I'll take care of it," she said with a smile.

Nick watched Amanda give Myles a quick check—she felt his forehead before letting him put his Yankees cap back on, poured him another small cup of Gatorade and brought it to him, fluffed the pillows behind him and even quickly ruffled his dark hair. She was so good with him. It just made him like her more. He knew an efficient nurse when he saw one, and she clearly was, but it was more than that. She really cared about this kid. Her heart and soul were in it, and it showed.

And while Nick knew how dangerous it was to let your heart and soul get involved in work where lives were on the line . . . he figured it was different for her. As a cop, he couldn't afford to get personally invested in the people he helped. Things happened fast on the street; he had to think, move, not feel. And with the system being how it was, and people being how they were . . . if he let himself care too much, it'd tear him to shreds.

But she was with this kid day in and day out, and had been for over a year. He'd watched her face when she'd told him about what Myles had gone through during treatment— two rounds each of chemo and radiation that hadn't worked—and how he'd rarely complained, just tried to keep positive. About how they played video games and board games and colored in adult coloring books together . . . She was more than his day nurse; she was his champion. Nick wondered if the Harrison family knew what a rare gem they'd found in this woman. And he didn't want to think of what it'd do to her if Myles didn't make it. He didn't want to think about that at all, actually.

He watched her as discreetly as possible throughout the evening, trying not to stare with open admiration. She'd nursed this boy through medical nightmares, and would continue to for as long as she was needed. She'd opened herself to Nick, and believed his story without even knowing him. She wanted him to feel comfortable there and had made it clear she was a safe space. That had made something heavy swirl in his chest, heavy but sweet at the same time.

Amanda Kozlov was genuine. Clearly capable, strong, and compassionate. Anyone who spoke to her for more than a few minutes could see all that. But add to that the way he burned for her when he looked at her for more than a few seconds? The way his blood had raced south when she'd innocently licked her lips? The way his heart pulsed when she sighed and her breasts rose and fell, tantalizing him? Goddamn, he wanted her.

Sweet Jesus, she was beautiful. Her honey-blond hair that fell past her shoulders looked soft, and he wanted to wrap it around his fingers to pull her closer. Her pale, creamy skin; her deliciously pink mouth; her enticing figure, hidden but visible beneath her shapeless uniform . . . all of it called to him. The curve of her ass alone made his body tingle and want. Her scrubs today were teal with white swirls, and the color set off her gorgeous sky-blue eyes.

But it was more than that. Talking to her had confirmed his initial assessment: she was smart, savvy, with a heady mixture of sweet and sexy that intrigued him. He just . . . really *liked* her. He liked the whole package.

He'd pulled his armchair to sit beside Myles's bed. They laughed and talked as the kid taught him the game. But every few minutes, he couldn't help but sneak a glance at Amanda. She sat in the chair still by the window, reading on her tablet. Nick knew why her brows were puckered as she read; it was the material she was absorbing. She'd told him how Myles would be "conditioned" for the bone marrow transplant, flooded with chemo and radiation, and she wanted to read more about what was ahead. He admired her dedication, her need to be as informed as possible, her desire to be prepared. He was the same way.

He was there to get to know his nephew. That was now his number-two reason for being in New York, behind donating and hopefully helping him get well. But yeah . . . getting to know Amanda too was a new and exhilarating prospect. She'd hit him like a tidal wave, knocking him on his ass. It was the last thing in the world he'd expected to find when he'd come to New York . . . but he couldn't deny it. He was drawn to her, and considering all the chaos and uncertainty swirling through his life right now, it was the one pleasant thing he could grab on to.

She flashed him a quick smile and it made his insides heat in response. Crushing hard on Myles's nurse wasn't the worst sin he could commit, right?

Chapter Eight

Nick rang the doorbell to the Harrison mansion. He hadn't planned on being back at the mansion the very next evening, but he'd been summoned by Charles. His guess was that the test results had already come back. Only that would have made Charles sound so serious . . . and a tiny bit humbled, if Nick wasn't wrong.

So here he was, on a cold Friday night. Well, it was cold to him. Everyone around him that day had been thrilled for temperatures that'd hit fifty-one degrees. To him, that was still too damn cold. He was a Florida boy through and through.

It was Ava who opened the door for him. She smiled and said, "Hiya, Unc."

Nick laughed. She was a firecracker, this kid. "Hi yourself."

She took his jacket, but he said, "Think I'm keeping the shoes on. I'm here to see your dad tonight, not your brother."

"Family powwow ahead," Ava whispered. "Be warned. My aunt and other uncles are here too."

A quick worry snaked through Nick, but he only whispered back, "Thanks for the heads-up."

Ava led him to the living room. He hadn't been in there before. It was much more grandiose than the den; more expensive furnishings and décor, all intended to impress. Nick supposed it was impressive . . . if he gave a shit about that stuff. Tess and Pierce sat on the longest couch, Dane was sprawled out on a love seat, and Charles was at the back wall, behind the wet bar, fixing himself a drink. "Well, well," Nick said. "Am I walking into an ambush here?"

"No," Tess said quickly, shooting to her feet. "No, please. We just want to talk. Not fight, or argue, or anything like that. All right?"

"What she said," Pierce chimed in. He and Dane set their beer bottles down on the coffee table at the same time.

Nick could feel the tension in the air, and it tugged at him. He gazed at Tess for a long beat, quickly scanned the three men's faces, and a surge of knowing rushed through him. "You got the test results back already, huh?"

"Yes," Charles said from behind the bar. He held up his glass, half full of golden liquid. "Scotch. You want some? Or a beer?"

"No thanks." He looked at Tess, saw the way she was studying him with something like wonder in her eyes. "It proved my mother's story, didn't it?"

Tess nodded and drew a shaky breath. "Without a doubt. You're a Harrison. He's your father."

The words set off something in his chest, a bizarre combination of elation and dread. His mother had been telling the truth, as had he, and they all had to eat that now. But at the same time . . . Jesus Christ, he was related to all these people. What did that mean to him? He didn't have the faintest fucking idea yet.

He just nodded, suddenly not knowing what to say or do. He could hear his heartbeat roaring in his ears. Everyone was looking at him.

"Are you okay?" Tess asked.

He nodded again. His throat had closed up, so he just looked at her.

She went to him, gently put her hand on his forearm, looked right into his eyes, and murmured, "Sit down, Nick."

He let her nudge him into the empty armchair and stared at his hands. His mind whirred, but it was blank. Just white noise in there.

Tess crouched in front of him, watching him, almost protective. "Talk to us. Your head must be spinning."

He shrugged, but met her eyes. "Ten days ago, I was just Nick Martell, a Miami cop, doing my thing. . . . I knew who my family was, who *I* was. . . . I guess it all just hit me." He raked his hands through his hair. "This whole thing is so fucked up, I don't know where to start."

"I'm sure it's overwhelming," she said.

"It's a shock for all of us," Dane said.

Dane's voice gave Nick a jolt, a small rush of irritation. Nick glanced at him. "Oh, I'm your brother, so you can talk to me now? How nice."

"I was wary of a stranger claiming to be a part of my family," Dane said. "I won't apologize for that. My family's been through too much, especially recently." His voice was calm, but his blue eyes glinted with steel. "However. Especially, yes, seeing as you were right—and the fact that I believe you when you say you're not after anything but the truth—I'm sorry if I came off like a dick. And would like to start over."

Nick sighed. Maybe a drink would have been a good idea.

Charles took a seat in the other chair as Tess took hold of Nick's hands. Her gentle touch startled him. She hadn't stopped looking into his eyes; even in his fog, he recognized she was clearly trying to soothe and support him. "There's so much I—we—want to know about you," she said softly. "I hope you'll let us."

"And if you don't," Pierce said from where he sat, "that's cool, too. You made it pretty clear you don't want to know us, and given the reception you got the other night, we can't blame you. Isn't that right, Charles?" His jab wasn't lost on anyone.

Nick couldn't help but grin. He liked Pierce; he couldn't deny it.

"I owe you an apology," Charles began.

"Save it," Nick said. "You made yourself clear." He stared right back, not giving an inch.

Charles's eyes blazed behind his glasses. "This family has more money and power than most people could ever dream of," he hissed. "And I've been at the number-two gatekeeper position for my entire life. I will protect my family to the ends of the earth. It's what I was born to do."

He huffed out a breath and a muscle twitched under his eye. "On top of everything else I've been dealing with, I had a strange man walk into my home and announce he's my long-lost brother. With the added bonus of he has serious leverage over me: he's the match that could save my son's life if it works. So tell me, Nick." His eyes narrowed and his voice sharpened. "What the hell would you have thought, in my shoes? How would you have reacted? I'd love to know. Because you know what? I'm willing to bet your reaction wouldn't have been that much different from mine."

Nick's jaw set tight. He hated to admit it, but he got it. Of course he did.

"Please try to understand all that," Tess said, still crouching before him. "We're sorry we offended you—we really are. But it was a huge shock to us too."

Nick nodded and gave her hands a squeeze. "Get up before your legs fall asleep."

"You obviously don't do yoga. I'm fine." She grinned and rose as gracefully as a ballerina, then went to retake her seat on the couch beside Pierce. "We'd like to get to know you, Nick, if you'll allow us to. I certainly want that."

"Seconded," Pierce said.

"Thirded," Dane said, raising a hand. "Is that a word?"

"No," Tess said with a grin.

"I just made it one, then," Dane proclaimed. His eyes set on Nick. "Give us another chance."

"Tell me what you know," Nick said, almost as a challenge. He looked around at all four of them. His gut hummed, wanting to believe them . . . but he couldn't shake the feeling that there was more, that something wasn't being addressed.

"What do you mean?" Dane asked.

"I mean," Nick said, "you've all had two whole days to do your homework on me. You got the DNA test rushed—thank you, money and power. You probably know more about me than my best friends do."

"I'm not going to insult you by denying it," Charles said. "I did an extensive search on you. Yes, I now know plenty of things. Facts. But we don't know *you*."

"That only comes from you," Tess said.

Nick wondered how and what they'd found. Then something hit him. His eyes rested on Charles. "Wait. You likely did your research on my mother too. Right?"

Charles gave one cool nod.

Nick's heart rate started rising and his fingers clenched. "You will *not* contact her. Under any circumstances. I want her kept out of this circus, if it turns into one. You hearing me? I'd say she's been through enough."

"I never even thought to contact her," Dane said. "Why would we?"

"To corroborate the story," Nick said. "To find out more about whatever happened back then."

"I am curious to hear some of those details," Charles admitted. "So yes, I had thought to contact her. But if you want us to leave her in peace, I'll do that. As a show of faith to you. How's that for trying?"

Nick's breath caught. Damn. Charles had thrown down the gauntlet.

"Nick," Tess said. "No one wants to hurt your mother."

"Your father will." Thinking of what his mom could be in

for now from that man . . . it made Nick's blood boil. "If he's as ruthless a bastard as she thinks he is . . . I want your word that you'll all leave her alone. If you have questions, ask me and I'll ask her. But I don't want this touching her."

"I understand your concern," Charles said. "You have my word. But your concerns about my father—"

"Are valid," Pierce interrupted. "C'mon, man. He's right, and you know it."

Dane nodded. Tess frowned and looked at Charles; the agreement in her eyes was crystal clear.

"I think it's pretty obvious," Nick said tightly, "that my mother never wanted anything from any of you. She's had twenty-nine years to come forward if she did."

"That's clear," Tess said. "Absolutely."

"The fact is," Pierce said, "if she raised you on your own, she is entitled to something, I bet." He looked to Charles. "Don't you think?"

"You're not hearing me," Nick pressed. "Keep your money. She wants nothing to do with anything Harrison. And I don't either. For now, while I'm here, not being treated like a criminal in your midst would be great. Let me get to know my nephew while I can. That's all I want. A little time with Myles."

Charles's eyes widened. "Of course you can get to know him," he said softly.

But Dane shifted in his seat, leaning in. "A criminal?" He sounded offended. "That's a little harsh. You're saying that's how we made you feel?"

Nick spat without hesitation, "Your words, not mine. I showed up on your doorstep to blackmail you, remember?"

Dane sighed. Charles leaned toward Nick and said, "I was trying to apologize for that before. You cut me off, remember?"

Nick slid him a withering look. "Let's get something straight. I'm a lot of things, but I'm not a liar. I believed in honesty and justice long before I became a cop, and now that

I am one, I take that even more seriously. So for you to imply otherwise? Yeah, it cut deeper than you realize. You all crossed a dangerous line with me."

Silence fell over the room. The four siblings looked to one another. Nick felt his heart thumping a little harder than usual. Man, this whole thing had him off his game.

"I'm sorry, Nick," Tess said. "I really am."

"Me too," Pierce said.

"I'm sorry too," Dane said.

"Same here," Charles said.

"But you're still wary of me," Nick said.

"We don't know you!" Dane stressed. "You don't trust us or know us yet either. We got off on the wrong foot. So . . . we all just need to take a deep breath here. And maybe, over time, we can all get to know each other and that'll change."

"He has no intention of staying," Charles said, eyes on Nick. "He said so last night. He wants to do the procedure, then go back to his life and leave us all behind."

Tess's eyes widened. Nick actually felt bad for a second.

"That's his right," Pierce said. "Um, hello. The guy just found out a week ago everything he thought he knew about his family isn't true. How about we give him some time to get used to the idea? A little slack, and backing the hell off?"

"Since when are you the voice of reason?" Dane said, incredulous.

"Since I've been in his shoes," Pierce said pointedly. He looked around at his three older siblings. "I spent a lot of years feeling like I was the enemy in my own family. And I kind of was. Damn, your memories are short."

Tess grimaced and grabbed Pierce's knee to squeeze it. The other two went silent. *Interesting.* Nick stared at him. "I really need to hear more about that some time."

Pierce grinned. "You got plans tomorrow night? We'll go get some beers if you're game. I'll tell you *allllll* about it."

Nick laughed. "Yeah, why not. I'm game."

"Excellent." Pierce's cheeky grin widened into a smile. "I have soccer games all day, so I'll have dinner with my wife and kids first. But then I'll pick you up at your hotel. How's eight o'clock?"

"All right." Nick looked at the other two men. Dane looked amused. Charles looked . . . perplexed. He arched a brow at Pierce.

"Try not to smear us too hard," Charles murmured, then sipped his drink.

Pierce laughed. "It's okay, Chuckles. You've more than made up for it since." He winked at him, then picked up his dark beer bottle from the coffee table and drank.

"So . . ." Nick said. "I'd like to see the papers with the test results, if there are any."

"Of course." Charles got to his feet and strode to the small table in the corner. He withdrew a manila envelope from its one drawer and brought it back to Nick. "Here's your copy of everything."

"Thank you." Nick opened it and gave the papers a quick scan. Yup, no doubt. There it was in black and white. Holy shit. He looked back up to see all four of them watching him. "Wow."

"Yeah," Tess said, and he could feel the waves of warmth she emanated his way.

He tried to smile at her, but as it hit him, he looked to Charles. "So who gets to tell the old man the big news?"

"That will be me." Charles sat again and took another sip of his drink.

Pierce cackled with dark glee. "Please let me be there. *Please.*"

"You're such a troublemaker," Dane laughed.

"Oh, c'mon," Pierce said. "I want to see his face. His head's gonna fucking explode."

"Maybe he'll deny it," Nick pointed out.

"He can't!" Pierce pointed to the papers Nick held. "BOOM!"

"It's going to be . . . interesting," Charles conceded.

"He could have another heart attack," Tess murmured. "Anyone thought of that?"

Pierce clamped his lips shut and shrugged.

"She's got a point," Dane said.

"I *had* thought of that, actually," Charles said. "But he still needs to know."

"You want me there when you do?" Nick asked. "I don't really care either way, so it's your call."

"Um . . ." Charles looked around at all of them. "I really think it'd be best if I just tell him first and let him absorb it. Then, we can set up a meeting. It'll be soon."

Nick nodded. "Okay. Let me know."

Dane got to his feet. "I'm ready for a stiffer drink now." As he strode to the wet bar, he asked, "Anyone else?"

Nick drew a long, deep breath. The whirring in his head had stopped. That was something. But he still felt like an outsider here. He wasn't ready to just throw down and hang out with the gang. Something inside him pushed, making him edgy. He got to his feet. "Maybe I should get going."

"Nonsense," Charles said. "Stay a while. I'm sure you have plenty of questions. We do too. Maybe we could all talk for a while. Unless you have somewhere to be?"

Nick had to grin. "Man, you're crafty. And pushy, too."

"He's got your number already," Dane chuckled.

Nick drew a long breath. He didn't feel right here. The whole thing was a total head trip. But . . . these people were okay. He could give them a chance in his head without them knowing it, still keep them at arm's length and protect himself. And why not? Getting to know them a little better, on good terms, and asking direct questions was quicker and easier than digging on the Internet. "I guess I can stay for a little bit. And I'll take you up on that beer now."

* * *

Two hours passed quickly. The five of them talked and talked. Nick heard about all his nieces and nephews, Tess's husband and his brothers' wives; some of what it was like growing up as a Harrison; a little about the family company, Harrison Enterprises, which Charles now ran; and about each of their individual careers. They, in turn, asked Nick a million questions, wanting to know everything about him, from his childhood and family to his career and his hobbies.

Lisette came and went, bringing snacks for them all. She thanked Nick for coming to play with Myles the night before and said that he'd loved it, prompting Nick to ask if he could again. Charles was quick to say yes to that, and it wasn't lost on Nick.

Ava, Thomas, and Charlotte came in for a few minutes for a proper introduction. The young teens looked so much like their father. Ava, confident and sharp, acted like they were old buddies already; Thomas was more wary, cautious, a slightly awkward thirteen. Little Charlotte, not yet six, automatically climbed onto his lap for a hug hello, a trusting and sweet soul with her mother's warm brown eyes. Nick was more moved by that than he wanted to cop to.

Overall, Nick had to admit that while they all were still being somewhat careful around each other . . . it wasn't a bad evening. His new half siblings were interesting, funny at times, and whip smart. People he could respect. And they really were trying, he could tell. He gave them credit for that.

At nine, he got to his feet and stretched. He didn't want to overstay his welcome, and he had a lot to process. He needed to be alone to do that. "I'm gonna get going," he said to the group. "But thanks for an enlightening evening."

They all rose too. "I'm going to tell him tomorrow," Charles said, obviously referring to their father. "I'll let you know afterward what transpired."

A shiver skittered over his skin, but Nick only nodded.

"So . . ." Charles held out his hand. "Truce?"

"Working on it," Nick said, but shook his hand firmly.

Tess moved in; she was so tall, he practically looked her in the eye. She kissed him on the cheek. "It's been a true pleasure. Thank you for staying." She smiled, and it was genuine. "This was lovely. I hope you think so too."

He got a little choked up at that. He nodded. "Better than I thought it'd be."

Her smile widened, a hint of triumph. "We're not a bad bunch."

"She's the best of us, though," Dane said.

Nick glanced at her with appreciation. "You own these guys, don't you?"

"Always have." Her eyes sparkled at that. "Knew you were smart."

He patted her shoulder. His newest sister was an impressive woman.

"Dude." Pierce leaned in, and they shook hands. "Eight tomorrow night. What hotel is it, again?"

"The Parker," Nick said. "In Great Neck."

"I'll be there. Don't stand me up."

Nick chuckled. "First round's on you."

Pierce smiled. "Game on."

"I'd ask to tag along," Dane said, "but another time." He and Nick shook hands. "Saturday nights, I have a standing date with my lady."

"Enjoy that, then," Nick said.

"Do you have a girlfriend back home?" Tess asked, as if it'd suddenly occurred to her to ask.

"Me?" Nick said. "No. Single, and fine with that."

The words were just out of his mouth when Amanda appeared at the doorway. "I'm leaving now, Charles. Just saying good-bye. Myles is asleep. He's fine."

"Thank you so much, Amanda." Charles went to her and

squeezed her shoulder. "Have a wonderful weekend. We'll see you on Monday."

Nick couldn't take his eyes off her. Her buttery hair was down, loose and pretty around her shoulders, and her scrubs today were lavender over white. She looked pretty and competent and adorable, and he wanted to devour her.

She caught his eyes across the room and gave him a little grin. "Hey."

"Hi. I was just leaving," he said in her direction. "Wait up—we'll go together. I'll walk you to your car."

"Okay." She smiled, and something flared in his chest. He finished his good-byes and walked to meet her in the foyer.

Lisette was there, holding their coats. Amanda shrugged into a puffy turquoise coat, the kind he'd seen a lot so far while in New York. He thanked Lisette for her hospitality, got his leather jacket on, and followed Amanda out into the night. It was very chilly now, a little blustery. He zipped up his jacket as they walked side by side down the front steps.

"I didn't know you were here," she said.

"I was summoned by Charles," he explained. "The DNA results came back. Congrats, Harrison family—like I told them, it's a boy."

Her eyes flew wide. "Whoa. And wow, they had that done *fast*."

"Guess that big money helps sometimes." He shoved his hands in his pockets as a soft wind ruffled his hair and made hers dance around her shoulders. "So we had a little family get-together. Played Twenty Questions. More like Twenty Million."

She peered up at him in the dark. "You okay?"

Warmed by her thoughtfulness, he smiled. "Yes. Thank you." He eyed the lined-up cars as they reached them. "Which one's yours?"

"You have to ask?" she said with a laugh, moving to the

older Honda Civic. "The only one that wouldn't cost a year's salary for me."

"Aha." He grinned again. Their eyes met and held.

"Thanks for walking me to my car," she said. "Very gentlemanly of you."

"I try. Besides, it was nice to see you." He wanted more. It was a pull; he couldn't think of any other way to describe it. He was drawn to her as if with magnetic force. *Do something*, a voice whispered in his head. *C'mon.* "Can I ask you a personal question?"

"Maybe," she hedged, but her eyes twinkled.

"Are you seeing anybody?"

She blinked but said, "No. Why do you ask?"

"Because I was curious." He met her growing grin with a matching one of his own.

"Ah. Well. No, I'm not." Her chin lifted the tiniest bit. "Are you?"

"Nope." His heart rate kicked up a notch. They looked at each other, the wind swirling around them, carrying the heavy, salty scent of the Long Island Sound.

"You doing anything right now?" he asked.

"No. I was just going to go home."

"Wanna get a cup of coffee first?"

She bit down on her lip. It made his blood race. Then she smiled. "Yeah. Sure."

"Great." He smiled broadly, his heart lifting. But then he stopped short. "Um. Thing is, I have no idea where the nearest coffee place is. Shit. So much for smooth."

She laughed. "I know where to go. Wanna follow me?"

His eyes held hers as a rush went through his entire body. "Yes, ma'am."

Chapter Nine

Amanda frowned for a second when she and Nick walked into Starbucks. It was pretty full, being almost nine-thirty on a Friday night, and she didn't see two seats together in the whole place. But an angel must've been watching over them; as soon as she and Nick stepped away from the counter with their coffees, a couple in the back corner got up from their chairs. Amanda rushed to claim them, waving him to follow.

"Damn, woman," he said with a grin, loping after her. "You moved in fast. Impressive."

She smiled triumphantly. "I don't mess around."

"I'll remember that."

Bluesy R&B music played over the sound system as they settled into the plush, patterned armchairs. Amanda had gotten a decaf caramel macchiato; if she had caffeine now, she'd be up all night. Besides, just being there with Nick had her adrenaline going, a heady rush. She still couldn't believe he'd asked her out, and that she'd said yes so easily. But something about him made her want to say yes to anything he suggested.

Down, girl, she thought as she shimmied out of her coat. She glanced over at him, all tall, dark, and sinfully hand-some, as he pushed his leather jacket behind him and got comfortable. Then she caught a glance at herself. Still in her scrubs. Sooooo not sexy. She winced, then had a thought. Setting her cup down on the tiny table between them, she pulled the short-sleeved scrubs top over her head, leaving only the tight white turtleneck beneath. "Just wanna shed at least part of the uniform," she said, feeling like she had to explain.

"I get it. Been there." His eyes quickly slid over her body. "You will *not* hear me complain." The tone of his voice, along with the flash of hunger she caught in his gaze, made it clear he liked what he saw.

She blushed lightly. The top was a little tight, but it was supposed to be underneath her scrubs, and . . . oh, screw it. She'd already done it, and he looked happy about it, so fine. She'd just ignore her not-sexy-at-all lavender pants. At least she was wearing her purple Converse sneakers—those were fun instead of boring. With a contented sigh, she took a sip of her coffee and leaned back into her chair.

"Must be long days for you," Nick said. "Being cooped up in Myles's room with him for hours at a shot."

"I don't mind it," she said. "As long as they feel they need me, I'm more than willing. For most of it, believe me, I've been too busy. That's been one sick little boy." She frowned, recalling it. "The last few weeks have been a bit of a reprieve for him, not going through any treatments. There are even some days . . . well, I don't mean this to sound disparaging in any way, but it's like I'm not even working. On the days he feels well, it's almost more like . . . babysitting."

"Then why do it?" Nick asked. "On those days . . . ?"

"Because they're terrified," Amanda said quietly. "And he's nowhere near done. He's weak, and with the transplant coming . . . if he even sneezes right now, they worry. They want someone watching over him all the time. If it's not me, they'd get someone else. And I've done more than my job's worth of medical care for that boy. So if they want someone there on the downtime, and they're paying well, and they're all wonderful people . . ."

"Say no more. I get it." He sipped from his cup. "You really care about him."

She nodded before admitting, "Maybe too much."

"That's not a bad thing," Nick said kindly.

She shrugged. "Well, it is what it is. Yes, I care deeply. I just want him to get well so one day he won't need me anymore."

Nick hesitated, staring into his cup for a long beat. Then he looked into her eyes. "What are his chances? Can you tell me?"

"Now that they found you, and you're doing this?" she said. "A lot better. But . . . yeah, it could go either way. No one ever knows. The fact that two rounds each of chemo and radiation didn't work is obviously a bad thing. His cancer is stubborn. And a bone marrow transplant isn't a guarantee. His body could reject it." She ran her fingertip around the rim of her cup, drawing a deep breath to stop herself. "But we can't give up hope. No way. He's got a decent chance. He does."

"I hope to God this works," Nick said solemnly.

"Me too." Amanda lifted the cup to her lips and took a sip. It didn't burn her tongue; that was good. "Is your family going to come to New York when the procedure takes place?"

Nick's brows furrowed. "I . . . hadn't thought of that. I don't think so. I won't want them to."

"Why not? The procedure is outpatient, but your recovery could take weeks. You'll need help."

"I'm a big boy. I'll be okay."

Amanda stared at him. She knew he considered himself a tough guy, but did he have any idea of what was in store for him? She asked him that outright.

"Yes," he said flatly. "And I'm not worried. Let's not talk about it now. Okay?"

She stopped herself again. It wasn't exactly coffee talk, was it? "Sorry."

"Don't be," he said. "I don't mind talking about it with you. I really don't. Just not *now*. I just want to hang out with you tonight, relax and chat about nothing heavy."

She smiled. "Understood."

"Good. I mean, you just worked all day. I just had a family reunion I wasn't planning on. . . ." He snorted out a laugh as he grinned wryly. "Really, we should've gone out for a drink. A real drink. Several of them."

"Next time," she said, and stole another sip.

His eyes heated. "Yeah?"

"Yeah. Why not?"

"Is this our *first* date, then?"

Her heart skipped a beat, then took off like a racehorse. What was she *doing*? But she found herself saying, "Maybe. Let's see how tonight goes."

His grin spread, revealing a dimple in his left cheek that made her stomach wobble. He lightly tapped his paper cup to hers. "To tonight going well, then."

Her breath caught as their eyes locked. God, he affected her.

"This is nice," he said. "I mean, I don't know anyone here. I've got a bunch of new relatives, yeah, but . . . I'm not at ease around them. Talking to you is so much easier than talking to them. And I like you, Amanda. So yeah . . . the idea of hanging out with you . . . that'd be great."

She only nodded, wanting to hear more.

"But I need to be up-front with you. I'm only here for a short time," he said quietly. His expression was somber, and earnest. He turned the cup in his hands. "Few weeks here, a week there, the surgery . . . you know how it might go. And when this is all done, I go back to Miami. Back to my life. So . . ."

"And here I thought you asked me out for coffee," she said. "Not to marry you."

The side of his mouth curved. "Yes. Absolutely. But I just felt like that needed to be said. I dunno."

"Short term. Hang out sometimes. Please have no expectations. Got it." She crossed her legs and took another sip. "Ya done?"

"Jesus." He dropped his head into his free hand. "That was . . . I sounded like a dick, didn't I?"

"No, you sounded honest. I like honest."

"I'm always honest. To a fault." He sighed and scrubbed that hand over his face. "Probably already blew that second date, huh?"

She didn't know what to make of him yet. But she liked his honesty. "Hey. Knock it off. This is the first date I've been on in a long time," she said, shifting to humor, her default setting. "Don't mess it up for me. I'm trying to enjoy it."

A surprised laugh burst from him. "Yes, ma'am." He laughed again and eased back into his chair. "How is that possible, by the way?"

"How is what possible?"

"That a woman as gorgeous as you hasn't been on a date in a long time?"

"My job's kind of taken over my life," she said, her insides warming from his compliment. "When I go home at night, I fall into bed. And even on my days off? I'm just either too tired or too sad to feel like hitting the bar scene. Not my style."

He nodded, taking that in. "We have that in common, then. I'm also over the bar scene, and I've been working too much myself. Just got a promotion, so it was worth it, but . . . I hear you."

She let her eyes run over his body, the muscles defined, taut and delectable in his charcoal-gray Henley and jeans. The man had the body of a god, the face of a model, and he oozed sex appeal. He was naturally charming and relatable, even though he screamed *alpha male*. She bet he had women throwing themselves at him all the time. "You know what? I call bullshit."

He barked out a laugh. "Excuse me?"

"Your sob story rings false. I bet you date. Probably a lot. I mean, look at you." She arched a brow mischievously.

"*Whaaat?*"

"'Fess up, Officer. Honest to a fault? C'mon, let's have it."

"Damn, woman." His grin was playful and sexy as hell. His dark eyes sparkled. "I mean . . . yeah, I've had dates. I go out. But nothing serious for a long time. My last real girlfriend was like . . . man, three years ago now."

"Mmhmmm." Amanda narrowed her eyes at him, equally playful.

"I swear that's the whole truth, and nothing but the truth." His brows arched as he added, "Related: I have nothing against short, hot flings. While I'm 'fessing up and all."

"Duly noted, Officer." She smiled, a fizzy feeling bubbling in her chest. She hadn't flirted with anyone in so long. It felt good. It was fun. He was fun. And so goddamn gorgeous . . . ohhh, she wanted him. She wanted him bad. A short, hot fling with him sounded like heaven on earth. Quick as lightning, a vision flashed through her mind of the two of them rolling around naked in a big bed, white sheets beneath them, taking each other hard and hot . . .

Oh, look, she thought. *There's me throwing my brain out the window. . . . Bye bye, brain.*

"You like razzing me," he said.

"Maybe a little," she confessed.

"Bold and forward New Yorker, giving the out-of-towner a hard time, huh?"

"You're a city boy, Miami Vice. You can take it."

The damn man smoldered at her, his dark eyes all hot and wicked.

Her insides turned to goop. There was insistent throbbing between her legs, just from how he looked at her. He made her burn with lust. He made her want to throw caution to the wind. Yup, she was definitely in trouble.

After almost two hours of easy conversation subtly laced with sexual tension, Nick and Amanda left Starbucks and walked through the small parking lot. The night was chilly and didn't feel very springlike, but Amanda was fine. Nick, she noticed, zippered up his jacket right away and shoved his hands into his pockets.

"You're cold, huh?" she asked.

"I don't think I've gotten warm since I got to New York," he said. "This chill goes right through my bones."

"You've lived in Florida your whole life?"

"Yup."

"You have no blood, then."

He laughed. "And my friends always say I'm hot-blooded."

She didn't doubt that. "I meant that you're not really used to temps lower than sixty-five, so—"

"I knew what you meant." His crooked grin was playful.

They stopped at her car. A soft breeze blew, making her hair dance lightly around her face. She turned to look up at him and say something, but his hands lifted to grasp her hair gently, pushing it back from her eyes and tucking it behind both of her ears. His large hands cradled her face as he gazed at her and edged a little closer.

Her heart started pounding, a thick *thump thump thump* that made it hard for her to breathe. His thumbs caressed her cheeks; while his hands were a little chilly, the heat coming off his body enveloped her, intoxicating her. She could smell a hint of his spicy cologne and wanted to burrow in close, wrap herself around him. Her mouth went dry and she licked her lips in anticipation. His eyes shot to her mouth, then back up again.

He stared into her eyes for a long beat, and the intensity

in his dark gaze held her captive. Her breath caught as she stared back, delicious anticipation unfurling through her. Slowly, he lowered his head, brushing his lips against hers, taking his time. The contact was featherlight, a sensual hint of things to come. . . . It set off fireworks inside her. She pressed closer, wanting more, parting her lips to invite him inside.

He deepened the kiss then, taking her mouth with slow, seductive sips. His tongue slipped inside and slid against hers, tasting her, learning her, consuming her. She whimpered softly into his mouth and he held her closer. His fingers sifted through her hair as her arms snaked around his waist.

She felt the car against her back and leaned into it, glad for something to ground her and hold her up. Because as he possessed her with his mouth, his deep, hot kisses made her legs go weak. She held on to his strong body, both to steady herself and because she couldn't get enough. Her fingers clutched at him, moving up to dig into his broad shoulders as her body pressed closer against his. But the leather jacket didn't give her the satisfaction of feeling him like she wanted, so her hands moved up the exposed skin of his neck to twist in his short black hair. As his tongue swirled with hers, his strong arms locked around her, holding her tightly against him.

She melted into his embrace, floating on sensation. He smelled good, tasted good, felt even better. They kissed for . . . was it only a few minutes, or longer? She had no idea, and she didn't care. She wasn't aware of anything but Nick.

The staccato slam of a car door nearby startled them both. He broke the kiss but panted softly as he leaned his forehead against hers. She couldn't catch her breath either. The space between them crackled with heat and desire.

"Jesus," he whispered, still holding her, seemingly unwilling to let go. His eyes searched hers. "That was . . ."

She couldn't form words at the moment, so she just smiled in mutual wonder.

He dove in for more, kissing her again, lingering as his tongue swept inside. God, his mouth . . . the feel of his body against hers . . . he was tall and solid and warm, and she wanted to drown in him. She could, easily. She knew it and, oddly, it didn't scare her. It actually left her feeling more exhilarated than she'd felt in ages. He didn't want her to have any expectations of him. That meant it worked both ways, and she found that freeing. She kissed him back recklessly, trying to give as good as she got.

"So about that second date?" His voice was all husky and low, his eyes were black with lust, and he was sexy as hell. "I'm asking. Please say yes."

She smiled wide and whispered, "Yes."

He kissed her again, nipping at her bottom lip before pulling back. "I was thinking of going into Manhattan on Sunday. I've never been there before."

Her eyes widened at that. "Really?"

"Yup." His fingertips caressed her cheek. "Any chance you'd want to go with me?"

"I'm free on Sunday," she said. "Besides, I couldn't let you go there all by yourself for the first time. Clearly you need my expert tour guide services."

"I was thinking that exact thing. Great minds . . ." His smile matched hers as his hands slid down to her waist. "I don't have the slightest clue where to start. There's a train station a few blocks from my hotel. I was just gonna take the train in, walk around, maybe hit Times Square . . . figure it out as I went."

"It's supposed to be nice out on Sunday," she said.

"Sunny and in the high fifties. Perfect weather for a day in the city. If you had any blood, I mean."

He chuckled. "I'll manage. So let's make a day of it, then. Together." He shifted and pressed his hips against hers, with just the slightest pressure, and it set off sparks in her body all over again. She could feel the rock-hard evidence of his arousal against her belly and it sent a heady shiver through her. Knowing she affected him as strongly as he did her made her feel powerful and giddy at the same time.

"You just want to see me in normal clothes," she joked, trying to distract herself. She wanted more and knew she had to hold back. "You want to see some evidence that I own clothing that's not scrubs. Tell the truth."

He laughed and played with a lock of her hair, wrapping it around his long index finger. "I just want to see *you*. Whether in scrubs, civilian clothes, or hey, even no clothes at all. That'd be fine by me too." His grin was wicked. "Totally up to you."

She snorted out a laugh. "I'll be dressed, sorry."

"Ahhh, all right." He shrugged, then winked. "It was worth a shot."

She smiled again. "Why don't I meet you at your hotel so I have somewhere to leave my car, and we'll go together from there?"

"Sounds good. What time works for you?"

"Um . . . we'll have to check the train schedule, but around eleven?"

"Perfect." He lowered his mouth to hers again, kissing her softly. "Thanks for coming out with me tonight."

"Thanks for buying me a coffee," she said, savoring the feel of his arms around her. But he blinked, as if a thought had hit him, and released her. Her body felt the loss of his solid warmth and missed it immediately.

"I'll need your number. . . ." He pulled his phone from his pocket and gave it to her.

She put in her number and handed it back to him. "This was nice," she said.

"It was." He grinned warmly as another gust of wind ruffled the top of his hair.

Something occurred to her. "Can I ask one thing?"

"Sure."

"This . . . I mean, yes, this is casual, but still, it should stay between us," she said, and looked at him straight on. "Okay?"

His brows furrowed, but he caught on quickly. "As in, don't mention this to my new siblings? Especially your boss?"

"Yes, please."

"Your personal life is none of their business."

"Of course it isn't. But Charles is very . . . proper. You know?"

"You mean uptight?" Nick quipped.

"A bit of that too," Amanda conceded. "So they might see this as . . . I don't know, a complication? Inappropriate. A step over boundaries. Do you know what I mean?"

"Well, it isn't any of those things, but I get what you're saying. And you're the one who has to work for them. So if you wanna keep this on the down low, whatever this is . . . that's fine with me." He stepped closer again, eyes sparkling at her as he whispered seductively, "It'll be our secret."

His warm breath against her skin made her weak with lust. She bit down on her lip, but the smile burst through anyway. "Thanks."

"No need to thank me. I understand." He lowered his head for one last long, sensual kiss that made her toes curl. "Good night, Amanda. Get home safe."

"Good night," she said. "See you on Sunday."

He waited until she'd found her keys in her bag and was safely inside her car before walking away. As she started the engine, she blew out a long, shaky breath. Goddamn, that was one sexy man. Her whole body was buzzing; she barely remembered the drive home, her mind was so filled with him. But before she knew it, she was pulling into the parking garage of her apartment complex.

She floated up to the apartment. It was dark and quiet; Gretchen wasn't home, already at work. Amanda took off her coat and shoes, flopped down onto her couch, and pulled her phone out of her bag to text her two best friends. But there was a text waiting for her, from a number she didn't recognize. Hi, it's Nick. There's an 11:17 a.m. train on Sunday. Is that good for you?

She couldn't contain her smile, or the zing of elation that burst in her chest. She sure did like a man who followed up. She quickly changed the contact information so it would show his name and keep the number, then texted back, That's perfect. I'll be in the lobby of your hotel at 10:45. Send me the name of it?

He answered immediately, Parker Hotel in Great Neck.

Okay, great. See you on Sunday morning.

I really enjoyed tonight, he wrote. You were, by a mile, the best part of my crazy day.

Her heart did a little soaring thing. Back atcha, she texted back. On both counts.

Glad to hear it. Enjoy your day off tomorrow!

I will, thanks. You too. Any plans?

Gym in the morning. A couple of phone calls that will take a while. Go for a drive. And get this—going out for beers with Pierce at night. His suggestion.

Wow. She wondered how that would go. From what she'd seen, Pierce was great with all the kids in the family, still a jock who liked to laugh. At least Nick might have some fun.

I hope you have a good time with him, she wrote, not sure what else to say.

Should be interesting, Nick responded. I'll tell you about it on Sunday.

Wear comfortable shoes! she warned. Or sneakers. Lots of walking in the city.

Sneakers, he wrote. Haha. You mean tennis shoes?

Whatever you're comfortable walking in, Miami Vice, she wrote back, grinning.

You razzing me again?

Maybe.

He sent back a winking emoji. She did the same.

After they signed off, she immediately opened the group text thread with Roni and Steph. Okay, ladies, she wrote. Sit back, buckle up, and grab your popcorn. I need to tell you about the unbearable temptation that is Nick Martell.

Chapter Ten

Nick's Saturday went by quickly. He'd had a good workout early in the morning, followed by relaxing in his hotel room and making phone calls. Those calls took up the bulk of his late morning and early afternoon.

He talked to both of his sisters, checking in and catching up. Then he finally reached out to his parents. He called their landline at the house so he could speak to both of them at the same time, but the answering machine picked up. They were out. He left them a message saying hi, he was fine, and he'd be in touch soon.

He still needed to turn over everything that had happened, process it better. So he went for a drive. The cloud front that had hovered over Long Island since his arrival had finally cleared out, and the bright blue skies and sunshine were like a balm to him.

He let loose with the Porsche, taking it for a spin on the parkway. The grasses seemed to have gotten greener, and he spotted little white and purple flowers along roads, big bushes blooming with yellow, daffodils . . . as if the sun had brought back color and life. With the sunroof open, Nick drove along the North Shore, all the way to the end of the parkway, then following the GPS directions even further along. He had no idea where he was going, and it suited him. Seemed like a metaphor for his present. Adventuring out into the great unknown with nothing but his wits.

He'd never realized Long Island was so big . . . but hey, he guessed that's why it'd been named *Long* Island. If he drove all the way from his hotel in Great Neck out to the eastern tip, it'd take him close to two hours. As it was, he drove over an hour east before stopping in a small town, having lunch at a tiny café near open farmland. It was rural here, so different from where he was staying. He grasped that the further east he went, the more the overcrowded houses turned into spread-out land, then farms. Amanda had mentioned that to him, how varied Long Island was with its packed suburbs, then more spread-out suburbs, and beaches, farms, even vineyards . . .

Amanda. He'd barely gotten her off his mind. He could still remember how sweet she tasted, how soft and warm her mouth was, how her body felt against his. What a delicious distraction she was from the chaos that had suddenly become his life.

She was so damn pretty, and he was very attracted to her, sure. But as strong as his physical pull to her was, there was more. She was smart, and caring, and easy to talk to. And she had such a quick, sharp sense of humor. He loved when she teased him, and he loved teasing her back. Getting her to blush felt like a victory. Flirting was good, but the joking and ease was even better.

It made him realize he didn't laugh enough these days. Being a cop wasn't fun, or easy. It was solid work to be proud of, and he wasn't afraid of hard work, but some days drove him damn near into the ground. Amanda made him laugh, and being with her was easy. If she lived in Miami, he'd pursue her, no question. But she lived here. He had to keep this light. The bottom line was their lives were both cemented in different places. Casual, easy, just for the short term . . .

But he couldn't stop recalling how good she felt in his arms, or the way she'd sighed into his mouth when they were kissing, setting fire to each other in the middle of a darkened parking lot like lusty teenagers. . . . It sent a hungry shiver through him every time he thought of it.

He was looking forward to tomorrow. Spending the day with her had been a great idea. He wasn't an overly social person, but he had started to feel a sense of isolation since he'd gotten to New York. Back home, he was always working, and his downtime was spent with a small circle of friends and his regular family dinners. He wasn't lonely yet, but he was . . . restless. Last night's impromptu date with Amanda had been a very bright spot in a very overwhelming week. Hell, a couple of overwhelming weeks. Between the promotion at work, the call from the bone marrow registry, his fight with his parents, and his involvement with the Harrisons . . . it was his craziest month ever, and it wasn't even over yet. Amanda made him feel good. Nothing wrong with latching on to that for a little while, especially if she was on the same page.

When he got back to the hotel, he stretched out in his suite and watched a movie. The Rock always had the power to hold his attention, distract for a while, and make him smile too. When it was over, he changed out of his Miami PD sweats, into a long-sleeved black T-shirt and jeans. He'd meet Pierce in the lobby in a little while. But his phone rang . . . and it was Charles. Before he even answered the call, his blood started to hum in his veins, instinct kicking in that this call would be something big.

"I told him," Charles said without preamble.

"How'd that go?"

"About how you'd expect."

Nick couldn't help but smirk. "That well, huh?"

"He wanted to know who your mother is, of course," Charles said, and the smirk vanished. "But I wouldn't tell him, because I wanted to keep my promise to you. I did everything I could to keep her name out of it. I told him it was someone who'd worked for him, but refused to give him her name."

Nick's stomach did an anxious little flip, even as he filed away the fact that Charles had done an honorable thing. "Thanks. I do appreciate that."

"Good. But he's probably trying to figure it out as we speak," Charles said. "You have to know that. Even though I assured him *you* will tell him yourself, when you meet. You know you'll have to do that."

Nick grunted affirmatively.

"So, if you want any control over this, I'd suggest you make that meeting as soon as possible. Busy tomorrow?"

"Actually, I am. I have plans for the whole day."

"Oh." Charles sounded surprised. "All right."

Nick didn't offer further explanation. He didn't have to. Instead, he said, "How about Monday?"

"Um . . . I can make that happen. Maybe we'll do it here, at my house. Neutral territory, kind of. That all right with you?"

"Sure." No, it wasn't. Nick didn't want to do this. Suddenly he felt uneasy and nervous, and he rarely felt like that outside of work instances. He hated it. But he couldn't get away from this meeting; it was inevitable. Might as well get it over with quickly. "Set it up, let me know. I have to go to the hospital at eleven on Monday to give more blood, but I'm free after that."

"Good to know," Charles said. "I'll get back to you as soon as I've worked it out." Charles paused. "You . . . might want to let your mother know. Just in case."

"What does that mean?" Nick said, but it was a dumb thing to say. He knew.

"When he finds out who she is," Charles said, "now that he knows what she did? He'll be out for blood. He was furious. More furious than I've seen him in a long time."

"You rein him in then," Nick demanded, his heart rate

rising. "Keep him in check. Because if I do it, he won't be standing when I'm done with him."

"I've been keeping him leashed for longer than you know," Charles said, sounding weary. "I've got this."

Nick couldn't help but feel like a time bomb had just been set off, and the ticks were suddenly loud and threatening. *Tick. Tick. Tick.* "When we meet, I'll make sure your father understands her position, and make it very clear he'd best leave her alone."

"But Nick . . ." Charles's voice was low and somber. "The fact is, she *did* bear his child and never tell him. Even you have to admit that was . . . well . . ."

"This conversation is over for tonight," Nick bit out. He knew what his mother had done was wrong on some moral level. But he'd be damned if he'd say it out loud to anyone with the last name Harrison. He was loyal to his mother. Period, the end. And anyone who tried to get at her or hurt her would find out just how fiercely protective Nick could be.

When Amanda entered the lobby of the Parker Hotel on Sunday morning, she spotted Nick immediately. He was sitting on a dark orange couch in the far corner but rose as soon as she walked in, grabbing his leather jacket and crossing to meet her. His long legs ate up the wide space in a few manly strides. Even when he walked, he oozed testosterone, at least to her. Maybe it was just that he muddled her brain whenever she looked at him. She wondered if pheromones ever went airborne. It would explain a lot in this situation.

"Hey." He smiled, showing his white, even teeth and the dimple she liked. "Good morning."

"Good morning to you."

His dark eyes slid over her in an unapologetic once-over. She wore her favorite brown suede jacket over a snug dark green top and skinny jeans. Her green and blue plaid Converse sneakers finished the outfit. He'd never gotten to really see her figure like this before; the shapeless scrubs had always hidden her body. She wondered if he liked what he saw.

"Hey," he joked. "You do own real clothes!"

"Told you so!" she said with a chuckle. She did a quick little turn, as if to model for him. "Ta-da!"

"I like it," he said.

"You like what?" she asked.

"The whole pretty package."

"Well, thanks." She smiled back as she watched him slide his leather jacket on over a tight burgundy Henley, trying not to notice how his biceps bulged a little with his movements. He patted his jeans pocket to check for his wallet, then nodded and said, "Okay, let's go."

It was a beautiful spring day, with a soft breeze, blue skies, and bright sunshine that spread warmth. But Nick winced briefly. He got his sunglasses from his inside jacket pocket and put them on. "Ahhh, better," he breathed with obvious relief.

She shot him a funny look as they walked down the street. "I thought you were from Florida, that you love the sun. What are you today, a vampire?"

"No." He snorted ruefully. "I'm a little bit hungover, if you wanna know the truth."

She laughed. "I see."

"Yeah, yeah, go ahead and laugh." But he chuckled too. "My own damn fault. Man, Pierce can drink. He must have a hollow leg."

"How many beers did you have?"

"I dunno. I mean, I wasn't totally trashed, but I did drink a little more than usual."

"Ah, why not. You needed to let loose a little."

"You have no idea how right you are."

"I bet. Did you have fun with him?"

The side of his mouth curved up as he said, almost surprising himself, "Yeah, I did. He's cool. As far as finding a new brother I never knew existed, I think I got lucky with him. I can see myself hanging out with him in the future. Is that weird?"

"That's great," she enthused, and she meant it.

She knew where the train station was, having passed it when she drove into town toward the hotel, so she led the way. They got there in under five minutes. After buying their tickets through the kiosk, they sat on a bench to wait.

"So," Nick said. "Do you have a plan once we get to Manhattan, O Esteemed and Mighty Tour Guide? Or are we winging it?"

"A little of both," she said with a grin. "How does that sound?"

"Sounds fine to me." He shrugged. "New York City's too big to cover in a day. So whatever we do today, it's all good." Birds sang from the cluster of nearby trees, a gentle breeze caressed them, and he slowly reached for her hand. Her heart gave a little leap as he interlaced their fingers. "Thanks for coming out with me today," he said.

"My pleasure," she said, unable to hold back a shy but pleased smile.

Over the train ride in, a short thirty-five minutes, Nick told her about his night out with Pierce. Amanda listened to how his new big brother had picked him up in a town car with a driver so neither one of them had to worry about driving home, and whisked him off to a bar in a nearby town. It was one of those wannabe English gastropubs, with fifty different beers and ales on tap, a menu full of fattening appetizers, and European soccer playing on all the flat-screens.

They'd talked nonstop. Pierce was eager to tell Nick about his miserable childhood, both to warn him what their father was like, and make him feel better about his mother's choices. Pierce had no problem telling it like it was about what he'd endured. It'd been unchecked emotional abuse, pure and simple.

"I just don't understand it," Amanda said, her mind

working. "He didn't treat the older three like that, right? Why was he so horrible only to Pierce? It doesn't make sense."

"Apparently," Nick said quietly, not wanting other passengers on the train to overhear, "their mother had affairs. Several of them." He moved closer, talking low by her ear. His leg pressed against hers; his shoulder leaned against hers. The nearness and the scent of his cologne gave her a heady thrill that shimmered through her. His deep voice and warm breath in her ear only made it more powerful. "By the time she got pregnant with Pierce, their marriage was in name only, so Charles didn't even think Pierce was his. He barely remembered the one drunken night he and Laura had . . . well, conceived Pierce. He demanded paternity tests. He never connected with him as a baby. And by the time Pierce was a toddler, he was just a symbol of everything that'd gone wrong between Charles and Laura. And he never shook that off."

"That's disgusting," Amanda spat. "None of that was Pierce's fault. He was just a child! How could anyone be like that to their own child?"

"I don't know." Nick shrugged, glancing out the window at the scenery that rushed by. "But that's my biological father. Sounds like a real prince, right? And Charles wonders why I don't want to meet the guy." He snorted disdainfully, then sighed before continuing.

"Pierce . . . he was all in. We had a good time, and we talked about some bullshit things, but then he really opened up. It was really . . ." He pursed his lips, and she saw his throat working. Whatever Pierce had said had moved him, hit home in a big way. "I could tell he just wants me to feel supported. Told me several times that no matter what the old man throws at me, he'll have my back. I don't think it was the beer talking—I think he meant it. Pretty amazing, huh? I mean, I just met the guy a few days ago."

"I think," she said, placing her hand on his knee, "if he

knows you're brothers, there's no reason why he shouldn't reach out to you. It's amazing, but it's also just . . . good." She gave his knee a little squeeze. "Good for him. And good for you."

Patterns of sunlight played along his face as he looked at her over the rims of his sunglasses. "Thanks." He placed his hand over the one she'd put on his knee. His skin was warm and firm. Slowly he interlaced their fingers again. His touch delighted her.

"Totally changing the subject," she declared. "Tell me a little about Florida."

When they got to the city, they hit the ground running. They walked from Penn Station to Times Square, the buildings looming high overhead and the crowded sidewalks an experience in themselves.

Nick was used to a big city—Miami was no Podunk town. But everything here felt bigger. Colossal. Just . . . *more*. And so damn gray. At least Miami was colorful. The most colorful things about New York City were its storefronts and its people. Maybe it'd be better when the sparse trees bloomed, but right now, the branches were still only buds. When they got to the center of Times Square, it was like being slammed with an overload of electricity and sound, even in the middle of the day. They moved along slowly as he tried to take it all in. He snapped pictures to send to his sister later, as he'd promised. Then they ducked into a pizza place for lunch. He insisted on paying, she insisted on splitting it, and he let her have her way.

They talked. He found it so easy to talk to her, even though he wanted to touch her every other minute. Her V-neck top gave just the slightest glimpse of cleavage if she moved the right way, but combined with those cute Converse shoes . . . it made her both sweet and sexy at the same time. That was the effect she had on him, and it was powerful. Her mixture of subtle siren and girl next door—with a drop of an edge—made her downright irresistible to him. Even watching her eat a slice of pizza was a slightly erotic act. Watching her teeth sink into the cheese and crust, or her little pink tongue dart out to lick her lips . . .

Focus, he chastised himself. *Eat your lunch, you animal.*

At one point, she mentioned something about her two best friends who were like sisters to her, and he got her to tell a few stories about them, giving him a glimpse of another side of her. She told him how just two weeks before, she and Roni had gone to Connecticut for the weekend to have a sleepover at Steph's house, something they tried to do every three or four months. Eagerly, she pulled up a picture on her phone of the three of them to show to Nick. He studied it, seeing the obvious lovefest there. Fair Amanda sandwiched between Steph, a petite, olive-skinned brunette, and Roni, a stunning African-American who towered over the other two, big giddy smiles on all three faces.

"How tall is Roni? Jesus, she makes you two look shrimpy."

Amanda laughed. "She's five-foot-nine. Compared to my five-four and Steph, who's only five-one? Yeah, it's noticeable. She's our warrior." She reached for another napkin from the metal dispenser on the table. "And men flock to her. She's dated more in the last year than I have in my whole life. So I've been dating my way through New York City vicariously through her."

He chuckled, but noted the tone of Amanda's voice when she spoke of her friends, filled with affection and deep feeling. "It's great you have friends like that."

"They're my lifeline," she admitted.

"Good friends usually are." He took the last bite of his slice.

"What about you? You have any close friends?"

He nodded, finishing chewing before he answered. "There's my best friend since high school, Tom. He got married and moved to Jacksonville two years ago, but we're still tight. We text and all that." Nick wiped his hands on another paper napkin. The pizza was outrageously good, he had to admit it. "And I have Darin. We met at the academy, trained together, and we just stuck. He works in the same precinct as me, but we're not partners. We hang out with a few other friends, but he's the one I trust the most. Guess you could call him a lifeline for me." He finished off his Coke. "Let's put it this way: the night I found out I was a Harrison? He's the one I called to talk about it."

Amanda nodded in understanding. "Are all your friends cops now?"

"Pretty much." He'd never really given that much thought. "Guess it's natural, right? I mean . . . I spend a lot of my time at work, and other cops understand what life is like on the job, so . . ." He shrugged. "Yeah, I guess so. You? Are most of your local friends nurses?"

"I suppose. I stopped working at the hospital three years ago to switch to private home care, but I've stayed in touch with some of my friends from there. That's actually how I got the job with the Harrisons."

Nick arched a brow at her in unspoken question.

"One of my friends from the hospital, Fiona, is a nurse. She's also Abby Harrison's sister," Amanda explained. "When Charles and Lisette decided to hire private nurses, Abby went to Fiona to see if she knew anyone she'd recommend. Fi told her about me, and the rest is history." Amanda brushed her hair back from her face. "So yeah, she and I are still friendly, and I am with others too. And you know, there's always Facebook, so you can keep up."

"I'm not a fan of Facebook," he said. "I'm on it, because of my sisters nagging me. But I'm rarely on there. Just saying."

"Duly noted." Amanda's grin faded a little as she pondered. "It's easy to keep up with friends online. And with my schedule, that's been a good thing, I guess. But actually going out and socializing . . . haven't done as much of that as I used to."

"You should go out more," he urged, as if it were obvious.

"Oh, okay. Gee, why didn't I think of that?" She rolled her eyes.

He laughed, crumpling up a napkin and tossing it at her playfully. She batted it away, sending it back to him with a triumphant grin.

"Can I ask you something?" he ventured.

"Sure."

"Your last boyfriend . . . how long ago was that?"

"About ten months or so now. Why?"

He narrowed his eyes on her, assessing. "Wondering if that ended badly, if you're still . . . I don't know, I'm curious."

"If I'm still what?" she asked. "Hung up on my ex? No. I'm the one who ended it."

"Was he a douchebag?" Nick asked.

"No," Amanda said with a tiny laugh. "Actually, the opposite. He was very nice. Perfectly nice. But . . ." She blew out a sigh and reached for her Sprite. "You sure you wanna hear this? Really?"

"Yeah, I'm curious," Nick admitted.

She didn't seem at all upset, which was a good sign. Finally, she said, "I broke up with him because I realized he was more into the *idea* of me than the real me. Long story. But, well, I deserved more. And so did he, since I wasn't really what he wanted when it came down to it. So I ended it."

Nick took that in. She didn't sound bitter or jaded, more like matter-of-fact and resigned. She wasn't nursing a broken heart; she wasn't pining for someone. . . . She was emotionally free. The relationship had ended on her terms, and for good reasons. All good. He wasn't sure why that mattered. Why he cared. But he did, and felt a twinge of something like relief at her words. He gave a short nod and said, "Power to you, then."

She shrugged. "Just seemed like the right thing to do. For

both our sakes. I mean, I could've gone along with it, just to have someone. But I'm not like that. So . . . yeah, that's it." She sipped through her straw until the bubbling sound of the last of her soda came out. "So. Real New York pizza. You liked it? You approve?"

"Big thumbs-up," Nick said with a grin as he thought, *And a big thumbs-up for you too, Amanda Kozlov. Biiiiig thumbs-up.*

They started walking again, window shopping as they went, and walked farther up Broadway until they got to what she told him was Columbus Circle. He'd heard of it. Since it was such a nice day, it was crowded. A thick stream of cars and taxis moved around the circle, seeming to never end. There were so many people walking around the high-traffic area, but also lots just sitting and hanging out, soaking in the sunshine.

They found seats on the famous cement that encircled the statue of Christopher Columbus and sat for a while, just people watching, taking in their surroundings, and still talking. They'd talked all along, at ease with each other. Finally, he slipped his arm around her shoulders and pulled her a little closer, the contact filling him with something warm and bright. Her dark honey hair was soft against his jaw. She smelled like flowers—it wasn't overpowering, just sweet and feminine enough to entice him. Her leg pressed up against his as she nestled carefully into his side. He savored the feel of her.

"This is nice," she said softly. "I've really enjoyed everything today."

"I'm glad," he said, smiling. "Me too. Really. This has been . . ." He ran a finger along her jaw, tipping her chin up. "Only one thing's needed to seal this day as off-the-charts fantastic . . ."

He leaned in and brushed his lips against hers, soft and sweet. She leaned into him. Then he kissed her more firmly, with a little more pressure. Her lips parted in invitation and he took it, slipping his tongue inside to touch hers, sweeping into her mouth to taste her. Her mouth was warm, her kisses intoxicating, pulling him under like he'd been drugged. She did that thing again, where she sighed into his mouth, and his blood raced through him, making his heart speed up and his cock grow heavy.

She turned in his arms to better hold him and be held by him. With a tiny groan, he pulled her even closer, her breasts pressing against his chest. Her fingers played along the hair at the back of his neck as the kisses deepened. He could have kissed her there until the sun went down. Except he wanted to do much more than kiss her. He wanted to take her back to his hotel and explore every sweet and sexy inch of her.

But he pulled back, reining himself in even though it was hard to catch his breath. He cradled her face in his hands, smiled, and murmured, "Yup, that's what I wanted. Now it's a perfect day."

"Then maybe you should do it again," she whispered. Her voice sounded breathless, and her gorgeous pink mouth was a little puffy from his kisses. Her light blue eyes seemed to glow around her dilated pupils as she gazed at him. He wanted to devour her.

"You don't mind PDAs, huh?" he asked, grinning.

"This is New York City. No one cares about us," she scoffed. "Kiss me again."

She didn't have to ask him twice.

Chapter Eleven

When Nick pulled into Charles's long sandy driveway on Monday evening, it was full. Amanda's car was parked at the end, so she was on duty. But there were eight cars there; apparently all the siblings would be there for this . . . this . . . whatever the fuck this introductory meeting would be. He'd been dreading it all day. The dread had simmered in his veins since he'd woken up that morning. An early, brutal workout hadn't made it go away. A quick trip to the hospital to give more blood and talk again with the doctor and his team had only made it more acute. A big lunch and vegging out in his suite watching TV hadn't made that feeling of dread disappear.

He wasn't afraid to meet Charles Roger Harrison II, for fuck's sake. Nick slammed the car door closed a little more forcefully than he'd intended. All his senses were on alert, like when he was on the job and in a potentially dangerous situation. That's exactly how he felt now, and he tried to chip away at why as he stood there and gazed up at his half brother's enormous mansion.

He wasn't afraid; what he was . . . was uneasy. On guard. Because he knew what kind of man his biological father was, and by all accounts, this wouldn't be a pleasant encounter.

No one *liked* walking into what they knew ahead of time wouldn't be a pleasant encounter. No one sane, anyway.

He was pretty sure Daddy Dearest wasn't going to be opening his arms for a big hug. No, Daddy was likely planning to take him apart, thinking like his eldest son originally had—that Nick was there for money and blackmail. Add to that getting caught on his shenanigans with the Latina housekeeper, bringing a smudge to his highly esteemed name? Charles Harrison II was likely more than livid, maybe rabid.

Blowing out a harsh breath, Nick raked his hands through his hair and stared up at the mansion. All he'd wanted to do was be a bone marrow donor for a sick kid. How had his life turned into this ridiculous drama?

He closed his eyes, took another breath, and reminded himself of who he was. Just plain old Nick Martell, sergeant on the Miami PD, from a modest background and close-knit family . . . his eyes opened as it hit him. Jesus, that just wasn't true anymore. And it never would be again. He was a Harrison, of the famous New York Harrisons, and even if he never did a damn thing with that, it didn't make it any less true. He was a member of one of the most wealthy and powerful families in the Northeast . . . hell, the whole country. He still hadn't figured out what that meant for him. It was insane.

Shaking his head, he marched up the stairs and rang the doorbell. He just wanted this done. Every muscle was a little tense, every nerve lit up and jangling, ready for whatever went down. He'd gone on undercover jobs over the past year where his life had actually been on the line. This meeting was pure bullshit in comparison. He had this.

The door opened, and both Lisette and Charles stood there.

"Great," Charles said. "We've all been waiting for you."

"Like a firing squad," Nick muttered under his breath in Spanish. "Let's fucking get this over with."

Charles blinked, stared at him for an extra beat, then looked to his wife. "What did he say?"

"He wants to get this over with," she said. "Can you blame him?"

Now it was Nick who stopped, blinked, and stared in surprise as he looked into Lisette's dark eyes. Well, goddamn.

"It's not a firing squad," she stage-whispered to him and winked.

"My wife is fluent in several languages," Charles said with open pride and a hint of a smirk on his face. He was clearly amused at having caught Nick off guard. "I guess you're glad you didn't curse me, huh?" Moving aside, he gestured inside. "Come in, please."

Nick had to chuckle. "What other languages do you speak?" he asked Lisette in Spanish, hoping both to hear her speak it in return and to irk her momentarily smug husband.

"Spanish, Portuguese, French. Little bit of Italian. But English is my first language," she said, answering in Spanish. "A long time ago, I was planning to be a translator for the government. I majored in linguistics in college."

Jesus. He felt like an idiot. "I've spoken both languages my whole life," he said, fumbling for something to say. "First at home, now at work too."

"Doesn't surprise me."

"I guess it wouldn't. But I admit, I didn't think anyone in this family would speak Spanish. That was wrong of me. I assumed. Sorry about that."

"No offense taken. You're kind of right, for what it's worth. None of them do, really. Just me." She grinned. "I've always spoken Spanish with Tina, who works here and is a close friend of mine, when we didn't want the kids to know what we were saying. But Ava started taking it in middle school so she could understand us. Be careful around her."

"Good to know," he said in English, noting the half-amused, half-curious look on Charles's face. "Thanks for the tips." He shot a glance at Charles and added, "Your wife's impressive."

"Damn right she is." Charles smiled and dropped a quick kiss on her forehead before saying to her, "I'm going to bring him to the firing squad now. You'll keep the kids away from the living room?"

"Of course." She looked up to Nick and said, "Good luck. I wish I could say you didn't need it, but . . . Charles II and I had some bad blood ourselves, back when he found out about my dating his precious heir. He usually comes out swinging."

Charles scowled briefly at the memory, then leaned down to give his wife a kiss. "See you after."

"Tell Myles I said hi," Nick said to her. "Maybe I can hang out with him again soon. How's he doing?"

"He's, um . . ." Any light that had been in Lisette's eyes faded. "He's starting the conditioning on Wednesday. He'll be pretty sick from that afterwards. . . ."

"How about tomorrow?" Charles suggested. "Some video games with his favorite new buddy might be just the thing."

Nick noticed Charles had gone all tense too at the mention of Myles's health. Damn, he felt for them. Amanda had told him how Myles would be prepared for the transplant: by flooding him with high doses of chemo and radiation, called "conditioning." He didn't even want to think about it. He noted how Charles reached out to caress Lisette's cheek for a minute, catching her eyes as they looked at each other. They must be so worried, so . . . no, he couldn't imagine how they felt, knowing what was ahead for their child. "Sure. You tell me what time. I have no plans tomorrow."

Two minutes later, he followed Charles down the hall to the living room.

Charles stopped him right outside the door, a hand on his shoulder. "Listen . . ." His voice was low, his gaze intent.

"Whatever my father says, know that we're behind you. He's full of bluster, gets nasty, and loves to manipulate. Don't let him get to you."

"I'll be fine." Nick's adrenaline levels were kicking up again; he could feel his blood in his veins, feel his pulse start to pound in his neck. "Let's just do this."

Charles opened the double doors wide. Tess and Dane sat on the couch to the left, Pierce was sprawled out casually on the couch to the right. But Nick couldn't take his eyes off the older gentleman in the big armchair by the fireplace, who slowly rose to stand as he stared right back at him.

Jesus Christ. He *did* look like the old man. It was devastating.

Charles II's hair was gray and thin, but impeccably groomed, no bald spot. His pale skin was weathered, lines on his face . . . goddamn, Nick realized that was his nose. And his square jawline, and the arch of his brows . . . all the contours of his face, even the shape of his eyes. But Charles Harrison II's eyes were cold, steely gray—like those of a hawk, shrewd, glittering, sizing up its prey. And as they focused on Nick like lasers, for a few seconds, the whole thing stole his breath.

"Jesus Christ," Charles II said softly. "He *does* look like me."

Nick's mouth went dry.

"Told you so," Pierce said, a hint of *neener-neener-neener* in his smug tone.

"Pierce," Tess whispered, a warning.

But it broke the tension for Nick, and he looked over gratefully at Pierce. He was going to have too much fun with this. Eh, why not?

"Hello," Nick said. And that was it. He was at a loss for words all of a sudden. What the hell was he supposed to say to this man? He was a stranger. They gazed at each other, assessing.

"How's it goin', man?" Pierce smiled and got up to shake his hand in greeting.

Dane also rose and leaned in for a handshake, giving Nick a pointed look and an extra clap on the arm as if to say, *You got this.* Tess went to him and kissed his cheek hello. Charles gave him a pat on the shoulder and walked to the wet bar in the corner. "Scotch for me. Want a drink, Nick?"

"No thanks." Nick wanted all his wits about him.

"I see you've already become friendly with your half siblings," Charles II said. "Isn't that nice."

Nick's mouth curved. That bothered the old man. Okay. "So far, so good."

"But you had no interest in coming forward to meet *me*," Charles II said. His tone was mild, but Nick could still feel the poison drip from it.

"Nope."

"Really. Why is that?"

"Simple, really," Nick said. "I already have a father. And if my mother thought you were a horrible enough person to leave the state and hide your identity from me for my entire life, that didn't exactly make me want to seek you out for a meeting."

The mere mention of her had made something shift in Charles II's eyes. Bloodthirst. "Then let's stop with the pretense. Who is your mother?" he demanded.

The open animosity toward his mother made a chill rush through Nick's veins. But he wasn't having it. Let the old man twist in the wind a bit longer. "You don't know?"

"I want to hear it from you!" Charles II huffed. "Not to mention I believe I have the right to know. And if we're going to prove your preposterous claim—"

"Preposterous?" Pierce laughed. "You just said yourself he looks just like you. Give it up, old man."

Charles II whirled on him, pointing down at him with an accusatory finger. "You haven't spoken to me in years. Don't start now. In fact, why don't you shut the hell up?"

Nick kept his cool, but his heart started pounding. There was the man Pierce had told him about in excruciating detail.

As if reading his mind, Pierce looked to Nick and said, "There he is. The *real* Charles Harrison the second. So polished and refined . . . father of the fucking century."

"Shut your damn mouth," Charles II growled at him.

"Don't you speak to him that way," Tess said sharply. "*You* shut your mouth."

Charles II looked at her with a combination of ire and hesitation. His lips pursed, and he shoved his hands into the pockets of his tailored slacks.

Fascinating, Nick thought. The man clearly, openly hated Pierce . . . and adored his daughter so much she could put him in his place with a few strong words. The layered family dynamics here were a psychologist's wet dream.

Pierce sent his sister a wink. "I'm fine, Tessie. But thanks."

"Dad," Dane said, "just gotta say, this is *not* a great way to make a first impression on your newest son."

Charles II's face darkened, the red rising from his neck to his hairline as he looked back to Nick. "Have we established that without a doubt? That he is?"

"Yes, we've more than established that," Charles said from behind the bar. With silver tongs, he dropped an ice cube into his glass. "You saw the paperwork. So why the bluster? Think you're going to scare him into recanting his lie? It's not a lie. The test proved it. And from what I've gathered so far, Nick doesn't scare easily. So just stop."

"*He's* proof of it," Tess said. "I knew it the second I looked at him, and so did you. Come *on*, Dad."

"Here's a good question," Nick said. He shifted into his power stance, spreading his legs a bit and crossing his arms over his chest as he lifted his chin, something that was effective as a cop. "Charles told you that my mother worked for you, right?"

Charles II's lips pursed again, and he gave a staccato nod.

"Well . . . then you should know exactly who she is." Nick

arched a brow, drawing it out. "Unless you were sleeping with more than one of your household employees." He let a smirk play on his mouth. "Of course, I'm sure such an up-standing gentleman like yourself wouldn't have done that, though. Right?"

Charles II's face got even redder as Tess gasped hard. Dane and Charles both went very still.

But Pierce barked out a laugh. "Oh my God, he's right! That's . . . that's priceless." He laughed again and said to his father, "You fucking hypocrite. Raking all of us over the coals . . . You gave Charles hell because Lisette was his nanny. Someone who worked for him in his home, a middle-class girl, and *so* beneath him."

"Stop," Charles said, but he'd paled a bit. He knocked back half of his drink.

"How many maids did you nail over the years, Dad?" Pierce grinned with malicious glee. "Two? Three? *More?* You randy son of a—"

"Stop it!" Tess demanded. "Pierce. Stop."

Charles II looked apoplectic. His obvious discomfort and rage pleased Nick more than it should have, but it did. "That's not true," the old man finally spat, but his voice seemed a little strangled.

"Know what? I don't really care." Nick shrugged. "Really, I should be thanking you for not being able to keep away from the hired help. I mean . . . I'm here. So thanks, you horny bastard who abused your position of power over my naïve mother, and God knows who else. Thanks to that, I exist."

"Well," Dane quipped from the couch. "This is going well, huh?"

Tess slumped, dropping her face into her hands.

"I'm sure you suspect who she is," Nick said, "but I'll in-dulge you, since you seem so . . . kind. Open. Since you've given me such a warm welcome, not at all wanting me to feel threatened or anything."

Pierce laughed again. "Man, you're good."

Nick stood up straight, tall, and proud. "My full name is Nicolas Esteban Martell. But before I was adopted by the best man on earth, for the first five years of my life, my last name was Sanchez." He made sure Charles II was looking into his eyes as he said, "My mother is Maria Sanchez. You got her pregnant in 1988. Do you even remember her?"

Charles Harrison II went stone-cold still. His face, which had been dark and mottled with growing rage, started to pale a bit as the blood drained. His mouth went slack, falling open for a few seconds. Nick watched him, fascinated, as the room went dead silent.

"Yes, I remember her," Charles II finally said. "Of course I remember her." He licked his lips, ran a hand along the back of his neck. "We were . . . involved . . . for a short time. Then she disappeared without a word."

"Did you try to find her when she left?" Nick asked. "I mean . . . if the woman I've been *involved* with totally disappears, I know I'd be curious to know what happened to her. But hey, maybe that's just me."

"We'd stopped the affair," Charles II said, "a few weeks before she left." He drew a deep breath, recomposing himself. The other four were quiet now, transfixed. "She stopped sleeping with me, and she stopped talking to me. Soon after that, she was gone. Never heard from her again. Why would I go searching after her?" His eyes turned ice cold. "Fact was, I didn't care. We didn't have some big love affair, if that's what she told you. No, it was just a few months of sex. And she was more than willing. A consenting adult. She was more than happy to get in my bed. Your mother's no saint, Mr. Martell."

Nick hadn't expected the sickening gut punch from those words, but it was like a boot in his solar plexus. His heart rate accelerated in thick, heavy beats.

"But now that I know what she did? I'm going to find her, all right." Charles II's voice was menacing, each word deliberate. "I'm going to find her, and I'm going to destroy her for keeping my child from me. The law can't do anything about it after all this time, but I sure can. She won't get away with what she did to me."

The whirring noise filled Nick's head. Red rage, hot and consuming, rushed through him. Without thought, he flew forward, closing the few feet between him and the old man in seconds. With both hands, he gripped the lapels of Charles II's jacket and yanked him close, taking pleasure in watching the old man's gray eyes bulge with shock and a bit of fear. Through gritted teeth, Nick growled low in his face, "Hear me." He gave the man a quick shake to make sure he had his full attention. "You lift a finger to hurt my mother in any way? I won't just make you regret that *I* was ever born, but that *you* were."

Chapter Twelve

"This man is threatening me!" Charles II yelled, looking around at his other children. "You're going to just sit there and let him manhandle me? Threaten my life?"

"I didn't hear any threats," Pierce said offhandedly. He shot Dane a mock-confused look. "You hear anything?"

But Dane moved to Nick's side and said calmly, "Let him go."

Nick didn't even budge. He kept his grip on the jacket, bunching it in his fingers as he glared at Charles II. At his father. God, his father.

The old man didn't give a shit about Nick; he just cared that he'd been duped. He just wanted revenge for being kept in the dark, being made to look foolish, not having any control. He was as awful as she'd said, as rancid as Pierce had warned . . . and they shared DNA. It made his stomach flip with nausea. His heart pounded hard. He wanted to hurt this man. Make him bleed. He wanted to pound him into the floor and make him beg for mercy.

"Nick," Dane tried again.

"Let go of me this instant," Charles II seethed at Nick, "or I'll press charges."

"You'd need witnesses to corroborate your story," Dane said. "You won't have any here. Not one of us. Understand?"

Charles II looked stunned.

Nick could barely breathe. It was as if everything he'd heard and seen and felt over the past week rose up in his core, an emotional tsunami, and swept him away. His body pulsed with energy, and his mind was focused on one thing: Charles Harrison II.

Charles came to stand behind Nick. "We won't let him hurt her," he said, and it sounded like a promise. He put a hand on Nick's back and spoke to him quietly, as if he sensed Nick was about to lose it. "Let him go. This won't accomplish anything."

Nick drew a shaky breath and swallowed hard. He knew Charles was right, and that he'd be in serious trouble if he hurt a civilian, but he couldn't help it. He took another deep breath. The thought of this powerful, hateful bastard going after his mom . . . "You stay away from her," he growled, his fingers clenching tighter in the old man's jacket. "You hear me? She wants nothing from you. She never did. You leave her alone, or so help me—"

"Nick." Tess's voice was soft, her big blue eyes pleading as she looked up at him from the sofa. "Please let go of him. We'll all make sure she's left in peace. I swear it."

Something about her words, the tone of her voice, broke through the throbbing haze in his head. He released Charles II but gave him a bit of a shove as he did, sending him staggering backward to fall clumsily into the armchair.

"I'll have your badge by the end of the day," Charles II vowed.

"You'll do no such thing," Charles III said harshly. "Shut up already, for God's sake. This is all even worse than I'd imagined it, solely because of you. I haven't seen you like this since the day of your heart attack. You should be ashamed of yourself."

"He'd have to have shame to be able to do that," Pierce remarked. "Or a soul."

"You stop too," Charles said to his brother. "It's not helping. I asked you to be here as a core member of the family and to support Nick, not to toss gasoline onto the fire. Please hold back somehow."

Pierce nodded and grumbled, "Sorry."

"Now." Charles looked from their father to Nick and back again. "Dad, he's your biological son. What you choose to do with that information in the future is up to you, but it's the truth. Maybe you two will come to some kind of understanding, maybe you won't. I think with some time to process all this, both of you might find you feel differently than you do right now.

"But as for Maria . . ." Charles's tone hardened as he held his father's eyes. "You won't go near her. Leave her be. This is official notice: if anything negative happens to Maria—or her husband, or her family—in *any* way, and it can be traced back to you? None of us—and I mean *none* of us—will ever speak to you again. And, on top of that, I'll personally help Nick pursue any means of retaliation that fit the action." He peered down at his father over the rims of his glasses. "I hope I'm making myself clear."

Charles II opened his mouth to speak, then closed it again as he glanced at his children, who all nodded in solid agreement with Charles's statement. Seeing their unified front, his jaw set and he sat up stiffly in his chair. "Fine."

"She's never asked for your money," Tess pointed out. "She isn't now. She wants nothing to do with you, or our family. You'd be the one dragging her back into this if you go after her, and that could make her change her mind. If she did, she'd have a case. She could sue you for all those years of child support, a whole list of things. Make this public, and make it ugly. You realize that?"

"I said *fine*," Charles II growled, pure malevolence radiating from him. "I won't pursue it. I'll *leave her be*." The old man glared at each of them, wanting them to make sure they felt his rage, but clamped his lips tightly together.

Nick felt a surge of emotion, a combination of gratitude toward his siblings, hatred for this man, and ambivalence about what would happen next. "How do I know he won't do something anyway?"

"He has too much to lose if he does," Dane said. "His entire family. Which he will, I promise you that."

"Assuming he cares more about the family than vengeance," Pierce said dryly. With a shrug, he added, "He doesn't give a fuck about me, Abby, or my kids, but he cares about all of them, so Maria's likely safe."

"Well, while we're all making things clear, this goes both ways," Charles II said, rising again to look into Nick's face. "What guarantee do I have that she, or you, won't try to sue me for anything in the future? Decide you want a few bucks after all?"

Nick snorted and shook his head. "Huh. Good point." He wanted to make this man twist. He grinned callously. "You know what? There is no guarantee, I guess. Funny how that works."

The old man turned purple. "Then why should I listen to any of you?" he said. "Why should I—"

"He's here to save my son's life!" Charles shouted, and the room went still. "That's why we found him at all—that's why he's here. You drive him away before the surgery, I'll spend the rest of my life making you pay for that. So just stop this!" His eyes were wild, and his breath came in short, hard gasps. "*Myles.* That's why he's here. For Myles. Your fucking grandson. Can you ever think of anyone other than yourself, for just a few minutes?"

"Hey." Nick turned to Charles and placed both hands on his shoulders. Jesus, the guy was trembling. Clearly he'd been pushed to the brink. "I won't leave. I'm committed to this. I'll do my part. Nothing could stop me. Okay? Take a breath."

Charles looked at him, blinked and nodded, and took a deep breath.

"I know you're on edge," Nick said. "I'm sorry if this fight made you snap. I'm sorry for my part. But you're right, gotta keep our eyes on the prize: getting Myles better." He gave a little squeeze, then dropped his hands. "We're all here for him. It's going to happen. He's going to kick ass and get better. It's all going to be all right."

"Thank you," Charles said, and drew another long breath.

"Spoken like a true Harrison," Tess murmured.

"I'm no Harrison," Nick said, stepping back from Charles and looking around. "I'm just me. And right now, frankly . . . I'm not sure what to do with all this. But I'll think about it later. Right now, my focus is doing my part for Myles. That keeps me on track. Gives me purpose in the middle of all this insanity."

His siblings all looked at him with things like respect, gratitude, support. . . . The old man looked stymied and sour. Nick's adrenaline ebbed, leaving him suddenly tired. He wanted to go back to his hotel room, lie in the dark and quiet. "I think we're done here for tonight, right? I'm gonna go now."

"Wait, stay a while," Tess said, getting to her feet as Dane voiced the same.

"We'll bring in something to eat," Charles said.

"Or at least have some drinks," Pierce added.

"No, not now, but thanks. I just need some air." Nick shot a look at Charles II. What a loathsome piece of shit he was. All Nick wanted was to get away from him. "You're on notice. Leave my mother alone."

"And what about you?" Charles II asked. "Leave you alone too?"

Nick paused for a second. "What?"

"Merely an inquiry," Charles II said. "Another talk is in order. You *are* my son. . . ."

"No, I'm not," Nick snapped. "Lew Martell is my father.

You were the sperm donor. I don't want to know you any more than you want to know me."

"You haven't even given me a chance to know you," Charles II said.

"Oh, please. Think tonight pretty much closed the door on that," Nick said. "I'm not interested. So at least on that note, you were successful. I want nothing to do with you." He walked to the door and said over his shoulder, "I'll see Myles tomorrow, Charles." He stopped in the doorway to add to the older man, "Stay away from my mother or I'll hunt you down, *Dad*. I swear that on my life. Good night, everyone."

Nick lay in the semi-dark for a while as he channel surfed. Nothing held his interest or could distract him; it was all like white noise, adding more static to what was already in his head. Finally, he muted the sound, leaving only the ghostly flickering light to play along the walls of the bedroom.

What a shit show that meeting had been. His biological father was every bit as awful as he'd been warned. As much as Nick wanted to know more, get answers to some burning questions, he knew he had to put as much space between himself and Charles II as possible. Asking things like "what drew you to my mother?" or "why did you pursue her at all?" or "what the hell were you thinking, hitting on the help, much less a woman twenty years younger than you?" would have to be stowed away.

He'd almost hurt him tonight. He'd wanted to, more than he was comfortable admitting. He was a police officer, for fuck's sake. And more than that, he was a decent human being. He knew he was too reactive sometimes, but he always reined in his temper—made the fire that burned inside work *for* him, not against him.

But tonight, Charles II and his smarmy face and his pointed barbs and threats had brought out the worst in Nick, with record speed. It was more than protectiveness toward his mother, which of course was at the root of it. It was just gut reaction to the look in Charles II's cold eyes, the haughty expression. . . . He'd almost lost his prized cool. He hated that. Now, that knowledge ate at him and made him restless. Like he couldn't get away from himself.

Grunting in frustration, he aimed the remote at the flat-screen and turned it off, tossing the remote aside as darkness filled the room. Still the white noise whirred in his head. He wasn't tired and knew he wouldn't sleep well, so it'd be a long night. His mind was filled with images and words and emotions, and he needed to wade through them. He didn't know what to do with it all. He didn't even know where to begin.

His cell phone buzzed on the nightstand. Warily, he picked it up and looked.

Hi. Where are u? A text from Amanda.

He grinned and felt something like a flicker of light spark inside. He saw it was 9:30. She must be done with work. In my hotel room. Why, where are u?

In your hotel lobby, she wrote back. Heard things didn't go well. Thought you could use a friend. Wanna go get a coffee? Or something stronger?

His grin turned into a smile as he sat up in the darkness. Yessss. I'll be down in 5.

Amanda stole a glance at Nick from beneath her lashes and took a sip from her glass. The Riesling was cool and crisp as it slid down her throat. She and Nick had walked along the main street of town, quiet in the slight chill of the night, going over six blocks until they finally found a place that was open. It was an upscale wine bar—not Nick's usual kind of place, and not hers either. He'd raised a thick brow at the door, mumbling about its clear hipster vibe. But he needed a drink, and desperate times called for desperate measures. So they'd gotten a table for two in the back of the dimly lit bar, and the now open bottle of Riesling sat between them on the round tabletop.

He took a first sip from his glass and said, "It's not terrible."

"Well, that's good."

"I wish it was a beer, but it'll work."

"That's the spirit," she said. "Take one for the team."

He tried to smile, but it came out as a grimace. "I don't have much spirit tonight. I'm likely bad company."

"Nah. I'd tell you if you were." She kept it light, hoping to break through his dark mood. She was on a mission tonight, and it was a simple one: distract Nick from his troubles for a few hours. Make him smile. Make him feel better. Because that's what she did, what she was good at: making people feel better when they were hurting. It was one of the reasons she'd become a nurse; she was a natural caretaker. She'd had years of experience, smoothing tensions between her parents, then friends, anyone really. She wasn't a doormat, or a blank listening ear. She cared about people, knew how to make them calm down, relax. . . . She was a soother, a healer. Nursing had seemed the obvious career path. And that had its origins in her personal life.

Nick, whether he wanted to admit it or not, needed soothing. Some care. He needed someone, something, to lean on right now. Why not her? They got along, she was good at helping others, and she wanted to give that to him now. And yes, she was drawn to him, attracted to him, and interested in him. She wasn't going to lie to herself. He was stunningly gorgeous, they had chemistry, and she was only human. She was glad he'd taken her up on the offer to come for a drink.

Staring into his glass, he took another sip, set it down, and sat still for a long beat. Finally, the side of his mouth curved up a bit. "I appreciate your coming to see me and dragging me out here." His warm brown eyes lifted to meet hers. "Thank you."

"You're welcome." She gestured over her royal blue scrubs as if presenting an award and added, "Hey, I wore my sexiest outfit for you. Least I could do."

That brought on a full smile, the kind that had the habit of stealing her breath. "Amanda," he said, "you're sexy in anything. Because *you're* sexy. Period, the end."

She felt a soft blush creep up her throat and heat her cheeks. "Well, thanks."

"It's the truth."

"Hard to feel like a seductress in scrubs, but I'll take your word for it."

He grinned and held up a hand as if swearing an oath. "I'm a man of honor. My word is gold."

"Good to know." She grinned back and took another sip of wine. "I'd love to see you in your uniform. Bet you're unbearably hot."

His brows shot up. "You think?"

"Not a doubt in my mind."

"You're one of those women? Get all hot and bothered over a man in uniform?"

"No, actually. But if it was *you* in uniform? Something tells me I might be. Got any pictures to show me so I can decide?"

He chuckled low and pulled his phone out of his pocket. She stole another sip of wine, gazing greedily at his handsome profile as he scrolled until he found what he was looking for. He held out his phone to her and said, "Me and a few of the guys at a charity event a few months ago."

She leaned in to look. There was Nick, out in the sunshine, a few palm trees in the distance, hot as hell in his full police uniform, standing with three other uniformed officers who may as well have been invisible. His tall, dark good looks eclipsed theirs completely. "Oh, holy hell," she breathed. Then, realizing she'd said that out loud, she blushed. When she met his eyes again, he was watching her, his eyes sparkling. "You cut a fine figure there, Officer."

"Thanks." He put his phone away and leaned in. "So I'm hot in my uniform?"

"Yes."

"Good to know. You're adorable in yours."

"Adorable?" She snorted out a laugh. "Really?"

"I think so. You've got that sweet-yet-sexy combo going on. Throws me for a loop." He smiled earnestly, and her heart did a little fluttery thing that made her feel giddy. "Have you ever been to Miami?"

"No. I've been to Orlando once, but never got that far south."

"Disney?"

"Yup. With the family when I was ten."

"Been a while, then."

"Yup again." She played with the edge of the coaster beneath her glass. It was thick cardboard, sturdy. "I've always wanted to go to Key West. That's on my bucket list."

"It's gorgeous there," he said approvingly. "You'd love it."

"How many times have you been?"

"A bunch. Seven or eight times, maybe? I love it there too."

"Color me jealous," she sighed. "Then again, I've barely been anywhere."

"Not a big traveler?" he asked.

"Nope." She picked up her glass again. "Money was a little tight growing up. Then I went to college, then nursing school, then started working. . . ." With a sigh, she took a sip. "Here I am at thirty-two, and I've barely been anywhere. I need to do something about that someday."

"Then do it."

"Oh, okay, poof! I'm going on a trip."

"Hey. Money was tight growing up for my family too. I get it."

The music over the sound system changed, the jazz saxophone replaced by the tinkling of piano keys. "When you've grown up like we have," she ventured, "to see how people like the Harrisons live . . . it's another world. Another universe."

He nodded slowly. "Bizarro world."

"And now you're part of that." She pushed a stray lock of her hair back, tucking it behind her ear. "That must be crazy. Trying to wrap your head around that."

His eyes snapped up to hold hers, narrowing with intensity. "*Yes.* And the truth is , . . I'm not doing a good job of it. I don't know what to do with all this. I don't know how I fit in there, what they all expect of me now, what my real family back home thinks now, what I'm supposed to do going forward. . . ." He heaved out a sigh and ran his hands through his hair. "It's noisy in my head when I try to figure it all out. So I'm just . . . kind of not thinking about it for now. Actually, I'm kind of avoiding it."

"I'd say deal with it however you need to. It's a lot to process."

"I'm focused on the transplant. Getting my part done. Thinking of Myles."

"Those are all good things to focus on."

"They're the only things that are important, and they're the only things I have any actual control over." His mouth flattened into a hard line. "The rest of it is drama. I don't do drama. Yet here I am, stuck in the middle of a huge drama. I hate it." He looked to her, deep into her eyes, as if he'd find some answers there. She met his gaze and smiled back, which brought a small smile from him before he said, "I was up in my hotel room drowning in it tonight. Your text was like a life raft. Thank you."

She leaned closer and covered his hand with hers. "You're welcome."

He laced his fingers with hers, setting off sparks of warmth in her core. His voice dropped low as he said, "You're a fantastic woman, Amanda. And, added bonus, I really like looking at you." He squeezed her hand gently, making desire shoot through her veins. "And touching you. And kissing you."

"Well, that's good," she said, "since that's all very mutual."

His eyes seemed to get even darker, his intensity off the charts. "There's nothing more I'd like to do than take you back to my room and lose myself in you tonight."

Her breath stuck in her lungs and her mouth went dry. Her panties liquefied.

"But I'm not going to do that," he said. "Because I'm leaving in a few days, on Sunday. I don't know when I'll be back, and when I do come back, for how long. And I . . . I don't know." He gave her hand a little squeeze, then pulled his away. "Don't want to jump too fast here, you know? No matter how right it feels. And it does feel right, but I also know I'm a little messed up right now. So that's not fair to you." A self-deprecating grin curved his mouth, showcasing his dimple. "I don't know what I'm trying to say. I'm trying to be a gentleman, even though the truth is I really don't want to be. Because the idea of asking you to come back to the hotel with me tonight is so damn tempting. *You* are so damn tempting."

She just nodded, not sure what to say. She wanted him too. The racing of her heart and the pulsing between her legs were proof of that. The chemistry was insane, the desire was clearly mutual . . . but yeah, it would be too much too soon if they jumped into something so quickly. She'd known him only a few days, strange as that seemed. She was comfortable with him. She trusted him enough to know she'd be safe with him if she did go to his hotel room. But still, cooler heads had to prevail.

Or . . . did they? Life was short and precarious. Her job reminded her of that every single day. "Nick," she murmured. "I'm a big girl."

He stared at her.

"I'm fine with . . . well, whatever. But you're more than a little messed up right now," she said kindly. "You're drowning—you just said it yourself. So *I'm* going to be the gentleman, and not take advantage of you while you're emotionally vulnerable. Because that would only . . . well, I don't see that ending well."

He stared at her, clearly conflicted. She understood it since she was battling the same thing: giving in to lust and desire versus being a moderate, levelheaded adult.

"For now . . ." She reached for his hand again, caressing his warm skin, keeping her eyes on his long fingers and how they looked and felt against hers. "Let's just hang out when you're here. Get a drink or a meal. Have some laughs. Steal some kisses. And if something more happens, it happens. Just know that I'm fine. I'm very clear on your being noncommittal and why. I'm not looking for a relationship either. Okay?"

He kept staring at her, his searing gaze hot and wanting. "You don't play fair."

She blinked at that. "What? I'm just being open and honest, same as you."

"I know. And now I just want you even more. Damn you." His eyes sparkled and he grinned. "You say you're fine. Does that mean I'm not fine?"

"I don't see how you can be," she said. "I think it's like you said yourself, there's a crapload of stuff going on. Not being fine seems like a normal reaction to me. I'd think you were nutty if you *were* totally fine. And I don't want to make things any more complicated for you. You and me—free and easy. I don't want you jumping into something you might regret later and resenting me somehow."

"Amanda." He said it like a command, and his eyes flashed. "I wouldn't regret sleeping with you. Ever. Impossible. In fact, my time with you has been the only good thing about coming to New York. Yes, I'm insanely attracted to you, but I also like you. A lot."

She smiled, ignoring the fluttering of her heart, the butterflies going crazy in her stomach, and the low, insistent throbbing between her legs. "Well. That's good to hear. For what it's worth, same here." Hearing him say things like that was making her dizzy. She withdrew her hands, grabbed her glass, and took a long swallow of wine.

He did the same, knocking back most of his glass. With a wry grin, he reached for the bottle and topped off her glass, then refilled his. "If we lived in the same place, we wouldn't be dancing around this. I'd seriously be trying to date you."

"But we don't, so that's that. Which is likely for the best. Takes the pressure off." She noted the look he gave her as she added ruefully, "It's kind of funny . . . because if we lived in the same place, and you tried to date me, I'd say no. So we wouldn't even be dancing around it. It'd be a done deal."

Nick's jaw dropped in open surprise. "Excuse me?"

Amanda bit down on her lip. "Sorry. Did that sound bad?"

"Um, yeah. A little." He gaped, searching her face. "You wouldn't want to date me, I got that right?"

"Well . . . yeah. I mean, no."

"Can I ask why?"

She sighed. This was going to go south fast if she wasn't careful with her words. "I don't date first responders," she said softly. "Cops, firemen . . . men who put their lives on the line over and over. It's a rule of mine."

Something shuttered in Nick's eyes, making her wince.

"Please let me better explain," she said.

"No need," he said, his voice clipped. "It's the danger factor, right?"

"Right. Yes. That. I can't . . ."

Nick sat back in his chair, jaw set tight. His long fingers played along the stem of his glass. "I understand."

She sighed. She felt her rule was valid, but could see how put off Nick was. "If I've offended you, I don't mean to. That's the last thing in the world I want to do," she said. "I totally respect and admire what you do. What *all* of you do. But to get emotionally invested, involved . . . I just can't. I won't. It's too big a risk. I'm just being honest with you."

His dark eyes blazed. "No, I get it now. It's been okay to flirt with me because I'm leaving. Free and easy, like you said."

Something in his gaze made her skin flush with heat. Was he mad, judging her, or just hurt? She didn't know, but his mood had shifted and it was palpable. "Well, can I remind you that *you're* the one, on the very first night, who made it clear you were leaving and for me to have no expectations. Right?"

A muscle jumped in his jaw, but he nodded. "Yup. True."

"So . . . you seem annoyed with me about that right now, and I'm sorry, but you really shouldn't be." Her voice felt smaller in her throat. But dammit, she was entitled to her feelings. "You said you're always honest. I am too."

He drew a long, slow breath as he looked at her. Finally he said, "You're right."

"Okay. So . . ." She lifted her glass and took a drink. Suddenly she wanted to gulp straight from the damn bottle.

"So, your ex-boyfriend," Nick said. "Not a cop or a fireman, I gather."

"Oh, hell no."

"Was he a doctor?"

"Noooo, I don't date doctors. Or surgeons. Walking ego trips with God complexes. No thanks."

His eyes narrowed. "Your list of who you won't date seems to be bigger than who you would."

"Not true! I just . . . have some rules in place. For self-protection. Nothing wrong with that," she asserted.

"I'm just wondering what kind of guys you *do* allow in."

She stopped at that. *Boring ones*, she had to admit to herself. *Safe ones.* "Justin was an accountant."

Nick rolled his eyes. "Yaaaawn."

Amanda giggled. "Yeah, a little. But he was nice. He treated me fine—I had no complaints there."

"Glad to hear it."

She shrugged.

"You dumped him anyway, though," Nick noted.

"I didn't dump him! I ended the relationship, and for good reasons."

"He must've sucked in bed, then."

"That had nothing to do with it," she said, but felt a flush creeping up her chest.

"If the sex is amazing, the person who gives it to you is a lot harder to give up."

"Maybe, maybe not," she grumbled, suddenly feeling sheepish.

"Was he good in bed?" Nick's question took her off guard, jolting her. His dark, commanding eyes held hers. "Did he rock your world?"

"Not that it's any of your business, but no," she admitted. "It was . . . fine, but no real fireworks. There, I admit it, okay? Is that what you wanted to hear?"

He nodded and leaned in, a new expression on his face. Something fierce, something like determination, and his eyes sparked with confidence. "Amanda . . ." He dropped his voice low, so she had to lean in to hear him. "When's the last time a man made you scream because you'd lost your mind to passion?" He grasped her hand and rubbed his thumb ever so lightly along her palm, sending shivers through her that zinged all her most sensitive spots. "What I want to hear is: when's the last time a man made you come so hard you could barely breathe?"

Her tongue turned to lead in her mouth as she gaped at him. She cleared her dry throat and squirmed in her seat. The sinful look on his face, the seductive tone of his voice . . . it was like he'd spun shimmering strands of sexual energy around her, drawing her in to his web of temptation. She was so wet now it was embarrassing.

"Tell me. Has anyone ever made you feel like that?" He was relentless. She couldn't break the gaze, or even move. "Has any man ever worshipped you properly in bed? Turned you into a clawing, panting animal, working on nothing but feeling?"

She felt exposed. And crazy turned on, and a little mad, and confused. But she couldn't break away. He'd put her under a spell. Hypnotized her with raw sex appeal.

And he didn't let up. He held her gaze for a long beat, still lightly stroking her palm with the pad of his thumb, sending shivers through her with every featherlight stroke. "I'd do that to you. Make you feel all those things. And I think you know it."

She stared back, her heart pounding wildly as she tried to breathe.

"I'd give anything to see you lose yourself like that." His voice was as seductive as his eyes . . . but he released her hand and leaned back. His gaze narrowed. "But for all your bold talk, I think you're scared of that. I think you're scared of guys who make you feel wild. So you'll put me off because I'm a cop. Easy to do. Right?"

"Wh-what?" she stammered.

"That's what you just said. I'm not a viable candidate. I'm just in a box with a label: 'Cop, Stay Away.'" He crossed his arms over his chest. "And you're entitled to your reservations, but I'm sorry, I *am* offended. I'm proud to be a cop."

Heat flooded her face as she pulled back. "You should be." She felt like she'd been driving a car at a hundred miles an hour, then crashed into a cement wall. She shook her head to clear the haze of lust, the spell he'd cast. Damn him. "I . . . I never insulted your profession."

"No, you didn't. But a blanket statement like 'I don't date cops' just . . . it sucks. You get that?"

He'd toyed with her. The man had fucking toyed with her. Her insides started to shake, and not from want now, but from anger. "I don't have to justify my reasons to you, though I tried to explain." With a shaky hand, she reached out and drained the rest of her glass. "In fact, I don't have to justify a damn thing about myself. To you or anyone else."

Other retorts ran through her head, but the overwhelming response was one of humiliation. He'd reprimanded her, but first he'd aroused her like crazy before throwing her into the wall. That was a mindfuck. She didn't do head games. Not ever.

She reached for her bag. He said her name softly, but she ignored him. She felt his eyes burning into her as she rummaged through it, fighting the surge of adrenaline that had her heart pounding at top speed. He said her name again, more insistently, and she ignored him. Finally, she found her wallet and dropped a twenty on the table. "Hot no-strings fling? No problem. Mind games? Big problem. Guess we're done. See you around, Officer." Grabbing her coat, she sprang up and marched out of the bar without a look back.

Chapter Thirteen

She only made it a block before he came up behind her, grasping her arm. "Amanda, wait."

"Get off me," she spat, shaking his hand free.

"Whoa." He held up both hands in surrender as he looked down at her, his features tense. "Okay, I won't touch you. Can you please just listen to me?"

"I don't know what's left to say."

"Plenty!"

"I don't think so." Fueled by embarrassment and anger, she kept walking. She'd left her car at the hotel, so she couldn't get rid of him, dammit.

Sure enough, he was right at her side. "If I looked you right in the face and said, 'I don't date nurses,' how would that make you feel?" he asked.

"I might not like it at first, but if you explained your reasons, I'd at least understand and respect your feelings."

"But you wouldn't like it. Well, I didn't either. It felt like a slap."

"So you slapped me back. Good for you. Mission accomplished." A gust of wind blew her hair into her face, and she swiped it back angrily. Her heart was pounding so fast it was hard to breathe. "Can you get lost now?"

"No. That wasn't my mission. I just . . ."

She picked up her pace, almost at a jog, but he kept up with her.

"I was only trying to make a point," he said, sounding a little desperate now.

"Point made." She kept her eyes ahead, refusing to look at him, and practically ran across the street to get to the next block.

"Amanda! Come on . . ." His long legs had no problem keeping up with her as she pounded the pavement. He muttered something in Spanish under his breath she didn't understand. Both things only fueled her anger.

A new burst of adrenaline surged through her as she bit out, "For the record, we never talked about *dating*. Right? We talked about hanging out, getting to know each other, and maybe sleeping together. That was it. Which you established from our first time out together, remember? And now you're going to play games with me? Draw me in, pull your sexy talk on me, get me all riled up, and then dropkick me like that to make me feel stupid? Fuck you, Nick. I'm not playing."

"I was upset," he said, his voice tight. "I was surprised at what you said. I . . . it kind of hurt me, so I handled it badly."

"Yes, you did," she snapped. She stopped walking to finally look at him as she demanded, "And it was petty. Own it."

His dark eyes blazed, his jaw clenched, and he was quiet for a long beat. Then he sighed, nodding slowly as he said, "You're right. It wasn't my best moment. I'm sorry."

Her breath caught. Justin had been nice, almost to the point of bland, but the thing she'd hated about him was he never owned it when he made mistakes. He'd always deflected, tried to turn it on to her, make everything her fault. Nick had listened to her, owned his mistake, and apologized within minutes. That was new for her. Astounding.

But she couldn't let it go. Humiliation still throbbed

inside, raw and ugly, and she couldn't get past it yet. "Okay. Thanks. But what exactly are you sorry for?" she asked. "Do you even know? Or are you just saying it to placate me?"

"Jesus Christ, Amanda . . ." A muscle twitched in his jaw.

"Are you sorry for being an asshole? For purposely making me feel like an idiot back there? Or are you just sorry because now you realize I won't sleep with you?"

His jaw clenched as his eyes flashed. "All of the above. And I *am* sorry."

"Fine." Her heart thumped away, and she started walking again. "Apology accepted." All she wanted was to get to her car and go home. Everything had gone wrong, and she wanted to be upset by herself, just get away from him. Her breath came in shallow pants as her sneakered feet hit the concrete with sure, quick steps.

And still he stayed by her side. "You say 'apology accepted,' but you're not forgiving me."

She bit down on her lip. Two blocks left.

"You asked me to own what I'd done," he said gruffly. "I did. Now own that you're still pissed at me."

"Ohhh, I own that."

They walked the rest of the way in tense silence. The main street of town was pretty quiet. Nick couldn't get over it. During the day, the town bustled with activity, but it was like the streets rolled up at night. He and Amanda were the only ones out walking. A few cars went by on the main road, but they were sporadic. He kept sneaking glances at her, knowing to stay quiet. She was clearly still furious with him, and he knew the truth was she had every right to be. He'd been a total dick. Seducing her one minute, pulling the rug out from under her the next . . . she was right when she'd said he was a little messed up. That was not cool. Not at all.

But man, did she get fired up when she was angry. It both frustrated him and turned him on a little, which only made it worse. Because not only would this night not end in a fun and possibly physical way, but also he'd made her so mad because, shit, he'd hurt her. Both her feelings and her pride. And now she couldn't get away from him fast enough. Great. Fucking great.

"I really am sorry," he said as they crossed the last street before his hotel.

"Okay."

"You're not going to talk to me now?"

"Not tonight, no. I'm done."

He knew she'd flip if he grabbed her arm again, so he quickly turned to block her, place himself in front of her. She bounced off him as he said, "Please, Amanda. Don't go like this."

"That was fucked up, what you did," she said. "That was manipulation."

"I lashed out, you're right. I guess I'm not fine, like you said." A wave of self-loathing whooshed through him. "And I've apologized. Several times now."

"I appreciate all that, but it doesn't make the sting disappear. I'm not over it yet." She glared up at him. "Are you going to let me pass?"

He swore under his breath and raked his hands through his hair in frustration. They were only a block away from his hotel now. He'd lost tonight, and had to accept it. "I'm walking you to your car," he said, his voice low and deliberate.

"Not necessary."

"That's not up for debate."

They walked in silence to where her car was parked. She immediately started rifling through her bag to look for her keys. He watched her, feeling powerless, which only made him edgier. Why was she letting one stupid thing blow up the rest? "You won't even look at me?"

Her head lifted and her eyes met his. He saw the pain there, and it made him cringe inside. He'd really cut her. "Amanda . . ."

"I came here to comfort you tonight," she said.

"And I appreciate that more than I can say." He stared down at her balefully. "It was great. I'm very sorry I ruined it."

"I am too."

"But . . . is there any chance you're overreacting a little bit?" he said.

Her eyes flashed with renewed anger. Shit. Clearly that'd been the wrong thing to say.

"No," she hissed, the word flying from her lips like a poisoned arrow.

"Okay, okay. *Fuck.* I just don't want us to stop . . . whatever this is we've started," he said earnestly. "It's been . . . really nice."

"Well, according to you, I'm not so nice. You think I'm a petty, small person for having generalized rules in place," she said, her chin lifting defiantly. "And it's only been a few days. We barely know each other, so I'm sure you won't feel the loss."

"You're wrong," he said firmly. "On both counts. I don't think that about you, what you said. And I feel the loss already."

Her mouth opened, then closed, apparently taken aback by that. She pulled her keys out of her bag. "Well, it's like you said—you're leaving in a few days. So while the idea of a fun, quick, hot fling might have been tempting, I see now it was probably a terrible—"

He grasped her face and kissed her, hot and hard. His fingers threaded through her hair, holding her head as he slanted his mouth over hers, and he tried to memorize how she tasted, smelled, felt against him. To his relief, she didn't pull away. His tongue swept inside her mouth as yearning pulsed through his whole body, as need battered him. The moment was charged, electric. When he pulled back, he stared into her eyes, which were a little dazed. Good. At least she'd felt the overwhelming power of that kiss too.

"Didn't mean to go all caveman on you there," he said

gruffly. He let his hands fall to his sides. "But if you're ending this, I had to have a kiss good-bye. I had to."

She blinked but didn't say a word. She looked how he felt: confused, frustrated, and turned on.

He searched her face for a hint of an opening. The narrow space between them still crackled. But he had to let it go. Let her go. He stepped back from her and licked his lips. He could still taste her sweetness, and it made him ache.

He huffed out a heavy sigh and said, "I'm sorry you've decided this is over, because I think it could've been something interesting." He shoved his fists into his jacket pockets. "But most of all, I'm sorry I hurt your feelings tonight. I was wrong. And I'd take it back if I could."

She stared at him for a long minute. He watched the conflict play out in her expressive eyes. For a few seconds, hope sparked inside him. Maybe this wasn't the end after all? But when she finally spoke, she only said, "Good night," and got into her car. He stood on the sidewalk and watched her drive away.

So. Tell me. Was I overreacting? Amanda asked at the end of her long text.

No, Steph answered.

Yes, Roni answered.

Well, shit, Amanda wrote with a snort-laugh. Which is it?

He was playing a head game, Steph wrote. That was manipulative, you were right. I don't like that.

Amanda reached to the coffee table for her glass of wine and sipped, tucking her legs beneath her on the couch. She'd been home for twenty minutes and was exhausted, but had had to run down the events to her girls. She needed to talk about it instead of just overanalyzing it to death by herself.

He lashed out because he was hurt, and he copped to

that, Roni wrote. Hello, he's a man. Men do dumb things. So do women, by the way. Just not as often.

I was about to do a dumb thing, Amanda texted. I wanted to start sleeping with a man I barely know.

You went into the city and spent the day with a man you barely knew, Roni pointed out. That was equally dangerous, if you think about it.

What? Amanda wrote, her brows furrowing.

But, Roni continued texting, these weren't, like, life-in-danger things. Sometimes, you have to take risks. Calculated risks. I go on dates. You spent a day in the city with him. Same thing, hon. You know him a little more now as a result. That's how you get to know a stranger a little better. It's also called living your life.

And if he's as hot as you say, Steph added, of course you want to sleep with him! You're only human. Don't beat yourself up for that. I was proud of you for getting back in the game.

What she said. And he's only human too, Roni pointed out. It was a dick move, what he did. But you have to decide if it's worth ending things over it. He did apologize, right?

Amanda sighed as she got Roni's points. More than once, she wrote. He knew he messed up. I'm the one who didn't let it go.

Okay. So think it over, Roni suggested. When you cool off, if you think he's worth giving another shot, do it.

Maybe she shouldn't, though, Steph chimed in. He IS leaving.

Aw hell, that just makes it easier, Roni wrote. Amanda could picture her sassy, wicked grin with a comment like that. If it goes south, she won't have to see him.

I think tonight it already went south, Amanda texted. Dead in the water.

Nope, Roni wrote. He told you he didn't want it to be

over. So still fixable. If you want it to be. It's on you now, sweets.

Amanda groaned out loud. I guess so. I'll think about it. Okay, I'm going to bed. Need my sleep. Rough week ahead.

Why? Steph asked. What's going on? Spill.

Myles is about to get a lot sicker, Amanda wrote. They're flooding him with chemo and radiation to get him ready for the BMT. It'll be awful.

I'm so sorry, Roni wrote.

That poor boy, Steph wrote. I can't imagine . . .

The last time he was very sick, Roni wrote, you got really depressed. I remember.

Of course I was, Amanda wrote. Hard to separate from being around that all day and coming home after, pretending like life is normal.

Well, lean on us if you need to, Roni said. We're here for you.

What she said, Steph wrote. If you get down again, tell us so we can support you. We love you. Stay strong.

Thanks. I will. I always do, Amanda said, but the sadness had already started trickling through her. Between the spat with Nick and thinking about what was immediately ahead for Myles, her heart suddenly squeezed with desolation and nausea rose in her throat. Dammit, why had she and Nick argued? He wasn't the only one who could use some comfort. Why did she always end up disappointed?

She sighed again and drained her wineglass. Thanks much, ladies. Love you. Going to bed now. xoxo

Amanda looked up from her e-reader at the soft knock on the door.

"He's back!" Myles said, sitting up a little more in bed.

She fixed a fake smile on her face. Lisette had told her Nick would be coming to visit. She'd put on a fresh coat of lip gloss and combed her hair, but was still torn inside. Let him back in, or let the whole thing go? She wasn't sure what to do. However he acted toward her would likely be the deciding factor, giving her the nudge she needed in either direction.

She opened the door and there was Nick, looking handsome as usual in jeans and a tight, navy long-sleeved T-shirt that showed off his muscled build. His eyes met hers and she saw a hint of . . . remorse? Hopefulness? Maybe both. "Hi," he said softly.

One velvety word and her insides quivered. Damn him and his overwhelming sex appeal. It wasn't fair. She'd never had such a strong physical response to a man in her entire life. "Hi," she said back and moved aside. "Come on in."

His eyes lingered on her for a long, heated moment before shifting to the boy in the bed. "Hey, you. How ya doin' today?"

Myles shrugged, but the smile on his face was bright. "Okay. The poison starts tomorrow. I'm just tired."

Her heart sank to her stomach. Myles certainly had a way with words. "Wait," she said to Nick, and went to get the hand sanitizer and the mask.

Nick stared down at her as she went through the quick routine. Want flowed off him in palpable waves. Before he put the mask on, he whispered, "Are you okay?"

"Fine," she managed over the lump in her throat. She stepped back. "I'll be over here on my throne, Myles. You guys have fun." She went back to the comfy armchair by the window, leaving them to their video games. The weight of Nick's stare burned into her; she could *feel* him, forcing her to look back at him. His eyes, so dark and intense over the white face mask, lingered for a few more seconds before his shoulders slumped a bit and he turned away. He went to sit in the chair by Myles's bedside.

She couldn't see them fully from her seat; the half wall cut off her view. This room had originally been a guest room, more like a suite, with the sitting area separate from the bed and its own bathroom. But when Myles had gotten sick, his parents switched him into this room so they could stay comfortably with him. His old bedroom, which was smaller, was now a guest room.

Amanda settled into her chair, pretending to read on her tablet. She had to pretend. She couldn't focus; the words swam in front of her. She listened to Myles and Nick chatter as they played games for almost two hours.

Nick told Myles he'd been invited to his Aunt Tess's house for dinner the following night, and was there anything he needed to know? Myles talked about how his aunt Tess was amazing and his uncle Logan was really nice for a super-huge mountain man, and then about his little cousins, Annabel, who was five, and the three-year-old twins, Evan and Emily. Myles said he'd liked to play with them when they were babies, but he didn't get to very much now. He told Nick how sometimes Aunt Tess and Annabel would bring board games up to Myles's room, like Candy Land and Chutes and Ladders, and how Myles was a little big for those now, but since Annabel was still little, he did it for her.

"That's good of you, being the big man," Nick commended him. "You're a good cousin."

"I try," Myles said, throwing his torso into the moves as he battled zombies.

"Well, thanks for the tips," Nick said. "Now I feel more prepared for tomorrow night. You're super helpful."

Amanda's heart squeezed. Nick was so good with him. He was a good guy—he really was. . . . All her original ideas about enjoying a fling with him came rushing back. He hadn't made any false promises, had made it clear from the start that while he liked her, their interaction had built-in limitations . . . all the things that had originally appealed to her about the whole situation. Okay, he'd lashed out and hurt her. But she'd called him on that bullshit immediately, and he'd apologized, and he'd made it pretty clear he still wanted to be with her, whatever that meant with the limits.

He liked her. She liked him too, even though he was covered in red flags. The truth was, maybe *that's* why she'd pushed him away so hard and fast. Damn.

"Hey, buddy, listen," Nick was saying to Myles. "I'm done with all the tests and stuff this time around. I'm going back to Florida on Sunday."

"Aw, man," Myles sighed. "Okay. But you'll come back?"

"Of course," Nick said. "Definitely when you're ready for the surgery. That time, I'll be here for about a month, probably. They said my recovery might take a few weeks, and they don't really want me in a germy airport, so I'm going to take time off work and just stay here for that."

"Here at the house?" Myles wondered aloud.

"No, bud, I'll be in my hotel."

"But who'll take care of you?"

A wave of affection flowed through Amanda. Myles was such a thoughtful kid.

"I'll be taking care of myself, buddy," Nick said. "Tough guy, remember?"

"Maybe Amanda could help you," Myles offered.

Nick paused before saying, "She's your nurse, bud. She'll be busy taking care of you."

"I don't know," Myles said. "They said after the surgery, I have to stay in the hospital for a while before I get to go home. So she'll be free. Maybe you should ask her? I'm sure she'd help you—she's the best. She's the nicest, really."

Nick chuckled warmly at the same time Amanda swallowed a laugh. Her heart swelled a size or two.

"I'll be fine," Nick said. "Don't you worry about me." He paused again and said, "I'm a little worried about you, though. No lie: I'll be thinking of you every day when I go back home."

"That's nice. But, you know, starting tomorrow, I'll be too

busy sleeping and throwing up and stuff," Myles said. "Probably not even feel well enough to play video games. You won't miss much." His voice cracked on the last word, and it sent a lance of agony through Amanda's heart. She sat up straighter in her chair, her fingers curling into fists.

"Are you scared?" Nick asked quietly.

"Yeah, a little."

"I would be too. That's normal." Nick's voice got a little thick. "I hate that you're gonna feel so sick, Myles. I'm sorry."

"It's okay. They have to do it. I understand why."

"You know what? You're the bravest person I've ever met."

"You're a cop," Myles said. "You're braver than me."

"I don't know, buddy. Faced with what you're facing, I think you're the one who's braver." Nick cleared his throat. "But I tell you what. We're gonna do this thing, and it's going to really suck at first, but then you're going to get better. I know you are. I feel it. You have to believe it too, okay?"

"Okay."

Amanda's heart thumped and she swallowed hard. She could feel her blood pulsing in her veins. She wanted to get up and hug both of them.

"Hey, Nick?" Myles said. "I'm glad you're my uncle."

"Hey, Myles?" Nick said back. "I am too. Come here, gimme a hug."

Tears stung Amanda's eyes. She sat very still, listening to the sheets rustle as Nick must have moved onto the bed to hug Myles. Her heart squeezed in her chest.

"When you're all better," Nick said, "I'm going to ask your parents if it's okay to bring you down to Miami to visit me. And if so, I'm going to take you on a boat ride. My friend has a speedboat, and we go fishing on weekends sometimes. You'll come with us. Deal?"

"I'd love that!" Myles cried. "And can we go fast on the speedboat, too?"

"Whatever you want, kid," Nick promised. "Whatever you want."

An hour later, Nick hadn't even gotten to his car in Charles's driveway when his phone dinged with a text. He looked at the screen.

You were amazing with him. It was from Amanda. It's not my place to thank you for that, but I just had to say something.

Nick stared at his phone, wondering how to respond. At least she was talking to him. She barely had all evening. He'd thought she was done with him. This felt like a reprieve. An olive branch.

He wrote back, Easy to be. He's an amazing kid. Then he paused, not sure what else to say. Deciding to go for it, he added, It was nice to see you. Added bonus. You looked pretty tonight. Thinking the last bit may be too much, he deleted the last sentence before sending the text.

She responded with only a smiley face emoji.

He sighed. From the start, it had been so easy to talk to her. This new awkwardness pained him. Good luck with him tomorrow, Nick finally wrote. Sounds like you'll be busy with him again for the next few weeks, unfortunately.

Very busy, she texted back, adding a sad face emoji.

Is it okay if I text you sometimes to check on him? Nick wrote. Just to see how he's doing? Or is that not allowed?

You can, she wrote back. Basic info would be fine. I'm sure Charles wouldn't mind.

Great, he wrote back. Thank you.

He took a deep breath and looked up at the stars. Longing swirled in his chest. He pictured her sitting in that chair by the window, the pale blue walls behind her setting off her gorgeous eyes, her dark honey hair flowing just past her shoulders. . . . When he'd left for the night, she'd risen to walk him out and he'd felt such a strong pull between them. It hadn't gone away. He'd fought the urge to pull her into his arms and kiss her with everything he had. Damn, damn, double damn . . .

Deciding to take one last shot, he texted, I don't know if I'm going to see Myles again before I leave on Sunday, so .... probably won't see you either. Okay to text you if it's not related to Myles? Or did I blow it completely?

He held his breath as he waited for her response. The seconds felt like hours. Jesus, he liked her too much already. Maybe he'd be better off if she turned him down. Maybe he—

I'd like to try again, she wrote. I've cooled off and fully accepted your apology now. So if you want to text me, that'd be fine.

He exhaled. She was still guarded—he could tell from her stiffer language—but she was willing. It felt like a second chance, and he felt a quick rush of elation. Then you'll hear from me tomorrow, he texted, smiling up at the stars. Good night, Amanda. And thanks.

Chapter Fourteen

On Wednesday evening, Nick went to Tess and Logan's home for dinner. Conveniently for Nick, they lived in the same neighborhood as Charles, so he was able to find it easily. Tess and Logan were gracious hosts, friendly, clearly going out of their way to make Nick feel welcome. Their three young kids were adorable and fun. Annabel regarded Nick shyly at first, but warmed up quickly. The twins were tiny bunches of boundless energy. After a delicious dinner, where they overfed him with steak, garlic mashed potatoes, and salad, Logan wrangled the kids to the playroom so Tess and Nick could sit in her study and talk.

He had to grin at the love she lavished on her tiny white dog, Bubbles.

"She's such an old lady now," Tess cooed as the Maltese lay in her lap quietly. Her hands stroked along Bubbles's fur over and over as she asked Nick many questions, but it wasn't an interrogation. She wanted to get to know him. He felt her warmth and natural curiosity, and he was at ease when they were just one on one, as he'd felt with Pierce after a beer or two. They sat and talked for a long while. He allowed himself to open up to her some, and by the time Nick left, he felt the beginnings of a true kinship with his new sister. She was sincere and likable. There was serious potential not only for them to have a relationship, but for it to be a good one . . . if that was what he wanted.

And as he drove back to the hotel, he thought yes, it more than likely could be what he wanted. First Pierce, now Tess . . . he did genuinely like these people. If he ended up changing his mind and having some kind of rapport with them, it might be a nice addition to his life.

But on Thursday, Nick woke with Myles on his mind. He shot a quick text to Amanda. **How was his first day? How's he doing?**

It took her about half an hour to respond. **He's feeling the effects. About what we expected. Will text you tonight.**

Nick's heart sank to his suddenly nauseous stomach.

He went down to the gym for a workout, trying to pound the worry out of himself. And he *was* worried. It may have been a short time, but he cared about Myles. They'd bonded. Nick felt sick thinking of the kid feeling sick. He hated it. And he was powerless to do anything, which he hated even more. He ran on the treadmill for a long time, pounding at it. He lifted weights and welcomed the burn. He did every machine on the circuit. Nothing helped.

He showered and went out to find some lunch. Two blocks away was a little bagel place that also served other kinds of food. Nick wolfed down a turkey club sandwich, people-watched aimlessly. . . . He just couldn't shake the disquiet that had gripped him. Not knowing exactly what was happening only made it worse, but he didn't want to contact Charles and pry. Amanda said she'd text him that night, he had to wait. He hated waiting, for anything.

So he went for yet another drive. It was a beautiful spring day, and Nick took the Porsche for another spin. Blue skies, sunshine, mild breezes . . . he opened the sunroof and blasted the music as he drove. But his mind was full. Myles. Amanda. His mom. Charles II. His new siblings. Sickness. Going back home, starting the new job, his promotion. His life had changed so drastically, so quickly. So much to process, so much to think about . . . he tried to make sense of things. Figure out his new place in his new world. There were so many components, so many moving parts. . . . He drove all the way out to Orient Point, almost a two-hour drive, before turning around to head back west.

By the time he got back to the hotel, it was almost dinnertime. Usually he didn't mind being alone, but tonight, he couldn't get away from himself and it all ate at him. An idea struck him and he went with it on impulse. He took the train into Manhattan. When he got there, it was just past seven-thirty, twilight edging in and all the buildings lit up. New York City with all the lights on was a sight to behold, that was for sure. He remembered how he'd walked with Amanda and headed up Seventh Avenue toward Times Square.

Recalling his day with her made him wistful. He'd rarely had a date—much less a first or second date, so early on in knowing a woman—that had been so great from start to finish. Amanda had been a fun tour guide . . . so alluring and sweet and brimming with presence . . . and making out with her in the middle of Columbus Circle on a gorgeous day was something he'd never forget when thinking of New York City. She'd effortlessly seared herself into his brain.

He grabbed two slices of pizza from the same place he'd eaten lunch with her, but took them to go. Sitting on the steps in the middle of Times Square where they sold half-price theater tickets, he ate and watched everything spin by and sparkle and blare noise around him.

Yet again, he wished Amanda were with him. She was so pretty, nice, smart, sassy. He liked how sometimes he'd catch her staring at him and meet her eyes directly; the way she'd blush when he caught her . . . he huffed out a frustrated sigh. He thought about her too much. He had to stop. It wouldn't turn into anything, and she was the type of woman where he could get in too deep. He sensed that, knew it even if he'd known her for only a short time. His life was in Florida; hers was here. But damn, he wanted her. Maybe if they just gave in to their burn-the-roof-down chemistry once, just one time, one night of abandon, he'd be able to get her out of his system?

He snorted at himself. Not likely. Something told him that one taste of Amanda would only leave him wanting more and more.

His phone vibrated in his pocket and he checked the screen. It was a text from Pierce. Hey, Nick. Heard you're leaving Sunday. True?

Nick grabbed a paper napkin to better wipe his hands, then texted back, True.

Okay, Pierce responded. You free tomorrow night? Come out for a few drinks with your big brothers. Well, 2 of 'em – me & Dane. Let us send you off right.

Nick had to grin as he stared at his phone. Why the hell not. It was better than sitting in his hotel room by himself, trying not to think about Amanda or Myles or his suddenly fucked-up life. Sure. What time?

7:00 work for you? We'll go into NYC. I'll pick you up.
Sounds good.

Nick sat back and gazed around. So many people, bright lights against the dark sky, surrounded by sound and color and motion. And he still couldn't get Amanda off his mind. Maybe he wouldn't until he left New York altogether. He hoped he would. This pining stuff wasn't like him; it was distracting him and tying him in little knots. And God knew with everything thrown at him over the past two weeks, he was off his game to begin with.

* * *

Nick was walking back toward Penn Station when his phone vibrated. He pulled it out to look at it.

Hi. From Amanda. That was it. His brows furrowed, gut humming. He moved out of the way of other pedestrians, leaning up against the cement wall of a skyscraper.

Hi yourself. How are you? he texted back.

Not great, she wrote. Hard day. With a sad face emoji.

His stomach twisted, knowing she meant Myles. Wanna talk about it?

Not really, she texted back. He's tired, he's sick, that's all you need to know. The chemo and radiation combo is brutally effective.

He swore under his breath and kicked the wall. That fucking sucks, he wrote.

Sure does. He has nurses around the clock again, don't worry. He's being closely watched.

I hate this.

Me too.

You sound off. I can feel it.

I am. Won't deny it. I'm sad for him. And I'm tired. I'm just … She ended with a sad face emoji again.

Want me to come over? Nick wrote without hesitation.

She didn't write back right away, giving him enough time to chastise himself for writing that. Not only was he still in the city—if she said yes, it'd take him an hour to get to her now—but he didn't want to push. It wasn't like they were—

Nice of you to offer, she texted. But no, I'm wiped out. I'm going to bed in a few.

Rain check, then?

Yes.

Something in him perked up at that. Yes to a rain check. That was good. I'm sorry you had a shit day.

I am too, she wrote. Tell me yours was better?

It was okay. I'm fine, other than being upset for Myles.

Good. Well, not good that you're upset, but good that you're fine.

He grinned softly. Pierce & Dane are taking me out drinking tomorrow night. Wish my liver luck.

LOL, she wrote back. Big, tough guy like you can't hold his own with 2 guys 10-15 years older? You wimp.

He laughed and quickly wrote, Thanks a lot! Now I feel like I've been challenged or something. Keep up with them or give back my man card, is that it?

Something like that. ;) Have a good time.

Thanks, I will. He paused, hesitated . . . then decided to go for it. So I leave on Sunday. My flight's at 2 p.m. out of JFK.

You mentioned that the other day.

Can I take you out to dinner on Saturday?

Her response didn't come in for a minute that felt longer than a minute. Finally she wrote, You think that's a good idea?

He winced but wrote back, All I know is I'd love to see you again before I leave. We could just hang out, Amanda. No pressure. Think it over, let me know.

With a sigh, he stared up at the lights around him. Flashing billboards advertising designer clothes, pretty girls in skimpy outfits, dancing around and showing off their bodies. All he wanted was some time with a down-to-earth woman who usually wore scrubs and tennis shoes. A woman he'd had a shot with before he'd done something dumb. A woman he wanted another shot with, because for whatever reason, she'd gotten under his skin.

He didn't want to think about that too much. Maybe it was best this way, her cutting him off after all. Fling or no fling, he didn't want to end up hurting her, and no matter what she said and how cool she played it sometimes, he knew that was a possibility. Because he'd already hurt her once, inadvertently and on a minor scale. The thought of hurting her on a grander scale made him skittish.

Three minutes passed. He sighed and went to put his phone away, but it buzzed with a new text. **I thought it over. Yes to dinner. What time?**

His smile bloomed wide and bright. All the "maybe we're better off" thoughts evaporated like mist, replaced by the buzz of excitement and something like hope.

Amanda nudged the food on her plate around with her fork. The food, as usual at this place, was great. But it was hard to eat when she had a bit of a nervous stomach, due to the very handsome man sitting across from her.

Nick had picked her up in front at six on the dot. He'd texted her when he arrived at her building and she'd gone right down to meet him. Simply dressed in a white button-down and jeans, he managed to make it sexy as hell. She'd enjoyed the ride with him more than she'd thought she would. He'd handled the sleek car with command, like he did everything else, and that was sexy too. She'd enjoyed sitting in the close, enclosed space, breathing in the smell of him, a hint of spicy cologne and something just brutally male that was all him. She'd liked that he'd asked her where she would like to go for dinner and taken her up on her suggestion without hesitation.

Now they sat in her favorite Chinese restaurant, the table covered with plates of steamed dumplings, chicken with broccoli, shrimp with bean sprouts, and pork lo mein, because he'd asked her to pick her favorites so they could share. He tried every dish and, thankfully, liked them all. He made her laugh with his stories of going out the night before with Pierce and Dane. Apparently, his two brothers had been quite the party boys back in their day, and still liked to uphold the rep whenever an opportunity arose. Nick assured her he'd kept up and his man card was in good standing, that he'd had the hangover this morning to prove it. He'd had a good time with them, and she was glad for him.

Talking with him was easy, as it'd been from the start, not at all stilted—which meant the bump in the road from earlier in the week was officially in the rearview mirror. The food here was delicious, as always. Her one glass of white wine was helping her relax. Amanda realized how completely she was enjoying her date with Nick, and it kind of jarred her. Being with him was just so . . . well, easy. She was comfortable with him, even though the butterflies hadn't let up, and she knew part of that was the unrestrained, dizzying lust that ran through her every damn time she looked at him. The man radiated sex appeal. He was so smoking hot it was ridiculous.

She didn't want to want him as much as she did. She didn't want to like him as much as she did. She wanted to keep things casual. She had to.

But she remembered what he'd said a few days before, about how if they lived in the same place, he'd be pursuing her, wanting to really date her. And that had gotten into her head and heart more than she wanted to admit.

"Amanda?" he asked, waving his hand in front of her face. "You zoned out. Am I boring you?"

Her face flushed even as she laughed. "No, no, you're not boring. I'm sorry."

"Thinking about Myles, maybe?" he asked softly.

That made her feel even worse for some reason. "Actually, it was the first time I *haven't* been. You've provided a wonderful, much-needed distraction tonight. I'm having a good time. Thanks for that."

He nodded, smiled warmly, and reached for his bottle of beer. As he tipped it back for a sip, she couldn't help but watch his throat work, his full lips around the bottle neck. . . . He made a simple white button-down shirt look downright dashing. It was tight around the muscles in his arms and across his broad shoulders and chest, the top two buttons undone to reveal a glimpse of his smooth, dark gold skin. She imagined what it'd be like to unbutton his shirt and slide it off him, her hands gliding over his body. . . . She swallowed hard.

She wanted to throw herself at him tonight.

She wanted to forget about the week she'd had, especially the last few long, hard days of caring for Myles. She wanted to be reckless and wild, to feel alive in the face of such sadness and sickness. She wanted to be with Nick . . . taste, lick, and nibble and touch every smoking-hot inch of him.

It wasn't smart. It wasn't like her. And she couldn't think of anything else.

"Lost you again," he said.

She drew a shaky breath, trying to get her heart to stop fluttering. "I . . . I'm distracted, I admit it."

"By what?"

"You."

One of his brows lifted the tiniest bit, and the side of his mouth curved just enough to make his dimple appear. Her nipples hardened instantly. God, she was toast.

"What about me?" His voice dropped, infused with flirty seduction.

"You're sitting there all gorgeous and it makes me have dirty thoughts." Had she said that? Yeah, judging from the way his eyes flashed, she'd said that out loud. She snorted at herself. *Might as well go for it. Just do it. Have a night with him. Feel alive, fight the darkness* . . . "You're leaving in the morning, right?" she blurted.

His head inclined as he said, "You know I am."

She glanced at the clock on her cell phone. It was seven-fifteen. They had all night, if they grabbed it. "So I'm going to say this, and it's probably a bad idea, but dammit, I'm saying it."

He stilled, but the half grin stayed and he didn't take his eyes off hers. "I'm listening."

"The more I look at you, the more I think about it, the more I . . . I want you. Tonight. Before you go, I want one round with you."

His dark eyes flared. "Just one?"

"Oh, God." A fluttery laugh escaped her as a rush of dampness throbbed between her legs. He was lethal. "Nick, I don't usually do reckless things."

"I believe that."

"You do? Why?"

"Because you're so levelheaded. Really smart. No pretense. Seem to have zero tolerance for bullshit."

"All that's true," she agreed.

"And I like those qualities. Also . . . well, there's your famously non-reckless dating choices." His thick brows lifted. "We've discussed that, though."

"You know what?" She leaned in on her elbows to hold his stare. "Not completely. You didn't let me fully explain last time, but I'm going to now, if that's all right."

"I'm all ears," he said, and speared a piece of chicken from his plate. "Hit me."

"When I was a sophomore in college," she said, "I had a boyfriend, a junior, who was wild. A real bad boy. And I was such a good girl. I'd never been with a guy like that before. We were opposites, but we were attracted as hell to each other. So we dated." Her mouth twitched wryly. "Remember when you asked me about the last time a man really rocked my world in bed? It was him. I'd never had sex like that, not before and not since. I'm just being honest."

Nick's eyes widened a drop, but he only nodded and took a sip of his beer.

"Anyway . . . Cooper," Amanda said, her voice gentling on his name, "Coop and I really, really cared about each other, and we couldn't keep our hands off each other. We were total opposites, but we really connected. So it was a thrill ride, and it *was* thrilling, but it was also kind of exhausting. Coop was intense. He was fun and exciting . . . but after a few months, it got dizzying." She stole a sip of her wine. "I was from here, he was from Tennessee. When we both went home for that summer, back to our families, I decided we needed to take a break."

"Forever, or just for the summer?" Nick asked. He kept eating while she talked.

"I guess we would've gotten back together in the fall, I don't know. I'd asked for some space. I needed to . . . ground myself again. My grades had gone down a bit that last semester, and I knew I needed to refocus, because I wasn't going to get into a good nursing program if my grades weren't good. Coop didn't like it, but he accepted it. We talked a few times, but didn't visit each other . . . so I never saw him again. Because one night that July, he went out on his motorcycle and got himself killed. No helmet. No, Coop was too cool for that. He was one of the most fearless people I've ever known. And an adrenaline junkie. And too fucking reckless. Dead at twenty."

"Damn," Nick said quietly. "I'm so sorry."

"I was too. Such a goddamn waste . . ." She sighed, willfully shoving the memories aside. "So . . . I mourned him for a long time. I focused on my schoolwork, and I didn't have another serious boyfriend for the rest of college. I was a little screwed up over it."

"Understandable."

"Then I started nursing school, and I just didn't have the

time to date. I mean, I went on a date here and there, but I really was too committed to the program to commit to a guy or even think about having a relationship at that point."

"I think I see where this is going," Nick said, putting down his fork.

"No, you don't. Let me finish." Amanda took a deep breath. "My first week doing a rotation in the ER, they brought in two cops who'd been shot. One made it, but the other didn't. The one who didn't had a pregnant wife out in the waiting room, and she'd left their toddler at home with her mother when she got the call." She closed her eyes briefly, licked her dry lips. "I'll never be able to get that woman's wails of grief out of my head for as long as I live. They bounced off the hospital walls, I swear. It was . . ."

Nick's jaw was tight as he reached for Amanda's hand. He gripped it and gave it a gentle squeeze.

"It brought back my memories of grieving over Coop," Amanda said, "which of course paled in comparison to this poor woman, seven months pregnant on her knees on the hospital floor, wailing for her husband to come back to her." *Please don't be dead, Vinny. . . . Please open your eyes, please don't be dead, come back to me. . . .* Would she ever be able to get that woman's anguished cries out of her head? She cleared her throat to dislodge the lump that had formed. "Nick, I swore to myself that night that I'd never again get involved with men who put themselves in the line of danger. It hurt bad enough when I lost Coop, but wouldn't it be a million times worse if I invested in another relationship with someone like that and lost him too? I just . . ."

Her face flushed as she took in his somber expression. She hoped she wasn't upsetting him, but how could she not be? She squeezed his hand hard. "I decided that long before I knew you existed. I have tremendous respect for cops, fire-fighters, all you guys. It's nothing against you personally. Can you understand that? Because I hate that I offended you the other day, and I wanted you to understand why

I've made the choices I have. I don't owe you or anyone an explanation . . . but I like you enough that I wanted to provide you with one."

He squeezed her hand back and said, low and gruff, "Of course I get it. And thank you for telling me. I . . . I like understanding you better. It helps."

With her free hand, Amanda reached for her wineglass and knocked back a hearty gulp of Chardonnay.

"So when I said I'd want to date you if you lived in Miami," he said slowly, "and we'd already talked about my job, and my promotion . . . it set off warning bells for you."

"That's exactly what happened."

"Okay. I get it now. I'm sorry."

"Don't be. The truth is, I like knowing you'd want to date me, not just sleep with me. It's flattering as hell. But I . . . if I dated you, I'd . . . I'd worry about you all the time. I don't want to."

He nodded, lips pressed together tight.

"And I know that's selfish. But you know what? It's not even up for debate anyway, because I live here, and you live in Miami. Case closed."

"Yup. Guess so."

They smiled at each other softly, their fingers interlaced.

"Thanks for telling me all that," he said, his voice gentle. "We're good."

"So . . ." She drew another deep breath. "What I started to say was, you're leaving tomorrow. You won't be here for very long when you come back before the surgery, your weeks of recovery. . . ." She set the wineglass down with care, trying to ignore the warmth of his large hand wrapped around hers. "Come home with me tonight. Let's have one really good night together. Just . . . be together and let go of it all for a night. Forget everything. I think we both probably need that. Yes?"

His lips parted in shock as his eyes flew wide. "Hell yes.

But *whoa*." He laughed and cleared his throat. "Give me a second here—I think my brain just exploded."

She couldn't help but laugh with him. "Kind of surprised myself with that one too. Well. How's that for an up-front girl?"

"I think my up-front girl is the sexiest girl I've met in a really long time," he said, his voice low and hungry.

My up-front girl. She shivered at how delicious that sounded.

His warm brown eyes darkened with growing desire. "Amanda, I want you too. So much. I've wanted you from the first night I saw you."

She smiled and her heart began beating faster.

"And yeah . . ." His slow grin was wicked. "We haven't known each other that long, and I'm a cop so I break your rules, and I'm leaving in the morning and all . . . so, on paper, it might be a bad idea for us to sleep together tonight."

"Terrible," she agreed. "It's rash. Clearly we're not thinking this through."

"Exactly. Totally impulsive, jumping into bed so soon. It's reckless."

"Yup. That. I mean, we've only gone on what, three dates?"

"Four, technically, but who's counting?"

"You, apparently."

His playful grin went into a full-blown smile, dazzling her. "So, okay, we're on the same page: this could be a bad idea. But we're two adults who are agreeing to this with eyes wide open, so it's fine." His eyes flared with heat and he licked his lips. "And the thought of having you has me so hard right now, I can't even stand up. But when I can, we're going back to your place, and I'm gonna take you in ten different ways."

Her mouth dropped open and her heart skipped a beat before taking off like a rocket. She felt the blood rush from her chest to her hairline as she smiled back. The throbbing between her legs had her shifting in her seat, making her aware of how wet she already was. "That . . . sounds really good to me."

Nick raised her hand to his lips and kissed it, his warm lips lingering on her skin. "Then let's finish dinner." His voice was as smoky as the look in his eyes. "I want you for dessert."

Chapter Fifteen

Nick could barely think, much less think clearly. The thought of getting his hands on Amanda had his blood stirring, every nerve ending lit up and alert. Once they got back in his car, he asked her to tell him where to turn to get back to her apartment building. At least after she said, "Umm . . . I don't have condoms at my place. Any chance you have one?" he had the presence of mind to pull into the first Walgreens he saw.

"Can we also get some snacks?" she asked with a grin.

He smacked a kiss on her mouth and tweaked her nose playfully. "Whatever you want, tell me now."

"Any kind of cheddar popcorn," she said. "And peanut M&M's."

"Seriously?"

"Yes. I have a feeling you're going to make me work up an appetite tonight."

"You know it." He kissed her again. "Be right back."

Fifteen minutes later, they stepped into the lobby of her building. Nick scanned his surroundings. The five-story building was small and modest, with a buzzer, security doors, and security cameras. Clean and well cared for . . . seemed like a good place.

"You approve, Officer?" Amanda asked, watching him with a bemused smirk.

He couldn't help but grin. "Yes. Did you read my mind?"

"You're casing the joint."

"I am not."

"You so are."

Still grinning, he finally shrugged. "Occupational hazard."

"This is a safe building, really. Also a nice one. I've lived here for four years and, luckily, never had any major issues," she said as they walked. "Never heard of any break-ins. The other tenants either say hi as they pass or mind their business, but no one's been nasty." She pressed the button at the elevator. "And the best part is, my roommate—who's lovely, by the way—is rarely home the same time I am."

"Hope she's not there tonight," Nick said as they stepped into the chamber. "Because she'll get an earful." As soon as the doors slid closed, he backed her against the wall and lowered his head for a deep, hungry kiss. His free hand stayed at her waist, but gave a little squeeze. As his tongue swept into her mouth, her hands came up to hold his face and run through his hair. His other hand, still holding the plastic bag, made a crinkling noise as his fingers curled into a fist. God, he wanted her. Blood raced through his veins and his cock already felt heavy. He kissed her until the doors opened.

When Amanda opened the door to her apartment, it was dark. "Yessss," she whispered victoriously. He chuckled as she flipped on the lights and he followed her inside, looking around as he set the plastic bag down on the glass coffee table. Small living room, decorated with a clearly feminine bent. Modern, neat, earthy colors.

His gaze traveled back to Amanda, who was removing her coat. His pulse pounded beneath his skin, and he worked to calm down. He wanted her too much. "Your roommate works on Saturday nights? That sucks for her."

"Not always, but I guess she is tonight. Or maybe she had plans. I really don't know." Amanda smiled. "Hey, we have the place to ourselves. That's what matters." She took his leather jacket from him and hung it in a closet by the front door, then turned to him. He let his eyes run over her again as she stood there in a formfitting white sweater over navy leggings and knee-high brown boots. Her hair tumbled over her shoulders and her face looked a little flushed. She smiled at him again and her eyes, so blue, sparkled at him. She had that thing—it just flattened him. . . . She was laidback, easy-going, yet drop-dead sexy at the same time. Jesus, this woman had him in knots. His heart rate started its slow climb again.

She smoothed her hands over her hips, blushing as she said, "So . . . what now?"

Warmth flooded him. He held out a hand. "C'mere, *mi reina.*"

Her brows puckered as she asked, "What'd you call me?"

"Mi reina." His smile turned seductive. "My queen."

"Oh." Her eyes widened a bit as she stepped to him and slipped her hand into his. "I . . . like the sound of that."

"It fits you." He pulled her gently to the couch and they sat. His heart started beating in heavier, harder thumps as he gazed at her. He lifted his hand to caress her cheek with the backs of his fingers. "You okay?"

"Completely." She smiled at him and he smiled back. "You said something," she murmured, "about ten different ways . . . ?"

Her voice was as sexy as her gaze from beneath her lashes, both hungry and challenging. It made his cock twitch in his jeans. "I believe I did."

"Can't wait to see what you have in mind."

"Then I best get started." He leaned down and unzipped her boots, one and then the other, and slid them off her legs. Then he grasped her hips with both hands and pulled her onto his lap, facing him. Relishing the look in her eyes, a combination of surprise and desire, he eased her down onto him, spreading her legs to help her straddle him, settling her open thighs along his. "Ahhhh." He slowly ran his hands up her legs, leaving his hands on her hips as he looked into her eyes. "That's better."

Her arms snaked around his neck as their gazes locked. "Well, hello," she said, smiling as she edged closer. His breath stuck in his lungs as she pushed down gently, positioning herself until the warm core of her settled on his erection. The position was intimate, raw . . . wicked. His hips lifted a bit to grind into her and her breath caught.

"You like that?" he whispered.

She nodded and licked her lips. Blood flushed her skin, spreading from her chest, up her throat, into her cheeks. Her fingertips played in the back of his short hair.

"Tell me," he whispered, husky and low. "Tell me what you like . . . what you want. . . . Don't be shy tonight, *mi reina*." He ground into her again, a little harder this time, and she let out the tiniest squeak. He watched her eyes darken with lust, felt her searing heat against his cock, and his eyes almost rolled back in his head.

"I like when you call me that," she revealed in a whisper. "And I won't be shy."

He leaned forward to take her mouth with a deep, commanding kiss. His fingers sifted through her silky hair, and she pressed herself against him as their kiss flared, a red-hot collision of want and need. They kissed hungrily, recklessly . . . like restraints had vanished and they were free at last to dive into each other. His arms banded around her as her hands ran over his hair, the planes of his face, his shoulders. She sighed into his mouth and it nearly undid him; his whole body burned whenever she did that.

He held her slowly undulating hips; she cradled his head as their tongues tangled. They wrapped around each other, holding each other close, and the kisses intensified, deepening as the minutes fell away. His hands glided along her lower back, sliding down to grab her ass. When he realized what he was feeling—no panty lines, but there, the tiniest bit of fabric . . . he groaned into her mouth. "Jesus," he managed. "You're wearing a thong?"

She flashed a triumphant smile of sin and seduction as she ground against him, circling her hips in a wanton way that made him almost dizzy. He kissed her hard, wanting to possess her, claim her, own her. He thrust his tongue in her mouth with the same rhythm as his hips beneath her. His fingers dug into her lush hips, gripping her ass tighter as he held her in place, letting her feel how rock hard he was. They kissed and rocked and fell into the abyss together.

He pulled out of the kiss to trail his open mouth along her neck, licking, kissing, taking little nips that made her suck in her breath and purr. His fingers slipped beneath her sweater to touch her skin, velvety soft and so warm. "Amanda . . ." he whispered against her skin. "Baby, you feel so good." As if in answer, she ground herself into him harder and he groaned. His hips met hers, rocking back against her as they kissed. He was lost in her, lost to nothing but sensation, and he welcomed it.

She leaned back enough to pull her sweater over her head and toss it aside. As his eyes feasted on the sight of her, he dropped kisses everywhere he could reach. His hands slid up the sides of her rib cage, savoring every inch, before moving around to cup and caress her breasts through her lacy pale pink bra. "Gorgeous," he murmured, kissing her, licking her, touching her. "So goddamn gorgeous."

She smiled at him, luminous, her eyes heavy-lidded with desire. "So are you."

Vaguely aware of her fingers undoing the buttons of his shirt and spreading it wide open, he reached around to unhook her bra and let it fall away from her body. He drew a deep breath at seeing her fully exposed to him for the first time. Her breasts were perfect, she was perfect. With a low grunt, he lowered his head to draw her nipple into his mouth.

She gave a soft cry as he sucked and nipped, her head lolling as her back arched, giving herself over to him. Her greedy hands swept across his chest, his shoulders, as his fingers dug into her hips to grind her against his cock again. Even through his jeans, he could feel her heat. A breathy moan floated out of her as she rocked against him, meeting him in a building rhythm heavy with tension and need.

"You . . ." She gasped, looking down at him through eyes clouded with pure lust. "You're staying all night, right?"

"Yes," he said, nipping at her chin. "Hell yes. Why?"

"Because I'm close already," she panted. "Too close . . ."

He grabbed her hips and ground her pelvis into his again, hard and merciless. She cried out, her fingers digging into his shoulders, her short nails biting into his skin. "I'm not kidding," she whispered.

"Good." He let her set the pace, find the sweet spot and work it. Natural rhythm kicked in and took over; he watched her face as her eyes closed and her lips parted, as her heavy breaths turned into soft moans. Her urgency drove his desire higher, and it was burning hot, making him sweat. He met her sinuously rolling hips with his own, rocking against her, kissing her skin, savoring the scent of her, learning her.

He'd suspected she'd be passionate, but this was better than he'd dreamed. She was on fire. He held her tight and enjoyed the ride. They moved together, wrapped around each other, simulating sex, shameless and dirty and needy and panting.

"Nick," she gasped. "Oh, God . . ."

"Go with it, *mi reina*," he whispered against her lips. She moaned, low and throaty. His arms banded around her as he kept moving against her, rubbing into her damp heat. The friction was so good, almost unbearable. "You're so fucking hot." He dipped his head and licked up the column of her throat, tasting her. "I wanna watch you come for me. Let go. Come *hard*."

She broke apart with a lusty shout, riding him, grinding

into him, moaning as her hands splayed against his chest. Listening to her moan with her head thrown back in ecstasy and watching her climax while he held her . . . it was the sexiest thing he'd seen in a very long time. Passion and need seared through him, making him so hard it almost hurt. The blood racing through his body had all pooled south, and he was as feverish as she was. But he tried to breathe deeply; he had to wait. He wanted to come inside *her*, not his jeans.

Panting hard, she finally fell against him, her heavy breaths hot against his neck. He rubbed her back and kissed the side of her face. "That was fun. And hot. You're so beautiful, Amanda."

"Ohhh, my God. That was . . . damn, I came too fast," she said with a laugh.

"No, you didn't. We just got that fast and furious one out of the way." He pushed her hair away from her dazed eyes and kissed her, long and sweet. Then he gingerly lifted her off him to lay her on her back across the couch. She was boneless, sated, and smiling, her gorgeous blue eyes locked on him. "I need to get these jeans off."

"Good, because I want more," she said between gasps for air. "I want you inside me. I need to feel you fill me."

"So soon? You sure?"

"Yes. Now."

Grabbing for the plastic bag on the coffee table, he got out the box of condoms and ripped one free of the strip. His eyes raked over her, lying there half naked and watching him, her cheeks and chest flushed pink and her sweet lips parted, curving into an admiring smile. Her body was all sweet curves and pale perfection. Christ, she was beautiful.

But he pulled her up to a sitting position. "Do you really want me to take you here on the couch?" he asked. "I mean . . . maybe we should lock ourselves in your room, in case your roommate comes home."

"Good point. Never know." She bit down on her bottom lip, then giggled and shook her head. "Come on!" Rising quickly, she practically ran. Condom in hand, he followed her to the last room at the end of a short hallway. They didn't even turn on the light as they quickly shucked the rest of their clothes. She peeled off her leggings and said, "Hey. Officer."

As his already opened shirt fell to the floor, his eyes met hers. She grinned wickedly and put her hands on her hips. She stood there almost naked . . . except for a scrap of pale pink lace. She did a little turn, showing off the thong completely. She even wiggled her ass a bit for his benefit. "You like it?"

The sight of her standing there wearing only that tiny piece of sexy fabric made him groan like a hungry animal. "Fuck yes, I like it. But . . ." He went to her and peeled it off her body, his fingers trailing down the soft skin of her legs. As he bent down, he nuzzled her thighs with his face. He sank to his knees, licking and kissing her incredibly smooth skin, reaching around to cup and squeeze her ass with both hands. "Now I'm even happier." Her fingers twisted in his hair. He could smell and taste her arousal. As he lapped at her and she moaned again, his whole body surged with a fresh wave of eager lust and aching need.

"Take me to bed," she gasped out.

Standing, he shoved off his jeans and boxer briefs. His rock-hard cock sprang free. She licked her lips and her eyes widened as they focused on it. "*That's* what felt so damn good. I could've rocked against that all night."

"Let's go for it." With a lustful groan, he reached for her and they fell onto her bed, a tangle of naked limbs as their mouths crashed in a searing, consuming kiss. Their greedy hands roamed over each other as they kissed, desperate and hungry.

"I need to touch you," she said. "I mean, I want to touch you everywhere . . ." Her hands traveled over his shoulders, his bulging biceps, his smooth chest. The man was like a damn sculpture. She'd never been with someone so built in her life, and she wanted to savor his physical beauty. But she also wanted to please him, to give him some of the earth-shaking pleasure she'd quickly stolen on his lap.

"Then go ahead and touch me," he said huskily against her neck, biting her earlobe as his hands closed over her breasts. "I *want* you to touch me everywhere. Do it." His hot mouth was everywhere. "Take what you want, baby. I'm all yours."

Sweet Jesus, when he talked like that . . . Her tummy gave a little flip as a new surge of wetness pooled between her legs. She kissed him as her hands skated down over the length of his smooth back to rest on his perfect ass. Jesus, his tight, rounded ass was a work of art. She squeezed it in full appreciation, pressing him down to grind his impressive erection against her. He groaned softly, then louder when her hand slipped between them to curl around his thick shaft. God, he was big.

As he kissed her neck, his hips rocked into her hand. He whispered dirty things in her ear as his hands squeezed her breasts, rolling her nipples between his fingers until she was panting along with him. She felt a little dirty and a lot wild, and she loved every second of it.

One of his hands moved lower and he slipped a finger inside her. "Christ, you're so wet. You *are* ready again."

"Told you," she said. They kissed and stroked each other and panted and moved. "See, you don't have to wait. So don't. Don't wait."

"Mmmm . . ." He added a second finger and slid them inside, drawing out a long, throaty moan from her. "You sure you don't want me to wait?" he asked. His eyes danced as he teased her, and her heart nearly beat right out of her chest.

"No, I don't want you to wait." Her voice came out all high and breathless. Her hips circled, straining for more, as he worked her.

"No?" He smiled, pure sin, as he lightly brushed her clit with his thumb. Her back arched right off the mattress as she moaned. He dropped his head to kiss her neck. "Tell me what you want, *mi reina*," he whispered in her ear, licking her skin, scraping with his teeth, making her crazy with lust. His voice, his words, his breath, his scent, his hands and mouth on her body . . . she'd never been this turned on in her whole life. He kissed her and commanded against her lips, "Tell me."

"I need you inside me now," she gasped out. "Take me. Now. Please . . ."

He grabbed the condom from where he'd dropped it on the bed and hastily got it on. With another deep kiss, he rolled on top of her and positioned himself. The tip of his cock teased at her entrance, sliding along the wet length of her, making her whimper as a long shudder racked her body. Her hands slid from his shoulders down his back to his ass, and she grabbed at him to push him in.

Finally, he slid inside her with a strong thrust. The feel of him filling her was the sweet relief she needed. Her insides welcomed him as he sank into her and they moaned together.

"Fuck, you feel so good," he gasped. "Jesus, Amanda . . ."

Her legs wrapped around him as her hips lifted to draw him deeper inside. She moved with him, the delicious friction dizzying, the tension building. "Harder. Go harder."

He growled against her skin, biting her neck as his hands clutched at her hips. Her entire body shuddered beneath him as she moaned. He pulled out, almost all the way, then slammed back into her, buried to the hilt. She cried out and clutched his shoulders to hold on. He did it again, and again, until she begged him to go faster. They panted as they moved together, wrapped tightly around each other, rocking in a hard, primal rhythm. Her moans seemed to only spur him on as he thrust faster, harder, again and again. She held on and let the incredible flood of feeling course over her and sweep her away.

"I can't hold back anymore," he bit out. "I can't, baby. Tell me you're close?"

"Yes." She saw the muscles in his neck and shoulders stand out as he strained over her, then met his eyes, so dark they were black. "Don't hold back—let go."

"Come with me," he panted. "I want to feel you come with me."

It was as if his guttural command made her snap. Gripping his shoulders, she cried out as the orgasm hit, the waves of sensation battering her, making her body go taut and her mind go blissfully blank. As soon as she went over the edge, he did too. He groaned loud and low as his body tensed, his broad frame stiffening in her arms. She rocked her hips to draw out his climax and his lusty moans made her buzz with elation. Feeling him lose control, knowing she had the same devastating effect on him he'd had on her, made her feel sexy and powerful. It was exhilarating, a heady rush like nothing she'd ever felt.

Slowly, his mouth sought out hers and he kissed her, lingering to sip from her lips while they tried to catch their breath. They both panted as if they'd run a race, and their bodies were coated in a light sheen of sweat. His head dropped into her neck as he carefully withdrew from her body.

"Jesus Christ," he whispered into her skin. "Jesus, Amanda . . ."

"Thank you for that," she murmured into his ear.

He lifted his head to look at her, his amused grin making that dimple show. She kissed it quickly, unable to help herself, and he chuckled. "You're thanking me?"

"Yeah," she said, smiling back. "When someone takes you like that, I think thanks are in order, no?"

He laughed and hugged her, his warm, dark eyes twinkling as he dropped a kiss on her mouth. "You're welcome, then. And thank you too. I'm still recovering here."

They lay side by side for a minute as they floated back to earth. She reached for his hand, wanting contact, and he didn't hesitate to intertwine their fingers. It made her heart give a happy little flutter. He lifted their joined hands to his lips, kissed the back of her hand, then pulled away from her to rise from the bed. "Let me just go take care of this, clean up . . ." His deep voice was rough and ragged, and she loved it. "Bathroom?"

"Second door on the right," she said, studying his insanely gorgeous body from behind as he left the room. Light from the hallway lit up his silhouette. There wasn't an extra ounce on him; it was all tight muscle, like pictures in magazines. He was a goddamned Adonis. Lucky, lucky her.

"Could you bring me a glass of water when you come back?" she called out.

"Absolutely," he called back.

She took a deep, cleansing breath and stretched her limbs. All her muscles burned and throbbed in the best ways and she knew she'd feel it tomorrow. The thought of that made her smile . . . but then the smile faltered. He was leaving tomorrow.

And she wished he wasn't.

Shit. She didn't want to think of that now. They still had a few hours ahead of them, and she wanted to just enjoy every minute they had together. She didn't want to think of her life, which veered between dark sadness at work and too much quiet when she got home. Or to think of him going back to work, where his job put him in danger on a daily basis. Or to think of him back in sunny Miami, where scantily clad women probably threw themselves at him every damn day. He may have said otherwise, but he was too handsome, too appealing, too off-the-charts hot for her to believe that wasn't the case. Just thinking about that made her a little jealous, and she knew she was being ridiculous. She had no right to be—she wasn't his girlfriend. She wasn't his anything.

Mi reina. Her eyes slipped closed. When he called her that, all sexy and wanting, she melted inside. Between the warmth in his eyes when he said it, and the sweetness in his voice when he purred it at her, she absolutely melted. She knew it didn't really mean anything, was just a term of endearment; that she shouldn't read too much into it or add significance that didn't exist. But that one little word, that one tiny gesture . . . the way his voice pitched low when he whispered it against her skin . . . had tipped the scales and helped to make her come undone.

Goddamn it. This was supposed to be casual. He'd warned her of that from their very first date. And she wanted the same. She wasn't looking for anything, and since he was leaving, and a cop, and hotter than hell, he'd been a perfect candidate for a fling and then a good-bye.

So why did she *feel* something more now? Yes, the sex had been mind-blowing, the best she'd ever had, but this . . . this emotion welling inside her, unwelcome and unwise, was something else. Frowning, she burrowed under her blanket and tried to swat it away, but these sudden feelings weren't letting go. She shivered as that realization washed over her.

One round with him hadn't made things better, but worse. Because she knew now one night wasn't going to be enough. She wanted more. More of his body, more of his thoughts, more of . . . oh, God. She wanted more of *him,* all of him.

And that wasn't going to happen. Their lives were in different places. This connection she felt, no matter how real it felt, was temporary. He was in emotional flux and grabbing on to her as a distraction from his problems. She had to remember that. She had to keep her heart out of this.

Nick walked back in then, gloriously naked, the white plastic bag in one hand and a glass of water in the other. "Here, beautiful." He leaned down to drop a light kiss on her lips as he handed her the glass. "Careful. Don't spill."

As she took it from him, she felt her heart slip deeper into his hold. She swigged down water as she cursed herself.

Oblivious to her turmoil, grinning leisurely, he got into bed beside her and made himself comfortable. He smelled of soap, sweat, and sex, a devastatingly masculine combination that made her head swim. His body was magnificent and the grin on his face was playful, but it was the warm and sated look in his deep brown eyes that did her in. Like there was nowhere in the world he'd rather be. It made her senses reel.

"So," he said jauntily, reaching into the bag, "what do we have here?" He pulled out the opened box of condoms first and offered it to her. "Ah, yes. Want that within reach." He winked.

Smiling, she took it from him and set it on her nightstand beside the half-empty glass.

He pulled out a big bag of cheddar popcorn, two small bags of peanut M&M's, and a bottle of orange Gatorade. "Gotta replace my electrolytes, you know." He handed her one bag of M&M's, gulped down a third of the bottle before recapping it, then tore open the second bag of candy for himself. As he popped three into his mouth, he gave a little moan of satisfaction. "Mmm. I haven't had these in a long time. Good call."

"They're my favorite."

"Cool. Now I'll think of you whenever I see them." He flashed another grin.

God, you're delicious. She leaned in, took his square jaw in her hand, and pulled his mouth to hers for a kiss. "Thanks for all this."

"You're welcome. Thanks for inviting me over." He gave yet another grin, making the dimple reappear. "Hope you're not tired yet. I'm far from done with you. Still have what . . . seven or eight ways to go?" He waggled his brows, making her laugh.

Yeah, she was a goner. She couldn't fight it, couldn't deny it to herself. . . . These were real feelings she was feeling now. And that would lead to disaster, and she knew it, because it would only end. And there was nothing to be done. Did she have to fall for someone who not only lived too far away to be a real possibility but also broke a bunch of her personal rules at the same time? Apparently so. The Universe was laughing at her.

Swallowing the rush of emotion down, she decided to feed her sticky new feelings. She opened her bag of M&M's and shoved a few into her mouth as she snuggled into his side. He was warm and solid, and felt like heaven. His arm wrapped around her and pulled her closer. He pressed a quick kiss to her lips, and her heart sighed in surrender.

Enjoy tonight, she told herself as she breathed him in, her fingertips playing along the ridges of his abs. *Enjoy what you can. He doesn't need to know you just broke the rules, both yours and his. He's got enough of his own stuff to deal with. He never needs to know that despite all your bravado and wiseass talk, you went and fell for him.*

Chapter Sixteen

Nick woke slowly, disoriented for a few seconds as his eyes adjusted and focused. In his haze, the unfamiliar room threw him. The walls were pale green, sunlight streamed through gauzy, feminine curtains . . . and there was a warm, soft, naked female body tucked against his back. Ahhh, yes. Smiling, he rolled over to look at Amanda, careful not to wake her. She slept soundly, her dark blond hair tangled and hiding half her face. Tenderly, with delicate care, he swept her hair back so he could gaze at her.

She wasn't a typical cookie-cutter beauty, but he thought she was absolutely beautiful. Something about her just hit him in a sweet spot. She'd told him she was an "Irish-Polish-Russian combo plate," which had made him laugh. Now that he had a chance to openly study her face, he did so with pleasure.

She looked so peaceful, and that made him happy. Not just because he knew his taking her all night long was the main reason she was sleeping so well, but because she'd been so tense for the past few days. He knew she'd been stressed about her work. Now, her features were relaxed; there was no little crease between her brows like he'd seen, or troubled look in her eyes. Seeing her at peace like this soothed and pleased him.

He pressed a featherlight kiss to her forehead. He suspected her job, though she loved it and rarely complained, brought her satisfaction and fulfillment but very little peace. He knew what that was like. All too well. It made him want to pamper her.

Her creamy skin was so soft, and so pale next to his. Her long lashes fanned out and her lips were slightly parted as she breathed slow and deep. Those lips . . . those gorgeous pink lips had wreaked havoc on him all night long. Memories of what she'd done to him with that mouth made his cock twitch and rise.

He trailed his fingers gently along her silky hair, the arch of her brows, her cheek, her neck, down her arm and back up again. Unable to help himself, he pulled the blanket down just enough to expose her breasts. . . . His mouth watered. He wanted to close his lips over her nipples and suck and lick them until she woke up. He wanted to hear her sigh, whimper, and moan. Just thinking about it had his morning hard-on ready to rock. He pressed his lips to the hollow of her throat and kissed her skin lightly.

Shit, did he even have time to wake her the way he wanted? He lifted his head to glance at the clock on her nightstand. It was a few minutes before seven. He worked backward mentally. His flight was at two, which meant he had to be at the airport at noon, which meant he had to leave his hotel at eleven-thirty, which meant he had to have the rental car back . . . shit. He had to leave her apartment by nine at the latest if he was going to get his act together.

He didn't want to leave her bed. He wasn't ready for this to end just yet.

His eyes drank her in as she slept. She was so damn pretty, even with bedhead after a long night of hot, crazy sex. Flashes of their night together went through his mind. How they'd talked in bed and ate M&M's as they cuddled . . .

how he'd been unable to keep his hands or his mouth off of her and gone down on her until she screamed his name, then pulled her on top of him. . . . She'd ridden him, looking down at him all gorgeous and sexy and taking control until he'd exploded. . . . They'd kissed and chatted and kissed some more until they drifted off to sleep sometime around midnight.

It'd been the best night he'd had since . . . God, really, had he ever had a night like that? Amanda was amazing. Yes, she was great in bed. So responsive, so passionate, willing to let him be in control or eager to take control herself, depending on the minute. She was right there with him at every beat, open and lusty, just plain fun.

His breath hitched. It was more than those things.

It was the way she'd looked into his eyes when she'd been on top . . . meeting his gaze directly as she moved like a fluid, seductive goddess, grinding into him and drawing him deep. He'd been unable to look away. Like she'd hypnotized him. Like she could see into his soul and felt the same connection he did. He wondered if she felt that too.

And not only could he talk to her with ease, but they laughed a lot, something he hadn't even realized he needed until he started spending time with her. His job was serious, his personal life had been blown apart and become serious . . . and she was really funny. She was a quick-witted smartass; it was like trading wisecracks with Darin or the guys at the station, but better, because he found her sexier with every comeback. She was also caring and grounded. She grounded him whenever he was with her. That was it— that was the draw. His life had become a swirl of chaos, but she made him feel steadier, supported, understood.

Finding her was like a lifeline, and he didn't want to let go.

But he had to. His flight left in just a few hours. Back to his real life.

He lowered his head to rain gentle kisses along her face, her jaw, down the side of her neck. His greedy hands skated possessively over her body. Damn it all, he'd have her for as long as he could, as much as he could get, down to the last minute.

She stirred slightly and her hand lifted to sift through his hair. So he kept going, kissing his way down her throat, over her chest, until his mouth closed over her nipple. She let out a little whimper as his teeth scraped the bud and his arm slid beneath her, around her, pulling her closer and holding her in place.

"Good morning," she whispered as her hands smoothed over his shoulders.

He hummed a response against her skin, making her suck in a sharp breath.

Her leg inched up so her thigh could brush his erection, sending heat through his whole body. "Mmmm." Her morning voice was deliciously ragged. "Is that for me?"

He lifted his head to look at her and grin. "Hell yes."

"Oh, good."

He moved to her other breast to lavish it with equal attention. Catching the tip in his mouth, he swept his tongue over her nipple before scraping his teeth gently and sucking. She arched her back and purred with satisfaction. He loved the erotic sounds she made, loved that she wasn't shy with him.

He shifted his position, rolling slightly to hold her with both arms. She sighed with pleasure as her hands traveled along his body. "You have more muscles than I know what to do with," she murmured. "It's fabulous. It's also . . . a little intimidating. There, I said it out loud."

That made his head snap up. "What? You're not intimidated by me. Come on."

"I'm not intimidated by you as a person, no," she said. "But your body is a goddamn work of art. You're ridiculously cut. I've never been with such a gym rat before. Makes me feel soft in all the wrong places."

"Not true." He squeezed her breast and smiled. "You're soft in all the *right* places. Believe me."

She smiled and rolled her eyes. "Okay, Captain Beefcake."

He barked out a laugh. "Look, I need to stay strong and fit for my job."

"I'm sure you do. But you're freakin' ripped, dude. Which means you also do it because you're one of those freaks who actually gets off on exercise."

He laughed again. "Guilty as charged. Uhh . . . I'm sorry?"

"You're not sorry," she accused, grinning back. "And *I'm* sure not sorry. I get this hot bod in my bed. You look like a Greek god, and you damn well know it."

"Whaaat?" He couldn't help but smile. "You think I look like a Greek god?"

"You know you do. Knock it off, don't be coy."

"Hmm. A Puerto Rican god, more like. Are there any of those?"

She pinched his ass, making him yelp and laugh.

He kissed her mouth. "What you said is very flattering. Thank you."

"I should be thanking you. I get to use your body like a theme park. I win."

He laughed again, then lowered his head to kiss the top, rounded, fleshier part of her breast. "I love looking at you too, you know. And touching you. You're beautiful, Amanda. You really are."

She smiled but didn't say anything, just pushed his head back down to her breast with soft insistence.

His arms held her tighter as he sucked on her nipples for a while, one then the other. His hands ran along the sides of her breasts, down to the curve of her waist and back again. . . . She writhed against him sinuously, clearly enjoying him. Together, they slowly brought the heat from a simmer to a bubbling boiling point.

He savored the feel of their naked bodies aligned . . . she felt so right against him. Desire coursed through him, needy and insistent in his blood. But when he finally moved to kiss her mouth, she turned her face away.

"Ack!" she yelped. "No! I haven't brushed my teeth!"

"I don't care," he said on a chuckle.

"I do. Ick. Let me just—"

She tried to roll away to get out of bed and he locked her in his embrace. "No way. Don't even think of getting out of this bed."

"But I—"

"Nope." His hands gripped her at the waist and flipped her over onto her stomach, bringing a shocked gasp from her. He swept her hair aside to kiss the back of her neck as he repositioned himself over her, pressing the length of his front along her back. He ground his hard-on into the back of her thigh, right below the soft curve of her ass, and growled softly into her ear, "Now you don't have to worry about morning breath. I'm gonna take you this way instead. Yes?"

"Yessss." Her moan made his whole body pulse. It was a guttural, passionate moan, wicked and wanting, firing his blood through his veins with a rush. She wriggled her ass against him and said, "God, yes."

His mind reeled, red-hot lust overtaking his senses. He kissed and licked and bit at her neck, her shoulders, her back, running his hands all over her as he ground his erection against her thigh, whispering dirty things in her ear that made her whimper and moan. Fueled by sensation, he reached over to grab the strip of condoms, tore another from the strip, and rolled it over his cock, already rock hard and straining.

She moved up to her hands and knees, and he let out a little groan at the sight of her. Wanting to make sure she was ready to take him, he slipped a finger inside her. Hell yes, she was ready, so wet and warm; she moaned and dropped her head.

Jesus, he needed to be inside her, all over her, *now*.

With a low growl, he gripped her legs and pulled her

back further, pushing her thighs wider apart with his knee. Then he rose up and slid into her with one easy thrust. His eyes closed at the incredible feel of her and they groaned together.

He started to move, gripping her hips as he thrust in and out of her. She pushed back against him, meeting him stroke for stroke. Her erotic sighs and moans drove him crazy. He couldn't get enough of her. He leaned over her, his chest against her back, so he could reach around and squeeze her breasts as his hips pumped faster. Her fingers twisted in the sheets, grabbing at them.

"God," she panted, "you feel so good, Nick. Soooo good."

"So do you, *mi reina*."

He thrust harder, faster, the sounds of their heavy breathing and skin slapping filling the room. With one hand still on her breast, he moved the other down to rub her clit as he moved inside her. Her moans turned into wild cries, letting him know how close she was.

"That's right," he growled in her ear. "Give it to me, all of it."

"Take it," she breathed. "Oh, God, take it. . . ."

He pounded into her, no holding back, and her steady cries let him know she loved it. He felt his whole body surge with heat, close to the edge. He couldn't hold back much longer.

"Let go now, baby," he said, voice thick. "Let it all go. Come with me."

Her body obeyed his gruff command. She grabbed a pillow and buried her face in it to scream out her release. The sound and feel of her pushed him right over the edge along with her. He thrust as deep as he could one last time and his climax hit, making him buck and grunt like an animal. His fingers dug hard into her skin, holding on fiercely as his body quaked and emptied inside her. The sensations slammed him, flooding him, bringing ecstasy and relief.

They collapsed onto the bed together in a panting, sweaty tangle. He rolled onto his side, still holding her close, spooning her as they fought to catch their breath. She was limp in his arms, slick with sweat, eyes closed. He nudged her hair aside with his chin and licked her skin, lapping at the curve of her neck with possessive sweeps of his tongue, sipping with his lips. She pressed her back into him, her hands on his forearms, and smiled. Her smile made him smile too.

"That was insanely good," she whispered, her voice raw and rough. "And *hot*."

"Sure as hell was," he murmured back, his own voice coming out hoarse like hers. Kissing her neck once more, he withdrew slowly from her body but held her for another minute, bathing in the afterglow and savoring it as they regained their minds.

"I wish I didn't have to leave soon," he said quietly. "But you know I do."

"I know." Her voice was just as low and quiet as his. She caressed his arms, still locked around her. "But that was a hell of a send-off, Miami Vice. *Daaaamn*."

He laughed and dropped a kiss on her shoulder. "Yes. It. Was." Rolling away carefully, he said, "Gotta clean up. I'm going to take a quick shower, if that's okay."

"Of course it's okay." She flopped onto her back and smiled up at him. Her face and chest were still flushed pink, her hair sweaty and tangled, her sky-blue eyes sparkling and sated. She was so gorgeous it stole his breath. "You have *several* tattoos," she said as her eyes ran over his body.

"Well, yeah," he said, amused. "You didn't see them last night?"

"It was dark in here, I couldn't see them well. Thought you only had the one on your shoulder. . . ." She studied him now, her gaze focused. "They're hot. Like you."

He laughed. "Thanks."

"I don't have any."

"I noticed."

She gave a little sigh. "You think I'm vanilla, don't you?"

A wolfish grin spread on his face. He leaned down, gently grasped a handful of her hair, and took her mouth with a firm, commanding kiss. "Nope. I can think of a lot of words to describe you, but after last night and this morning? 'Vanilla' isn't anywhere on the list." He moved his lips to her ear and nipped at the lobe, making her breath catch.

She drew in a shuddery breath, met his eyes . . . and smiled with a devastating mixture of triumph, satisfaction, and sensuality. God, he wanted to take her again, just from that look on her face.

But she said, "Towels are in the linen closet, right next to the bathroom. Whatever you need, use it."

The only thing I need is more time with you. The thought was so instant and hit him with such a pang, it made him shiver. *Oh, shit. That's . . . shit, that's not good.* He pushed the thought and feelings away. "How about you join me in the shower?"

Her eyes lit up and she smiled again. "I could do that. It *would* save us time. . . ."

Amanda loved the feel of Nick's hand in hers as they walked through the lobby and outside. It was a beautiful spring day—bright blue skies and sunshine, a light breeze, not too warm and not too cool. Her favorite kind of weather. Why did it have to be so perfect when she had to say good-bye to him?

They'd shared a deliciously sexy shower, making sure to be quiet so they wouldn't wake Gretchen. Her door was closed and the red scrunchie was on her doorknob; Amanda explained to Nick that was their signal to each other that she was home after a night shift and sleeping.

He'd pulled on his clothes from the night before and his button-down shirt was rumpled, making him adorable.

Amanda had pulled her damp hair into a ponytail, quickly dressed in a royal-blue long-sleeved T-shirt and gray leggings, and tried to act casual. She'd scrambled some eggs and toasted whole-wheat bread while he'd used the Keurig to make coffee for both of them. As they'd sat and ate together, they kept looking at each other and grinning, but didn't talk much. It hadn't been awkward or uncomfortable, but clearly neither one of them was sure of what to say that didn't lead to *good-bye*.

Now, as they reached his car, he pulled her into his arms and laid a long, deep, toe-curling kiss on her. Damn, she'd miss him. She really would.

He looked into her eyes as his lips curved up. "This was amazing. *You* are amazing." His thumb caressed her cheek. "Thanks for a great night. And morning. And breakfast."

Delight and something stronger seared through her, and she couldn't hold back her smile. "Back atcha. Everything you said." She pressed her lips to his for another kiss. "Safe travels home, Officer."

"Thanks." His eyes shadowed a bit at the mention of home, and he drew a deep breath. "Things are so different now. Gonna be interesting to go home and . . . figure things out. New job, new relatives . . ." He shook his head. "Back into the fray. No more avoiding some things."

"Well," she said, caressing his shoulders, "if you need someone to talk to, you know where to find me."

He peered into her eyes. "Yeah?"

"Yeah. I mean it."

His dark gaze lowered to her mouth for a second. She saw the flash of hunger there before he looked into her eyes again. "What are we to each other now, Amanda?"

The exact question she'd been asking herself all morning. "I'm not sure what we are," she said softly. "We don't need to label it. Let's just take it as it comes. Yes?"

"Yes." He stared at her for a long beat, caressed her cheek. "So I can text you?"

"You better."

"Can I call you?"

"I'd like that too."

"Amanda . . . this was . . . you're really . . ."

Her heart stuttered in her chest, and she didn't move, waiting to hear what he was trying to say. The look in his warm brown eyes was so . . . longing. It seemed like longing. Or was she imagining that because she wanted to?

"Back atcha," she finally whispered, saving him with a soft, sweet kiss.

His mouth curved up. "I'll text you. We'll talk. Promise."

"Okay."

He didn't release her. She was glad; she loved how he felt. "Also, I'll want updates on Myles. Are you allowed to tell me things?"

"I'm not sure," she admitted. "Usually, I'd say no details. But these circumstances are so unique. Do you want me to ask Charles?"

Nick hesitated, then shook his head. "You don't want him to know we're involved, remember?"

She winced. "True. Right. Um . . ."

"I'll get detailed updates from him," Nick said, rubbing her back. "You can keep things vague when I ask you. And I'll try not to ask you too much, okay? I don't want to put you in a position that compromises you."

"I believe *that* happened about two hours ago," she joked.

He chuckled softly and grinned. "Hell yeah. And I loved it."

"So did I." She winked, trying to keep things light, so he wouldn't know how this was affecting her. How she was already aching because he was leaving.

He nodded again, then lowered his head to take her mouth one last time. Their arms wrapped around each other as they shared deep, slow, sumptuous kisses.

Finally, he pulled away, leaning his forehead against hers. "Take care, *mi reina*."

"You too," she whispered, her heart squeezing in her chest.

She watched him get in the Porsche and zoom away. A light breeze stirred the ends of her hair and caressed her face. The street was quiet and still in the way it always was on a Sunday morning. Amanda wrapped her arms around herself and drew a long, deep breath, letting it out slowly as she closed her eyes and tipped her face up to the sun. She recalled the delicious tone of his voice and look in his eyes when he called her *mi reina*, like it meant more than just an endearment. . . . She licked her lips to savor the taste of him that lingered, then turned to go back inside.

The day would feel lonely without him, but she had incredible images to hold on to and replay all day long. They'd sustain her as she relaxed and enjoyed a lazy Sunday, and they'd sustain her in the long weeks ahead.

Chapter Seventeen

Nick turned off the car, leaned his head back, and closed his eyes, just wanting to relax and gather himself for a minute. The last time he'd come to his parents' house for dinner, his whole world had been upended.

He'd been back in Florida for three days now. Gone to work and started his new position on Monday, thrown right into long hours on two new cases. Relaxed a bit by going for beers with Darin after work on Tuesday. Now it was time to face some tough questions and tougher answers, but also time to make peace.

Peace wasn't something he had a lot of these days. He had to find it where he could.

As soon as he entered his parents' house, his sister Erica flung herself at him in a big hug. He smiled from the inside out as he returned her embrace. "*Ay, mamita,* you missed me, eh?"

"Of course I did, dummy," Erica said. "It's really good to see you."

"Good to see you too." He stepped back to look her over. His beautiful baby sister wasn't a baby anymore. Her curvy body was encased in a tight little dress with the middle cut out, exposing most of her midriff. He frowned. "Your clothes need more clothes."

She rolled her eyes and said, "You sound like Dad."

"There are worse things," Nick said. "And Dad's a smart guy. You should listen to him."

"Well, that's good to hear." Lew leaned in the doorway between the kitchen and the family room, his pale eyes on Nick.

"I'll go get Livvie," Erica said, looking between them. She left the room.

The two men stood quietly, looking at each other. Things had been awkward between them since the blowout.

"How's the new job going?" Lew asked.

"Good. Busy. Lots to absorb."

"Yeah, but you'll get it."

"I know. I'm not worried. It's just a lot." Nick shoved his hands in the pockets of his shorts. "Weird wearing a shirt and tie every day instead of the uniform. That's gonna take me a while to get used to."

"Once a patrolman, always a patrolman," Lew said with the quiet wisdom of experience. His mouth twisted in a wry grin.

"Dad, I'm sorry," Nick blurted out. "I'm sorry for blowing up at you when I found out about Mom and me, and. . . . I'm sorry for letting my temper get the best of me, and not hearing you out. And being a rude prick. That wasn't fair to you."

"I understood," Lew said. He pushed off the doorframe and stepped closer. "I understood all of it, even though I hated it."

Nick nodded and huffed out a sigh. "It was a shock. I . . ."

"Stop. Apology accepted." Lew looked him over. "You okay?"

"Yeah. I'm just a little . . ." Unable to think of the right words, Nick used his hands to gesture like his head was exploding.

"Seems about right." Lew stepped forward and clasped his son in a bear hug.

Nick hugged him back, some of the tension in his body easing.

"I love you like you're my own," Lew said gruffly at his ear. He pulled back and put both hands on Nick's shoulders. "You're my son. End of story."

"I know. And I'm proud to be." Nick's throat felt thick and he swallowed hard. "You've always been there for me. You're my father. End of story."

Lew smiled, and to Nick's shock, his eyes looked a little glassy.

Maria walked in then, stopping at the sight of them. Her dark eyes rounded and set on her son.

"Ma . . ." Nick turned away from Lew to go to her, pulling her into his arms.

She broke down crying as she grasped at him. "Oh, *mijo* . . . I thought I lost you."

"Never," he murmured, closing his eyes against the sudden sting of tears. He kissed the top of her head and held her tight. *"Te quiero, mamí. Te quiero mucho."* He rubbed her back as she cried. "Shhh. You're stuck with me forever."

She sobbed with relief. Erica and Olivia came into the room, saw them, and walked right out. Nick held her for a few minutes until her tears subsided, then led her to the couch. Lew handed her a box of tissues. She gave a little laugh as she grabbed a few and wiped her face.

"Now I'm a mess," she said. "And who cares."

"Not me," Nick said with a shrug as he sat beside her and took her free hand.

She turned to him as Lew sat in the armchair across from them. "Tell us about New York, Nick. Tell us everything."

Nick felt like he talked for a long time. He told them about all of the Harrisons and their families. He told them about how he'd go back to New York in a month or so for the surgery and what recovery would be like, at least according to the reps he'd spoken to. He told them about things he'd seen in New York City.

But he didn't tell them about Amanda. She was . . . that was all for him. He'd only texted her twice since he'd gotten back. They'd both gotten so busy, and their chats had been brief. But he wanted to keep her to himself. His delicious, secret girl . . . it wasn't to be shared with the world. Not yet, anyway.

"I'm getting hungry," Olivia said from the doorway.

Nick glanced at his watch. Sure enough, he'd been talking for an hour. "You know what? I am too. Dinner almost ready?"

"I kept an eye on the kitchen," Olivia said. She was finishing her senior year at a nearby college, and was a little more mature than Erica. "The food didn't burn or anything."

"Thank you, sweetie," Maria cooed.

Lew rose from his chair, stretching his stiff limbs. "The girls and I will get everything to the table. You two take another minute."

Maria watched him go, then looked back to Nick. "Your father. Your biological father. Did you see him?" Concern and worry played across her face. "You talked about everyone else but him."

Nick's jaw tensed. "Yeah, we met. One time. And that was enough."

Her eyes widened. "It was bad?"

"Let's just say I see why you never told him about me. He's a real asshole." Nick raked a hand through his hair. "Let's have dinner, and I'll tell you the rest after, okay?"

She sighed but nodded and got to her feet.

The five of them enjoyed the meal. Nick relished the familiarity of it: Olivia and Erica both talking too much and annoying him at times, Lew quiet but solidly there, his mom smiling and making sure everyone ate enough and tossing out wisecracks with him and his sisters. It was comfortable, close, and wonderfully known.

This was his family. These were his people, and he was walloped by a wave of emotion as he looked around. He was so damn grateful to have them all. He didn't know, ultimately, how he'd find a place in his life for his new . . . siblings. And they definitely seemed to want a place there. But these four people were his home base, his compass. They'd always been there for him and helped make him who he was. His younger sisters had never known anything from their parents but love, support, and kindness. His parents were compassionate people who adored all of their kids and always put them first. His four New York siblings may have had tons of money, but they weren't as lucky as Nick and his sisters. The Martell family was blessed. His eyes stung and he took a deep breath. This was where he belonged.

"Hey," he said, his voice gruff. The table quieted instantly, four pairs of eyes on him. "I love you guys. I really do. It's good to be home."

Maria's eyes shone. "We love you too."

"Very much," Olivia added with a tender smile.

"I don't care what those New Yorkers want from now on," Erica asserted. "We had you first. You're ours. We have dibs."

Nick laughed, relief cresting over him at the break in heavy emotion. "That's not up for debate. This is my family. Always has been, always will be."

Lew nodded and reached for his beer. "Damn right."

Later, after the table had been cleared, Olivia and Erica went back to their rooms while Nick again sat in the family room with his parents. "I need to talk about some of the tougher stuff now," he said.

Maria and Lew sat together on the couch. Lew reached

over and took his wife's hand in his. She drew a visibly shaky breath, but nodded. "Go on, *mijo*."

"I don't think Charles II is going to come after you," Nick said. "But I have no guarantee. I made it very clear that if he did anything at all, he'd answer to me."

"Oh, Nick," she whispered.

"He's a bastard, Ma. You were right. Even to his own kids . . . The youngest, Pierce? The one you told me about? Well, they have no relationship. They hate each other. Pierce came to the family meeting when I met the old man as a show of support to *me*, and it was the first time they'd talked in like seven years. And Charles was nasty to him. You would have been appalled at how he spoke to his own son."

Maria shook her head. "He never learned. That's so sad."

"Well, don't be sad. I don't want you to be afraid, Ma, but . . . he implied he'd love to come after you for keeping me a secret from him. You need to know this."

Lew's free hand clenched into a fist. "If he comes anywhere near her—"

"Not just her, Dad. He'd probably like to mess with all of us, just to feel like he has some control in this situation, since it was taken from him. The man lives to control." Nick met his eyes. "He's a narcissist, a power freak. But like I said, I made it clear to him that he better not. And his four kids all backed me. Told him if he lifted a finger to hurt anyone in our family, they'd cut him off from the rest of *their* family. That they'd make sure he paid for it and was held accountable."

"That's kind of amazing," Lew said.

"Yeah. I was stunned," Nick admitted. "But it was a nice show of support."

"Sounds like they grew into decent people," Maria murmured. "In spite of him."

"They are, Ma. I think they are. So . . ." Nick rubbed his palms together, fidgety and restless. "I think it's gonna be fine. That the old man will stay away from you. From us. But if anything happens . . . anything unusual, anything bad? You need to tell me right away so I can check it out, and then handle it. Okay?"

"What do you think he'd do?" Lew asked, brows furrowed.

"I have no idea, because I don't think like him. So I'm just saying. Keep an eye out. Just . . . be aware we all have an enemy now. A powerful one."

"He'd do something to *you*?" she said tremulously. "His own son?"

"I'm not his son," Nick said. "I'm flesh and blood, but I'm not his son." He looked into his mother's eyes. "Ma . . . I know I should be mad at you for keeping me a secret from him, and him from me. That on some level, it was wrong."

Her face flushed, but she didn't look away. Her eyes held his.

"I know that in my head," Nick continued. "But in my heart . . ." He shrugged and dropped his hands onto his knees. "I'm not mad, and I'm not judging you. I wish I'd known sooner, yes. But I'm not mad at you anymore. I'm not holding a grudge, none of that. I wasn't in your shoes. That was your decision. It was what it was. You did the best you could. So . . . I don't want to dwell on it. We just go forward from here, okay?"

Her eyes welled and tears spilled onto her cheeks. "It's better than I deserve."

"No, no, stop that," he demanded. "You did right by me. You raised me in a good home, to be a good man. You did good, Ma. I'm letting this go; you have to also."

"Are you really?" she asked, peering harder at him. "How can you?"

"I . . . still need to figure some things out," he said. "But I know who I am. So I'll be okay."

She grasped both his hands with hers and squeezed as she sniffled. "Of course you will, *mijo*."

"We're here for you," Lew said. "I'm glad you're letting us be."

"I'm glad you forgive me," Maria said.

"I should be thanking *you*," Nick said to them. "You've been great parents. I have a good life. I'm a lucky man. So . . . onward." He drew a deep breath and exhaled it slowly. He felt better about repairing his relationship with his parents. But really, that was the easiest part. He still felt the slight tension in the muscles of his neck and shoulders. . . . The rest of the moving parts in his life weren't an easy fix, and he knew it.

Hey, gorgeous. How's my favorite nurse tonight?

Amanda looked at the text from Nick and her insides warmed. She'd heard from him a few times over the past week since he'd gone back to Florida. He'd texted when he touched down in Miami, as he'd promised. He checked in every other day, and they'd chatted via texts for a few minutes. But it didn't feel like enough.

She wanted more. Longer text chats, or more of them, or to hear his voice . . . to hear something from him that indicated the connection she'd felt between them was real, and he'd felt it too. But so far, not so much. And it frustrated her.

She wasn't sure what frustrated her more: that they weren't going deeper on an emotional level, or that she was the one bending the unspoken rules by wanting that at all. Both had her overthinking the situation and coming up short. She had to swallow it.

Here it was, ten o'clock on a Friday night. She was back in her apartment after a long, hard week, and all she wanted was to sink into Nick's arms and have him soothe her headache and heartache away. The Chinese takeout for dinner had filled her, the glass of wine she'd had with it helped to calm her, but nothing could get rid of the gnawing inside.

She longed for comfort. Texting with Nick would have to be a good substitute.

She changed into her pajamas first, refilling her wineglass and bringing it to her nightstand along with her phone. The lights stayed off, lending a touch of intimacy to her surroundings as she prepared to dig in for a long chat.

Hey there, Miami Vice. I'm okay, she texted back, then climbed into her bed. She sighed aloud in contentment as her body relaxed into her mattress. *Keep it casual*, she reminded herself. *Nick just wants casual. You told him you wanted that too. So be that.*

Nick's text came back right away. Is that true?
Is what true? she wrote back.

Are you really okay? I know things with Myles this week must've been hard.

Her throat thickened unexpectedly. She swallowed and texted, Truth? Yes, it was a rough week. But I'm okay.

I'm sure, Nick wrote. On both counts. But … wanna talk about it?

Nope. How'd your first full week go, Detective? she wrote, hoping to deflect away from herself. If he was nice to her, she'd spill all over him, and she didn't want to. She scowled at herself and reached over to grab her glass. Why did he make her feel so much, when she didn't want to feel anything at all?

It was fine, thanks. But you're deflecting, he wrote. Talk to me. I have time. Not working. Home alone, got all night.

The lump in her throat felt like it got bigger. She swallowed down a sip of wine. Home alone on a Friday night? After your first week on the new job? That doesn't seem right. You should be out celebrating.

A few friends wanted to take me out, but I was tired. Maybe tomorrow night.

Go clubbing, she wrote. Dance with a hot girl. Laugh with your friends. Drink like you're out with Pierce. You deserve it.

LOL, Nick responded. Pierce can drink. That's more like a challenge than a suggestion.

Amanda sent back a wink emoji.

Then he texted: Are you telling me to go hook up?

Amanda's heart skipped a beat, and embarrassment flooded her. Shit. What should she say?

I'm not looking to hook up right now, Amanda, Nick wrote. Got enough on my plate. Just saying.

She felt her face turn crimson, grateful he couldn't see her. Okay.

That's it? Nope. Say what you meant.

I didn't mean anything by that, she wrote, her stomach churning now.

Then why'd you say it? Seems odd.

I just meant I wanted you to go out and have fun. That's all.

I'm kinda too tired to have fun right now. And . . .

She waited. After thirty seconds, she realized she was holding her breath and expelled it in a gust. And what? she typed.

And I'm not looking to hook up with a stranger right now, because if I close my eyes, I can still remember how you felt in bed. How you tasted, how you smelled, how you sounded. I want to hold on to that right now. It's enough.

Amanda almost spilled her wine all over herself. Her heart pounding, she swallowed a huge gulp, put the glass back on the nightstand, then called Nick.

"Hey." His voice was low and sexy, sending a shiver through her.

"You made me melt," she said quietly. "I needed to hear your voice."

"Hmm. I like that." She could hear the smile in his voice, pictured it on his gorgeous face. "I'm glad you called, then. It's good to hear your voice too."

She drew a shaky breath, heart still beating fast, and nestled further into her pillows. "Did you mean that? What you just wrote?"

"Yup." He paused, then blurted out, "I've thought about you every day. I know I'm not supposed to, but to hell with that. And I . . . I know you had a hard week, so I just thought I'd tell you that. Maybe it'd help, or make you smile, or—"

"It did. It does." Her heart squeezed, and her stomach did a flighty little flip. She ached for him. "I missed your voice. This week was hell," she confessed. "I wish you were here tonight to help me forget it."

"I'm sorry to hear it," he said gently. "Talk to me. I'm listening."

"Well, he started losing his hair again." Her voice was barely above a murmur, but it suddenly felt thick in her throat. "It happened quicker than last time, and it upset him pretty bad. When he wasn't sleeping. His blood sugar was all over the place because of the chemo, the steroids, and . . . dammit, I don't know how much I should be telling you. It sucked—how's that?"

She heard Nick swear under his breath. "I called Charles on Wednesday morning to see how Myles was doing. He said it was hard, and sounded stressed. But he said you were taking good care of him. Didn't give me a lot of details."

"You don't need any more details," she said. "You can guess the rest."

"You're so strong, Amanda," Nick said, his voice a caress. "You know that, right? Charles and Lisette are so glad Myles has you. And so am I. You're an angel."

"No, I'm not. I'm just doing my job."

"The job of an angel. I couldn't do what you do. You're amazing."

Tears pricked her eyes and she drew a long, shallow breath. "Thanks. But I don't feel so amazing at the moment. I feel sad and worried and exhausted and emotionally wrung out. I might not get out of bed for the rest of the weekend so I can recharge my battery and go back on Monday with a smile for that kid. That's the truth."

"And that's okay. Do that if you have to." He paused before adding, "I wish I was holding you, in that case."

Her breath caught. God, he was being so sweet. "Me too. That sounds nice."

"It does." They were quiet for a few seconds before he added, "I wish I was doing a little more than holding you, truth be told. Or, if I was, that at least you'd be naked. Can I envision holding you but you're naked? Oops, too late. Already doing it."

A giggle popped out of her. "I wish you were too, I admit it."

"Sounds good, right?" He paused. "So, um . . . have you . . . ever had phone sex?"

Heat seared through her body, making her skin tingle. "Maybe. Why?"

"Why do you think?" His voice dipped low, playful yet seductive. "I can't hold you, but I can do something else for you. Could be a great way to help you relax."

"Relax? You getting me all worked up is not my idea of relaxing."

He laughed softly. "Well . . . I'd talk you through and get you all worked up until you come. Hopefully, come *hard*. After which, you'd relax. Get it?"

"Jesus," she breathed. Just hearing him say something like that, with that sex-on-a-stick deep voice of his, had her wet already.

"So, Favorite Nurse. You game?"

"Um. Hold on." Heart rate rising, she reached for her

wineglass again. She drank down three huge gulps, then set it back down. Her whole body was already pulsing with lusty desire. "Okay, Miami Vice. Show me your A game. Why not, right?"

"You sound a little nervous."

"I . . . no. I'm not. You just got me all flustered over here."

"Good. I mean . . . it's not like I haven't heard you come before, *mi reina*." His voice was pure sin. "And I loved it. Every time."

A jolt of electricity shot through her, ending right between her legs. She squirmed in her bed, pressing her thighs together.

"You keep talking like that," she warned, "it won't take me long at all."

He chuckled. "What's the rush? We have all night. This is going to be fun."

"It is, huh?"

"Fuck yeah. Hearing you when you're turned on is so hot. Thinking about you touching yourself? I'm hard already."

A soft moan fluttered out of her. "Jesus, Nick. Your voice alone should be illegal, much less the dirty things that come out of your mouth."

He gave a little snort-laugh of triumph. "But you like when I talk dirty to you, don't you?"

She shivered. "Yes. Like you couldn't tell."

"I have to admit . . . I could tell. Which is why I'll keep doing it."

Fifteen minutes later, she was moaning out a powerful orgasm, one hand pressing the phone against her ear while the other worked herself into a frenzy. She panted as she regained her senses, then realized what she'd done, what she must have sounded like, and let out a hoarse laugh. "Ohhh my God."

"That," Nick said roughly, "was unbelievably fucking hot."

She smiled as she tried to catch her breath. "Glad you enjoyed."

"I'm glad *you* did, babe. Damn, you're sexy."

Still a little woozy, she said, "Well, I don't know if I can match your dirty talk, but I'll give it my best shot. Your turn."

He groaned. "I'm halfway there, you kidding? Won't take much."

She hoped she'd be able to cast a spell over him the way he had over her. His powers of seduction, even just with sexy talk over the phone, were epic as far as she was concerned. But she felt suddenly shy. She hadn't done this since college.

He must have sensed her sudden nerves, her hesitation. In a low, sexy rumble, he coaxed, "Just tell me what you'd do to me if you were here right now. Go on . . ."

She started out slowly, feeling awkward, but eased into it with his guidance. Luckily, he must've been as turned on as he claimed, because it only took about five minutes before he came. The sounds of his heavy breathing and groaning climax made her insides clench and want to go another round.

"Jesus," he panted. "See, you're good at this. Knew you had it in you."

"Did you? I didn't."

"Oh, I did. You're my bold New York girl."

"I loved hearing you," she admitted. "That was *hot*."

He laughed. "I'm glad. Give me a minute?"

She reached over and drained what was left in her wineglass. Between the slight buzz from the Chardonnay and the after-buzz of her orgasm, she felt floaty and content.

"I'm back," he said. "You know what? If I can't see you, this was the next best thing. It was fun, anyway. Right?"

She giggled and rolled onto her side. "Yes, it was."

"You warmed up to it quickly. You weren't shy after the first minute or two."

"Because you led me down the path to ruin like a master."

"Did I? Awesome. I feel like a king now. Or a naughty Pied Piper. Not sure."

She laughed, and "I miss you" came spilling out of her mouth. She cringed and squeezed her eyes shut. Damn, damn, double damn, why had she told him that?

"I miss you too," he said softly.

"You don't have to say that because I did."

"I wouldn't. I don't say things I don't mean." He paused, and she could hear the rustle of sheets. She figured he was easing back into his bed. "So you miss me?"

She sighed. "Yeah. I do. I wasn't going to tell you that. Sorry."

"Why wouldn't you tell me that?"

"Because we . . . we're not like that."

"Like what? Two people who like each other? Yeah, we are."

She bit down on her lip before saying, "I don't really know what we are."

"I don't either. But I miss you too, if that makes you feel better about saying it." Nick paused. "I've been busy as hell this week, but I've thought about you."

She smiled and her trepidation lessened. "That's nice to hear." With a yawn, she rolled onto her side and burrowed deeper into her bed. "Between the wine and the O, I'm so nice and sleepy now."

"Maybe I should let you go, then."

"Not yet. Soon, but not yet. I like talking to you."

"Amanda, you know what . . ." His voice trailed off, and she waited. "It's okay that we're into each other. We're hiding it from the others, but we shouldn't have to hide it from each other. We spent a night together. An amazing night. And we're staying in touch. So . . . I don't know what this is either, but I know I'm into you, so I'm just gonna go with that for now. There, I said it. Okay?"

"Works for me," she murmured, her heart growing a size or two.

Chapter Eighteen

Nick rubbed his eyes, then raked his hand over his hair as he pored over the file yet again. This case was eating at him. Three weeks ago, it'd been the first case he'd been given as an investigator, and he desperately wanted to solve it. Not just to prove something to himself or his superiors, but for the victim's family. They deserved answers and hopefully, eventually, some closure. Clearly the twenty-four-year-old murder victim had been a case of mistaken identity—poor bastard had been in the wrong place at the wrong time. If the killer had made that mistake, there had to be other mistakes too. Nick just had to find them. But he wasn't used to the new pace. Things worked much more slowly, with more steps, and though he knew it was necessary, it frustrated him. He had to learn to dial it back and get used to it.

His cell phone rang on the desk beside him. He didn't even look at the screen when he answered it, eyes still on the computer screen. "Martell."

"Hi . . . Mr. Martell? Nick Martell?"

"Yes."

"Okay, good. This is Dr. Greenberg, from Northwell Hospital."

Nick snapped to attention. "Sure, right. Hi."

"Hi. Do you have a few minutes to talk? I realize you may be at work."

Nick's whole body went tight. The doctor in charge of Myles's medical team was calling him? Something had to be up. "Yes, I'm at work, but that's fine. Sure, I have a few minutes. What's up?"

"We're ready for you to come back to New York," the doctor said. "Myles is done with the conditioning and we're just about ready to do the surgery. How soon can you come back? Any idea?"

"I'll be there tomorrow if you need me to be," Nick said without pause.

Fifteen minutes later, Nick was walking into his boss's office to request the leave of absence they'd known would be coming. After that, he sat down at his desk to book a flight to New York when his phone rang. Charles's number lit up the screen.

"Hey," Nick said. "I was going to call you in a bit. Just had a meeting with my superior, got the clearance. I'm on my way."

"Wonderful. I heard from Dr. Greenberg that you said you'd be coming," Charles said. "So everything's swinging into action. Thank you for coming so quickly."

"Of course," Nick said. "I was actually about to book my flight. I'm going to work tomorrow to finish out the week, but I'll take an evening flight, get there late tomorrow night."

"Glad I caught you, then," Charles said, "because that's not necessary. That's why I called. My private plane will bring you to New York. Don't book anything."

"What?"

"My jet. It'll be at the Miami airport for you, whenever you're ready to go. You just tell me when you were planning to leave. How's seven-thirty, eight P.M. sound?"

Nick almost sputtered. "You don't have to do that."

"I want to do that. Please let me."

Nick sighed. He suspected that now that the surgery was a go, Charles was probably freaking out and needed to do something. Nick knew him well enough now to know that . . . but it still felt like leeching off him. "Charles . . ."

"So I'll fly you in. My next question is," Charles barreled on, "do you want to stay here at the house while you recover? After the procedure, you're going to need to be watched for a few days. Maybe even weeks. You know that."

"I'll be fine, and I'll be in a hotel," Nick asserted. "I appreciate your concern, really. So don't take offense, but I'll want my own space. I need that." The thought of an audience around him while he recovered was not going to fucking happen. Not to mention the Amanda factor. For three weeks, he'd been texting and talking to her, growing a little closer every day. He couldn't wait to see her again. He couldn't wait to get her into bed again. And they couldn't do any of that freely if he was staying under Charles's roof. "I'm not budging on that, so don't try, okay? I'll stay at a hotel."

"Okay, but you *are* going to need some help those first few days," Charles asserted. "I respect and understand that you want your own space, but I'm going to hire a nurse for you anyway. Warning you now."

"Jeez, Harrison," Nick joked. "You're a pushy bastard, aren't you?"

"On all this stuff? Absolutely." Charles's voice softened as he said, "I want to help. I want to do something. This is what I can do. Please . . . just let me help you, okay?"

Nick understood him, and was more moved than he wanted to admit. "Okay. All right, fine. So what are we talking about, exactly?"

Charles actually sighed with relief. "Starting with my plane, we'll firm up the time later and get you here. I'll book you a room at the same hotel as last time, if that's all right? You liked it there?"

"Yes," Nick said, "that'll be fine." He leaned back in his chair, giving in.

"Consider it done. And I'll make sure a rental car is there for you." Charles's tone turned playful as he asked, "Want a Porsche again? Or something else? Name your ride, baby brother."

Nick laughed, but something in his chest twinged at the *baby brother* bit. It was the first time Charles had called him that. "Something fast and sweet. Surprise me."

"Oh, that'll be fun," Charles said, his voice infused with a new zeal. "That I'll do myself, not leave to my assistant."

"Have fun with that."

"I will. You will too, I promise. Um . . . since you're getting in late Friday night, would you be amenable to coming to my house on Saturday for lunch to see our other siblings? Or dinner? Up to you. I know Myles would love it."

Our other siblings. Nick was going back into the fold of his new, other family. The short amount of time and space hadn't brought him much in the way of answers. He still wasn't sure exactly how he fit in with the Harrisons, or how much he wanted to. But the thought of seeing Myles made Nick's gut clench. He wanted to see that kid more than anything. "I'd love to see Myles too. Tell him I'll be there. But . . . can we make it lunch? I may have plans in the evening."

Charles paused a second, and Nick knew he was surprised. He also sensed Charles wanted to ask what kind of plans, but his refined manners wouldn't let him. "Of course," Charles said. "We can even make it a brunch, if that works better for you."

"Hmm . . . I'll hit the gym in the morning and be over to your place at noon, if that works."

"That's fine. Listen, Nick . . ." Charles cleared his throat. "The surgery is Wednesday. You'll have pretesting and all that on Monday and Tuesday. So . . . I'd like it to be a family get-together on Saturday. With all the siblings. Have everyone there except for my father. Between you *and* Pierce being there, he shouldn't be. So that's all right with you, right? I'm asking first. I'm not sure how much of the family you want around you, especially if you're at all tense about the surgery."

"I'm not tense about the surgery," Nick said automatically.

"Great. But you may still be tense about being a Harrison. And I understand that. So . . . if it's too much, and it isn't what you want, tell me. And I'll make the family get-together for Sunday, without you, so you can just visit with Myles alone on Saturday." Charles added, "I'm trying to be considerate. Because I don't know what you're thinking or feeling. So I'm not trying to shove us all down your throat. Understand?"

Nick went quiet. The swirl of others talking around him, the varied noises of the station, seemed to overwhelm him for a few seconds. He wished he had a better handle on what he was thinking or feeling himself. When he was immersed in his work, it was easy not to think about Myles, or the Harrisons, or Amanda, or any of these new factors that played into his life. The fact still was, he had no idea where he stood, and he wasn't sure what to do with that. So he'd just keep barreling forward until he did. "The thing with everyone on Saturday is fine with me. And the plane, the hotel, and the rest of it too. And . . . thank you for wanting to do all that. I'll let you this time."

"You're very welcome. Wait—*this* time?" Charles asked. "That makes it sound like you'll be coming back to New York after the surgery. Are you planning to be?"

"I have no real plans," Nick said. "But it's likely, at some point. I've got a few relatives there."

"You do indeed," Charles said warmly.

"But if I do, I pay my own way, make my own reservations, all of that. Got it?"

"Got it."

"Okay then. I'll be in touch later about the flight. I just need to check on a few things."

"And I just need to figure out if I should pick a Ferrari or a Lamborghini for you," Charles said. "Decisions, decisions . . ."

Nick laughed. "Don't go nuts. See you on Saturday."

Amanda made sure Myles was comfortable. He'd fallen asleep sitting up, and she eased him to lie down, gently pulling the video game console from his hands so as not to wake him. She felt his ears to make sure he had no temperature; to her relief, they were cool to the touch. "Thatta boy," she whispered. If he got sick now, the surgery would be postponed, not to mention the havoc it would wreak on his weakened immune system. Every day now, that was her biggest concern. She found herself thinking, *Stay healthy, stay healthy, stay healthy* several times a day.

With a sigh, she stretched her arms over her head and went to the side window to look outside. It was a lovely spring day. The mid-May flowers seemed to be everywhere; the Harrisons' landscaping was a gorgeous cascade of color. Tulips of all shades lined the mansion and the wide backyard, bursts of bright reds, yellows, pinks, and purples against the greens of the shrubbery and lawn. Spring was blooming out there . . . and Myles was wilting in here. Life wasn't fair sometimes. It just wasn't.

Sighing, she grabbed her water bottle and took a few sips. She rolled her head, trying to loosen the tight muscles in her neck, then pulled out her ponytail, ran a quick comb through her hair, and put it back up again. Reaching into her deep tote bag for her lip balm, she also grabbed her phone to check her messages. A text from her mom, one from Roni, and one from Nick. His made her brows lift.

Hey there, beautiful. Got any plans for Saturday night?

She sank into the chair by the bay window with a smile. Sunlight warmed the back of her head and shoulders as she texted him: No. Why, are you making sure I'll be home for another round of texting or phone seduction?

His text came back immediately. Ha! No, much better. I'm coming back to New York tomorrow night. But I'll get in pretty late, so I can't see you til Saturday. Would love to take you out to dinner if that's ok with you.

She smiled with delight as a burst of excitement rushed through her veins. It's more than okay. I'd love to see you.

Great. Then we're on.

Knew you were coming back soon, she wrote, but wasn't sure when. Heard today they scheduled the surgery for Wed. Was going to call you later.

Can you talk? I'll call and tell you everything.

Can't talk now. Still at work & Myles is sleeping nearby.

Ah, ok. Thought maybe you were on a dinner break. How is he?

Same. But holding steady.

Good. And you? You holding steady too?

Yup. She added, And now that I have a date on Saturday night, I'm a little perked up.

Only a little?

She sent back a winking emoji.

Minx. So here's the plan, he wrote. **I'll be at Charles's house on Saturday afternoon for a family thing. Mostly to see Myles. But then I'll come pick you up. How's 6:00?**
Perfect. She wiggled a bit in her seat, another wave of happiness washing over her. Where are we going?

Wherever you want. So the thing is . . . I'd like to take you out to dinner. But then I want to bring you back to my hotel. I want you. Stay the night with me. Would you please?

Her heart skipped a beat as her skin heated, adrenaline shooting through her. I'd like that. All of that. Yes.

Oh, good. Plus, if you stay with me, we don't have to worry about being quiet for your roommate. Heh heh

LOL! A little shiver rolled over her as she thought of the ways he'd make her unquiet. Which hotel? Same as last time?
Yes. **And I have all day Sunday to focus on nothing but you,** he wrote. **I might not let you out of bed. Pack accordingly.**
A bolt of electricity zipped through her, stopping with a zing between her legs. Smiling, she texted back, Sounds good, but . . . won't you feed me at some point on Sunday? I get hungry when I'm screwed senseless.

Fiiiiiine. So demanding. I'll make sure you're fed. And definitely screwed senseless. Deal?

Deal, she typed, smiling broadly. Um ... protection? You or me?

I've got that, no worries, he wrote back. But you'll stay all day Sunday? I want that time with you before ... you know. Everything.

She swallowed a sigh. After the surgery, he wouldn't be up to much for a while, whether he wanted to admit it or not. But he was telling her flat out he wanted her, and wanted her to stay with him. All night, and all the next day. That was ... a rush. Happy-making. Thrilling. Her cheeks bloomed pink, and she bit down on her lip. Yes. I'll stay. Sounds fantastic. Looking forward to it.

Can't wait to see you, Favorite Nurse.

Back atcha, Miami Vice. She turned to look out the window, squinting into the sunshine. Her day had just improved by a gazillion. She smiled with excited anticipation as she gazed out at the trees and flowers, her mind filled with visions of Nick. She couldn't wait to see him again, touch him again, let herself sink into oblivion with him ... for a short time. All she had to do was not focus on why he was there in the first place, and everything that would follow immediately after their secret rendezvous. She'd just live in the moment. Nothing was guaranteed beyond that anyway. She glanced over her shoulder to check on Myles, who slept soundly. No ... nothing was guaranteed.

"You have *got* to be kidding me." Amanda approached Nick with wide eyes. At the curb in front of her apartment building, he looked hotter than hot standing alongside a sleek black Ferrari. Dark sunglasses on, saucy grin on his handsome face, his long, muscled frame in a tight navy T-shirt and jeans slung low on his narrow hips as he perched on the hood . . . she swallowed hard. It was like a cover shoot for a magazine or something. Ridiculously sexy. The whole picture made her weak with lust.

Was she that shallow, to be swayed and affected so much by a hot guy in front of a hot car? Apparently so, and who cared, power to her, the man was smoking. Off the charts.

And hers for the night.

"Hey." His grin widened into a smile and he stood, straightening to his full six feet as she reached him.

God, he was gorgeous. She had a fleeting moment of awkward hesitation, an unexpected jab of sudden shyness. Did she kiss him hello? Offer a friendly hug? Not touch him yet at all? But he didn't even pause. His hands went to her waist, pulling her in as he smiled down at her. "I remember you." His voice was warm as he pushed his sunglasses to the top of his head, revealing happiness in those deep brown eyes.

"You look vaguely familiar," she murmured, captivated, sucked in to his presence and his embrace like she'd been put under a spell.

"You look so pretty," he said softly. "I like this dress." His eyes traveled over her body in heated appreciation as his hands clasped her waist a little tighter. "It's flattering as hell on you. And brings out your eyes."

"Thank you." She gave herself a mental gold star for choosing the pale blue shift dress rather than jeans and a top. She wanted to look and feel feminine, attractive, and a little bit sexy, and this dress did the trick. A low V-neck, fluttery short sleeves, hem that stopped just above her knees . . . it was a very different look from her scrubs, which Nick had seen her in one too many times. She'd wanted to set a certain tone for the night; clearly the dress and her nude peep-toe heels had done their job.

"It's really good to see you," he whispered. One hand stayed at her waist, curling around her lower back to pull her closer as the other hand lifted to cup her face. He lowered his head, brushing his lips against hers gently at first, then with a little more pressure and heat. His tongue ran along her bottom lip, asking for entry. She parted her lips to invite him in and her arms snaked around his neck and locked there. With a soft groan, he deepened the kiss and she pressed against him, arching into him.

His warm mouth against hers and his strong arms around her felt so good. It was both a re-acquaintance of touch, getting to know each other again, and fresh new sparks igniting. Her fingers ran through his short hair, clutched at his shoulders as the kisses smoldered, burning hotter, until she remembered they were out on the street and broke the kiss.

"Whoa." Nick leaned his forehead against hers and smiled, his eyes dark with desire. It pleased her to see she wasn't the only one breathing a little heavy. He moved his hand to brush a stray lock of her hair back from her eyes. He tucked it behind her ear as he said, his voice pitched low, "Better stop now, or I'm just gonna sweep you upstairs and into bed."

"Would that be so bad?" she said with a grin.

"No." His grin matched hers. "No, it wouldn't. But dinner first. I need fuel for what I plan to do to you all night." A soft breeze made her hair dance again, and his eyes lit as he stared at her face. "It's good to see you, Amanda."

"Good to see you too." She smiled, touched his cheek, then pulled back a little. Her whole body burned for him, but if he could hold back, so could she. "So. This car? Seriously?"

"I know." He laughed as he released her, then grabbed his sunglasses from where they were perched on top of his head and put them back on. "Charles did this. It's kind of a running joke now, I think. I never would've picked this out."

"Too flashy?" Amanda guessed.

"Too expensive to justify the rental. But he . . ." Nick laughed again and shrugged. "He thinks I'm a young alpha male who likes like fast, shiny cars."

"Are you?"

"Hell yeah. But still, this . . . it's a fucking Ferrari. I mean, Jesus, you know?"

"I know. It's hot. And I've never even been this close to one, much less in one." She slid him a playfully sexy look. "You gonna take me for a spin in it or what?"

He immediately opened the passenger door for her. "Absolutely, gorgeous."

She slid into the leather seat, admiring as she looked around. She was sitting in a *Ferrari*. This was bizarre. She grinned to herself as Nick started the car and the engine purred to life. "Damn, this car is sexy," she said.

"It really is," he admitted.

Amanda felt invigorated. She opened the window halfway to let in the warm spring air. "We need to take a drive before dinner. Would that be okay?"

"Sure, that'd be fine." He grinned as he pulled away from the curb and eased onto the street. "Just tell me where you want to go."

She thought about it for a few seconds. "I know where I'd love to go, because I think you might like it, but it'd take some extra time to get there. I think it'd be worth it, but you said you're hungry. . . ."

"I can wait." He glanced at her over the rims of his sunglasses. "Look, the night is ours. Let's make the most of it. I want to be out with you. It's a gorgeous night. We'll take a drive, then we'll get some dinner, and then . . ." His grin turned wicked. "You're mine, all mine. Every luscious inch of you." He winked. "So, go ahead, tell me where we're going."

Nick loved everything about the drive. The feel of the wind, the wheel in his hands, the way the sun dropped slowly in the sky, turning it into shades of dark pink, orange, blue-tinged purple . . . but best of all was the gorgeous woman sitting beside him. Beautiful, alluring, and with a smile she hadn't been able to take off her face from the moment she'd first seen him.

He'd missed her. Almost a month of texting and phone conversations had helped them get to know each other better, helped them grow a little closer, but it wasn't the same as actually being together. Getting to look at each other when they talked, being able to reach out and touch her skin or her hair, to hold her hand as he steered the car down the open road . . .

She'd taken them along a few parkways, going from the North Shore of Long Island down to the South Shore. She was originally from the South Shore, and apparently that was a thing. She told him the cool girls were from the South Shore, and that the beaches were better. The North Shore had the Long Island Sound, but the south had the Atlantic Ocean, and did he want to drive along that? Hell yes, he did. She told him where to go, and in a little while they were soaring down the Ocean Parkway.

The landscape was different here, he could tell. The North Shore had been greener, lusher. Here there was lots of brush by the beach, and it wasn't as green. The car sailed along the asphalt like a dream, and the ocean was visible as they went, so close. They drove for a while with the windows down and the music up, enjoying the power of both the car and the sexual tension that crackled between them.

It was just what he'd needed. It helped him take his mind off what he'd left behind at Charles's mansion.

Amanda had warned him that Myles looked different, but Nick hadn't been prepared for what he'd seen today. Myles was hairless now, and the sallow tone of his skin made him sad. But the kid had brightened when he'd seen Nick, which had made his heart do a funny twist in his chest. And his attitude had been as positive as it could be, causing Nick to admire his nephew more than he could express. Nick had brought him gifts—a Miami PD T-shirt and sweatshirt, and a Marlins ball cap just to mess with him. Myles had thanked

him and switched out his Yankees cap right away. The sight
of his bald head had made Nick's stomach clench. Nick had
helped him adjust it, then asked if he could hug him. When
he had, he'd felt the kid's bones. He'd breathed him in.

But it was more than all that. It was the thick tension that
had been in the air, that palpable worry that had pervaded
the house. Nick had felt it the minute he'd set foot in the
mansion. Charles and Lisette had been wound up tight. They
mostly did a good job of concealing their worry, but he'd
seen it in their eyes. He'd seen it in the way Ava shot her
mouth off at her father and the way Thomas retreated into
the corner with his phone, barely looking up as he curled
into a chair. He'd seen it in how clingy little Charlotte had
been with both of her parents, much more so than last time.

When the rest of the family had arrived, it'd helped to distract them all from the unease in the atmosphere. Tess,
Logan, and their three kids, Pierce and Abby with their two
tiny boys . . . the house had filled with sound, a cushion
against the dark presence that hung like a veil over everyone.
Dane and Julia had shown up last, carrying boxes of cookies
and pastries for everyone, which had brought cheers. And
every one of them had seemed genuinely glad to see Nick.
Each had given him a warm welcome, asked him how his
new job was going, all the good things.

But throughout the afternoon Lisette and Charles had
taken turns disappearing up to Myles's room. Neither of
them had been willing, or even able, to leave his side for
long. Nick had watched them discreetly as they'd trade
shifts. Charles would kiss the top of her head or pull her into
a hug; Lisette would rub his shoulder or his arm or his
back . . . tiny gestures of love, meant to comfort one another.

They were terrified. It had hurt Nick to see it.

"You with me?" Amanda asked.

He shot her a quick glance. "I am. Sorry. I was just thinking about them. The whole family. They're on edge . . . and
I felt for them. I care." He adjusted his sunglasses, absently

ran his fingers through his hair. "Isn't that bizarre, that I barely know them all, but they mean enough to me that I care?"

"No." Amanda squeezed his hand. "It's not bizarre. It's lovely, really."

He squeezed her hand back.

She leaned over and turned the volume up a bit, letting the music fill the comfortable silence. The scenery whirred by. . . . Nick got lost in his head again, stuck on the thing that had burrowed under his skin as much as seeing Myles so weakened.

At one point, needing a breather, Nick had wandered into the kitchen looking to grab a beer. A short Latina woman, around his mother's age, had stood at the stove stirring something in a huge silver pot. Her black hair, threaded with silver, had been pulled back in a ponytail and she'd hummed to herself as she worked.

"That smells amazing," Nick had said to her. "Whatever it is."

"Soup for Myles. Chicken, carrots, barley. It's his favorite." She'd turned her head, looked him up and down. "You're the new long-lost brother, aren't you?"

"I am." He'd extended a hand. "Nick Martell."

"Nice to meet you. I'm Tina Rodriguez." She'd shaken his hand and flashed a quick smile. "I've worked here forever. I didn't meet you last time you were here, but I heard about you." Then she'd added, in Spanish, "Lisette told me how you found out she spoke Spanish. That's funny as hell."

It shouldn't have surprised him, but she'd caught him off guard. He'd laughed and leaned a hip against the counter, switching to Spanish as well. "Ay, you think so, eh? She handed me my head, but with such class. Served me right."

"Lisette is nothing but class. But I would've given anything to see your face when she answered you." Tina's eyes had sparkled as she set down the long wooden spoon. "My God, look at you. I can see the resemblance since I know, but . . ." She'd shaken her head in wonder. "It's really something, when I think about it."

"What is?"

"That one of us is one of them." Tina had given a little grin, one of a secret ally. "Blew my mind when I heard that. That Charles's asshole father had . . . well." She'd tsked at herself. "I don't mean to be rude—forgive me. It's just seeing you in person . . . I've known this family a long time. It's just wild, the whole story."

Nick had stared at Tina, stopped cold as it hit him. She was a Latina, working in the Harrisons' kitchen. . . . That could've been his mom thirty years ago. It had stolen his breath. *One of us is one of them.*

"You're not here again." Amanda's voice burst into his thoughts.

He blinked, glancing at her before looking back out at the road. "Sorry. Just got caught up. . . ." He shook his head.

"Wanna talk about it?" she asked, her voice gentling.

He sighed. "Part of it, you already understand. Part of it . . . you couldn't possibly understand."

She rolled up her window so she could hear him better, lowered the volume of the music, then turned to him with a firm but kind gaze. "Try me."

He told her everything about seeing the family, being with Myles, the pervading worry. Then, after some hesitation, he told her about meeting Tina, and what she'd said that he couldn't get out of his head. "It just brought up a lot of things. . . . I don't know how to explain it. Old demons."

"You don't have to talk about it if you don't want to." Amanda reached over and took his hand again, her skin soft and warm as she interlaced their fingers. "But if you want to, I'm listening. I'm here."

Something expanded in his chest at that. He stole a glance at her, caught the genuine friendship and kindness in her eyes. . . . He felt safe enough to be open with her. "I don't think a lot about being biracial. Really, I never have.

I am who I am. I just live my life, whatever. But once in a while, it comes up. Like today. And I have to admit that, deep down, it's always felt like . . ." He sighed as he searched for the right words, keeping his eyes on the road, the fading colors of the sky. Her hand was warm in his.

"I have one foot in each world," he admitted quietly. "I'm just . . . never a hundred percent in one world. You wouldn't understand, but it's just . . . sometimes, when I think about it? It just makes me weary. Maybe a little sad, or mad, or something. I don't know. There's too much. Neither side of my family ever really clubbed me over the head with it, but there's been tiny things, subtle things, over the years. . . . I was aware of it. So I just don't think about it too long or too hard, but . . ." He shook his head. "Whatever. I don't like sounding like I'm whining. Sorry."

"You're not whining. You're talking about your feelings."

"Yeah, well, I'm not great at that."

"Gee, I'm so surprised." Her voice was gently teasing.

He couldn't help but grin. "Yeah, well. Typical guy, I guess."

"There's nothing typical about you, Nick." Her tone changed, warmth infusing her words. "It's why I was drawn to you in the first place. Don't sell yourself short with that bullshit. You run deeper than you admit to."

He loved her straight-talking ways. His fingers involuntarily squeezed hers.

"Why wouldn't I understand what you said, how you feel?" she said. "You articulated it pretty well."

He just shook his head. She hadn't experienced that feeling of displacement, so no matter how well he articulated it, there was a level of distance she'd never get past. He eased the car down the road, focusing on how it curved slightly.

"Tell you what," she said. "You're right—I can't understand what that's been like. But I can listen, and you can talk to me about it. And I'm not judging you. You weren't whining, and I'd never think that. I'm here to talk to, to lean on. You can do that with me. Because I care about you."

Something heavy snaked through his chest and he swallowed hard. Her words struck something deep inside him. It was like he'd been hit by a lightning bolt; he was that shaken to the core. Overwhelmed, he felt warmth flow through him, and he wanted to hold her, pull her into his arms and not let go.

With a sharp turn, Nick pulled over to the side of the road, the tiny little strip for emergencies, and threw the car into park. Her eyes were round; clearly, she wasn't sure why he'd stopped or what was happening. But he turned to her and said intently, "Thank you. Thanks for that." He reached up to hold her face with both hands, gazing at her in soft wonder. "I appreciate what you said. You're great, and . . . I care about you too."

He pressed his lips to hers in a long, sweet kiss, reverent and adoring.

"I'm getting hungry now," she said softly. "Let's go get some dinner. I know a great place right on the beach. We passed it a few miles back. We'll turn around. Okay?"

He caressed her face, her beautiful face. . . . He couldn't stop staring at her. Something forceful surged through him, feelings he couldn't name, crushing and elating at the same time. He just couldn't tear his eyes from her, locked there with a gravitational pull. They gazed into each other's eyes for a few long, charged moments. She reached up to trace her fingertip along his ear, then moved her hand to the back of his neck to play with his hair, her expression neutral except for the soft smile that played at the corners of her mouth. Something he couldn't label was gnawing at him, restless and straining. . . .

"You're okay," she whispered. "Everything is going to be okay."

The knot in his chest unraveled, a quiet ease replacing it. At a loss for words, he shifted in his seat so he could take her mouth again. The kiss was deep, firm, filled with the passion and emotion he felt inside that he couldn't put words to. He'd been meant to meet her. Meant to find her. It was a whisper in his head, in his heart.

"I missed you when we were apart," he whispered against her mouth. *"Mi reina. Mi reina bella . . ."*

She gave a little shiver and her smile twitched, as if she was pleased to hear his words but didn't want to admit it. So he kissed her again, threading his fingers through her silky hair as his mouth consumed hers. He wanted to kiss her for hours. . . . He wanted to curl around her, draw her into him, become one. These feelings were insane, sending him spinning. . . .

But she pulled back, her hands on his face. "Let's get some dinner," she said. "The sooner we do, the sooner you can take me to bed and show me just how much you missed me."

A fresh surge of lusty heat shot through his veins, making his limbs tingle, and he grinned. He drew a deep breath and willfully shook off whatever spell had gripped him. It felt dangerously like attachment, deep connection, or even . . .

No, no, hell no. Falling in love with her? That would be the worst thing he could do. Borderline devastation. He was leaving in a few weeks, and that would be it for them. He knew that in his head. But in his heart . . .

Shit. Get it together, man. Focus! Dinner. Sex. Temporary companionship. That's all she wants—that's what you agreed to. Stop swooning. Get your head back in the game.

He cleared his throat, let his eyes linger on her gorgeous face for another few seconds, then took his sunglasses back. "You just tell me where to go." He threw the car back into drive and got back on the road.

Chapter Nineteen

Amanda was stirred from her sleep by Nick's low voice murmuring . . . in Spanish. She rolled over and opened her eyes. It was dark in the room, thanks to the blackout curtains, but the thin sliver of light that glowed where the curtains met offered a hint of the bright day outside. Nick sat on the edge of the bed, his muscled back to her, one hand holding his cell phone to his ear.

She shifted beneath the covers, burrowing further into the pillows. Unwilling to be totally awake yet, she watched him through heavy-lidded eyes. The man was intoxicating. He'd clearly taken great pleasure in seducing her when they'd gotten back to his room the night before. He couldn't keep his hands off her any more than she could him. They'd gone at it like wildfire, then lay in bed talking for a while, never able to stop dropping kisses or caressing each other. The second round of lovemaking had been slow and leisurely, a languorous exploration. . . .

She closed her eyes as she recalled how last night had felt, both the rush of the physical and the depth of the emotional. It hadn't felt like a hookup between friends, or whatever they were at this point. It had felt like a reunion of lovers.

She was crazy about him. In deep. She knew it. She just hoped he didn't know it.

When Nick ended the call, his head dropped and he sighed.

She watched him. He reached up and rubbed the back of his neck, trying to ease tension, or maybe it was just a fidgety sign of helplessness. Whatever that call had been about, it had upset him a little—that was clear. She sat up and draped herself over his back, pressing her naked breasts against him as she ran her hands along his smooth skin. Her arms wrapped around his broad shoulders as she kissed the side of his neck. He felt warm and solid, so good she wanted to purr. "You okay?"

"Yeah." His hands lifted to cover hers and hold them. "Sorry I woke you."

"Don't worry about it. What happened? You seem tense."

He sighed again, lifted her hands to his mouth to kiss them. "That was the mother of the victim of one of the cases I've been working on. She was a wreck."

"So she calls you this early on a Sunday morning?"

"It happens." He shrugged, but she could feel the coiled tension in his muscles.

She just held him for a minute, sensing he needed some comfort. "You're never fully off the clock with this gig, are you?"

"Sometimes it feels that way," he murmured. "Comes with the territory."

She knew how that felt. Having a job where you took the work home with you, where it never really left your head . . . she understood. She smoothed her hands over his skin, caressing the firm muscles in his shoulders, his arms, his back. He made a sound of contentment as she did.

"Come back to bed," she said softly. She kissed his neck, nipped at his earlobe. "I'll take your mind off it."

He turned to grin at her, eyes warm. "That sounds promising. . . ."

They cocooned under the blankets. In the darkened room,

they held each other and kissed, long, slow, deep kisses that took them out of the moment and into a pleasantly hazy dream state . . . until she pulled away and made her way down his neck and throat, then his chest, her hands everywhere, raining kisses on every inch of him.

"Where you goin'?" His voice was a lazy rumble as she traveled lower, trailing her lips and tongue along the ridged muscles of his abs. She licked and lightly bit down on his hip bone, and he sucked in a breath.

Lifting her head, she gave him a wicked, wanton smile, then continued moving south. A new rush surged through him, a fresh burst of desire heating his blood. Anticipation made his whole body pulsate and harden. By the time he felt her hair brush his belly and her warm breath on his cock, it was standing up for her, begging for her attention.

She ran her tongue around the head, circling it, flicking at it. He groaned low in his throat and sifted his fingers through her silky hair.

Stretching out, she positioned herself between his legs, running her fingertips up and down his thighs while her breath feathered over him. Taking her sweet time, she explored his lower body with her hands, her lips, her tongue and teeth, a full-out assault on his senses.

His mind clouded with lust and need, he watched her as she took him over. Watched as she grasped the base of his cock, stroking slowly as her tongue ran up and down the shaft. Watched as her tongue darted out to lap up the shiny drop that pearled at the tip before those gorgeous pink lips parted. His hand cradled the back of her head, gentle yet urgent, a silent plea. Finally, when he thought he couldn't take another second, she took him fully into her warm, wet mouth. His eyes slipped closed, his head fell back, and a low, guttural groan rumbled from deep in his chest as he willingly let her take control of him.

She worked him slowly at first, setting a lazy pace until the friction made his rocking hips thrust, straining upward.

They were in sync now; she felt when his lust took on that urgent edge, when his thrusts became more insistent and his hands twisted in her hair . . . and she kept going, in command, owning him. Christ, how she owned him right then. His hands moved over her neck, her shoulders, back to her hair. . . . His hips rocked desperately, and his breath came in short, hard pants. . . . It was so good, too damn good.

"Amanda," he gasped out when he was getting close. "Baby, you should stop or—"

Making a short noise that clearly meant "nope," she went faster. Unfazed, she hummed as she sucked him, the vibrations against his skin making him growl like an animal. Her mouth and hands worked in tandem, her warmth and wetness and suction and caresses leaving him mindless. His breath caught and again his head fell back onto the pillows as he thrust faster, harder, as the pleasure grew and the sweet tension built.

She was a damn seductress who obviously enjoyed what she was doing, and he was one lucky bastard. His mind went blank as the incredible sensations washed over him. His breathing turned harsh, raw need battering him . . . until he groaned hard, unable to hold back anymore. "Amanda," he panted, a last warning. "God, baby, I'm gonna come. . . ."

Not stopping her fierce pace, her hand moved down to cup his balls and squeeze. His orgasm hit hard, leaving him grunting and panting as the climax sent him flying over the edge. One hand fisted in her hair while the other clutched her shoulder. She took it all, only releasing him when he was done, licking and kissing him as he gasped for breath.

"Jesus fucking Christ, woman," he managed in a gravelly voice.

She gave him a lazy, sexy smile as she moved back up his body. He grasped her head in his hands and kissed her, long and hard.

"I love doing that," she confessed. "And I love making

you lose yourself to me, taking you over . . . hearing you and feeling you like that. That was *hot*."

He groaned softly and stared at her. "You're a goddess." He kissed her again, then pulled her close, wrapping his arms around her possessively. The adrenaline was ebbing; sleepiness set in fast, making his limbs as heavy as his eyes. His whole body felt weighted, relaxed, at peace. "Please don't be mad, but I think I'm going to pass out now. You destroyed me."

"Good. Why would I be mad?"

"Leaving you hanging."

"Nope, this one was for you, remember?" She nestled into his side, dropping a kiss on his shoulder before resting her head there. "Besides, we have all day."

"Yes, we do." His hands swept slowly up and down her back. "When we wake up, I'll take care of you. Then we'll get something to eat." He gave her a quick kiss. "I promised to feed you. I didn't forget."

"See that you don't," she murmured. Her arm slid across his stomach to snake around and hold him, and her foot dipped between his. His arms banded around her. They were sweetly, comfortably entwined, a warm tangle of limbs. Her breath slowed, his tired eyes slid closed, and he knew they'd sleep for a good few hours before surfacing again. That was fine. Like she'd said, they had the whole day.

Surprisingly, she fell asleep before he did. He held her close and enjoyed it. She felt so right in his arms. For the first time in weeks, things felt okay. He knew it was temporary, and the week ahead would be harrowing. But he'd take it where he could get it right now, and right now, he felt good.

Nick had more than come through on his promises. Amanda honestly couldn't remember enjoying a day this delicious. They spent most of the day in bed, luxuriating in each other's bodies, talking about trivial things, laughing, whispering in a way that felt like . . . real intimacy. It made her bloom inside, made her want more, even though she knew she shouldn't. She was getting tired of reminding herself this was a fling, it was temporary, he just wanted things to be casual, when with every look, kiss, touch, and word, it seemed like those things were morphing into something else. Something real, if she let herself get swept away by it.

They ordered in brunch, and later dinner, eating at the table while wrapped in the hotel's plush robes, not wanting to get dressed. The whole day was like a dream. After showering together in the evening, they stretched out again in bed, just holding each other as the sky slowly darkened.

Amanda felt like she was glowing as she nestled into his embrace, rubbing up against his side like a cat, practically purring. Radiating with a softly humming energy that flowed through her limbs, shimmering with it, floaty . . . happy and sated, deep in her bones.

"I don't want to take you home," he murmured against her temple, kissing her forehead as his large hand swept slowly up and down her back. "I don't want this amazing day to be over. It's the best day I've had in a really long time."

Her heart melted. "Same here," she whispered. She trailed her fingertips up and down his muscled arm, across his broad chest. She didn't want to stop touching him, breathing him in, much less leave the room. After being together for twenty-four hours straight, she figured she should be tired of him by now, ready to go back to her own space. But no. She couldn't get enough of him.

He nudged her chin up so he could kiss her, taking her mouth in a long, sweet kiss. His dark eyes, filled with warmth, focused on her face as he said, "So . . . about this week. We have to talk about it."

She sighed. It was the only thing they hadn't talked about. They'd danced around it, an unspoken accord not to let reality crash in on their perfect fantasy day. Now she felt the crack in the façade, and the first drops of tension seeped into her.

"You're going to be fine," she said firmly.

"I know that. And so is Myles."

"Well, he's going to be watched around the clock. You aren't. And you're going to need help."

"Nah," he said dismissively. "I'll be fine, like you just said. Maybe sore for the first day or two, but I'm sure that—"

"Stubborn ass." She turned onto her side and leaned up on one elbow to hold his gaze, which she saw had quickly grown wary. He didn't want to talk about it either. "It could be more than that. It could be a *week* or two. You don't know. And I hate to tell you this, Miami Vice, but you don't have a say."

He shrugged.

"I won't be working at the mansion, you know. Not for a while. As long as Myles stays in the hospital—"

"I know all that—you told me."

"So let me help you." She rubbed his arm as she said, "I can come over every day, spend some time here, just check and make sure that you're—"

"No."

His fierce, low charge startled her. Suddenly the cracks into their cocoon expanded into a wide open breach, and the unforgiving bright light of reality splashed over her. As if she'd spent days in a dark, cozy room and then been thrust outside into the midday sunlight, squinting, wanting to shield her eyes until they adjusted to the brightness. Nick's one clipped word, a sharp reprimand, had had that effect on her.

Her hand stilled on his skin as a chill prickled over hers. "Why not?"

"Because I told you. I'll be fine."

"Yeah, well, I'm a nurse. I know what could happen."

He moved back an inch, but it might as well have been a mile. She felt him pulling away, body and mind. "I'm not your patient, and I'm not going to be."

She narrowed her eyes at him, studying him for a long beat. "You're too proud to let me help you? Is that it?"

He huffed out a breath and grumbled, "Charles already said he's hiring someone to check on me that first week. Against my wishes, but I caved. So someone will be here." He scrubbed a hand through his hair and added, "He needed to feel like he was doing something."

"Maybe I do too." The words flew out of her mouth before she'd even processed how true they were.

"That's sweet," Nick said, almost dismissive. "But I don't want you to."

Her heart skipped a beat. It was like the blood in her veins, the air in the room, slowed. She swallowed hard, not sure what she was feeling, but it was something unwelcome and uncomfortable. Something that made her skin chill and her throat thicken as a lump lodged there. And it must have shown on her face, because as she drew back, he frowned hard.

"Amanda . . ."

"You don't want my help. I heard you." Something had shifted inside her. The gauzy, luminescent shimmer she'd bathed in all day was gone, leaving her chilled and vulnerable. She got out of bed.

He sighed, almost a groan. "Come back here. Don't just take off."

"I have to get dressed." She went to the small suitcase she'd brought. Suddenly, she didn't want to be naked in front of him. She felt naked on the inside at the moment, and being naked on the outside too was unbearable. "It's time for me to go home. We both know that."

He threw the covers back, got to her in three long strides, and gently gripped her shoulders. He bent a little to make sure they had eye contact. "You're mad at me now."

"I'm not mad," she said, even as her stomach churned. "Frustrated, a little annoyed, but I'm not mad." She shook him off. She didn't want to have this conversation at all, much less with both of them standing there naked.

"The whole vibe in here just changed," he said. "You're a lousy liar."

She shrugged, unwilling to look him in the eye, mad at him and madder at herself. Why was she feeling this way? She reached for her bra and panties, but he hooked her elbow to bring her back to him.

"Talk to me," he demanded.

"Nothing left to say. I offered help, you said no. Okay, fine. That conversation's closed." She wiggled her arm free.

He stared down at her as his arms crossed over his broad chest, making his biceps bulge a little. When he stood there naked, with that stormy look on his face . . . his presence was so commanding, it stole her breath for a second. Then her irritation kicked back in and she shook her head at him. At herself.

"Amanda." His voice was almost a growl. "I'm . . . I'm not good at asking for help. And I'm even worse at accepting it. Obviously."

She stood still for a long moment, trying to process a good response. But all she came up with was, "You didn't ask. I offered."

"And I appreciate that." His voice softened, but his stance stayed rigid. "I really do. But since Charles is hiring someone, let that faceless, nameless person do it. Not you. All right?"

She swallowed hard. She wasn't crazy about this side of him; she had to admit it. His male ego was a little more fragile than she'd thought. His stubborn pride was fiercer than she'd realized. He didn't want to seem weak, vulnerable or needing, in front of her, was that it? It made her want to shake him, or try to debate further. . . .

But hey, he wasn't her boyfriend, or even her lover, not really. He wasn't her anything, and she wasn't his. They'd shared some nice times together, especially today, but clearly it was more special to her than to him. She'd thought they'd connected on a deeper level, had moments of intimacy so true and real that they . . . A rush rose up in her throat, clogging it. Apparently not. Nope. It was all good when they were having hot, crazy-good sex, or talking about things that didn't really matter, or just hanging out. Bend her over the mattress and have his way with her, sure, no problem. Talk about TV shows, okay. But when she tried to offer help, something of substance, something real she could give him? He wasn't interested. It wasn't even up for discussion. Just: *"No."*

She was hurt. And that made her madder than anything else. Mad at herself.

She flicked him a nod, then reached for her panties and pulled them on. Her heart rate jittery, she got into her leggings.

He watched her dress in unsettled silence. As she pulled on a mint-green T-shirt, he sighed, then turned away to go to the dresser and grab his own clothes.

She double-checked that she had everything she'd brought with her. It was all there except for one thing. As he got into his jeans, she went to the bathroom to retrieve her toothbrush, came back and dropped it into her suitcase, and zipped it up. *Rejected*, she thought with a start. I feel rejected, that's why I'm being like this. Recognizing it didn't make it any better. It was a sticky, uncomfortable feeling, and she hated it.

"What I was originally going to say . . ." He pulled a black T-shirt over his head, yanked it down. ". . . is I'd like you to come visit me after the first few days. When I'm more myself again. You will, right?"

"Sure," she said.

"Yeah?" He peered at her as he sat on the edge of the bed to pull on a pair of socks. "You don't look or sound like you want to."

"Stop it. Of course I'll come by," she said. "You'll text

me when you're up to visitors. Feeling a little more like yourself." *Maybe by then, I'll feel more like myself too.*

He arched a brow at how she'd thrown his words back at him. "Not mad, huh?"

"Nick . . ." She ran her fingers through her hair, brushing it back from her face. "Last night and today were wonderful. A perfect little break from reality. A fantasy, right? Let's not ruin it with arguments at the end. Your reality isn't mine. Your recovery isn't any of my business. Clearly I overstepped."

He stared at her for a few seconds, eyes narrowed as he studied her. "What the hell does that mean?"

"It means I should've kept it light," she said, ignoring the way her heart bounced around in her chest. "We're bed buddies. That's all. Got it."

"*What?*" His eyes flashed; he looked confused and frustrated, similar to how she felt. He stared her down for a few long beats before swearing under his breath. "You're blowing this way out of proportion. I shouldn't have been so curt when I said no, and I'm sorry if I seemed ungrateful."

"Oh, God." She could feel the flush from her chest up into her face. "Stop. Don't patronize me."

"I'm not!" He crossed the room, took her into his arms, and said, "I don't want to argue either. I don't know how we got here. Five minutes ago, you were curled up into me, and now—"

"Now it's time for me to go home." She steeled her insides against him, against how she felt, against the unwanted feelings zinging around in her brain and the sting of misery she was trying to ignore.

He threaded his hands through her hair, coffee-colored eyes still scrutinizing her features. "Can we play nurse another time? After I'm better?"

That made her bristle from the inside out. Not only didn't he want her help, he didn't take her seriously. Anger rose quick and hot. "I don't play at my job, thank you very much."

She shoved out of his embrace with both hands against his chest.

"Whoa, wait. I was just joking, Amanda."

"It wasn't funny. Or I guess I'm not in a joking mood anymore," she said, knowing how cold her voice sounded and not caring.

"Hey." He reached for her, but she stepped back. He blinked and said in a low, deliberate voice, "I was kidding. I'd never want to offend you, Amanda. Not about your job. You're good at what you do, and I respect you. I think you're wonderful. Don't you know that?"

She bit down on her bottom lip, annoyed at herself that she'd gotten carried away. Why was she overreacting like this? A fresh lance of withering fury pierced her. This was on her. He'd never made promises. This weekend was just about fun and sex—that was it. *She* was the one who had unwanted, sticky feelings. *She* was the one who was . . .

Realization hit and broke over her like a tidal wave with merciless brute force. Oh, God, she was in love with him. That's why she was going overboard with this. Her limbs felt heavy, wavy, and her knees went weak. She gripped the nearby armchair to stay upright.

Her eyes slipped closed. She had to get a grip. What the hell . . . she was in love with him? How *stupid*. And that was unacceptable, because she wasn't stupid. She was smarter than that, stronger than that. She wasn't in love with him. This was a serious infatuation—that was all. They were caught up in an emotional storm, both on edge because of Myles and the surgery and his sudden new family and everything that went along with all of that that had thrown them both off-kilter.

She'd let herself get caught up in the fantasy. He was temporary, passing through her life. He'd told her that from their first date. After the surgery, he'd go back to Miami and that'd be it. He'd forget all about her. And she'd miss him, and pine for him, and . . . goddamn it, she was a hot mess all of a sudden.

"Hey." He held her chin with gentle fingertips, willing her to open her eyes and look into his. "You're trembling. What's going on?"

She stared up at him. Her tongue felt thick in her mouth, her throat dry. She was sure her feelings were so obvious, plastered all over her, but he was scouring her face like he couldn't figure her out. That was good.

Frustrated with herself, feeling scattered, vulnerable, thrown, she said in a harder tone than she'd intended, "I'm just tired. It hit me all of a sudden. I'm really tired now, and I have work tomorrow. Could you please take me home?"

On the drive from his hotel to her apartment complex, Nick felt his blood buzz and his limbs hum with excess energy. His gut was tight, nerves jangling. Amanda had pulled away from him, right in front of his eyes. The whole day had been incredible—one of the best of his life, honestly. He'd been entertaining thoughts of more days like this, more time with her. Maybe trying to tell her his feelings had deepened.

But at the end, the whole vibe had changed. Because he'd snapped at her. He kept replaying the look in her eyes, the way her soft skin had gone all goose bumpy under his hands . . . and then that stupid crack about playing nurse, which she'd taken as an insult. He'd upset her. Of course he hadn't meant to, but he had.

He didn't know what to do. He'd fallen for her so hard. All day, he'd so gladly drowned in her softness, her sensuality, her playfulness, her wit and charm and smarts and beauty. When he held her close, when he moved inside her and looked deep into her eyes and she gazed back . . . it felt dangerously close to something deep and real.

And a few harsh words had sent her scurrying.

He'd insulted her skills by turning down her offer to care for him, and then again with the dumb joke. She took pride in what she did, and thought he'd belittled it somehow— which belittled *her*. He got that; hadn't he been all bent out of shape when he'd perceived her "no dating cops" rule as a subtle insult against his profession and his life's work, no matter how unintended her slight? And he'd just turned around and done it to her.

He shot her a glance as she gazed out the window. She was sitting next to him, but may as well have been a thousand miles away.

"You're wound up so tight I'm afraid to touch you," he blurted out.

That made her head turn toward him.

"You're obviously hurt or mad," he said. "I offended you. I didn't mean to, and I'm sorry. You have to know that."

"I do know that," she said. "I'm fine, Nick. I'm just tired."

"No, that's bullshit," he spat. "You think I don't know you well enough by now to know when you're pissed off? Or I can't feel the difference between when you want to be next to me and when you don't? It's one of the things I like the most about you: you have no filter. You don't hide what you think or how you feel. So when you do, that's . . . it's bad." He took the turn around the corner a little too fast, making them both shift in their seats.

Unable to hold back, he pulled over to the curb and threw the gearshift into park. He saw her eyes widen as he did, as he turned to her and said fiercely, "This was the most incredible day I've had in years, and I don't want it to end on a low note. I don't want you to get out of this car and be upset with me. I . . ." He gripped her hand.

She just blinked at him, those beautiful sky-blue eyes filled with emotions he couldn't figure out.

He leaned in, gripping the back of her head with a sweep of his free hand, and sealed his mouth to hers. He kissed her hot and hard, a little urgent, trying to get back the woman who'd been with him all day long. She kissed him back, her lips parting with a whimper from deep in her throat. Fueled by the sound, his tongue swept inside her mouth, possessive, a claim. He affected her, and he wouldn't let her forget it.

His fingers threaded through her hair, holding her head as he kissed her, pulling her in. When he released her, he looked deep into her eyes and whispered, "I'm crazy about you, Amanda. Whatever happens on Wednesday, you need to know that."

"What? Nick, you're going to be fine," she said.

"Are you hearing me?" he demanded. He wanted something in return that she wasn't giving him. It made him want to grab her shoulders and shake her. *Tell me I mean something to you too. Tell me what I felt today is real, that it's not just me.*

"I hear you," she whispered. Her eyes dropped from his. "But you . . . we're just caught up right now. With the surgery coming, worrying about Myles . . . people get caught up in high emotions, swept away. We had a wonderful day, Nick, a fantasy day. But . . . maybe we just need to step back and breathe. We got swept away. It happens—you hear about it all the time. When people are in an intense situation, they kind of throw themselves into it, at each other, and . . ."

He stared at her, dumbfounded. Was she for real with this crap?

She fidgeted with the hem of her T-shirt. "Maybe the surgery's actually good timing, you know? Enforced space between us. You've got a lot on your plate."

He froze and released her, staring. Now who was the one being brushed off? Only her brush-off, unlike his, was intentional. "So I don't know how I feel, is that it?"

"I don't either," she whispered. "This is all . . . I think we're just getting carried away. Everything feels extreme because so much is at stake. But it's not . . ." Her voice trailed off and she looked away.

He stared at her for a few seconds; the sound of his blood rushing through his ears rose to a roar. With a disgusted grunt, he let her go, threw the car into drive, and pulled away from the curb with a screech of the tires.

She curled her arms around her middle and turned away as much as she could, staring out the window.

His heart hammered in his chest, anger searing through him as he focused on the road. What the fuck? He knew how he felt, dammit. Yes, things were crazy right now, but he knew how he felt. He sure as hell didn't like having his feelings brushed aside, being told what he was feeling. For fuck's sake . . .

When he pulled up to her building a few minutes later, he tried to draw a deep breath. "Amanda."

She looked at him. He stared back. The conflicted look on her face made the fiery words he'd planned to spew die on his tongue. He sighed and admitted, "I don't even know what to say right now."

"Me neither." She leaned in and dropped a quick kiss on his lips, held his face. "You're going to be fine. Pre-op and all that tomorrow and Tuesday, right?"

He nodded. *Tell me I mean something to you.*

"And I'll be with Myles. So . . . text me to check in when you can, I guess."

He stared at her gorgeous face. *Give me something to go on here, dammit.*

"When you feel up to visitors, let me know."

Don't throw my words back in my face. The force of his ire surprised him. *You're running away from me. I want you . . . need you . . . and you're running.*

"I'll be thinking of you," she whispered. "I'll be around. . . . Call if you need me."

Something flashed in those sky-blue eyes. She too was feeling more than she was letting on; he just knew it. Goddamn it. But she said nothing and kissed him again, long and lingering. He couldn't resist her, even when he wanted to shake her. His hands flew up of their own volition to cradle her head and hold her to him. They kissed for a few minutes, their urgent, needy mouths and caresses expressing what neither of them seemed to be able to say out loud.

"See you soon," she whispered. "You got this."

"Yup," he whispered back, the longing and pent-up frustration in his chest threatening to blow him apart.

She untangled herself from him, opened the door, and got out of the car. He watched as she pulled her suitcase from the trunk, as she turned to look at him one last time, then walked away.

He sat there quietly for a few minutes, unsure of what had happened. Everything had been so right, then gone sideways so fast . . . then that kiss at the end . . .

He scrubbed his hands over his face, rubbed his eyes. What the fuck was wrong with him? Falling in love with her on top of everything else—he didn't have enough going on? And how dumb could he get? She clearly didn't feel the same things that he did. The closeness, the connection, that click . . . all one-sided. She didn't feel the same if she could separate herself from that after a few harsh words, even after he'd apologized.

It stung like hell, but luckily, he didn't have much time to dwell on it beyond tonight. A little more than forty-eight hours from now, he'd be in an operating room, on a table. That's what he had to focus on now. Not Amanda. Not on this want and raw emotion that were rising in him so fast and hard he was almost choking on them.

He'd have plenty of time to dissect his feelings for her later, if he wanted to. And the truth was, he didn't really want to.

He put the car in drive and eased away from the curb.

Chapter Twenty

Nick slowly opened his eyes. His mouth was dry and his tongue was stuck to the roof of his mouth, making him grunt.

"You're awake," said an unfamiliar woman's voice. "How do you feel, Mr. Martell?"

He looked to his side. A nurse stood over him . . . the one who'd helped prep him for the surgery. The one who'd been there yesterday. He couldn't remember her name now. . . . He thought hard through the throbbing in his skull. Sadie? Sophie, that was it. A quick glance around showed him he was still in the hospital, in a room, in a bed. His head was pounding harder than it ever had in his life. "Head hurts," he managed. "And I'm thirsty." He barely recognized his own voice.

"Here, let me help you." Sophie grabbed a cord and raised the head of his bed just a little, enough to get him upright. Then she brought a plastic cup to him, even put the straw between his dry lips. "Here you go."

He drank down the water like a man who'd been in the desert for days. Jesus Christ, he'd never had a headache like this. Like his brain was an alien life form trying to shove out of his skull. He tried to sit up more, and a wave of sensation radiated from his lower left side and up his back, quick as lightning and equally powerful, stealing his breath. Nausea gripped him. The straw fell from his mouth as he hissed.

"Still sore," she noted. "That's to be expected."

"It's not . . ." He moved more carefully. "It's actually not as bad as it was yesterday. It is a new day, right?"

"Yup. Well, that's good." She looked into his eyes, felt around. "You look better than you did yesterday, I'll tell you that. Glad you got some sleep at last."

He took a quick account of his body and decided for the most part, he *did* feel better than he had yesterday. The surgery itself, he didn't remember at all. Who knew waking up from the anesthesia would be harder than that? It was a cruel twist.

His lower back, by his hip, was still sore as hell, like someone had kicked him hard. But it wasn't brutal. The pounding headache and nausea from the anesthesia had been far worse. He'd spent the night in the hospital. Even shot off a text to his mom at some point to let her know that he was all right. Then he'd floated in and out of it all evening . . . vomited two or three times. . . . He remembered Pierce, Dane, Tess, and Charles all coming by to check on him, but Nick had been kind of out of it. . . . He'd tried to be still and slept a lot.

Now, a glance toward the window showed sunshine, and though his headache remained, it wasn't as bad as it'd been the day before. "I'm better," he said, his voice rough. Then his head throbbed again, making his eyes close. They'd warned he might have a headache, but this was brutal. He wouldn't let on, though. If he did, they wouldn't spring him, and all he wanted was to hole up in his hotel room and be miserable in peace, without being poked and prodded.

"I'm glad to hear it. But if you want to be released today," Sophie warned, "you need to be honest about how you feel. None of the macho stuff you tried to pull yesterday. Okay?"

He sighed. "Okay."

"I'm just going to check you over now," she said. "Now that you're up, I'll let the doctor know so he can check on you too. When he gives the all-clear, you can be released, but that won't be for a few hours."

"Got it." He opened his eyes and gave her a weak smile. "Thank you."

"You're welcome. You did great, Mr. Martell. All you have to do right now is rest."

"Okay," he whispered. He was worse off than he'd thought it would be. Damn everyone who'd been right about that. It pissed him off. "Myles . . . is he okay?"

"He's in recovery," she said.

"I need more than that. I need to know how he is. . . ." Nick struggled to sit up but he moved too fast, making both his head and the back of his left hip throb at the same time. He groaned low and hard, holding still.

Six hours later, Nick was released from the hospital. Charles had planned everything ahead with the tactical efficiency of a wartime general. Pierce was the one to help Nick from the hospital room to the wheelchair—damn hospital policy—to the car. Pierce drove him to the hotel while Nick closed his eyes and tried to keep his throbbing brain inside his skull. He asked Pierce a few questions. So far, Myles was holding his own, and that was about all there was to say. The family was holding vigil at the hospital; Charles and Lisette had barely left Myles's side, while the others had all taken turns checking in.

Nick felt heavy-limbed, sluggish, and woozy. He was more grateful than he wanted to admit when Pierce practically lifted him out of the car and slung an arm around him to keep him upright.

"I'm the strongest of the family," he said to Nick as they slowly walked to the elevator. "Or, I was before Logan came in, but that walking mountain is out of town on business. So I was picked for this. Someone had to help drag you along."

"I don't need a babysitter," Nick growled good-naturedly.

"Shut up," Pierce said. "You do too." They crossed the lobby at a slow, careful pace. "Besides, I'm only babysitting you for the first shift. Julia's coming tomorrow."

Nick lifted a brow at that. He hadn't spent any time with Dane's supposedly fiery wife; he didn't know her at all. "Why her?"

"She volunteered." Pierce didn't let go of Nick as he pressed the button for the elevator. "She takes no crap, so she's a perfect pick. You're a little grouchy."

Nick grunted. His head hurt too much to argue, and his back was sore. They stepped into the elevator and he leaned against the wall.

"In all seriousness," Pierce said, his voice more somber than usual, "you did a great thing. We're all so damn grateful, Nick. You know that, right?"

"I do." He shifted so his bad hip wasn't against the wall. "It was my honor, and I just hope to God that it works. I care about that kid. You know that, right?"

"We all do." Pierce looked him over. "I'm sorry you're uncomfortable."

"Yesterday was worse. That was a nine; this is like a six. I'm okay."

"You're so full of shit. You look like hell and you're in pain, tough guy."

Nick laughed hoarsely. "My headache's the worst of it, to be honest. Worse than my back and hip. That just feels like I got bruised, you know? But it feels like my brain is playing conga drums and trying to escape my head at the same time, and it's messing me up."

"Doctor said that was normal, unfortunately."

"Yeah, I know. Apparently, anesthesia and I don't get along."

The doors slid open and Pierce immediately went to Nick, helping him down the hall. He got him to his room, through the suite, and into the bedroom. As Nick collapsed gingerly onto the bed, Pierce glanced at his watch. "This is good. The nurse Charles hired for you should be here soon."

"Wonderful," Nick grunted.

Pierce chuckled. "I have a feeling you're a terrible patient."

"I don't like being hovered over," Nick said.

"I get that. But when you need help, you should admit it. And you do right now. So take it."

Nick grunted again.

"I'm going to run back downstairs," Pierce said as he watched Nick kick off his shoes, "to get your bag from the car. Then I'll come back and hang with you 'til the nurse comes."

Nick watched him leave, then slid out of his clothes down to his briefs. He left them in a pile on the floor and climbed into bed. Fuck, his head . . . all he wanted was to lie still.

When Pierce got back, he asked if Nick needed anything. "Bottle of water or Gatorade on the nightstand," Nick said quietly. "And if you could pull those blackout curtains, I'll be your best friend for life. That's it."

Pierce did as he'd been asked before leaving Nick to go sit in the front room of the suite. Nick was just starting to fall asleep when he heard voices from out there. Pierce was talking to a woman. Probably the nurse. Nick didn't care; he just wanted to be left alone. He lay motionless, his eyes closed, trying not to worry about Myles or think about Amanda or his mom or anything that would make his brain do actual work.

He heard the door open, then close. A few moments later, a cool hand gently touched his forehead, then his ears. The woman's soft hand felt like heaven.

"He's going to be okay, right?" Pierce's voice, a little concerned, on his right.

"Of course he will," said the voice on his left. "No temperature, so that's good."

What the fuck? He knew that voice. With a jolt, his eyes snapped open. Amanda was there, standing over him, a little crease between her brows as those sky-blue eyes studied him.

"Hi," she said.

"You're my nurse?" Nick growled.

"Charles asked me," she said.

"She's not working with Myles right now," Pierce said, "so it makes sense."

"I don't want you to—" Nick started to say, then stopped himself. A few more words and he'd out them to Pierce. Damn it all to hell.

She pressed a fingertip to his pulse, which he felt hammering away. "Shhhh."

Nick's insides bubbled with anger that didn't make sense, and he knew it.

"Nick, look," Pierce said, blissfully clueless, "Amanda is a great nurse. She's been amazing with Myles. I know you're cranky, but just let her do her job, okay?"

Nick swallowed down everything and let his eyes slide closed. "You win for now. Headache's real bad—I don't have it in me to fight."

"Should we be worried about that headache?" Pierce asked Amanda.

"The headache's a normal side effect of the anesthesia," Amanda said, sounding cool and assured. "Also one of the drugs they used during surgery. I'm watching him—don't worry. Charles wants me here until eleven tonight, and I will be. So you can go if you want."

Pierce touched Nick's arm lightly. "You're in good hands, so I'm going to take off. You just want to sleep anyway, I'm sure."

Nick opened his eyes and nodded. "Yeah. But do me a favor?"

"Anything."

"Keep me posted on Myles?"

"You got it, no problem. I'll text you or call you." Pierce gave Nick's arm a little squeeze. "Feel better, man. Julia will come by tomorrow. She's the morning shift, Amanda's the afternoon and evening."

Nick just sighed.

"Don't abuse your nurse," Pierce mock warned. "I like this nurse a lot, so give her a break, all right?"

Nick harrumphed but said, "Thanks for getting me back here. For everything today. Appreciate it, man."

"Glad I could help. Rest up. Talk to you soon." Pierce said his good-bye to Amanda, then left.

As soon as Nick heard the door close, he looked at Amanda. "I thought I told you—"

"You knew Charles was hiring a nurse. Well, he asked me to do this," she said evenly. "As a personal favor to him. I won't be needed at the mansion for a few weeks, maybe more. I've been *hired*; he's paying me. You don't like it, take it up with him. I answer to him, not to you."

Nick wanted to growl, he was so mad. "You knew I didn't want you here."

She stilled, and he saw her eyes flare. Fuck, that was mean. He was being downright mean. That wasn't fair to her.

But before he could say another word, she snapped, "Sorry. You're stuck with me for tonight." She moved to the nightstand and opened the bottle of water.

As she poured some into a plastic cup, he watched her. Did she have to look so damn pretty? Half of him hated that she was there. The other half was so glad to see her, it bordered on ridiculous. They'd exchanged texts before he'd gone into the hospital on Wednesday morning, but he hadn't seen her since Sunday night. Seeing her now made him acutely aware that he'd missed her. Her silky hair was pulled back in a ponytail, her baby blue T-shirt brought out her eyes, and her gray checked leggings showcased her legs, making him recall how fantastic they'd felt locked around his hips.

He'd missed her. Her presence was a balm even when he was furious.

"You're not in scrubs," he managed, every word making his head thump. "Thought you're on duty."

"I am, but I figured I could dress casual for this one. You gonna report me?"

"Hell no."

She brought the cup over. "Drink some," she commanded as she stood over him.

"Amanda," he said, leaning up slowly on his elbows. "I'm sorry for being rude."

She just pushed the cup at him.

He took a few sips, then fell back onto the pillows. "Listen. I know you're a good nurse. I just . . . dammit, Amanda, I didn't want you to do this. Anyone but you."

She stiffened as she gazed down at him. "Well, then you're shit outta luck, aren't you." A quick twist of a grin that didn't reach her eyes, sharp and hollow, made him wince.

He was messing this up royally. If only his brain would stop trying to pound its way out of his skull . . . He reached out and grasped her hand, holding tight. "I just . . . ah, fuck!" He closed his eyes for a second against the fresh wave of pain in his head that brought some nausea along for the ride. He swallowed hard. "Nauseous," he muttered.

"I'll get the bowl so you don't have to get up." She pulled her hand free and left.

For about an hour, he lay as still as possible, trying not to vomit. She went to sit in the front room, leaving him in peace so he didn't have to get madder at the idea of possibly puking in front of her, which he appreciated. He was miserable; that was for damn sure. But that didn't give him the right to be such an asshole to her, and he stewed over it as he lay in the dark room. He tried to not think at all, just breathe.

After a while, the door opened, bringing cracks of light into his dim cave. Amanda approached the bed. "Bowl's empty. That's good." She laid her hand against his forehead.

"You're a drop warm. I'm sorry, Nick, but I'm staying right here to keep an eye on you whether you like it or not. You spike a fever, that's a different set of problems."

"All right," he murmured.

"How do you feel?"

"Like total shit."

She only nodded as her eyes scoured his face.

"Go ahead," he said.

Her brows furrowed. "Go ahead what?"

"Say 'I told you so'," he said. "You must be dying to. You warned me I'd need help after the surgery. I brushed you off. All of you."

"Your discomfort doesn't bring me pleasure," she said, a hard edge to her voice.

"Not even now, when I've been such a dick since you got here?"

"Not even now."

"Amanda . . ." He swallowed his pride and said gruffly, "I didn't want you to see me this way. I didn't want *anyone* to see me this way, but especially *you*. I didn't want you to see me all weak and needy. Gross, pukey, and laid out. Didn't want to . . . diminish myself in your eyes. Can you understand that?"

She stared at him and murmured, "I do now. I'm sorry you feel that way."

"I'm sorry I'm a lousy patient and will probably be insufferable the next day or two," he said. "Apparently pain, feeling powerless, and being hovered over make me a little mean." He sighed as his head pounded away. "I didn't want to look weak to you. My ego and pride can't stand it. There, I said it." He licked his dry lips as he met her eyes. "I also didn't want to maybe be a dick to you and say or do something I couldn't take back. You mean too much to me. Okay?"

She sat on the edge of the bed, next to him, her hip barely

touching his good side. "You could've just told me all that the other day. Why didn't you?"

"You didn't exactly give me a chance to."

She pressed her lips together into a hard line. "Maybe not."

"I also didn't say so because I'm not proud of it, Amanda. Because I'm too proud, I guess."

"I am too. I felt slighted."

"I know. And I'm really sorry for that. Can you forgive me?"

She gazed down at him for a long moment, then murmured, "Forgiven. But you need to work on your communication skills."

"We both do. You shut me out and wouldn't admit to it."

"I was hurt," she admitted in a whisper. "When I'm hurt, I . . . go inside myself. Like a turtle. I turtle up."

"I'll make sure to remember that in the future." He reached for her hand, and she let him take it as their eyes met and held. "I really am sorry. I just . . ." His head pulsated, his hip throbbed, and his eyes squeezed shut as he drew a deep breath.

"Shhh." She held his hand in both of hers and caressed it gently. It was so damn soothing; he bathed in her small but tender touch. "I know you're really hurting right now, but it'll be better tomorrow, and then even better the next day. Promise."

"Okay," he ground out. "This sucks. Can't lie."

"I know." She kept caressing his hand. He held tight. She felt like a lifeline. It occurred to him she'd felt like one since he'd met her. Emotionally, physically. As a friend, as a sexy bed partner. In a short time, she'd come to mean a lot to him, dragging him out of emotional holes . . . a true lifeline. They sat in the dark, holding hands in comfortable silence, and damned if it didn't make him feel a little better. Soothed.

Finally he said, "My head hurts like fucking hell, Amanda.

It really does. The hip's not as bad, but it's sore as hell too and . . . I'm not good company. I'm sorry."

"Don't be sorry. Shhh." She kept stroking the top of his hand, his fingers. He focused on her touch, trying to concentrate on that instead of how awful he felt. Then she added, "I'm not expecting you to be good company. It'd be nice if you're not a dick, but if you are, I can take it. It's part of my job, and I'm good at my job, Nick."

"I know you are. I do, baby."

"All right. So just let me take care of you, okay?"

"Okay." His eyes slid closed. "Thank you." He felt her lean in, felt her lips press ever so lightly against his cheek. His other hand lifted to stroke the back of her neck and hold her there. They stayed that way for a minute, a kind of half hug. His fingers twisted into her ponytail as he breathed her in. "You smell good," he whispered.

"Flirting with your nurse?" she joked. "Jeez, you're so the type."

He laughed, but it made his head hurt and it turned into a groan as he finally fell asleep.

Chapter Twenty-One

Charles had only asked Amanda to stay until eleven o'clock, but no way was she leaving. Nick had a temperature. At nine o'clock, it'd only been 100.7; by eleven, it'd gone up to 101.6. She didn't want him there alone, especially if his fever got any higher.

She sat by his side, too concerned to read the book she'd brought. She just sat and watched over him. He lay there quietly. He didn't want to talk, and that was fine. But after a while, he reached out to hold her hand. He was still gruff, not an easy patient, but he clearly needed comfort, wanted it from her, and she gladly gave it. Around midnight, exhausted, Amanda decided to sleep right next to him. The king-sized bed had more than enough room for her to do so without touching him; she wouldn't bump his bandaged hip. Still, she slept lightly, part of her consciousness aware of him even then.

Most of the night, he tossed around, restless and slightly feverish, drifting in and out of sleep. Even half-asleep, she kept touching his forehead, his ears, checking on him. Close to dawn, when his body bucked hard beside her, her eyes opened instantly. Fat drops of sweat rolled from his hairline down his forehead and the sides of his face. His breathing was heavy, as if he'd snapped out of a trance.

"What the hell?" His voice was rough in the dark.

"I'm right here, Nick." She gripped his hand with one of hers, felt his face with the other. He was pouring sweat, but his skin was cooler. Whatever fever had set in had broken as quickly as it'd arrived. "You're okay. Let me get you a drink."

He released her hand and she set into action. She checked his temperature. Back down to 98.9—that was good. She brought him a cup of Gatorade and more acetaminophen, then went to the bathroom to drench two washcloths in cool water and return to him. He was frowning, lying there in his damp sheets, hair mussed, a few days' scruff covering his jaw. . . . He was a total mess, but he still appealed to her. He'd shoved the covers down to his waistline, and she couldn't help letting her eyes travel over his sculpted body . . . the chiseled muscles in his shoulders, chest, arms, abs. He was a pain-in-the-ass patient, but he was one unbearably sexy, gorgeous man who rocked her socks, no denying it.

"This might get your pillows and bed a little wetter," she said, "but they're already drenched from you anyway." She folded one of the wet cloths and draped it over his forehead; he exhaled a gentle sound of relief, almost childlike, making her heart twinge. "I'll call housekeeping in a few and ask them to change the sheets, but this first." She sat beside him and swept the other cool, wet cloth over his body, starting at the top of his chest. She moved it over his broad pecs, down his torso and up again. "Feel good?"

"Yes," he said on a sigh. "Amazing, actually."

"Don't think you're up to a shower right now," she said, "so I thought this would help."

"It does." His dark eyes focused on her face. She liked seeing they were clear, not hazy with fever as they'd been last night. "I love when you touch me," he said. "Keep doing it. Whatever you want."

She held back a grin. That was the Nick she knew. "I'm

only touching you as a nurse right now. I'm not trying to turn you on."

"Then it's wrong to tell you I'm getting hard?" He shifted a bit. "Because I am."

She couldn't help but laugh. "You're shameless."

"When it comes to you? A little." The sides of his full mouth curved up. "Sorry. What can I say, your hands are on me. That's all it takes. You turn me on like crazy."

"You're definitely feeling better," she noted, pushing down the delight inside. She ran the damp cloth along his rock-solid arms, across the broad expanse of his chest, down over his carved abs, then back up his chest to the sides of his neck, secretly enjoying herself. He clearly enjoyed it too; his eyes drifted closed under her gentle ministrations. "There you go," she said when she finished, folding up the cloth.

"How about a little lower?" he asked, shooting her a mischievous look. "You missed a few important spots."

She snorted. "You're passing shameless now, going straight for incorrigible."

"Amanda . . ." He took the washcloth off his forehead and swiped it over his face before reaching for her hand. Looking at her earnestly, almost sheepishly, he said, "Thank you. This was a rotten fucking night, but thank you for being here. I know Charles paid you to be here, but I'm grateful. And I'm glad it was you. I mean—"

"Stop. You're welcome. I'm glad I was here for you. And I'm relieved that fever broke. You had me worried." *Because I love you, you goddamn pain in the ass.* "I'm just glad you're better."

He lifted her hand to his mouth and kissed the back of it.

When Nick's eyes opened again, a woman with fiery red hair was sitting in the armchair in his bedroom. Her head was down as she stared at her cell phone. He cleared his throat and her head snapped up. "Hey," she said with a grin, "you're up. How do you feel?"

"Been worse." His throat felt dry, and his voice came out gravelly. "Julia, right?"

"Yes. I know—we only met once and very briefly." She smiled and rose from the chair, heading for his nightstand. "Want a drink?"

"Please." Nick couldn't help but look her over; her hour-glass figure was insane, even in just a simple black top and olive pants. A beautiful face, with creamy skin, pouty lips, and big hazel eyes that shone with intelligence. Nick knew from his research that Dane's wife was close to fifty, but hell, she looked maybe thirty-five. Her presence filled the room; the woman emanated waves of sex appeal and self-confidence. Damn, she was stunning. He sent silent kudos to his brother.

But even still, his thoughts went back to another woman, the one whose sexy ways appealed to him the most. Not even this sensuous woman could make him forget the only woman he wanted by his side. "Where's Amanda?"

"Went home to shower and sleep. I made her promise me she would. She looked exhausted." Julia poured a cup of Gatorade and gave it to him. "She'll be back at five. She said you had a rough night. I'm supposed to watch for if the fever returns."

"Yeah, it was a long night. It sucked." He yawned and carefully stretched out his limbs. The answering throb in his hip wasn't as searing as it'd been the day before, but it was still nasty. "Last thing I remember is her going to answer the knock on the door."

"That was me. When we came in here, you were out cold again."

He recalled Amanda getting him to the couch around 6 AM while housekeeping changed the sheets on the bed . . . her bringing a dry, clean T-shirt and underwear, helping him back into bed, and him pulling her down with him. He'd wrapped his arm around her and held her close against his good side, feeling more secure with her there. Comforted.

"What time is it?"

"Noon. You hungry?"

His stomach growled as if on cue. "Yeah, actually, I am."

"That's a good sign, right?" She went out to the front room, then came back with a shopping bag. "I brought heros. Dane thought a big, strapping guy like you would go for a sub. But I had no idea what you liked, so I brought four kinds. Turkey club, ham and cheese, meatball, and chicken cutlet. Take whatever you like." She peered at him, those golden eyes studying him. "Can you sit up?"

She helped him maneuver into a sitting position. It wasn't as bad as it'd been the day before, but his hip still throbbed. His headache was down to barely noticeable. He'd take it. "Do me a favor?"

"Sure, what?"

"Grab me a pair of shorts from the dresser? We'll eat at the table. I have to get up—I'm getting stiff from all this lying around."

It was painful, but he slowly made his way out to the front room without leaning on Julia. They ate lunch together and talked. While she told him a little about her standing singing gig at Dane's upscale Manhattan hotel and how she and Dane had met, Nick inhaled his food, choosing half of the ham and cheese, half of the meatball, and half of the chicken cutlet. Julia had brought a Cobb salad for herself.

He liked her, felt a spark of immediate affinity that he hadn't with his siblings. He figured it was because she was more like him. He remembered that from his info dig on the family: she was from a middle-class background, similar upbringing, similar lifestyle. Well, a similar lifestyle before she'd married a billionaire hotel mogul, anyway.

Nick was finishing up the chicken cutlet sub when she said, "My father was a cop, you know."

He swallowed his mouthful first before saying, "No, I didn't know. Was?" he added tentatively.

"Killed in the line of duty when I was ten," she said. "Robbery at a bodega."

Nick winced and said softly, "I'm very sorry to hear it. My deepest condolences."

"Thanks." She pushed her salad around with her fork. "It was a long time ago."

"Must have been rough growing up without him," he murmured.

"Yup. But I survived. I got my toughness from him." She gave a proud little grin. "So, if you're an investigator now, does that mean you're off the street?"

"Pretty much. Certainly not like I was."

"Good. Now that I'm going to know you, not having to worry as much will be nice." She took a bite of her salad. "Your mother must not sleep well, you being a cop."

"Well, my dad was a cop too. On the job twenty-five years before he retired. So unfortunately, I don't think she's *ever* slept well."

"I bet." Julia peered at him. "She did right by you, though."

"Oh, yeah?" He took his last bite, then wiped his hands on a napkin.

"Yeah. She obviously raised you right. And away from here." Julia sipped her water. "Can I tell you something? Strictly between us?"

Nick nodded, listening.

"Dane and your other siblings want you to be part of the family." She folded her manicured hands on the tabletop and leaned in. "They can be a forceful, strong-willed bunch. But they're not going to push you on anything, because they're scared it'll only push you away. They recognize you're pretty strong-willed yourself. So . . . just know they care, they'd like you to be part of the clan somehow, and they're trying."

Nick met her direct gaze. "Why are you telling me this?"

"Because I love my husband and I always want him to

be happy. You being in the family, in any way, would make him happy," she said. "And I could be wrong, but I feel like . . . we get each other. I can be straight with you. You and me, we weren't raised like them. We had normal lives." Julia smirked as she added, "Well, for the most part, anyway."

Nick smiled back.

"In spite of all the money, power, privilege, and their insane parents, those four are really good people with good hearts. They seek out goodness in others. They know what's really important in life: family, friends, honor, compassion. They're generous, loyal, and trustworthy. They have integrity, Nick." She leaned in and touched his forearm, her gaze level. "I have a feeling you're the same as them in all those aspects. So give them a chance. Get to know them. You'll not only like them, but you might even be glad to be part of this family one day."

"Never know," he admitted. "Anything's possible."

She nodded. "I'm probably overstepping. Something tells me you can handle it."

"I appreciate your candor," he said. "And this lunch. I needed it. Thank you."

"You ever have any questions about the clan, or want to talk? Call me. Okay?"

"I might take you up on that."

A week passed quickly. Myles was still in the hospital; his body hadn't rejected Nick's bone marrow, and he seemed to be holding steady. Charles texted updates every day, and Nick had even gotten to say hi to the kid via phone call. Nick was relieved beyond words. If this kept up, Myles would probably make it and, on the other side, be healthy again. If he stayed on this course, remission was a real possibility.

Lying in bed, Nick prayed every morning for Myles's full recovery.

Amanda came every day. By the fourth day, Nick was feeling better and going stir-crazy. The two of them ventured outside and sat on a bench in the courtyard of the hotel, soaking up sunshine and fresh air for half an hour before he got tired and went back up to bed. Every day after that, he moved a little more, pushed himself. He took walks around the block, working through the occasional stabs of discomfort in his hip.

The recovery time frustrated him, but the time with Amanda more than made up for that. They only had another week. After that, he'd be on his way back to Miami, and they'd go back to their separate lives.

With each day, he knew he wanted more of her, from her, with her. Hell, they couldn't even have sex because of his hip—he'd tried on the fourth day, not a smart move—and he was content to lie on his bed and make out with her like a frustrated, horny teenager, as long as he was holding her, touching her. He enjoyed talking to her, lying around and watching TV with her . . . anything. Anything, as long as she was there.

This wasn't just the emotion of the situation sweeping him away. He felt a real connection. He just wasn't sure what she was feeling, because she kept it inside. When they kissed, she'd melt into him. When they whispered naughty, flirty things, her eyes lit up for him. When they talked about their families or their jobs or politics or anything, she was engaged and right there with him. But when he even hinted at the future, she would brusquely change the subject or even just get up and walk away, suddenly needing something in the other room.

For a smart, strong, take-no-bullshit woman, Amanda was running scared. He knew that, but wasn't sure exactly what she was scared of. For a man who was an investigator by profession, he was having a lot of trouble figuring her out.

She drove him to his one-week checkup at the hospital. She waited for him during it, and after it, the two of them went to visit Myles for the first time. Seeing him hooked up to machines and still in bed, pale and bloated and weak, made Nick's heart seize and plummet to his stomach. But he limped in and put on his best face for the kid, who lit up like a Christmas tree when he saw Nick and Amanda. His happiness was palpable; it touched Nick like few things had in his whole life. His nephew was so brave, and he loved him.

As they headed down the main hallway toward the front exit, ready to leave and enjoy the rest of the day, Charles II walked into the hospital. Amanda gasped softly and looked up at Nick.

"I see him," Nick murmured. His jaw tightened.

The older man was dressed in a navy suit and striped tie, looking polished and radiating power as always. But when he saw Nick, he stopped in his tracks. His gray eyes pinned Nick and held.

"What do you want to do?" she whispered.

"See what he wants," Nick whispered back.

They slowed to stop in front of him.

Charles II nodded in greeting at Amanda, but said to Nick, "Got a minute?"

"Sure." He looked down to Amanda. "Why don't I meet you outside?"

"No problem." She cast one concerned glance at him, but walked away.

"What do you want?" Nick asked calmly, even as the muscles in his body tensed.

Charles II paused, studying him for a long moment before saying, "I wanted to thank you for what you did. Coming here, the transplant . . . if it works, you'll have saved Myles's life. Thank you."

Nick swallowed hard. He hadn't expected civility, much

less anything resembling a heartfelt statement. "I just hope it works," he said gruffly.

"Of course. We all do." He paused again before saying, "You and I . . . we're not going to have a relationship, are we?"

"I don't think so," Nick said.

"We got off on the wrong foot."

"I'd say it's a little more than that."

"You threatened me."

"You threatened me and my family first," Nick countered. "Reminder, while we're on the subject: stay away from them."

Charles merely inclined his head in acknowledgment.

Nick felt his blood rush, his muscles coil, but kept his voice even. "Look . . . I have a family. You have a family. We don't need each other. We don't like each other."

"We don't know each other," Charles stressed.

"We know enough."

"Perhaps. But perhaps, in another life, we could have known each other. We were denied that opportunity."

Nick's heart started beating in heavy, thick thumps. He'd thought of that a few times. He'd mulled over a few 'what-ifs' that stung. But after meeting his biological father, and disliking him so intensely, he was fine with it. "I guess that's how it goes."

"I guess it is." Charles's gray eyes still held him in place. "I respect that you haven't come after a payoff, your siblings speak highly of you, and I'm grateful what you did for Myles. So . . . I'll leave you be. That's what you want, right?"

His chest tightened. Was there a hook here? Was the old man actually being sincere, or was there a sucker punch coming? All he said was, "Right."

"All right, then. That will be my gesture of goodwill toward you," Charles said. "I'm going to visit my grandson now." He gave Nick a stiff nod and brushed past him, continuing on down the corridor.

Nick turned and stared after him, watching until the old man disappeared.

When he left the fluorescent grind of the hospital and emerged into the late May sunshine, he tipped his face to the sky to let it warm him and breathed deep lungfuls of fresh air. It felt good to be alive.

Amanda was waiting right outside the doors. She gripped his arm and asked, "Are you okay?"

"Fine. Honestly." He dropped a quick kiss on her head. "We need to celebrate. Doc gave me a thumbs-up. I'm taking you out to dinner."

"Sounds good," she said. "But you sure you're up to it?"

"Yep. And when we're done and go back to my room? We have some catching up to do." He gave her a deliberate look.

"You sure you're up to *that*?" Her eyes took on a new sparkle.

"We'll find out. I want to try." He lowered his head to whisper in her ear, "I've missed being inside you." Nipping her earlobe, he kissed her mouth. "I mean, *really* inside you. My fingers adore you, but . . ." He winked.

Spots of color flushed her cheeks. "I've missed that too," she said.

And after I ravage you, he thought, *we're going to talk about what comes next for us.*

Amanda watched Nick walk into the bedroom, gauging his pain level from his movements. He'd gotten through dinner, and even though his eyes were shadowed, a bit tired, he was definitely on the mend. The only thing affecting him now was his lower back and hip, still tender. The doctor said he might feel twinges for a few weeks. Nick claimed it wasn't as bad as it'd been at first, and while she believed him, she knew it was still sore. Even now, she saw the quick wince as he bent over to pull off his socks.

The other night, when their make-out and groping session had gotten heated, he'd rolled on top of her to take it further. Feeling the hard length of him against her belly, wanting him as much as he clearly wanted her, she'd forgotten herself and wrapped her legs around him to draw him closer—and he'd grunted in pain, a loud, low groan that made her freeze. His hip was still too tender. In spite of his protestations, she hadn't allowed him to try again since then.

Not that it had stopped Nick's libido. They found plenty of other ways to please each other over the week. There was something about having limits, making it something of a challenge, that seemed to spur them on to different heights and make it even more sensual. She used her mouth on him without mercy, and he begged for more. When he cradled her into his good side, whispering naughty, dirty things into her ear as he held her close and worked her into a frenzy with his talented fingers, she'd had some of the most powerful orgasms she'd ever experienced.

But tonight she really, really hoped he was better. She wanted to make love with him so badly it was ridiculous. She missed the feel of their bodies in full alignment, all of him around her and inside her, the way they moved together. . . . Need swamped her now as she watched him shed layers and reveal that incredible body to her once again. She couldn't imagine she'd ever get tired of looking at him. Everything about his body made her blood heat, tantalizing her. The defined, cut muscles of his physique . . . the sharp angles and hard solidity of him, so very male . . . the trail of dark hair that led from his navel into his black boxer briefs.

He was down to those when he glanced over at her. "You still dressed?"

And that voice. Hearing his deep, sexy voice could get her wet even faster than looking at him. "Just making sure you're up to this, Miami Vice."

"Take your clothes off and get in my bed, woman." His eyes were hot and bright. "I'll show you how up to this I am."

She reached for the hem of her T-shirt and pulled it up over her head, letting it drop to the floor. The capris came next, pooling around her ankles before she stepped out of them. Noting how intently he watched her undress, she stopped to bask in the heat and appreciation of his hungry gaze. As she stood there in her matching pink bra and panties, he clearly liked what he saw.

He stepped to her, letting his fingertips skate over the straps on her shoulders, then down to the cups of her lacy bra. "You're so beautiful." His hands moved down her sides, reached around to her ass, and gave it a squeeze over her panties as his mouth took hers. "Get." He kissed her. "In." Kissed her again. "My." He nipped at her bottom lip, bringing a tiny squeak from her. "Bed." He kissed her hard and hot, edging her backward to the bed behind them.

"I don't want to hurt you," she said as he lowered himself on top of her. "How can we do this without hurting you?"

"It's the best kind of pain, baby," he murmured against her lips. "I can take it." He took her mouth in a searing, sumptuous kiss as one hand slid down her leg. His hand hooked under her knee and swung her leg over his hips, on his good side. "Maybe one leg around me, the other alongside but not over me. We'll try it. . . ." The rest of his words were lost in his hungry kisses.

They kissed and caressed slowly at first, testing the waters even as their mutual fire burned. "I missed holding you like this," he whispered.

"I missed it too," she whispered back. Her hips undulated beneath him, rocking against his erection. "But if it's too much, tell me and we'll switch positions, find another way."

"Stop worrying about me," he commanded as he trailed hot, openmouthed kisses along her throat. "If you can worry . . ." He licked her skin, nibbled on it. "If you can think clearly about anything other than what I'm doing . . ." More kisses, a little bite on her earlobe. "Then I'm not doing this right."

"You're doing this amazingly right," she assured him.

She felt his smile against her skin. "Good to know," he

said as one of his hands fondled her breast while the other ran through her hair. "Didn't want to think I'd lost my touch or anything."

"Impossible. Never happen." She rolled her hips against his again, and they both moaned from the delicious friction. "No man has ever affected me in bed like you do."

His eyes flared with satisfaction. "Good. Because I've never wanted a woman as much as I want you." He stared into her eyes for a long beat, and she felt like he was staring into her mind and soul, seeing the affection and adoration for him she was fighting so hard to hide. She gripped his head and brought his mouth back to hers.

Every kiss, every touch, felt infused with deeper meaning. They were communicating without words in a way only true lovers did. It moved her profoundly and made her edgy at the same time. She didn't want to be in love with him. She didn't ever want this moment to end. She didn't know what the hell her brain was doing.

He grasped her hands, bringing them over her head and interlacing their fingers, holding her as he entered her with a smooth thrust. Her breath hitched. He'd possessed her, body and soul. The way he looked at her as he moved inside her, right into her eyes, his breath mixing with hers and the lazy rhythm his hips set and the feel of him all around her . . . it was more intimate than anything she'd ever felt in her life. It made her shiver, and her eyes slipped closed as the power of it overwhelmed her.

"Christ, I missed you." He dropped kisses on her lips, her chin, her cheeks. His fingers squeezed hers as they rocked together and she squeezed his back.

"Is your hip okay?" she asked.

"Shhhh, it's fine."

"Sorry, can't help it."

He smiled down at her. "I know." He kissed her, long and

sweet, and released her hands to cup her face. "Because you're beautiful, inside and out."

"Because I care," she whispered, feeling both bold and vulnerable at the same time. Her hands skimmed over his shoulders and held. "I care about you, Nick."

"I care about you too," he whispered back. "More than you know, *mi reina*."

Her heart skipped a beat. The way he said those words, the way he looked at her . . . there was so much more going on. She felt it. She knew it. But as much as she wanted to hear more, to say more, she just couldn't. She pressed her lips to his and wrapped her arms around him, holding him close and savoring every second.

Afterwards, Nick fell asleep quickly, his breathing going slow and heavy in under two minutes. His body still was recovering. Exhaustion had won out over any conversation, and she was grateful.

She needed the silence. She needed to deal with the whirlwind in her head.

When he'd made love to her, he'd truly made love to her, in every sense of the term. It had been insanely intense; what they'd just shared went beyond sex. Feelings were there, deep, raw, and real. She recalled the look in his eyes as he'd moved inside her and shuddered. He hadn't said he was in love with her, but she'd felt it. That look had touched a place deep in her heart that no man ever had, not ever.

She wanted him too much. She had to leave.

She needed to process all this, and she couldn't do it wrapped in his embrace. He was like a drug she couldn't get enough of. She was drunk on him, stupid with it, and she needed to sober up. The emotions rolling through her now felt dangerous. If she wasn't careful, she could be swallowed whole by this fantasy as he'd been, could make herself believe it was real. She just didn't trust it. Being with him was too easy, felt too right. Too risky.

They'd only known each other less than two months. She shouldn't be having *forever* thoughts. That would lead to crushing disappointment . . . maybe even disaster. She had to go home and regroup.

She carefully slipped out of his arms, out of his bed, and out of the room.

Chapter Twenty-Two

Amanda didn't sleep well, her overloaded heart and brain making her restless. Finally, she drifted into deeper sleep around 4 AM for a few hours straight; exhaustion had won out. She woke just after nine. The incredible sex last night was surely a factor in the deeper sleep, along with knowing she had nowhere to be today. Nick was fine now. He didn't need her to take care of him anymore, and Myles wouldn't be out of the hospital for weeks. As Charles had said, for the next few weeks, her time was her own, and he'd insisted on paying her for two weeks of her time off as if she were a corporate salaried employee. She appreciated his generosity. She had enough in her savings that even if she didn't go back to working with Myles for a whole month, she could lay low and afford it. Some time off would be great.

The feeling of freedom, the idea of not adhering to a daily schedule, was so alien. She hadn't had a real vacation in six months. When Myles had had a good streak, Charles had insisted she take two weeks off, fully paid. The first week, she'd stayed home and just lazed around, but the second week, she'd gone to a resort in Jamaica with Roni and Steph. It'd been Roni's idea, of course, and they'd gotten the plans together in record time. The best trip of her life, it'd been the only time she'd ever gone away without family. She was thirty-two, for God's sake—she needed to go places, do more. She needed more of a life.

She lay in bed and started thinking about where she could go next week on such short notice, and not spend a bundle doing it. Maybe up to the Cape? Out east to a spa on the tip of Long Island? Just go to the beach every day? The first week of June was gorgeous weather-wise, holding infinite possibilities close to home. She wondered if her friends would be able to get away for a few days. She knew she'd need them.

Because once Nick was back in Miami, only six days from now, she'd need to get away from here for a bit to shake him off. She wondered if that was even possible. She doubted it. She loved him, and holding that back had proved too much over the past few days. At least when they were back to their separate lives, she could pine in peace.

Deciding to text her friends, she rolled over to reach for her cell phone and turn it on. Sunlight dappled the walls as a soft, warm breeze blew in from the window. Soon she'd need the air-conditioning, would no longer be able to keep the window open.

But a waiting text from Nick made her stomach flip. It's 3 a.m. I rolled over & the bed is empty. Why'd you leave? Not happy here. Please call me when you see this.

She sighed deeply and decided to take a shower before responding. But as she got out of her bed and stretched, the buzzer from the lobby went off. Her whole body tightened. She wasn't expecting anyone . . . so she knew who it had to be.

She padded out to the living room. Gretchen wasn't home, so she clicked the intercom. "Who's there?"

"It's me." Nick's voice sounded tight. "Can I come up, please?"

She pressed the button to let him through and ran to the bathroom to quickly brush her teeth. Her reflection in the mirror made her wince. She wrangled her messy hair into a ponytail just as he knocked on the door. She looked down at the thin lavender camisole and matching sleep shorts she'd worn to bed. Clearly, she wasn't ready for company, but she opened the door to Nick standing there, tension radiating off him. He wore a white T-shirt, navy athletic shorts, and a stormy look on his face.

"I thought you can't drive," she said. "What are you doing here?"

"I took an Uber," he said tersely. "The better question is, what are *you* doing here, instead of being in my room? Without anything but a good-bye note on your pillow?"

She'd put off having this talk as long as she could. Apparently, it was going to happen now. Steeling herself, she moved aside and said, "Come in."

She'd barely closed and locked the door when he said, "Why'd you leave?"

She turned to him with a sigh. "I needed to."

"*Why?* Last night was . . . different. It felt like . . ." His voice softened as he stared down at her. "It was beautiful, Amanda. We were beautiful together. It was more than just sex, and you know it."

Realizing he'd felt it too made her insides start to shake.

He looked at her, imploring, earnest. "I've never felt that completely connected, body and soul, to anyone in my whole life. I fell asleep at peace in a way I never have before. Because of you." His dark eyes flashed. "And when I woke up, you were gone."

Her heart started pounding in heavier thumps. He'd felt what she'd felt. She hadn't imagined it or built it up out of silly romantic wishing. Maybe—

"Isn't it bad enough I have to leave in a few days?" he asked. "Why are you cutting our limited time together even shorter?" He stopped and scrubbed his hands over his face. "I don't mean to sound pissy, but I'm tired. I didn't sleep well after I saw you were gone. I laid there with my brain going, trying to figure out why you left."

She swallowed what she'd been about to say. He was leaving. To draw this out now would be even more painful. It had to end. Why not now? End it clean, let him go, cry in private.

"I'll tell you something else I thought about, lying there in the dark and thinking about you. Before the surgery, that night we argued, you implied that anything I feel for you isn't real. That because everything's kind of crazy right now—finding out I'm a Harrison, getting to know Myles, the surgery—that I'm just all swept up in emotion."

"Aren't you?" she said. It came out harsher than she'd intended.

"Hell no!" he snapped. "I know what I feel is real. Don't tell me how I feel, goddamn it—you're not in my head. Christ, that pissed me off then, and it does now too."

Her stomach roiled as she stood there, trying to stay strong under his withering, tangible frustration. *You're leaving*, she chanted to herself. *You're leaving. This is hopeless.*

"Last night . . ." He stared at her balefully. "That was real, Amanda. As real as it gets. Real and intense and fucking beautiful." His eyes pinned hers, and she felt caught. "Tell me you didn't feel it too and I'll leave right now, and it'll be over. Because if you tell me that, you're a goddamn liar."

She drew a shaky breath and stared back, unable to think of a clever response.

"You can't, can you?" he murmured. His dark, heated gaze seared through her. "Because you felt it too. And it scares the hell out of you. That's why you left last night."

"You're leaving in a few days," she whispered hotly.

"Yeah, and it sucks, but—"

"But nothing! It doesn't matter what we felt last night, what we feel now." Panic rose up in her throat. "This wasn't supposed to—we weren't supposed to—" Her hands fluttered at her chest, rubbing to ease the sudden tightness there. "I can't do this."

"You can't do what?"

"Have feelings for you. Want this. Any of it."

He moved closer, watching her, his voice low. "Why not?"

"You're *leaving*," she ground out. "You live in Florida. I live in New York. End of story. Game over."

"It doesn't have to be the end of the story."

She stilled, confused, blinking at him.

"Come with me," he said. "Move to Miami and be with me."

Chapter Twenty-Three

"You can't be serious," Amanda sputtered.

"I'm dead serious," Nick said, staring back at her, realizing with a jolt he absolutely meant it. "I don't want this to end. We're great together. Long-distance relationships suck. Move to Miami, sweetheart."

"Just like that." Her voice was strangely calm, a contrast to the growing excitement he felt.

"Yeah! I just got promoted. I can't leave now. You're a per diem nurse. You can find work anywhere." The more he thought about it, the more sense it made. They could do this—they could make it work.

"Never mind the fact that I already have a job here I'm not done with," she said. "Or the fact that the patient in question means a lot to me, and has become attached to me as well, and he's going to need my services again very soon. And when he does, I'll be working with him for months. Or the fact that I have a good standing relationship with a great hospital, should I need to go back to regular shift work in the future."

"Those are all valid points." He paused, mind scrambling. A moment ago, he'd felt like he was getting through to her, but now . . . she just looked pissed off. "Okay, so don't move to Miami next week. But maybe in a few months, when Myles is better—"

"I have friends and family here, Nick," she said. Color bloomed on her cheeks, the spots of pink another warning. "I have a life."

"You're the one always saying you *don't* have a life," he reminded her. "So would it be that hard to consider moving, starting over somewhere new? With a guy who's in love with you? I am, Amanda. I'm so in love with you I can't think straight."

Her eyes widened and her lips parted. He'd shocked her with that last part. He'd shocked himself too. He hadn't meant to tell her like that, just blurt it out that way. But desperate times called for desperate measures, and maybe now she'd see how serious he was about this.

She gaped at him for a long moment, then said quietly, "You need to leave."

Now it was his turn to be shocked. "Excuse me?"

"Go. Just go." She turned away and went to the door, opening it for him.

His gut started churning, nerves on red alert. "Did you hear what I said?"

"Every word. Every manipulative, thoughtless, selfish word." Her face flushed, hot pink flooding her pale skin as her eyes narrowed on him.

He blinked, stunned speechless for a long moment. Then he said, "Telling you I love you is manipulative, thoughtless, and selfish?"

"When you do it as a means to an end? Absolutely."

"Are you serious?"

"As a heart attack." Her hand went to her cocked hip. "How convenient that you tell me you love me for the first time as you're trying to convince me to do something you want. Something as big as walking away from my whole life here."

"Let me get this straight," he said, feeling his heart rate rise. "I tell you I love you and you think I'm trying to manipulate you?"

"You are!" she cried, hurling the words at him. "And either you meant to, which is despicable, or you didn't mean to, which is troubling at best, but still fucked up. Either way, you need to get out of my sight right now."

This was going to hell fast. His stomach twisted harder as he saw the steel in her eyes. "No! No, we need to talk about this."

"Why should I? According to you, I have no life," she spat. "Nothing worth staying here for. I should be thankful that a big, gorgeous guy like you wants to save me from my nonexistent, boring world. I should just throw everything to the wind and move a thousand miles away, where I know no one and have nothing in place, just so you can keep getting laid. Because you love me. You love me so much you don't give a shit about me or anything in my life, only what I can do for you."

He swore under his breath. Christ, had he messed this up. He'd never seen her so angry, and he'd seen her pretty mad. How could he fix this, make her see? "None of that is true. I want you to move a thousand miles away," he said, "because I'm in love with you and the thought of not being with you has me tied up in knots. You can find work—I know you can. I know we could be happy."

She just kept glaring at him.

"By the way, I can get laid any time, by anyone. But I—"

"Congratulations."

"Goddamn it, you didn't let me finish. That's not what I want. I want only you. I want *us*, together."

"Then you move here," she countered.

"I can't," he said. "I just started my new job a few weeks ago. If I put in for a transfer now, I don't know that I'd be the same rank. I don't—"

"But you have family here," she pointed out. "You already know people here. I don't know a goddamn soul in Florida. Do you care? I don't think so."

Shit, this was bad. "Amanda. Stop. Listen to me."

"I think I've heard enough." Her knuckles went white on the doorknob.

"I just want—"

"I, I, I. Do you even *hear* yourself, Nick? It's always about you."

All the air left his chest. She might as well have kicked him in the stomach.

"This was fun, what we had," she said. "So good, and too fast. I got caught up in it too. But to give up my life and move somewhere new, with a man who didn't even think through what that would mean for me? Who throws out a serious, life-changing idea on a whim? Who never tells me he loves me until he uses it to manipulate me? I deserve better than that." Her voice was flat, but her eyes glowered with outrage. "Please go now. I mean it."

His head whirred, his heart hammered, and all he could do was stare at her. Holy shit, how had this gone so wrong so fast? "Baby, please. I'm not trying to manipulate you. *I love you.* I may not have thought this through properly, but that's because I—"

"I, I, I, again!" she said. "All. About. You."

He hissed out an exhale as his stomach flipped over, as frustration and anger overtook him. His hands curled into fists. "*You*, Amanda Kozlov, mean more to me than you can imagine." He stuffed his fists into his pockets. "*You* are beautiful and kind, smart and sexy, fierce as fucking hell. You take care of a deathly ill child and master it. You took care of me even when I was a dick to you." He speared her with his gaze, hoping he was getting through to her. She didn't look away, so he barreled on. "You give so much of yourself. You have a quick, razor-sharp sense of humor that makes me laugh all the time. I don't just love you, I like you.

I like being with you, even when we do nothing but lie around. Hell, *especially* when we just lie around. But know what else there is about you?"

He stepped closer, his heart thumping. "For all your tough talk, I think you're afraid. I think you love me too and you're afraid to admit it. I've tried to talk about what comes next for us several times this week, and you shut me down. Just like you're shutting me down right now. That's what's driving this argument. *You.*" He pointed a finger at her, punctuating his words. "You. Are. Scared."

"Fine! I do love you," she said, and tears sprung to her eyes. "And yes, that scares me." She cleared her throat, sniffed hard. "And it doesn't matter. Because if you think we're only fighting right now because of me, this won't work. So we're done. Good-bye, Nick." Her voice broke on *good-bye.*

He lurched toward her, but she held out a hand and barked, "Don't."

"Please," he said, urgency flooding him. "You—"

"Good-bye, Nick."

"If you love me too, don't do this. Dammit, Amanda—"

"*Good-bye*, Nick." She ground out the words from between her teeth, a last warning, like if he didn't leave right then she'd go ballistic. Her glassy-eyed glare was blistering.

His mind raced as wildly as his heart. She'd totally shut down, that was clear. But he couldn't just leave. He didn't know how she could tell him she loved him and throw him out at the same time. He didn't know anything right now.

"This can't be over," he said, searching her eyes for a hint of an opening.

"It is," she said, not moving, not giving him anything.

His heart dropped to his stomach. Nothing made sense; it was all chaos and waves and white noise. Swearing under his breath, he stormed out. Even halfway down the hallway, the sound of the door closing behind him made misery shoot through him, stealing his breath.

* * *

Nick didn't give up on anything he cared about without a hell of a fight. For the next few days, he called Amanda every day, texted every day—but calls went to voice mail and texts went unanswered. He didn't bother going to her apartment building, because he knew she wouldn't buzz him in past the lobby. There was no way to reach her. She'd barricaded herself. In full-blown "turtle mode," as she herself had called it.

He tried not to go crazy. He took walks and took naps. He got visits from a different sibling each day. They'd been really great about keeping him in the loop about Myles's progress and checking on him; he had to admit it. He liked this group more every day. But he still had plenty of time alone to think about what had happened. Time to realize what a complete selfish asshole he'd been.

Amanda was absolutely right; he hadn't taken her life into consideration when he'd asked her to move. She'd often made cracks about how she had no life, how it centered around the job with Myles. . . . He'd taken that a little too literally. Of course she had roots in New York, but even if she didn't, a cross-country move was a huge decision, not to be taken lightly or made on a whim. What the hell had he been thinking, dropping it on her the way he had? The answer was simple: he hadn't been thinking. He'd gotten carried away and done it all wrong. And that pricked him with self-loathing every time he replayed their fight in his mind.

But dammit, he'd been right about two crucial things: that she loved him too, and that it scared her to death. He understood how loving him smashed every self-protective rule she'd put carefully into place. Which was why she'd run like hell. Combine that with his colossal screw-up, and things looked bleak.

He didn't want to give up on her, but if she wouldn't

answer him in any way, how long could he try before having to concede defeat? He wasn't a quitter, but he also wasn't a fool. He was leaving the day after tomorrow, and there was nothing to do but . . . leave. Go back to his life. Miss her every damn day and wish he'd done things differently. Wish that she'd be open with him and honest with herself and that . . . so many things. So many goddamn things.

Early June was nice here—warm, the way he liked it, but not humid yet. Flowers bloomed everywhere; trees were lushly green—lots of color. Long Island was so much nicer now than when he'd first arrived on a gray day in April. New York had grown on him. It was a gorgeous evening, so he sat on the bench in the hotel courtyard, stared up at the clear blue sky, and felt the heartache and misery of missing Amanda wash over him for the thousandth time.

His cell phone rang, and he pulled it out of his pocket, the split second of hope crashing when he saw it wasn't her calling. "Hey, Charles, how's it goin'?"

"Fine," Charles said. "I'm still at the hospital. Myles had a good day—I thought you'd want to know."

Nick smiled for the first time all day. "That's really great. Thanks for telling me."

"He's holding his own. Every day he does is a victory, and a step toward his getting out of here," Charles said. "So listen. I know you're leaving on Friday. Up for a good-bye family dinner tomorrow? At my house?"

"Sure," Nick said. "That'd be fine. I can handle that."

"Fantastic," Charles said. "I'll make the calls. Say . . . seven o'clock?"

"I'll be there." Nick paused, then added, "Can I ask you something?"

"Of course."

"Have you spoken to Amanda in the past few days?"

"Yes, two days ago. She wanted to let me know she

was going away for a week with her friends. A spa trip, somewhere in Maine."

Nick felt nauseous. Not only wasn't she answering him, she'd fled the state.

Blissfully unaware, Charles continued, "She wanted to let me know on the off chance that Myles was released from the hospital and I needed her, but I assured her that isn't likely and told her to go have some long-overdue fun. Why do you ask?"

Nick swallowed a sigh and swiped a hand over his face. "Just curious."

"You know . . . I did ask. She said you were a rough patient at first, but you mellowed out by the end of the week. She said she enjoyed hanging out with you once you were better." Charles let out a wry chuckle. "You could've taken it easy on her, tough guy. She's not just a great nurse—she's a truly wonderful person."

"I know." Nick's eyes squeezed shut as he winced. "Couldn't agree more."

Amanda cradled the wineglass as she leaned over the railing. Her room at the spa was small and adorable, and had a little terrace that overlooked the beach and ocean. The view was breathtaking, and the sounds of the crashing waves soothed her. She could have stayed there all evening, until the sun disappeared and the stars came out.

She missed Nick. She hated herself for it, because it was her own fault.

He'd tried to call, text, everything. She'd ignored him. She should have talked to him like a rational adult, but she'd shut him out. Because nothing about her feelings for him felt rational. She hadn't even known him for two months; she had no business thinking she was in love with him. Much less so in love with him that she'd even considered his ridiculous idea of moving to Florida.

She'd love to write off his crazy presentation as his submitting to a wildly romantic impulse, but the whole thing had just left her unnerved. So, radio silence.

She'd had enough time to realize the truth and admit it to herself: he'd been right. She was scared. She'd pushed him away because she wanted it too much. And wanting anything too much scared the hell out of her, because sometimes she lost herself. It'd happened with Cooper, it'd happened with nursing school, it'd even happened with caring for Myles. She went all in and lost herself in the process. Loving Nick felt like that. She didn't want to go into a free fall when she wasn't sure if he'd be there to catch her even if he wanted to be. So she'd ended it, just like that.

Not fair to him. Not even fair to herself. She hadn't given it a real chance.

A seagull screeched overhead as it soared through the sky, hanging in the air for a long moment before diving toward the water. She watched it fly until she couldn't see it anymore. Sipped her wine. Inhaled the sea air. Chastised herself for being a lovesick fool.

Over dinner, Roni shot Amanda a sharp look and said, "Stop wallowing."

"I know," Amanda said. "I hate myself for it. After all, I'm the one who ended it. I have no right to wallow."

"Then knock it off," Roni said, but gave her hand a quick squeeze.

"I haven't seen you this sad over a guy since Cooper," Steph said gently.

Amanda opened her mouth to say something . . . but found herself at a loss for words. She looked at her friends, closed her mouth, and nodded.

"Then just call Nick," Roni said. "You love him, he loves you. Work it out."

"He flies back to Miami today," Amanda said. "He's probably on the plane right now, actually."

"So what?" Roni nudged her under the table with a little kick. "Text him."

"What's the last thing you heard from him?" Steph asked.

"Voice mail this morning." Amanda's stomach did a little wobbly flip as she thought of the voice mail. She'd listened to it three times; she'd all but memorized it.

"I'm leaving today, Amanda. I've tried calling, texting. . . . You're not having it. I get it. So after today, I won't try anymore. I don't give up, usually. I fight. But I'll respect your wishes and stay away. I just had to try one last time. I just had to tell you that I love you. And I think we could've been something amazing together. I hate that we'll never find out." A long pause before he'd cleared his throat and added in a thick voice, *"Voy a pensar en que siempre. Te amo, mi reina."*

"He said he won't try to contact me anymore," Amanda said quietly. She picked up her fork and aimlessly pushed around the salad on her plate. "That since I've made it clear I don't want him, he'll leave me alone. And he . . . ended it with horribly sweet things. In Spanish."

"Oh, swooooon," Steph said.

Roni blinked at her. "You got that big hunk of alpha male falling over himself like that over you," she said sharply, "and you're here with us? Girl. *Girl.*"

"He wanted me to just drop my life and fly off with him!" Amanda reminded her friends.

"That romantic bastard," Roni said in fake outrage, putting her hand to her head.

Amanda gaped at her. "You both *agreed* that was a selfish, dick move."

"Yes, it was," Roni said. "But he's tried to reach you every damn day since. Right?"

"Yeah," Amanda mumbled.

"Maaaybe he thought about it and realized that. And wanted to work something out anyway." Roni slanted her a look and reached for her wineglass. She drained it before pronouncing, "We're gonna need more of this."

"We've gone over this," Steph said. "Dumb move, yes. But don't all people in love do dumb things? Make mistakes? The point is he kept trying to reach you. You . . . you could've just heard him out. You were afraid to. You don't like not having control over your life. Falling in love is about as out of control as it gets. No wonder you're fighting it. You always did. You forget, we've known you forever."

Roni clinked her empty glass to Steph's. "Amen."

With a sinking feeling, Amanda drained her wineglass too. They were both right and she knew it. She'd been fighting her feelings for Nick from the beginning, telling herself it'd just be a fun fling—who the hell had she been kidding? No, he wasn't perfect. But he was wonderful, and she'd pushed him away.

"*Voy a pensar en que siempre.*" She'd Googled it to understand what he'd said. *I'll think of you always.*

Her heart dropped to her stomach as she sighed.

"I looked up some things online," she said quietly, staring into her empty glass. "I probably could get work down there pretty easily. He was right about that much."

"Is that so?" Roni said.

"Yes." Amanda turned her empty glass in circles as her heart thumped away.

"You're so in love with him," Steph said.

"Yeah," Amanda whispered. "And I'm terrified. So I blew it." Tears sprang to her eyes and she sniffed them back.

Roni caught the eye of a waiter, charming him with a smile to bring him over. She asked for another bottle of the Riesling, then turned back to Amanda with an intent stare. "Okay. Listen up. I'm going to make a proposal to you."

"You're not my type," Amanda joked. Steph snorted out a laugh, and Roni rolled her eyes.

"Go visit him there," Roni said. "Stay with him for a week or two. Check out job opportunities, the local hospitals, all of that. Wake up with him with morning breath, see how he reacts when you ask him to help with the dishes or take out the garbage. Be with him enough to get real. See what it's like. See if you two work outside of this high-emotion chaos you've been in since you met, see that you can do normal life."

"So far," Steph said, leaning in on her elbows, "I really like this proposal."

"Give serious thought to moving there," Roni said pointedly. "Because all three of us know if you really wanted to, very little is holding you back here. And honey, he knew that too."

Irritation pricked Amanda as she said, "How about my job?"

"Do it after Myles recovers, of course," Roni said.

"Maybe have a long-distance relationship at first," Steph said. "To see if you two can even do that before taking it further."

"Right," Roni agreed. "Finish the job with Myles, then do this. Because I'm sorry, but you're not the only nurse on Long Island."

"You're the one who just said you could probably find work easily there," Steph pointed out. "Sorry, your bullshit excuse is officially declared bullshit."

"What about my family and my friends?" Amanda asked.

"You can barely stand your family for more than an hour at a time," Roni reminded her. "And your friends will always be your friends. You're stuck with us, sister. Here's proof . . ." She pinned Amanda with such a commanding look, Amanda felt a whoosh of uneasiness, knew something big was coming.

"If you decide to move down there," Roni said, "and give

it a shot with him, do it one hundred percent. And if you give it your all, and if it doesn't work out?" Roni reached out and took her hand. "It's not the end of the world. You move back to New York. You get a job at the hospital, and you can stay with me until you find a new place to live. I won't let you feel stuck down there. You hearing me?"

The lump that formed in Amanda's throat felt more like a boulder.

"I love this proposal," Steph said, smiling wide as she took Amanda's other hand. "I'll up the ante: I'll personally help you move back to New York if you need to. I'll fly down to Florida and help you pack up all your things so you won't feel overwhelmed or alone. Husband and kids will live without me for as long as that takes. I'm in too."

Again, Amanda's eyes filled with tears. She swallowed hard and whispered, "You're both incredible. I . . . my God. Wow."

"Think it over," Steph said.

"You have nothing to lose," Roni said, "but so much to gain."

"We love you," Steph said. "We want you to be happy."

"We will always, always have your back," Roni swore.

The tears finally spilled over. Amanda swiped them off her cheeks impatiently. "It doesn't matter," she said. "It's too late—he left."

"He would take you back in a heartbeat," Roni said.

"I don't know about that anymore," Amanda said. "I think his pride kicked in. He sounded done."

"He tried to seduce you with Spanish," Roni said. "*Hello.* He's not done."

Amanda snorted out a tiny laugh at that.

"Think it all over," Steph suggested. "We're here for another day and a half. Plenty of time for you to just think about everything."

"That's already all I've been doing," Amanda mumbled.

"Well, now you have even more to think about," Steph said as the waiter approached the table.

"And more wine," Roni said, smiling brightly. "Which is always a good thing."

Amanda looked at her friends, squeezed their hands before releasing them, and whispered, "Thank you. I love you both so much."

Chapter Twenty-Four

Nick pulled himself out of his car, tired and weary after a long day at work. In contrast to the air-conditioning in his car, the humidity in the parking garage swamped him, making him break into a sweat in about ten seconds. He unknotted his tie as he walked and popped open the top button of his shirt. It was Friday, and his buddies wanted to take him out to welcome him home, but he'd turned them down and asked for a rain check. All he wanted was to get up to his apartment, take a shower, grab a cold beer, and sit on his terrace to watch the evening sky darken into night.

He'd been back for a week now. His hip twinged once in a while, but he was fine. He'd gone back to work immediately and thrown himself into his caseload. He sometimes got tired, but he pushed through it. No way would he show that at work.

His mom had come by on Monday night to make him dinner and hover over him. The home-cooked meal had been nice, but spending some one-on-one time with his mom was even nicer. They talked about the surgery, the Harrisons, and what he wanted for his future where they were concerned. Turned out, he did want them in his life.

He even told her about Amanda. She'd been surprised, but offered support and not too much advice, which he appreciated.

"Give her some time, *mijo*," his mom had instructed. "Let her miss you. Let her think about you. And in a few weeks, try again."

He'd taken a sip of his soda as he mulled that over. "You'd like her, Ma. She's down to earth, not a phony or pretentious bone in her body. She's amazing."

His mom had only nodded. "So, in time, you'll go after her again. If you want to."

"I'll want to," he'd mumbled. "I miss her like crazy, Ma. I'm . . . Christ, I'm helplessly in love with her. I never felt like this before. I think she's the one for me."

"Wow. Okay. Well . . . if it's meant to be, it'll be," she'd said, and spooned another serving of rice onto his plate. "But I have to say, if she lets a man like you go, amazing or not, it's her loss."

"You're totally biased," he'd said with a grin.

"Of course I am!" She had smiled back. "But it's still true."

He worked long hours. He went back to the gym, taking it slow but getting in his workouts. At night, he fell into bed, utterly exhausted. But Amanda was never far from his thoughts. She showed up in his dreams. Awake or asleep, no matter what he was doing, she was there, in his head and in his heart. She owned him.

He hadn't heard from her at all. The pain of it was like nothing he'd ever felt before, only showing him that yes, he was truly in love with her. He'd never felt like this about another woman. And the fucking misery of it, the ache of knowing how deeply he felt about someone who had cut him off, was a palpable thing that never let go. He didn't know how to let go of her, because he didn't want to.

He'd try again soon. But for now, he'd live with the

heartache and push through. Other than the pictures and texts on his phone, the heartache was all he had left of her.

As he emerged from the garage, the late-evening sun slanted at an angle that blinded him, even with his sunglasses on. The leaves of the palm trees overhead barely swayed; there was no breeze. It was just hot and humid, typical mid-June weather. Nick thought about jumping in the pool for a quick swim before a beer. He wasn't hungry; he'd had a late lunch at the station. *Maybe a swim would be good*, he thought as he approached the front door of his modest building. Swim, beer, scroll through his pictures of Amanda and miss her some more like the pathetic idiot he was, Netflix, bed.

Yup, those were his plans for the night, done, he decided as he pulled open the door to the small foyer.

He stopped cold. Amanda stood there, between the metal front door and the glass door that allowed people access to the building's lobby.

He blinked, his brain taking a few seconds to process that. She straightened up, her eyes widening a drop. She bit down on her bottom lip for a second before clearing her throat. The corners of her mouth ticked up shyly. "Hi."

His heart rate started climbing. "Hi."

"I wanted to wait for you somewhere I knew I'd definitely catch you," she said. "But I didn't want to bother you at work, so I decided to wait here."

He gave her a quick once-over. Her silky blond hair was pulled back in a ponytail. She wore a simple light blue tank dress and green flip-flops. Her pale skin was dewy with sweat; the air-conditioning in the small foyer was on, but weak. A burgundy suitcase stood perched beside her feet, her flowered tote bag resting on top of it. She licked her lips and stared back at him.

She was the most welcome, beautiful sight he'd ever seen in his life.

"How'd you know where I lived?" he asked.

"I asked Charles for your address," she said. "I told him I wanted to send you a 'hope you're feeling well' card. Blatant lie, but you know . . . desperate times call for desperate measures and all that. I'm not sorry."

"I'm not either." Warmth bloomed in Nick's chest, along with a surge of hope. *She was there*. "How long have you been here?"

She grabbed her cell phone from where it poked out of the pocket of her tote and glanced at it. "About an hour. I thought you said you usually work until six o'clock, so . . ."

He winced. It was just past seven now. "I worked late every night this week. Sorry to make you wait."

"Don't be! You didn't make me wait—you had no idea I was here."

He couldn't stop staring at her. She'd come all this way, for him.

She fidgeted with her silver bracelet. "I hate seeming like a stalker, but I didn't want to miss you. I know this must seem a little creepy, but I . . ." A shadow of ambivalence crossed her features.

"No, it's okay," he said quickly. "You're the one stalker I'm happy to see."

She blinked, and a hint of a hopeful grin lifted her lips. "I didn't know if you'd even want to see me. I didn't know if I blew it for good, if you'd even take my call if I called." She reached up to adjust her ponytail and brush it off her shoulder, an endearingly nervous gesture. "This week, I picked up the phone so many times, but I didn't know what to say. How to break through the wall I put up between us. I did that, so it was on me to reach out. You stopped trying, so I thought you were done, and so I . . . did something a little crazy. I just took a chance." Her eyes widened a little. "I had to try, Nick. I just hope it's not too late?"

He gripped her face with both hands, pulled her against him, and took her mouth with a heated, consuming kiss. She whimpered into his mouth and opened for him, kissing him back with equal passion, matching his fervor as her arms snaked around his waist to hold him tight.

He kissed her long and hard, the feel of her mouth and arms and body making his blood race. He kissed her without holding back as adrenaline and pure joy shot through him. He'd never felt such elation in his life.

When he broke the kiss to gaze down at her, they were both breathless. He leaned his forehead against hers and smiled. "Ahhh. Yes."

"I guess that means it's okay I just showed up at your door."

"It's more than okay," he said. "Christ, I missed you, baby. I've been a wreck."

"You still want me," she said, but it was more like a question, seeking assurance.

"Hell yes," he said, still cradling her head with his hands. "More than anything." He caressed her cheeks with his thumbs and kissed her again. She tasted minty and sweet and like heaven on earth. "And I guess you want me too, since you're here."

"Of course I do," she said. "I missed you too. Every minute, really."

He kissed her again, needing to taste her sweet mouth, feel her breathe into him.

"I've been thinking about everything since I threw you out of my apartment." Her hands swept up and down his arms, his back, gazing at him like she was drinking him in. "I'm sorry about how I handled that. But I hated that you tossed me that 'hey, move to Miami' on a whim. We do need to talk about that."

"Agreed. I screwed that up so badly." He groaned, shaking his head. "You were right to kick my ass over it. I was selfish and stupid. But the sentiment was real. It came from a good place, Amanda, I swear. I just didn't want to lose you. I didn't want it to be over. I got desperate, because that whole week, every time I tried to talk about it—"

"I know. I screwed up too, Nick. You were right—I got

scared. So I shut you down and pushed you away." Her eyes held his, unwavering. "I pushed you away because I didn't want to lose myself in something that wasn't real, that wasn't going to last. And I didn't see how we could last. But . . . I can't see *not* being with you. I want *us*, together."

"I do too. That's all I want, us together. We can figure it out if we just talk about it, can't we?"

"Yes. I'm so sorry. I hope you can forgive me for shutting you out."

"Forgiven," he said. His hands smoothed down her back, stopping just above her ass to hold her tighter against him. She felt so good in his arms. "Does this mean you've forgiven me for dropping the move idea on you so stupidly?"

"Forgiven," she said without pause. "I have to admit, it *was* kind of romantic. . . ."

He grinned, but something else occurred to him. "One last thing. You really gonna be okay with dating a cop? It breaks your big rule. . . ."

"It does." She looked right into his eyes. "But I don't care anymore, because I just want you. I'll worry about you every damn day, but I'll learn to deal with it. I'm willing to take the risk. Because I'll have you, and that's what matters most."

"Okay then." He held her close and pressed a kiss to her forehead. "You're here. We're together. We're going to work this out. *That's* all that matters, *mi reina*."

"Okay then." She echoed him with a smile. "I was worried you gave up on me."

"I gave up on calling or texting," he admitted, "but only for a while. I was letting you do your turtle thing, waiting—hoping—that you'd cool down and realize I really do love you. I was giving you some time, then I was going to come after you again. I never gave up on you—I kept loving you." He tucked a stray lock of her hair behind her ear. "I didn't know how to stop loving you, and I didn't want to. I couldn't if I tried."

"Thank God." She sighed and let her head drop to rest on his chest as she hugged him.

His hands skated over her hair, her back, everywhere he could touch. "The suitcase is a good sign," he said, resting his chin on top of her head.

She chuckled and said, "We have a lot to talk about. I was hoping you'd let me stay long enough to do that. Might take a few days to figure this all out."

"I'd love that." He kissed her hair and hugged her. "Baby, I know we can make this work somehow. Maybe try a long-distance relationship for a few months, then . . . see where we go from there?"

"I was thinking something like that too. Whatever it takes." She pulled back to look up into his eyes. "Because I love you, Nick. I'm yours. I have been from the start. I just hated to admit how much I wanted it. It scared me. I'm not scared of that anymore. The only thing that scared me now was the thought that I'd lost you for good."

He smiled as his blood raced through his veins. "Say that again?"

Her brows puckered in confusion. "Which part?"

"The loving me part," he murmured. "First time you finally admitted it, we were fighting. This time, it sounded like music."

Her smile spread wide and bright as her eyes sparkled with joy. "I love you, Miami Vice. I love you so much I got on a plane and came here to work it out with nothing but a wing and a prayer, hoping it wasn't too late."

"I'm so glad you did." His hands lifted to hold her face as he smiled back at her. *"Te amo, mi reina bella."* He lowered his mouth to hers, kissing her softly. *"Mi amor, mi cielo . . ."* Another kiss, long and sweet, as his hands ran over her hair, down her back. *"Mi vida . . ."*

"I love when you call me *mi reina*," she murmured against his lips. "And I understand *mi amor*." She smiled. "But the other things? I need translation, please."

"*Mi cielo*, my sky." He kissed the tip of her nose. "*Mi vida . . .*" He gently nipped her bottom lip. "Love of my life."

"Ohhh. I really like that one," she whispered, beaming. Her head cocked to the side, as if an idea hit her. "You know, if I'm eventually going to move down here, I better learn some Spanish. I think I'm going to start taking lessons."

The idea made him smile so wide his cheeks hurt. "That sounds great. But I'll gladly be your personal tutor, if you want."

"Hmm. I'm serious about learning, but if you want to help me too, that could be fun. You'll likely distract me, but . . ." She squeezed his ass and asked playfully, "How should I compensate you for your lessons?"

"Heh. I can think of several ways. . . ."

He drew her in tight, sifted his fingers along her hair, and kissed her again and again. She pressed herself against him, melting into his arms as their mouths met, their deep, passionate kisses saying all the things they couldn't express with words.

Nick's mind reeled as they willingly drowned in their embrace. They were together. She'd come around and admitted how she felt, both to herself and to him. She definitely loved him as much as he loved her, if the woman who hated taking risks took one like this to fly to Miami and seek him out. He'd made mistakes—they both had—but their love had won out, because it was real. They had connected in a way they would never deny again. It may have started in chaos, but they'd found each other in the storm.

They were meant to find each other. Nick believed that with all his heart.

So yeah, they'd talk tonight, and over the next few days. But he knew they'd work everything out, and that their future together was going to be incredible. There wasn't a doubt in his mind. Amanda was his forever.

Epilogue

Three years later

Being a Harrison definitely had its perks.

Nick found that to be true when he had the funds needed to give his bride the destination wedding of their dreams. Marrying Amanda on the beach in Key West, following it with a reception at a luxurious resort, was like a fairy tale. But as he looked around the reception at everyone around them, he knew the perks were, of course, way more than financial. He'd gained a whole other family, filled with great people who had enriched his life for knowing them.

All of his family was there: his mom and dad, his two younger sisters, and his four older siblings with all their spouses and kids. Most of his aunts and uncles and cousins were there. Amanda's parents and brother were there, and some of her aunts, uncles, and cousins. There were a few close friends too. Darin and Tom had made sure to be there for him, and Roni and Steph for Amanda, like anything would've kept them away. They were her wedding party.

And heartwarming as could be, his best man sat at a table, sipping soda as he laughed—Myles, now fifteen and a half, was strong and healthy. The journey after the transplant had been an arduous one, but he'd not only recovered, he'd gone into full remission. He had a good life, and a real future. Nick loved the kid like a little brother. Myles meant the world to him, and they were close. Even now, as he caught Myles's eye, Nick tossed him a wink and a smile, which the teen returned.

The only direct relative not in attendance was his biological father, Charles Harrison II. The patriarch had passed away the year before, after suffering a massive heart attack at the office. He and Nick had barely spoken over the months in between, sharing only a few tense chats when Nick came to visit New York. Nick hadn't felt a deep sense of loss. He'd never been sad that he and the old man didn't have a relationship, and they'd at least gotten to a point of cold civility instead of open hostility.

And a week after the funeral, an attorney called Nick with the shocking news. Charles II had left ten million dollars to Nick, and a million to Maria.

At first, Maria refused to take it. Charles and Tess flew down to Florida and personally convinced her to do so. Nick wasn't comfortable with his inheritance either. His four older siblings had had to persuade him to take it. He had, but he'd never get used to knowing he had money like that. He vowed that it would never change who he was. At least he knew Amanda loved him for who he was, not what had suddenly, fortuitously been dropped in his lap.

They'd dated long distance for eleven months. Amanda had been Myles's private nurse from the day he got out of the hospital and went home, never leaving him as he fought through recovery. Nick had made trips to Long Island to see her for a weekend every two months, also seeing Myles and all the Harrisons when he visited. His relationship with Amanda had bloomed, deepened, and thrived. They'd made plans for the future. And two weeks after Myles's medical team pronounced him well enough not to need any private care—a celebratory all-clear—Amanda had packed up her things and moved down to Florida to live with Nick.

Three months after that, he'd bought a diamond ring that was worthy of her, whisked her off on a surprise trip to Key West, and proposed.

Their life was full. She'd easily found work in Miami as a per diem nurse and transitioned well. His career as an investigator was as fulfilling as he'd hoped it would be. They bought a house with three bedrooms, thinking of filling them with kids in the future. Downtime was spent hanging out at home or enjoying time with his family and the friends Nick had, along with the new friends Amanda made. Each of the Harrison siblings came to visit him over the winter, and those relationships blossomed too.

Life was good, Nick thought as he looked around his wedding reception. He looked from one face to another, seeing people he cared about and who cared about him and his bride. His gaze came to rest on his beautiful Amanda, the love of his life. She looked radiant, a stunningly beautiful and happy bride. Her blond hair was pulled back from her face and held in place with flowers, but the rest of it flowed down her back in bouncy waves. The strapless ivory gown she wore was simple but gorgeous, and she looked like an angel, or a princess, or like magic itself. She laughed at something Roni and Steph said, and Nick couldn't help but smile at her joyous smile.

He crossed the dance floor as the music played, as a soft, warm breeze blew and the palm trees shaded them from the sunshine. Eyes only for his bride, he moved in behind her to circle her waist with his hands. "Hey, Mrs. Martell," he whispered in her ear. "Dance with me."

She turned around, already smiling as she looked up at him. "I'd love to."

They moved to the dance floor as a sweet ballad played. He pulled her close, dropping a light kiss on her lips as they began to move to the music together. Her arms looped around his neck as his slid around her waist.

"Are you having a good time?" she asked.

"The best ever," he assured her. "Hope you are too?"

"Of course. I'm with the hottest guy in the place, and I get to go home with him. The food's amazing. My dress rocks. . . ." She smiled brightly. "It's a good day, yeah."

He chuckled. "You know, I was looking around at everyone . . . thinking about the last three years. So many crazy turns. Unbelievable, some of them . . ."

"That's for sure," she agreed.

"But in the end, all good." He kissed her forehead. "The best of it all, two things. Myles is alive and well, and I found you." He pressed her closer. "I'm the luckiest man in the world because I found you."

She smiled again. "I feel pretty lucky too."

He gave her a little twirl, a dip, and yanked her back to him with a dazzling smile.

"Remember how when we met, it seemed too good to be true?" he asked. "Too right, too fast, too hot, too much . . . we tried to deny it."

"I tried to leave you because it felt too good to be true," she reminded him.

"No, you didn't leave—you shoved me out the door. That's a little different."

She snorted. "Semantics, Miami Vice."

"I think that's an important distinction, Favorite Nurse."

"I think it doesn't matter now because we're married."

"Okay." A wide, warm smile spread. He felt like he hadn't stopped smiling all day. "Hey. We're married."

"We are." She moved in and pulled his head down so she could kiss his lips.

"*Te amo, mi reina bella,*" he whispered against her mouth.

"Te amo mucho," she whispered back.

While the Harrisons, Martells, Kozlovs, and their friends watched in enchantment, Nick and Amanda danced, kissed, and smiled as breezes made the palm trees sway and the sun slowly lowered in the sky.

Keep reading for an extra treat—
the full Harrisons novella

***Happily Ever After*,**

where we see Pierce and Abby tie the knot!

Loved getting to know the Harrison clan?
Then be sure to check out the entire series:

More Than You Know
Someone Like You
'Tis the Season
Between You and Me

Chapter One

Pierce Harrison looked around with something he'd only gotten used to feeling since he'd met Abby McCord: content satisfaction. It was a bone-deep, easy warmth, that contentment and sureness . . . and now the only person who'd ever enabled him to feel that way was about to become his wife.

He'd promised he'd give her the wedding of her dreams, and it seemed like it was going to be. So far, anyway. Everything had gone pretty smoothly, without much of the typical wedding planning drama he'd heard about from others. He'd simply given Abby carte blanche to do whatever she wanted. Being a millionaire had its benefits at times like these.

But his woman was no diva, and her friends and family were as down-to-earth as she was. There were times Pierce had actually had to insist that Abby choose the more expensive option if it was something she really liked, be it the entrée choices at the reception or the flowers for the tables. Abby had made his world a better place; he wanted her to have the wedding she wanted.

They'd gotten engaged the previous Thanksgiving, high on a mountain in Sedona. After a morning hike up the red rocks, under a crisp blue sky, he'd dropped to his knee and asked her to spend the rest of her life with him. Thankfully, she'd said yes and thrown her arms around him so hard, he'd fallen off balance and they'd gone crashing to the ground. They'd laughed and kissed and held each other in the red dirt, happy beyond measure. Every time he thought of it, he smiled again, infused with love.

The past nine months had flown by. She'd asked for an August wedding because she was a first-grade teacher and a summer wedding and honeymoon meant she wouldn't miss even a day of work. It made sense. But that was Abby: sensible, focused, smart . . . how Pierce had gotten someone like her to fall in love with someone like him, he sometimes still didn't know, but he thanked his lucky stars every day. This strong, grounded woman had seen past his bad-boy reputation, not cared about his tumultuous history—both in the English tabloids and within his own family—and seen the real him . . . the decent man he'd never realized was inside him until he met her.

Now he stood on the terrace of the bridal suite of the lavish, elegant Oceanview Hotel and Resort, drinking a bottle of his favorite IPA while admiring the panoramic view from seven floors up. Located in Westhampton, on the eastern end of Long Island, the five-star resort boasted magnificent lawns and grounds, with the beach and Atlantic Ocean fanning out only a few hundred feet beyond. He and Abby had arrived half an hour before, his idea. It was Wednesday afternoon and things were quiet. He wanted the two of them to have some time alone before all the friends and family descended.

There would be more than 120 guests coming to the wedding, most of whom were staying in the hotel at the resort. A select few—his older brother Charles and his family, for example—had rented some of the eight luxurious guest cottages on the property. The rehearsal dinner was Friday night and the wedding was Saturday evening. Afterward, there'd be a bonfire on the beach for the after-party and a brunch on

Sunday morning . . . a long, busy weekend of celebration. Pierce had wanted to savor the last bit of calm before the storm.

Out on the terrace, he stared out at the ocean for a while, thinking about how different his life was now than it'd been before. Two years ago this month, he'd returned to Long Island with his life in shreds. Since leaving his professional football career in tatters and leaving England altogether, life in New York had been the 180-degree turn he'd desperately needed.

He had bought partial ownership of the New York professional soccer team and gotten immersed in management there. He was heavily involved in the Edgewater Soccer Club, the local kids' league where he'd first met Abby. It was his way of giving back. Along with coaching and giving clinics, he'd been asked to join their board of directors for the new season and accepted, knowing he could make a difference. His relationships with his two older brothers had not only improved but he felt close to them, almost as solid as his always-strong bond with his sister, Tess. He spent time with his nephews and nieces . . . he was truly part of the family at long last, and it was more satisfying than he'd ever thought it could be.

And, of course, there was Abby. Loving her, and being loved by her, had been the single best thing that had ever happened to him. They now lived in a lovely four-bedroom house in Edgewater, right on the Sound, and only half a mile from her parents' house—which was what they'd wanted, for whenever the family needed babysitting help for her nephew, Dylan. Abby loved her job as a first-grade teacher, still volunteered as a soccer coach for Dylan's team, and was involved in community activities. Pierce couldn't be prouder of her or more in love with her, and that just seemed to grow with every day.

If someone had told him two years before that this was

what his life would be like, he would've laughed in their face. Small-town living? Getting married? No way.

He'd felt alone and misunderstood for most of his life. He'd acted out and rebelled in every way, even leaving the country altogether for over a decade. He'd found fame and fortune in England, living the fast life until he'd crashed and burned. And still, somehow, he'd ended up back on Long Island, with the support of his family, a career he enjoyed, and an amazing, special woman at his side. His life was richer, better, and so different from what he'd envisioned for himself. He was the last guy in the world he'd thought would have a happy ending . . . yet it was happening for him.

A soft breeze off the water ruffled the front of his dark hair, and he narrowed his eyes at the crashing waves, out to the horizon beyond. On the other side of that ocean was the life he'd left behind. He was very lucky to be where he was now, and he knew it. Small, quiet miracles . . .

He tipped back another swallow of beer, set the bottle down on the little glass table, and went back inside the bridal suite. It was elegant and lavish, all whites, taupe, glass, and chrome. A big, soft couch and plush armchairs, a tremendous flat-screen TV, a small bar in the corner . . . but no fiancée. "Abby?"

"Back here," she called from the bedroom.

Was she still unpacking? Pierce crossed the wide front room to find out. The carpet was blissfully lush beneath his bare feet. He peeked into the bedroom to find her bent over as she rustled through a suitcase on the floor. The back of her pale blue tank dress lifted a little, showing the backs of her legs. Unable to resist, he moved in behind her, gripped her hips, and rubbed himself against her. The feel of her soft, sweet ass against his cock stirred his blood.

"Oh!" she gasped, rising up and whirling around in the circle of his arms. She laughed, her dark blue eyes sparkling as she wrapped her arms around his neck. "You're naughty."

"Damn right." He grinned and squeezed her ass, pressing

her close. Blood surged south and he ground his pelvis against hers as he quipped, "It's one of the many reasons you're marrying me."

"Damn right." She grinned back, running her fingers through the back of his hair, which was a drop shorter than usual, freshly cut for the wedding. Her fingertips caressing him sent a little shiver over his skin. "I'm so glad you wanted to do this. I mean, us getting here early, being alone today and tonight before the chaos takes over . . ." She brushed her lips against his and smiled warmly. "Even driving out here with you—the windows down, the scenery, just the quiet of it—was a pleasure. Thank you for thinking of it." She kissed him, long and sweet, then looked into his eyes. He saw the deep affection there and it warmed his heart. "Thank you for *everything*," she whispered and kissed him a little harder this time. "I love you."

"I love you more." Pierce pressed his lips to hers, savoring the feel of her. Of her sweet mouth, her silky blond hair in his fingers, her warm body against his. This woman was everything. All he wanted to do this long, special weekend was show her how much she meant to him. Remind her that the coming chaos was about one single thing: them. And their love for each other. Edging her backward as they kissed, he lowered her onto the bed, himself on top of her.

"Let's get this wedding weekend started properly . . ." he whispered in her ear, nipping the lobe before he worked his way down her neck with hot, openmouthed kisses. A low hum of pleasure floated from her as his hands glided over her body. "I mean . . . I have to make the most of this." He caressed her breasts with both hands, listening to her breath catch as his thumbs stroked over her nipples. "I only get to make love to my fiancée a few more times and that's it."

"Really?" Abby asked breathlessly. Her soft hands slipped under his T-shirt and she lightly raked her fingernails down his back, sending delicious shivers along his spine. "Why? What happens then?"

"Then I get to spend the rest of my life making love to my beautiful *wife*." He kissed her hard, possessing her, and she met his heat with a matching fervor of her own. As their tongues tangled, he grasped the hem of her cotton sundress and pushed it up to bunch around her waist. "Which will make me . . ." He started moving down, dropping kisses everywhere as he went. ". . . the luckiest man on the god-damn planet." He pushed her panties to the side and sealed his mouth to where she liked it the most.

Abby opened her eyes slowly. It was dark in the room; Pierce had pulled the blackout shade at some point during the night. He loved it as dark as possible when he slept. She'd gotten used to that quickly, but it always threw her for a few seconds when she first woke up because she had no idea what time it was. A glance at the glowing blue numbers on the nightstand told her it was 8:05 A.M. They'd spent the afternoon making love, then gone downstairs for a five-star seafood dinner. They'd walked along the beach as the sun set, sat on the sand, and talked with the waves as their background music. When it finally had gotten dark, they'd gone up to their suite and back into bed. By the time she fell asleep, it was only ten o'clock, but she was so tired she'd slept like the dead. Now, feeling refreshed and glad to be able to wake up at her own pace, she stretched and rolled over to look at her fiancé.

This beautiful man had given her everything. When she'd first met him, she'd immediately written him off as an enti-tled, self-involved player, everything the gossip tabloids had said about him . . . but she was wrong. Maybe that was who he'd been before she met him, but he constantly surprised her. He had more depth and heart than he showed to most of the world. A lifetime of having to protect himself, having to guard his feelings and heart, had hardened him. Beneath the swagger, the bad-boy rep, and the façade was a kind, thoughtful man who strove to be better every single day. He'd shown her that. She'd watched him struggle, then evolve. He'd proven to her he'd be the kind of man she wanted and needed. And she'd fallen head over heels in love with his genuine efforts, with his fierce devotion . . . with him.

Now they were getting married. Three mornings from this minute, she'd wake up as Mrs. Pierce Harrison. He'd be her *husband*. The word held weight, and the thought of it sent that familiar delicious thrill rolling through her. She'd fallen in love with him thinking even though he loved her back, he wasn't the marrying type. Again he'd surprised her, turning her ideas about him on their head. He'd planned a romantic proposal on a Sedona mountaintop. He'd bought them a gorgeous house she could only dream about before, claiming he wanted to fill those extra bedrooms with kids someday. He'd bought it in her hometown because he knew how important her family was to her. He'd gladly, seamlessly found a way to make sure her parents, sister, and nephew stayed a top priority for her while not taking anything away from their growth as a couple.

He supported her, championed her, and loved her. She was marrying the man of her dreams, dreams she'd given up on before she'd met him. She was lucky and she knew it, always grateful for what she had, never taking it for granted.

She only hoped she made him feel as unequivocally supported, adored, and loved as he did her. He'd had such a lack of love and affection for most of his life; she was happy— almost eager—to give him what he needed because he'd given that to her.

Now her eyes caressed his features as he slept beside her. He was the most handsome man she knew and way sexier than his very handsome older brothers, in an edgier way, always hinting at sin—again, lucky her. Her fingers ran through his tousled dark hair as she gazed at the thick, black lashes that feathered over his chiseled cheekbones, his sensual lips, the dark scruff on his square jaw. Her hands trailed down over his strong, tattooed shoulders, his muscled, tattooed arms, his smooth chest, then slipped around his waist. She let her head drop to his chest as she snuggled close, wrapping herself around his sexy body. The sound of his slow, steady heartbeat beneath her ear soothed her now as it always did.

She had a lot to do. *So* much to do. Excitement whooshed through her as she thought of all the things ahead in the next three days . . .

Pierce's hand moved up and squeezed her ass. Still mostly asleep, he kissed her forehead and turned so he could hold her closer. Her cluster of thoughts evaporated for a moment. He often had that effect on her: making her worries dial down from a bubbling boil to a low simmer. They wrapped themselves in a cocoon of intertwined limbs and warm flesh. She kissed his neck and sighed in pure contentment as they lay together in silence.

His cell phone rang on his nightstand. They ignored it. When the noise stopped, they both exhaled and snuggled closer.

A minute later, it rang again. "Fuck them," he growled, his voice raspy with sleep. "Whoever's calling me this early, fuck them."

"That's what voice mail is for," she murmured into his skin. He grunted.

The room went quiet again. But a minute later, the phone rang again.

"Maybe it's important," Abby said. "Maybe you should answer it?"

Pierce groaned and didn't even open his eyes as he reached for the phone. "Hello?" he ground out.

Abby watched as his eyes snapped open and his expression changed into an instant combination of surprise and anger.

"Mom," he said. One small word, yet so many emotions conveyed.

Abby's insides tightened for him. He'd been avoiding his mother as much as possible since their engagement had been announced. He didn't want either of his parents involved with the wedding, or even in attendance.

She totally understood why he didn't want his father anywhere near the wedding, and the truth was, she was grateful for that. She didn't want the Harrison patriarch there either. He was nasty, harsh, and had made it clear from the start he considered Abby and her middle-class family to be beneath the mega-wealthy Harrisons. The relationship between Pierce and his father was toxic, and they weren't on speaking terms. To have Charles Harrison II there was ludicrous, and the only person who'd thought otherwise was Charles II himself. Luckily, Pierce's three wonderful siblings had run interference for him over the past months, doing damage control throughout the wedding planning. They'd surrounded their baby brother like knights or soldiers, and she knew it meant more to Pierce than he could express.

But Abby had never met his mother. She had heard about the infamous Laura Dunham Harrison Evans Baisley, who spent her time jet-setting from one tropical paradise to another. Charles II had divorced Laura and thrown her out when Pierce was only six. She'd left without looking back, barely staying in contact with her four children. In recent years, the contact had only lessened, and she hadn't shown any interest in any of her grown children or small grandchildren. She hadn't even been at Charles and Lisette's surprise wedding a few months before; she hadn't been called. Pierce's mother, as he'd often said, was a mother in name only. She hadn't raised him; the nannies had. He'd come to terms with that, but his resentment lingered, even now, as a thirty-three-year-old man.

Most of the time he didn't talk about it, and knowing him as she did, he didn't think about it. But Abby knew that deep down, the pain of his mom leaving him behind, combined with leaving him in the care of his father, who had no love for him and alternated between ignoring him and excoriating him, would be a deep wound forever. It was one of the reasons he'd opened himself to Abby's family so readily; hers was a true, close-knit, loving family, and Pierce responded to that.

Even so, when he'd initially told Abby he wanted neither of his parents at the wedding, she wasn't sure it was the way to go. She didn't want him to possibly regret that decision later. But she stood by his choices 100 percent. If he didn't want them there, fine with her, end of story. She wanted him happy.

"What do you want, Mom?" he half growled. "You woke me up and I'm not a morning person. Calling three times this early without just leaving a message is obnoxious. I don't appreciate it."

Abby's insides tensed at the hardness of his voice, and how quickly he'd opened the gate to an argument. He had a temper he usually managed to keep under wraps. But when it flared, he was formidable, intimidating, a powerful force. She felt the tension now coiling in his body as she still held him. He closed his eyes and sighed while he listened to whatever Laura was saying, and Abby hugged him gently to show her support. His hand ran up and down her back in response.

"Stop it," he spat into the phone. "You're a piece of work, calling me this early, two days before my wedding, to lay a fucking guilt trip on me. Which just shows why I don't want you here in the first place." He laughed, a caustic, hollow sound, and Abby's heart rate started to rise for him.

"Seriously, Mom? You really want to hear me say the words? Is that what it'll take? Fine." His eyes opened and he pushed away from Abby, as if the surge of anger was too much and he had to expend the burst of adrenaline. He threw back the covers, sprang out of bed, and began to pace the room as he spoke into the phone.

"You left me—you left us all—and you never looked back," he said flatly. "No . . . no, you didn't . . . holy crap, stop it. Don't start with the phony tears and the blame and the bullshit. I don't want to hear it . . . what? . . . Yes, Dad made it hard for you to see us. But you could have if you wanted to. You didn't want to. That's fine. But you don't get to play spurned mommy now. . . . Yes, I know, you were hurt. Poor you. Like you didn't have *four kids* who were hurting, who wanted and needed their mother. Luckily, we don't any-more . . . no. None of us want you around and we sure as hell don't need you . . . what? That's harsh? It's the truth . . . no. Fuck no. That's one hundred percent on *you*."

Suddenly, whatever Laura was saying made him stop in his tracks. "You've got to be kidding me." His jaw clenched and he gritted his teeth, then said in a low, deliberate tone, "I'm warning you right now. *Hear me.* Do not show up here on Saturday. Do. Not. Am I being very clear?"

Abby's eyes flew wide at that. Was Laura planning to come to the wedding? Whoa, she was ballsy.

"Because I'll throw you out myself." Pierce raked his free hand through his hair, pure frustration apparent as his marine-blue eyes flashed. "Oh, believe it. Try me . . . yes, I feel that strongly about it. . . . You really don't get it. This only proves how selfish you are! . . . Yeah, Mom, it *is* selfish, actually. Because I've made it pretty fucking clear I don't want you here. Don't you think? . . . All right, enough. Stop. Here's the deal." He spread his feet, digging in his stance, as if she were there and he was telling her to her face. "You don't get to come to my wedding, the most important day of my life, and parade around like you're someone special. You aren't. And I want no drama and no bullshit. You? Are pure drama and bullshit . . . yeah, you are." He started pacing again as he listened, then burst out, "Only the people who mean something to me will be here to share in this, and that sure as hell isn't you. So don't waste your plane fare with a surprise appearance. You. Are. Not. Welcome. Here."

Abby's heart squeezed for him. She'd known he thought these things because he'd told her, in the calm quiet of their home, with her arms wrapped securely around him. But he'd never before said them out loud to his mother. Now his free hand clenched in a fist. Years of repressed rage were pouring out and the air around them had gone electric with it. She sat up as she watched him pace furiously, aching for him.

"No, Mom. Sorry, but no." He snorted out a laugh. "It's really a lot simpler than that. The way I see it, if you weren't around for me in my bad times—hell, around *at all*—you don't get to be with me for the good times. That's all there is to it."

He glanced over at Abby for a second. It was all she could do not to go to him, take the phone out of his hand, throw it off the terrace, and hold him tight. But she knew him well enough to let him get it out and just be there. Her presence was enough.

"Yeah? Really?" His voice was lethal. Abby hadn't seen him this angry in a long time. "I haven't heard from you in months. But you call me two days before my wedding to get at me and I'm supposed to feel bad that you're hurt? I don't . . . no, in fact, I'm glad it's all out there and you know exactly how I feel. It's cathartic really . . . right. That's right. Okay, then. We're done now. Buh-bye." He ended the call and threw the phone across the room with all his might. It sailed through the air and hit the pillows. He swore violently and raked his hands through his hair, then scrubbed them over his face as he swore again.

"Pierce," Abby said. "Take a deep breath."

He looked at her, his eyes wild and bright.

"You're okay."

He snorted, the angst coming off him in waves.

"She won't come here," Abby said gently. "Neither of your parents will. Everything will be fine."

"I gotta get outta here." He strode to the dresser and rummaged through the drawers. "I'm sorry, babe."

"Don't be. I understand. Go ahead."

"I need to go for a run. I just . . . I gotta go."

"Good idea," she said. "Go run on the beach. Pound at the sand."

"That's where I'm going." He yanked on his clothes with hard, jerky motions, his jaw clenched tight and his face flushed. Then he went to the closet, found where Abby had put his sneakers, and got them on. "I'll see you later."

She watched him, her heart beating fast. His stress was hers. His pain was hers. "I love you," she said.

He was halfway to the door but stopped cold at her soft words. Then he came to her, stroked both hands over her hair, and dropped a kiss on the top of her head. "Thank God for that." He kissed her mouth, a quick peck. "I'm too fired up. Let me go let off steam. When I get back, I'll be fine. I'm not going to let her ruin our day. Promise."

"Go," she said, stroking his cheek.

He practically flew out of the room. She heard the slam of the door and sighed. Damn his parents, both of them. What a stellar job they'd done. They'd never done right by their youngest son and they still had the power to upset him, even now that he had his own life. It tore her apart to know he was hurting, and he was. Even talking to either of his parents seemed to bring back all the unresolved hurt and anger with only a few words. Abby could only hope it wouldn't be like that forever. For *his* sake.

She swallowed back the anger and bitter sadness, then went to take a shower and start the day. If Pierce could find a way to sweep their sins aside, she had to do that too.

Chapter Two

Pierce knocked on the door of the guest cottage closest to the hotel. He could hear sounds on the other side of the door, his nephews' voices, loud and wild. The door opened and his oldest brother stood there, looking slightly harried.

"Hey! Great to see you." Charles affectionately clapped his shoulder and brought him inside. Pierce saw Thomas and Myles running around the front room, circling the leather sofa with Nerf guns and yelling as Ava sat with her head down over her tablet.

"Barely controlled chaos," Pierce remarked.

"As usual," Charles said. "I was about to take the boys to play outside, but I'm waiting for Tess to get here. I thought you were her."

"She's here?" Pierce asked, waving hi to Ava as she looked up at him and smiled.

"She should be," Charles said. "She said she'd be here by noon because we were planning to be. She's been great about helping Lisette with the baby. Comes over almost every day."

Pierce nodded. Their sister was one of the kindest people he'd ever known. That Tess would take time out of her schedule to help with their newest niece, even though Charles had hired a new nanny and had a full household staff, didn't surprise him one bit. "Well, you want me to get the boys out of here before they wreck the place?"

"That would be great, actually." Charles sighed and pushed his hand through his dark, wavy hair, then adjusted his black-rimmed glasses. "Maybe you could just take them out front, onto the grass? And I'll join you guys as soon as Tess gets here. I just don't want to leave Lisette here alone with the baby in case she needs anything."

As if on cue, there was a knock on the door. Charles practically raced to it.

"Oh, thank God," he breathed, hugging his sister hello.

"That bad?" Tess asked with a laugh.

"The kids are stir-crazy," Charles said. "And I didn't want to leave Lisette alone."

"I'm here, you're free, 'bye now," Tess singsonged. She swept back her long mane of dark curls as she walked in, then realized her younger brother was standing there. "Hey! It's the groom!" She embraced Pierce tightly. "How are you holding up?"

"Truth?" Pierce asked. "I was fine until early this morning." He saw both his siblings' faces change to expressions of concern and rushed to add, "I'm okay now. Just . . . still a little edgy." He briefly told them about the phone call from their mother.

"I'll handle it," Charles said firmly, immediately shifting into oldest brother protective mode. His eyes flashed with cool fury. "I don't want you to think about anything but your wedding and Abby. You leave the family drama to me, all right?"

"And me," Tess said. She put her hands on Pierce's shoulders. "We've got this. Don't waste another thought on her. Go be happy."

"I will. But first, I'm going to help Charles with these rowdy kids." Pierce leaned forward to scoop up little Myles into his arms as he ran by.

Myles laughed and wiggled. "Put me down, Uncle Pierce!"

"Nope. Outside, you rugrats!" Pierce joked. "Let's go!" He shifted the seven-year-old over his shoulder like a sack of potatoes and headed for the door. Charles opened it for him and they went outside.

"Come on, you," Charles commanded his other son, and Thomas followed. He looked over to his daughter. "Ava? Want to come outside with us for a while?"

"No," Ava said, not lifting her eyes from the tablet in her hands. "I'll stay here with Aunt Tess and Lisette. And Charlotte."

Charles grinned. Ava was over-the-moon in love with her new baby half sister, and he was grateful for that. "Okay, sweetie. But if you change your mind, I think we're going down to the beach. Feel free to join us."

"Mm-hmm." Ava didn't look up.

He chuckled, then looked to Tess, and the grin fell away. "So. Let's talk for a minute about Mom."

Tess hissed out a disdainful breath. "I'll call her now."

"No, I'll do it when I get back. I'd do it this second, but the boys—"

"Stop. I'll do it." Tess moved closer and dropped her voice so Ava wouldn't hear. "You've been running interference between Pierce and Dad for months. You had to listen to her squawking when she found out you got married and didn't let her know until after it'd happened. Let me take this one. Share the burden."

He held her gaze for a long beat, then sighed in acquiescence. "All right." Charles patted her arm. "Family drama tag. You're it."

She snorted out a laugh. "It never ends, does it?"

"I thought we had it handled with my keeping Dad away from all this. But Mom? Goddammit. If she shows up here . . ." Charles drew a deep breath, as if to re-center himself. "No. She won't. We'll see to that."

"That's right. So go. It's a gorgeous day out, this property is gorgeous, and we're all here to have a nice time," Tess said. "Go enjoy the kids, have fun. And keep Pierce's mind off it too. That's what you can do right now. You have your orders."

"Yes, ma'am." He gave a jaunty salute. "Lisette's with the baby, last bedroom in the back, down the hall. They were trying to take a nap, but the boys were so loud, I don't know if they actually fell asleep or not."

A few minutes later, Tess tiptoed into the master bedroom at the back of the three-bedroom cottage. It was a lovely room, decorated in white, taupe, and sky blue, a beach motif. The king-size bed had gauzy white fabric draped over the four wooden posts. Lisette lay on her side toward the edge of the mattress, very still, within arm's reach of the small white bassinet beside the bed. Tess was glad to see her sister-in-law was asleep. Like any new mom, Lisette hadn't gotten much sleep since giving birth to Charlotte only three weeks before, even with the help of a new nanny, Charles, and Tess herself. She'd made a point of going there for a few hours almost every day.

Tess moved around the bed to the bassinet and peeked inside at Charlotte—also asleep. Her heart smiled. There was her tiny new niece, the precious, perfect sweet pea, cute as could be as she slept on her back. Tess watched the newborn's chest move up and down, up and down, mesmerized. She had fallen head over heels in love with this baby. Charlotte was eight pounds of pure love and joy. It was all Tess could do not to pick her up and hold her, but she would never disturb her as she slept. She gazed down at her for another minute, then tiptoed toward the door.

But as she got there, as if on cue, Charlotte squeaked in her bassinet. Tess rushed back, hoping to get to the baby before she woke her mother.

Lisette stirred, her eyes opening halfway, weary and clouded.

"I've got her," Tess whispered as she reached into the bassinet. She lifted Charlotte into her arms and held her close to her chest, cradling her. "Get some sleep; you need it. I've got her, it's fine. Go back to sleep."

"Thank you so much," Lisette murmured, and her dark eyes slid closed.

Tess's heart gave a little pang for her. Lisette usually woke up when Charlotte did, ready to care for her even if she was tired; if Lisette had given in that easily, she must've been truly exhausted.

Even though Charlotte was such a newborn, and Pierce and Abby had made it clear they understood if Lisette wasn't up to coming to the wedding, Lisette had brushed that off. There was no way they'd miss it. And with the added benefit of the family being cozily ensconced in their own private cottage—away from germy strangers and not having to worry about the noise of a newborn at all hours—Lisette had insisted on the whole clan going for the long weekend. Tess admired her tenacity but sympathized with the truth of how drained she must be. Tess was more than happy to help them out however she could.

Charlotte squawked and fussed. Her tiny cries sounded like the mewling of a kitten, and Tess left the room holding her before Lisette woke up again. She walked into the next empty room—the one the boys were sharing—and rocked Charlotte gently as she *shh-shh-shhed* her. In a minute, the baby was fast asleep on her aunt, her little face pressed to the exposed skin at the base of Tess's neck. Tess moved to sit on one of the two twin beds, leaning against the wall for back support as she held her precious niece close.

She ran her fingers ever so lightly over the baby's dark hair, then her back, then up and over again. She inhaled her sweet baby smell and listened to the wondrous sound of her breathing. Holding Charlotte made Tess's ovaries ache. She wanted this. She wanted a baby of her own so badly. The more time she spent with her new niece, the louder her biological clock seemed to tick. She was thirty-seven now, with no prospects for a loving partner, much less a baby daddy. The now familiar pangs of longing and sadness hit her heart and sank in their claws once again.

Maybe one day, hopefully much sooner than later, she'd meet someone. She used to yearn to find a wonderful man to fall in love with, have a family with . . . that hadn't worked out. Nowadays, she merely longed for the family part. She'd always wanted kids. Was it in the cards for her? Time would tell.

Swallowing a sigh, she held Charlotte close and savored the feel of her.

On Thursday night, Pierce and Abby sat together as they watched some of their friends and family hang out. The resort had a separate cottage, right on the beach, equipped with a manned bar, a billiards table, flat-screen TVs and Xbox One games, and a karaoke machine. Pierce and Abby's guests had all but taken over the whole resort; the rest of the guests would make it a complete occupation on Friday and Saturday.

Pierce's brother Dane and his wife, Julia, had arrived about two hours before. Dane had commandeered the billiards table, taking on first his wife, then her son, Colin, and now Troy, Pierce's best friend. He laughed as he heard their trash talk. Pierce had met Troy at fifteen, when he'd started a new private high school after being thrown out of an elite prep school. Pierce was all about making trouble back then, the very picture of a rebellious teen acting out against his father. Pierce and Troy, a whip-smart kid from a normal, middle-class family, were the two best soccer players in the school, even as sophomores. But instead of becoming fierce competitors, they'd become fast friends, a force to be reckoned with. When Pierce left for England right after high school graduation, he and Troy had stayed solid. After all, Pierce hadn't had many true friends in his life—it was hard to find and trust kids who liked him for who he was, instead of what perks the Harrison name could bring. He wasn't going to let that friendship fall by the wayside. He could be himself with Troy, and that was a gift. Now, Troy was his best man for his wedding; that way, he hadn't had to choose between his two older brothers. They were his two grooms-men instead.

The wedding party was small, for which Pierce was grateful. Bigger wedding parties meant bigger potential for drama, and he had no patience for that. Abby's maid of honor was her older sister, Fiona, and her two bridesmaids were her best friend, Allison, and Tess. Ava, Pierce's niece, would be their flower girl, and Dylan, Abby's nephew, would be the ring bearer. That was it. It was a close-knit family affair, which was what both Pierce and Abby had wanted. The closest thing to a drama queen in that mix was feisty Fiona, but she'd been nothing but supportive throughout the wedding planning. All had gone smoothly and well.

The only drama, Pierce mused as he reached for his beer, had come from his side. From his obnoxious parents. He knew Charles had basically put himself in front of their father like a stone pillar, blocking his attempts to get at Pierce or interfere in any way. Pierce was more grateful for that than he could express. But now, just when he'd been at ease knowing his father wouldn't crash the rehearsal dinner or wedding, to get a call as he had from his mother that morning . . . man, had that pissed him off. He'd gone for a run on the beach, pounding the sand beneath his feet, not happy until he felt the burn in his muscles and his lungs. Why had she rattled him so hard? He wasn't sure why. And more than that, he still hadn't shaken it off completely.

"Hello?" Abby waved her hand in front of his face. "You didn't hear a word I just said, did you?"

"No," he admitted. "Sorry, zoned out there." He slid an arm around her shoulders and pulled her close. "What'd you say?"

She leaned in closer and whispered in his ear, "Your best man keeps stealing glances at my maid of honor."

He pulled back, his eyebrows lifting in surprise. "Seriously?"

"Totally." Abby tried to suppress a grin and failed. "Your bestie's hot for my sister. Should we do something about it?"

"Like what?"

"I don't know . . . help them along?"

Pierce snorted out a laugh and sipped his beer. "No." He watched Troy from across the room, playing pool with Dane. Fiona was sitting with Tess and Julia, talking and laughing. Pierce waited . . . waited . . . there it was. Sure enough, Troy discreetly darted a glance over at Fiona. Pierce knew that look. Shit, the guy was burning for her. Busted.

"I'll be damned," Pierce murmured, more amused than anything.

"You know," Abby said, keeping her voice low, "if they hooked up, I'd be more than fine with it."

"Oh yeah?" Pierce laughed. "I'm sure Troy will totally go for it now, knowing he has your approval."

Abby pinched his thigh under the table, making Pierce yelp.

"Smart-ass," she muttered with a chuckle. "But really. Think about it. They have a lot in common. They both grew up in Edgewater, even though they didn't know each other because they went to different schools."

Pierce sat back, sensing she had a list.

"They've both been divorced for a long time," Abby continued, "so it's not a rebound thing. He has a daughter, she has a son, close in age—so they both understand what it's like to be a single parent. They're both really nice. And they both probably really need a hot fling. So why not?"

Pierce gave her a long, bemused look. "You've been thinking about this, huh?"

"Well yeah, ever since I caught him checking her out last week. But it's adorable." Abby's voice dropped to a whisper. "They'd be great together. We should work on this."

"Ha! Um, no. The only thing I want to work on right now," Pierce said, "is getting married." He dropped a quick kiss on her lips. "Besides, Troy doesn't need any help. If he wants her, and he wants to do something about it, he will. He's a big boy."

"I hope so," Abby said. "Because now that I can picture them together, I really want it to happen."

"Leave them alone, Abby."

She huffed out a sigh. "Fiiiine. Excuse me for wanting to play matchmaker."

Pierce chuckled and drew her in for another kiss. "You're such a sap."

"I *am* a sap," she admitted. She looked into his eyes. "I'm happy, so I want everyone around me to be happy too."

"A noble desire. But not realistic."

"Why not?" Abby's dark blue eyes sparked as she added, "You know what? My sister is fabulous; she really is. And she got a raw deal in the love department. I just want her to find someone who makes her happy, someone who loves and supports her." She touched his scruffy cheek. "Like what I have with you."

"Aww." He was teasing, but his heart warmed from her words. "You're gonna make me blush."

"I mean it," she said. "You think I'm being a Pollyanna."

"Maybe a little. But I know you mean it. You have a huge, wonderful heart. And sometimes, when you say things like that, it's easier for me to tease you because . . . it hits home." He trailed the backs of his fingers along her soft cheek as she looked back at him. "You say things like that and it reminds me how lucky I am. How lucky *we* are. That we found each other and made it work. I look at us now, think of where we're going together, and . . ." He swallowed hard. His throat had thickened with a sudden rush of emotion. "I'm so glad I make you happy. That means the world to me. *You* mean the world to me, Abby." He stared at her, sifted through her golden hair with gentle fingers, and took her mouth in a deep kiss, hoping it conveyed what he felt.

Chapter Three

Pierce started Friday morning with a run on the beach with Dane at his side. His brother was six years older than him but was as serious about staying in shape as he was. Since Dane had moved to Blue Harbor and Pierce had moved to Edgewater—only a few miles apart—they often met for morning runs by the Long Island Sound. Pierce no longer had to be as fit as when he was playing pro soccer but found he felt sluggish and off when he didn't keep up some kind of fitness routine. Dane claimed the same. That, and his running joke: that he had "a sexually insatiable wife he needed to stay in shape for." Julia always laughed as she smacked him for that, but Pierce noticed she hadn't once denied it.

The brothers dropped to the sand after roughly six miles, panting and sweating. They gulped water and did cool-down stretches.

"Still can't believe you're getting married tomorrow," Dane said with a grin.

"Me neither," Pierce admitted. He glanced out at the ocean from behind his sunglasses, taking in the fantastic view. "Can I ask you something? I've always been curious."

"Sure." Dane adjusted his baseball cap to keep the sun out of his eyes.

"When you proposed to Julia . . . you were totally sure about it, right?"

"Without an ounce of doubt." Dane peered at his brother. "Why, are you having doubts?"

"No. No, not at all," Pierce assured him. "I was wondering why you eloped."

"Aha." Dane grinned. "Because once I proposed and she said yes, the thought of having to wait a year to throw a big wedding . . . it wasn't what I wanted. She didn't want a big wedding either. So, we wanted to be married, decided the other stuff wasn't for us, and that was it." He shrugged as he added, "Also, I've always had a bit of a problem with impulse control."

Pierce laughed. "You and I share that trait."

"We share more than a few, actually," Dane remarked. "You and me . . . we were the serial daters."

"I didn't even date," Pierce said quietly. "I slept around. Hit and ran."

"And Abby changed all that."

"Well . . . I was trying to change it just before I met her, but yeah, once I met her . . . I didn't want anyone else. I knew she was it for me." Pierce kicked at the sand in front of him. "I sound like a sap, don't I?"

"Nope. Either that or I did too, because that's exactly how I felt when I fell for Julia. No one compared." Dane leaned in. "They still don't. My wife is extraordinary."

"I feel that way about Abby."

"Good. You should. Means you're doing the right thing." Dane stared at his younger brother for a long beat. "You're gonna do okay, you know."

Pierce met his gaze. "I worry sometimes. I think about Mom and Dad and . . ."

"I know. I get it. I did too." Dane nodded, then lightened his tone. "But if I can carry this marriage thing off with such panache, so will you. Abby is an amazing woman. She's grounded and she keeps you grounded. You're already involved with her family, who are a really decent, good group of people. Not only am I *not* worried about you, I'm thrilled for you." Dane put a hand on his brother's forearm and added kindly, "I hope with them—the McCords, I mean—you're feeling the kind of extended family love and support you never had growing up."

Pierce blinked in surprise. "Yeah, I didn't, but I feel it now. Always had Tess, but now I have you and Charles too. And your wives and his kids. That all matters. A lot."

Dane nodded. "Good. Good, I'm glad."

"I know you've all been keeping Dad away from the wedding too."

"Well, Chuckles gets most of the credit for that, really."

"You and Tess helped. I know that. I'm trying to say I'm grateful." Pierce rubbed the back of his neck as he thought. "I was thinking the other day how different my life is now from just two years ago. It's a total one-eighty, you know?"

"Yeah," Dane said. "Because you worked hard for it. That credit goes to *you*."

"I guess. I just . . ." Pierce looked out at the water again. "I've just been very aware lately of . . . how lucky I am. I'm so damn grateful for Abby and the life we have. It's, um . . . a little overwhelming sometimes."

Dane nodded slowly, seeming to take that in. Then he murmured, "You deserve this good life, Pierce. You hear me?"

Pierce's eyes flew back to his. He didn't say anything.

"You deserve this happiness," Dane said. "You deserve Abby, you deserve what you've built together, and you deserve peace. I thought you knew that by now."

Pierce swallowed hard. His throat had thickened and his mouth had gone dry. "I don't want to let her down," he whispered.

"You won't," Dane assured him.

"I don't want to suck at this," Pierce said. "It's too important."

"You feel that strongly about it," Dane said, "you won't."

Pierce licked his dry lips. "I hope so."

"Look. This is a marathon, not a sprint. Marriage takes work. There are boring times. There are hard times. But it'll also transform your life. Because . . ." Dane paused, searching for the right words. "Guys like us? Who thought we'd never settle down, like getting married was a fate worse than death? When we found the right women, it changed us for the better, right? We changed. We grew. We'll keep evolving and growing. And we're gonna fuck up sometimes because we're human, and that's okay. As long as we keep trying." Dane snorted out a laugh as he added, "We've got the prime example of what we don't want: Mom and Dad. So use that. Learn from their mistakes. Whatever they did, do the opposite."

Pierce chuckled at that. "Good tip."

"It's true, though." Dane took off his cap, scratched at his damp curls, then put it back on. "They were both selfish. Never put the other one first. Demanded everything and gave each other nothing. So when in doubt, I remember that. And I love Julia so much, it's easy to want to give and listen and work at it, because she makes me want to. You have that with Abby, from what I've seen and what you're telling me. She also happens to love you as much as you love her, also from what I've seen. So stop worrying." Dane squeezed his shoulder in support. "You're gonna be fine, bro. I know it."

"Thanks." Pierce nodded and exhaled. "I think . . . I think you were the one I needed to have this talk with."

"I get that. Like I said, we have a lot in common."

"Nah, you're nicer than me," Pierce joked. "Not as surly."

"So true," Dane joked back. "I'm also wiser, more stylish, better-looking, and infinitely more charming. Don't forget all that."

"Like you'd let me." Pierce smiled wide. "But hey, you're also older. Like *so* much older. You just turned thirty-nine . . . before we know it, you'll be *forty*. Geezer."

Dane grimaced. "All right, shut up, you. And get off my lawn."

Abby floated back up to her room at one o'clock. She'd just come from the spa, where she'd enjoyed one of the best massages she'd ever had in her life. It had been a gift from Tess: massages for Abby, Fiona, and their mother. Tess was always so thoughtful and generous. Abby adored her.

After all, Tess was the one person who'd always watched over Pierce and made him feel like someone cared about him, from when they were small kids all the way through adulthood. Tess was the one family member Pierce trusted and counted on, back before he'd restored his relationships with his brothers. When Pierce's soccer career tanked and he needed a safe haven to lie low while he licked his wounds, he'd gone to the one person and place in the world he felt secure: to Tess. If he hadn't come back to Long Island to stay with his beloved sister, he and Abby would never have met. Tess and Abby both adored Pierce and had bonded over that. Needless to say, Tess held a special place in Abby's heart.

Abby sat on the plush couch that faced the back wall, with its wide windows and magnificent views of the property and the beach and the ocean just beyond. As she sighed in contentment for the umpteenth time, she picked up her cell phone and texted a gushing thanks to Tess for the massage, then texted her fiancé. Hey there, handsome. Where are you?

Pierce's text came back immediately. At the pool with Charles and the kids. Come on down!

Sounds good, she wrote, but no thanks. The massage left me boneless. I'm basking in the afterglow, melting into a puddle of happy goo in our suite. Might take a nap. You enjoy.

I'll be up soon, he responded. Might want to take advantage of you in goo mode.

Stay if you're having fun! she wrote back. Seriously, I might
fall asleep.

Okay. Enjoy your afterglow. See you later. Love you.

Love you too. xo

Abby put down the phone to enjoy the view of the sea and
sky for a few minutes. When her eyes grew heavy, she got
up and went into the bedroom to burrow into the luxurious
bed. As if on cue, there was a knock at the door.

She wasn't expecting anyone, but anyone coming to see
her was friendly, so she opened it without hesitation.

"Miss McCord?" said a hotel employee from behind a
tremendous bouquet of colorful flowers.

"That's me."

"Then these are for you."

"How nice! Come on in."

Abby watched as the young man placed the bouquet on
the glass table in the middle of the sitting area. She thanked
him, closed the door behind him, then went to the flowers
with an enchanted smile on her face. The flowers were beautiful, and she dipped her face down to smell them before
plucking the small white card from its holder.

> *Dear Abby,*
> *Wishing you well as you*
> *officially join the family.*
> *Hope the wedding is lovely.*
> *Best, CRH II*

Abby was so shocked she dropped the card. Pierce's
father had sent these? He'd made no attempt to hide his dis-
taste for her from the beginning. His words floated through
her head as she recalled some of his choice phrases: "gold
digger . . . blue collar . . . nothing special." She'd disliked

him for his disparaging comments about her, but they didn't really matter. What she hated him for was the way he'd purposely tried to drive a wedge between her and Pierce simply because the man couldn't stand to see his son happy. It'd almost worked too. But his attacks had only served to draw them closer together.

Pierce . . . oh God. Abby frowned hard. When he saw the flowers and the card, Pierce would *not* be happy. In fact, he might go ballistic.

Abby stared at them, thinking about what she should do. Do nothing and keep the flowers? Send them back? Get rid of them? She just wanted to keep Pierce happy. The wedding was only twenty-eight hours away now . . .

Her phone dinged with a text and she went to check it. It was from Tess saying, I'm so glad you loved it! That makes me happy. Mission accomplished!

Could you call me? Abby wrote back. I need to ask you something.

The phone rang in fifteen seconds. "What's up?" Tess asked.

"Umm . . . I don't want to sound like a drama queen," Abby said, "or possibly be making a big deal out of something that isn't a big deal. But . . . I just got a huge bouquet of flowers, here in the room. From your father."

"Oh God," Tess groaned. "Pierce will flip out."

Abby exhaled. "That was my exact reaction. I feel better now. But what should I do? I don't want to hide anything from him, but he was already upset yesterday by your mother's call. I'm thinking if he sees this now . . ."

"I'll be there in a few minutes," Tess said. "I'll take them back to my room. Done deal."

Relief washed over Abby. "I'm not overreacting, then?"

"Nope. Pierce has a short fuse when it comes to our parents on a good day. Seeing those flowers today could make him blow up. He's already a little high-strung because of the wedding."

"I noticed," Abby said. "I mean, the whole time he's been so laid-back about everything. All the wedding planning, you know? Until we got here. Now . . . I thought *I'd* be the one who'd be tense with all the last-minute things, but *he's* the one who's tense."

"It's not about you, if that's what you're thinking," Tess assured her. "It's that he desperately wants everything to be perfect. *For you.* He wants to give you the wedding of your dreams . . . and his parents are reminders of his unhappy past. He doesn't want that—or them—touching this weekend. He wants perfection. They remind him of how far from perfect he was before he found you. Does that make any sense?"

Abby sighed. "I suppose."

"I'm so glad I texted when I did," Tess said. "I'll be there in two minutes."

While Abby waited, she thought over what Tess had said. The rehearsal dinner was only a few hours away. Getting him alone might be difficult. But at some point, she needed to have a heart-to-heart talk with her soon-to-be husband.

Chapter Four

Abby looked around, utterly enchanted with everything she saw. Their rehearsal dinner was being held out on the massive back patio, on a deck canopied by trees that went right up to the edge of the beach. Six round tables were topped in cream-colored linens, bright flowers, and candles. Music played from some hidden sound system, soft acoustic guitar over ethereal keyboards. Paper lanterns hung from the surrounding trees and thousands of tiny white lights had been strung everywhere, making the twilight sparkle and shimmer, transforming the space into something magical. She couldn't help but sigh in sheer delight.

Pierce slid his arm around her waist to pull her closer and murmured into her ear, "You like it?"

"I love it," she gushed. "It's beautiful. I can't believe it."

"I'm so glad it's how you hoped it'd be." He pressed a kiss to her temple.

She turned into him for a long, tight hug. Her head rested on his chest as their arms wrapped around each other. "I love this," she said. "And I love you."

"Oh, good. I mean, because we're getting married tomorrow and all."

"I can't wait." She pulled back to smile at him. "We were standing there during the rehearsal and I kept staring at you and thinking, 'This time tomorrow, it'll be real. We'll be married.' And Pierce . . . I can't wait."

He smiled down at her, his fingers caressing her cheek, before he lowered his head to press his lips to hers. "Me too, baby. Me too." He kissed her again, long and sweet. Her arm curled around his neck to hold him as they kissed.

"All right, all right, enough of that." Dane's jovial voice broke into their moment. "Come on, you lovesick kids. Time to eat, drink, and be merry. You can get it on later."

Pierce shook his head and snorted, giving his brother's arm a light punch as he passed. Dane grunted and rubbed his arm, then kept walking to join his wife.

The sixty guests mingled, enjoying the evening as the sun fell farther into the horizon. Soft breezes blew off the ocean, bringing its salty scent. Drinks and hors d'oeuvres were passed around, people talked and laughed, and music played.

Pierce glanced around, taking note of where his nearest and dearest were situated. Charles and Lisette had the table closest to the wall. Dane and Tess were with them; Dane had tiny Charlotte in his arms, making silly faces and trying to charm their newest family member. Tess laughed at whatever he was saying to the baby, her smile radiant. Julia was by the railing with Abby and her sister, talking and looking gorgeous. Charles's three kids and Abby's nephew, Dylan, all sat in a huddle at the edge of the deck. Thomas held a tablet in his lap and they were watching a video or playing a game or something. While Pierce felt bad because the kids were likely bored at something like this, he was glad his niece and nephews had made Dylan feel so welcome, instantly a part of them. Abby's parents sat at one of the tables with her aunts and uncles, talking and laughing. Various friends filled in the spaces. Seemed like everyone was enjoying themselves. Pierce allowed himself to exhale.

Troy came up to his side and said, "You still throw a good party."

"Thanks," Pierce replied, "but I can't take credit. Abby planned all this, chose everything." He smirked. "Besides, this is really nice but tame. Too elegant for you to think I planned it."

"Good point."

"I mean, it's not like I can really let loose with my soon-to-be in-laws here."

"Another good point."

"The bonfire on the beach tomorrow night, after the wedding? *That*'ll be fun."

"Want tequila shots there?"

"Sounds like a plan."

"I'll make sure to bring them, then."

"You're the best best man ever."

They clinked their beer bottles and sipped.

"Still can't believe you're getting married," Troy said. "But I have to say . . . I've never seen you so . . . well, content. Like you've finally found peace." He looked across the deck to where Abby and Fiona stood as Julia walked away from them. "I'm happy for you, man. Seriously."

"Thanks." Pierce gazed across the deck to his fiancée. Abby's straight blond hair swayed as a breeze lifted the ends. The same breeze made the hem of her gauzy sky-blue dress seem to float around her ankles. She smiled broadly at something Fiona said. "It's all her," Pierce murmured. "Everything."

"I know," Troy said. "Well, we Edgewater folks are pretty damn awesome."

"That's the truth. Speaking of Edgewater folks . . ." Pierce lifted a wicked brow at his best friend. "Fiona's pretty nice to look at, huh?"

Troy blinked, then huffed out a breath. "Shit. Am I that obvious?"

"Only a little." Pierce chuckled. "Fiona's gorgeous, no

question. Smart, with a good heart. You have some things in common. Could be fun. Could be more than fun. But I'm warning you, she's feisty as hell. Think you can handle her?"

"I'd love to find out." Troy took a swig from his bottle.

"Well, then." Pierce fixed him with a look. "You gonna do anything about it this weekend?"

"Hell yes."

"Attaboy."

After the salad plates had been cleared away, Dane turned, scanned the length of the wide patio, and realized his wife still wasn't there. Maybe she'd slipped away to use the restroom? He nabbed a waiter and ordered another beer. After he got it, he chatted briefly with Abby's parents. They were nice people, smart, down-to-earth. Dane could see where Abby got such a good base from, and a wave of sentimentality whopped him. He'd found himself expressing personal thanks to them for welcoming Pierce into their family as warmly and completely as they had. Carolyn and Jesse had seemed genuinely moved by that. It was a nice talk . . . but then he'd realized he'd almost finished his beer and Julia still hadn't returned.

A glance at his watch showed she'd been gone for almost half an hour. Where the hell was she?

Determined, he left the deck and went into the hotel. His long legs carried him down the hallway toward the restrooms. Never shy, he pushed open the door to the ladies' room just a few inches and called out, "Red, you in there?"

"Dane?" Tess emerged from one of the stalls and gave him a strange look. "What are you doing?"

"Looking for my wife, obviously."

Tess went to the sinks to wash her hands as she said, "I thought I saw her go down to the beach. Figured she was meeting you there or something. But that was a while ago."

"Well, at least I know she's not in here," he quipped. "Thanks, Tesstastic. Catch you later."

He cut through the hotel, out to a side door, around to one of the staircases. From the grass, he could see the enormous raised back patio a few feet away; the sounds of the rehearsal dinner floated on the air. He walked until the lawn beneath his feet ended at the sand, then kicked off his shoes to step onto the beach. The crashing waves of the ocean sounded nearby, just beyond, hidden in the black of night. His eyes hadn't fully adjusted to the dark yet, but he scanned the area as best he could.

"Julia?" he called out. "Are you out here?"

"Yes. Over here."

He turned at the sound of his wife's rich alto, peering harder into the darkness. "Can't see you, babe. Where are you?"

"Walk straight about another eight or ten steps, then turn a tiny bit left."

He did as she said, squinting in the night, and found her sitting on the sand, her dress floating around her, her knees drawn up and her arms around them. "*There* you are."

"Yup," she said plainly. "Here I am."

He dropped to the sand to sit beside her, then studied her. Julia sat very still, her thick red hair drifting off her shoulders from the breeze, her gaze out on the ocean. She would likely seem relaxed to someone who didn't know her well. But he knew her better than anyone. "What's wrong, Red?"

A hint of a smile flitted across her face because she knew he knew her too well. "Just thinking. Needed some quiet."

"And you've had it. I've been looking for you for a while now." He reached for her hand in the dark and found it, intertwining his fingers through hers. Her skin was warm, soft . . . home. He affectionately caressed the top of her hand with his thumb. "It's not like you to just leave a party like this. So I know something's up. Talk to me."

She kept staring out at the ocean for a minute. He let

her, waiting patiently even as concern stirred his blood. Moonlight glimmered on the crests of the waves, the whooshing sound soothing, hypnotic. By the time his eyes had completely adjusted to the dark, he recognized sadness in her expression, tightening the lines of her face. He squeezed her hand. "Come on, Red," he murmured. "Please talk to me."

She finally looked back at him. "I need you to tell me something and I need you to be a hundred percent honest with me. Even if you think it'll hurt me."

His brow furrowed as his gut hummed with intuition. "I always am, Julia."

"I know." She drew a deep breath, then asked, "Do you ever wish you had kids of your own?"

Something in his chest tightened. But not for him; for *her*. "No," he said succinctly. "No, I don't. Not really."

"What does that mean exactly?" She leaned in a bit, her eyes locked on his.

"It means once in a rare while," he said, "I wonder what a baby you and I made together would have looked like. Which is natural, I think. That curiosity."

She nodded and said, "Of course. I've wondered that too." But he saw her wince the tiniest bit before she looked away, back out to the ocean.

"Hey." He squeezed her hand, willing her to meet his eyes again. "I don't long for kids, Julia. I told you that and I meant it. I can visit my nephews and nieces any time if I need a kiddo fix. Then I get to go home. To you."

"Is that enough?" she whispered.

"More than enough," he said firmly, edging in closer. "You're my family. You're all I need, all I want." With his free hand, he stroked her hair back from her face, then cupped her chin. "Not everyone needs children to feel complete."

"I know that."

"So what's going on?"

"I saw you holding Charlotte," Julia said quietly. "You

looked like you were in love. And I . . . I felt that pang. The one I get when I wonder if I . . ." Her voice trailed off.

"If you what?" He gentled his voice but was insistent. "Tell me."

"If I should have let you marry me," she whispered. "You won't have children of your own because of me. Most of the time I'm okay with that. But sometimes . . ."

His stomach wobbled at her words, and the forlorn tone of her voice. "Julia Shay Harrison, you listen to me. Right now." He gripped her chin again, firmer this time, a demand that she meet his gaze. "First of all, *let* me marry you? No one *lets* me do anything; I do what I want. And no one could have stopped me. I wanted you. I chose you. And I knew, when I did that, that we wouldn't have kids together." Something like desperate frustration bubbled inside him. "Because we talked about this, at length. Don't you remember that night? Out on the boat, a month before I proposed?"

She nodded, but she also sniffled, and it tore at him.

"We made that decision together," he reminded her calmly. "I asked you if you wanted another child. You said no."

"I didn't," she whispered. "Besides, I was too old."

"I said it then and I'm saying it again now: that's bullshit."

"No, it wasn't. I was already forty-two when we got married."

"You weren't too old," he insisted. "I said we could have our own or adopt if you wanted. But you really didn't want any more kids. And I didn't want any. We agreed on that." He paused, then asked, "Or . . . did you lie to me?"

"No!" she said staunchly.

"Okay. Well, I didn't lie to you either. I meant what I said." He kept holding her face, caressing her skin with the pad of his thumb. "I like my freedom. Always have. I just wanted you. Us." He dipped his head to look deeper into her troubled hazel eyes. "We covered this. We've been great. So where is this coming from? I don't understand."

Her shoulders lifted and fell in a listless shrug and she wouldn't look at him. "I admit it. Once in a blue moon, I think if you married someone else . . . someone younger than you, instead of older than you . . . you could've had that, and I feel guilty. Like, maybe if you'd gotten another wife pregnant, you would've warmed to the idea of having kids and been fine with it. So when you married me . . . I wonder if I . . . if I was selfish to ask that of you. Or to let you agree to what we agreed to."

His blood rushed through him as powerfully as the crashing of the waves. "If I married someone else, I'd be miserable," he said firmly. "Because *you* are my soul mate. My other half. My everything. Are you hearing me?"

Her eyes filled with tears.

"Jesus. Oh, honey . . ." He pulled her closer, wrapped his arms around her shoulders. His heart pounded as he brushed her hair back so he could rest his cheek against hers. He murmured right into her ear, "You don't need kids to be a family. *You* are my family and I'm yours."

She nodded against him but said nothing.

He struggled to stay calm. He'd never known she'd thought these things, occasionally racking herself with guilt over them. Even if it was *once in a blue moon*, it was too much. And knowing she was hurting over this, beating herself up about it, tore him up inside. "I really, really love our life together, Julia. Everything's the way I want it to be. Not having kids gives us a certain freedom others don't have. We have freedoms Charles and Lisette will never know. Our life is *ours*. We travel, we go out whenever we want, we do things—"

"I know. And yes, it's great. But . . ."

"But nothing. Besides, hello, you *have* a son. And Colin is a great guy."

"Yes, I have a son." Her eyes shone in the moonlight. "I missed fifteen years of his life, but yes, I have a son. *You don't*. And tonight, I just . . ." She drew a shaky sigh. "I saw you with Charlotte and it just hit me. That one day you might regret that you don't have children of your own." A tear rolled down her face and she swiped it away as she added in a whisper, "And you'll resent me for it."

His heart lurched. "Julia. Jesus, honey. Hear me." He tipped her chin back up so he could meet her glassy eyes. Holding her face, he vowed, "I have no regrets. And I never will. I could never resent you—you're the single best thing that's ever happened to me. *Ever*." He wiped away the tears that rolled down her face. "I love our life. I knew when I married you what the deal with kids was and I was one hundred percent fine with it. I swear that to you."

"Okay." She sniffed back the tears and nodded. "I believe you. I do."

"Promise?"

"Yes. Yes. Thank you for reassuring me." She sighed and sank into him, letting her head drop onto his shoulder. "Truthfully, I usually don't think about this anymore. I haven't in a long time. It just walloped me tonight. I don't know why. I'm sorry."

"Don't be sorry. You need reassurance, I give it freely." He wrapped his arms around her, holding her close and tight. "But I hope you really believe what I'm telling you. Tonight, once and for all, beyond the shadow of a doubt, so you'll never have this pang or worry again. Seriously. All right?"

She huffed out a long exhalation and nodded again. "Yeah. Just had a weak moment. Sorry."

He watched as she worked to compose herself. "Julia," he murmured. "Baby." He cupped her cheek, making her look into his eyes. "You're my family. My home, my heart." He kissed her lips with exquisite tenderness. "You're everything to me."

She smiled faintly. "Same here. On all of that. Honestly."

"Good." His thumb stroked her velvety skin. "Know what? I'm going to be one of those creepy people who dies the day after his spouse because he couldn't live without her. Just dies of a broken heart."

"Well, I *am* a few years older than you," she quipped, "so it's likely I'll kick off before you do. Sure you want to hold yourself to that?"

"Yup. Because I don't want a life without you in it. I don't want a *day* without you in it. I love you that much." He stared into her eyes, saw that his words had taken hold, then grazed his lips across hers.

"I feel the same way about you." She deepened the kiss, her warm mouth opening to welcome him. They kissed for a while, reconnecting and luxuriating, before she finally relaxed. He felt the tension leave her body, and again her head dropped onto his shoulder.

Running his hand down the thick curtain of her hair, up and down her back, they held each other tight. They sat that way for a long time, sharing closeness in the dark, the sounds of the waves crashing beyond, soothing them as they settled down.

"One last thing," he said softly. "If this ever crops up again . . . I hope it doesn't, but if it does, please tell me. And I'll reassure you again. I will as many times as I have to, if you need me to. Just promise you'll never slip away to cry in the dark by yourself over this, ever again. You come to me instead. Okay?"

She hugged him tightly and whispered, "Okay."

"I love you, Red."

"I love you too, Boss."

He snorted and said, "That nickname's gotta go. I'm not the boss here; you are."

She laughed softly and snuggled in closer, dropping a kiss on his neck. "No. We're equals. A total partnership, a team. That's why we work."

"That's right." He kissed her lips, nipped at the bottom one. "And don't you forget it."

She kissed him again and ran her hand down the front of

his button-down shirt. "So . . . wanna have a hot quickie here on the beach?"

His return grin was wicked. "Like you have to ask."

Pierce and Abby stepped out of the elevator. As they walked down the hallway, he reached for her hand and intertwined their fingers.

"It's this one," Abby said, stopping in front of a door at the end of the corridor.

He huffed out a sigh of exasperation. "I still don't see why you have to do this."

"I *want* to do this," she said with a grin.

"I know, but still. We live together. Have for a while. *Now* you're going all old-fashioned on me?" He snorted out a laugh. "It's a little late for that."

"I like the premise." Abby leaned into him, her dark blue eyes sparkling as she reached up to lock her arms around his neck. "I like you not seeing me until I walk down the aisle tomorrow. A tiny last bit of anticipation."

"You just want me to miss you." His hands ran down her sides to rest at her waist as the side of his mouth curved up in a playful grin. "I will, you know."

"I love that." She kissed him. "I love you."

"I love you too, Coach." He winked.

Her grin blossomed into a radiant smile.

"Have fun with your sleepover with your sister."

"Thanks, I will. Hey, at least it's not with my parents."

"Your dad would drive you bonkers."

"That's right. That's why I'm staying with Fiona."

Pierce huffed out another sigh and an exaggerated pout. "I can't see you at all tomorrow?"

"That's the idea. So don't be late." She quirked another grin. "You know. Down at the beach. Five o'clock sharp. You, me, wedding ceremony. Be there or be square."

"You didn't really just say that."

"Actually, I did."

"You're too damn adorable." He lowered his head to take her mouth in a sumptuous kiss. They stood there kissing for a minute before she pulled away.

"What will you do tomorrow?" she asked.

"Run on the beach in the morning," he said. "Go for a swim. Eat things. I'm sure Troy and Dane will be around. Maybe even hang out again with Charles and the kids; it gives Lisette a break while she's taking care of the baby. I'll take a nap at some point." He tweaked the tip of her nose. "I won't be bored while I'm missing you, don't worry."

"I'm not worried. Not at all. About anything." She caressed his cheek and smiled a dreamy smile. "This time tomorrow, we'll be married, dancing at our fabulous reception with everyone we love. I don't have a worry or a care in the world."

"That makes me really happy," he murmured, then kissed her good night.

Chapter Five

Abby woke to a bright, sunshiny day on Saturday. Looking out the wide-open window beyond, feeling the breezes on her skin, it seemed like the weather was perfect; warm, but not too hot, and there wasn't a cloud in the clear blue sky. The wedding weather gods had smiled on them and she was overjoyed.

She looked across the room; her sister was still sound asleep in the other double bed. They'd stayed up talking until almost one in the morning. Abby smiled as she recalled some of their funnier moments, and some of the heart-warming ones. Fiona was more than her older sister; she was her best friend and she cherished her.

It's my wedding day, Abby thought. *It's my WEDDING DAY!*

Excitement rushed through her. Smiling brightly, she rolled over to grab her cell phone off the nightstand between the beds. She intended to send Pierce a good-morning text, but there was one already waiting for her. An hour before, he'd written: Good morning, Miss McCord. This time to-morrow, I'll be waking you up by making love to you as I say, Good morning, Mrs. Harrison. Hope you slept well. Love you.

Jesus Christ, she loved that man. She texted back: **I love you more.**

He didn't answer right away. She figured he was either on the beach or in the pool, as he'd said he would be. So she got out of bed and crossed the room to the terrace. Sliding open the glass door, she stepped onto the balcony, leaned on the railing, and tipped her face up to the sun. Seagulls screeched as they soared overhead, and the crashing waves of the ocean ebbed in and out. Abby smiled, closed her eyes, and took a long, deep breath. Life was beautiful. Today would be a wonderful, wonderful day.

After his shower, Pierce wrapped the towel around his waist and walked into the large sitting room. The suite felt empty without Abby. He really did miss her. Knowing she was with her family somewhere on the resort property appeased him somewhat, but still . . . He'd hated going to sleep without her and hated waking up without her. Holy shit, was he a changed man. *Good thing I'm marrying her*, he thought with a wry grin.

He was supposed to meet Tess, Dane, and Julia for lunch at noon down at the outdoor restaurant. After that, he'd try to catch a catnap before the festivities kicked in. Whistling as he strode across the room, the knot of his towel loosened and dropped to the floor. With a snort of a laugh, he bent to pick it up, but something under the coffee table caught his eye. Looked like a business card or something, and two pink flower petals. He reached for the card with his left hand, then snatched up the towel with his right. His eyes ran over the words on the card . . . and the grin fell off his face.

"What the actual fuck?" he murmured as his heart rate ratcheted up a notch. He glanced around the room. There were no flowers anywhere. So what was this? Had his father sent flowers? Or contacted her? Why wouldn't Abby tell him about that? Why would she hide it from him? Why would she hide *anything* from him? His gut churned.

By the time he entered the restaurant for lunch, his mood was shit.

"Hi!" Tess smiled as she greeted him at their table, reaching out for a hug. Immediately she stopped, her hands gripping his upper arms instead. "You don't look right. What's wrong?"

"I need to talk to you," he said tightly.

"Sit," Tess commanded, and they both did.

He pulled the card from the pocket of his shorts and handed it to her. "I found this about half an hour ago. Under the coffee table in my suite."

Tess looked at it and sighed deeply. "Oh dear."

"That bastard's trying to contact her behind my back?" he ground out. "And she didn't even tell me?"

"I told her not to tell you," Tess said. "Calm down."

He felt a muscle jump in his jaw. "When did this happen?"

"Yesterday afternoon. He sent her a big bouquet of flowers." She folded her hands on the tabletop. "They're lovely, actually. They're in my room."

Pierce sat there, seething.

Tess sighed again. "She called me when they arrived and asked what she should do. I took them back to my room and told her not to mention it until after the wedding. Guess the card fell out."

"Oops." It came out as a snarl.

"Stop it," Tess said firmly. "We decided it was best not to tell you so you wouldn't get upset. You're only proving us right. Look at you."

"I think I have a right to be upset."

"Really? Why?"

Pierce practically gritted his teeth. "Are you fucking kidding me? My parents are awful people; that's why I don't want them at my wedding. And they keep popping up their ugly heads anyway. They want to ruin the day."

Tess leaned in close and looked her younger brother right in the eye. "The only one who could ruin this wedding is you. If you let them get in your head and upset you. And hey . . . look what's happening."

Pierce scowled.

"Charles has done a damn good job of keeping Dad away from you, from the wedding, from Abby, all of it. Believe me, he's been a gatekeeper all these months."

"I know," Pierce admitted in a low voice.

"Dane and I have pitched in too," Tess continued. "Both with him and with Mom. All three of us called her separately yesterday and lit into her, by the way."

Pierce let out a heavy sigh. "I appreciate that."

"They're not going to be at the wedding. Which is what you wanted." Tess reached for his hands and gripped them. "We love you. We've got your back. Mom and Dad . . . they never did right by you. No one can undo a miserable childhood. The damage was done. I've tried to compensate for that your whole life and these past few years, your big brothers finally caught up and have done the same. We didn't have it nearly as bad as you did, and yes, we'll always feel residual guilt about that, even though all of us know it wasn't any of our faults." Tess stared hard. "I know you know all this."

Pierce nodded, but his eyes flashed and his jaw still held tight. "I do know. And what you especially have always done for me, and now them too . . . it means more to me than I can ever express. Honestly."

"I know that."

"But . . . this isn't about you guys. Abby's going to be my wife. She hid this from me . . . dammit, she can't hide things from me."

"This isn't some big lie," Tess said. "It was a little white lie, for a short time. She didn't want you upset before the wedding. That's all. She was going to tell you after. C'mon,

Soccer Boy. Take some deep breaths. I thought you were past the days of letting your temper get the best of you."

Pierce sat with that, working to take it down from a boil to a simmer.

"Pierce. Sweetheart . . ." Tess's voice was quiet and gentle as she gazed at him, still holding his hands. "You haven't been insecure like this in a long time. Talk to me. Maybe I can help."

He blinked. "Is that what this is?"

"I think so. I think you're scared."

"I want to marry her more than anything. I'm not scared of marriage to her."

"I know. But once you get married . . . there's a lot more to lose. And you're scared to lose her. And the reminders of Mom and Dad, so close to the wedding . . ." Tess grimaced sadly. "They trigger you. Push your buttons. Remind you of how lost and scared you felt when you were young, and how bad their marriage was, and of everything you fear most. Triggers are wreaking havoc on you."

Pierce went very still. His heartbeat seemed to slow in his chest. "Jesus, that went deep."

"I know you very well. I understand you better than just about anyone." Tess gave his hands a squeeze. "Psychological triggers are a powerful thing. You just . . . you have to fight them, remind yourself things are different now. That you're a grown man, with a good life you've worked hard to build for yourself. And an amazing, wonderful woman is about to become your wife, and she understands you too. She loves you as much as you love her. That's why things *are* going to work out. And because you can't remind yourself of that at this moment, I'm here to remind you. I've got you."

His mouth went dry and a lump rose in his throat.

"Our parents really suck. That's the sad truth. But they can only get to you if you let them," Tess asserted gently. "Don't let them."

"I usually don't," Pierce finally said. "Not anymore. I've been good. But I guess . . . what you're saying has merit." His stomach churned as he thought about it. "I just want this to be perfect for her. I don't want them tainting it in any way . . ." His throat thickened as he got out the rest. ". . . and make her regret marrying me. Choosing me."

"Never happen. Can I remind you of something?" Tess asked, rubbing his hands. "The very first night you introduced her to the family, at that disastrous wedding party Dad threw for Dane and Julia. Dad attacked you viciously in front of everyone, and he attacked her too. What did she do?"

"Gave it right back to him," Pierce said quietly. "Stood up for me. And for herself."

"That's right. That's no shrinking violet you've got there. Dad can be intimidating as hell. She told him off her first night out." Tess smiled. "She's got guts, she's really smart and insightful, and she has a big, warm heart."

He nodded. "She's the most amazing woman I've ever met. Other than you, of course."

Tess grinned before continuing. "That night, she made it clear she had your back. But you were so thrown by it all, you tried to push her away. Even got her to break up with you." Tess squeezed his hands as he winced, remembering. "You almost did irreversible damage. You had to really work for it, beg her to come back. And she did. Because she knew, deep down, why you'd done it in the first place. She knew you that well, even then. She chose you too. Right?"

Again Pierce nodded, releasing a shaky breath.

"She knows you, she understands you, she chooses you, and she loves you. Not she loves you *anyway*, Pierce. She just loves you. Do you get the distinction?"

He nodded yet again and said, "I'm the luckiest bastard on earth that she does."

"She's pretty lucky too. You're a great guy." Tess's voice dropped to a fervent whisper as she asked, "When are you truly, truly going to believe that? I know Mom left you and Dad abused you. But you are worthy of love and worthy of Abby and worthy of the good life you have now and will continue to have. *Believe that.*"

It was like she'd gut-punched him. Jesus, if she was wrong, it wouldn't have hurt. Her astute words wouldn't have stolen his breath or made tears sting his eyes.

"Oh, honey." Tess rubbed his hands, gripped them harder. "The triggers did this to you. *Fight.* You're a fighter. So understand what's getting to you and work on overcoming them. But don't be upset with Abby over this little thing."

"That's what Dad wanted," he said, realizing it as he said it out loud. "For me, and her, to be upset on our wedding day, even if only for a few minutes."

"Right," Tess said on a sigh. "Look, she didn't lie to you. She's not always hiding things from you. She hid this one little thing because she was protecting you. Because she loves you so much. Like you would do for her if the situation was reversed."

Unable to speak, he nodded again. His throat had thickened and he swallowed hard. His jaw clenched.

Tess rose and pulled him to his feet. When he stood, she moved close and hugged him tight. He hugged her back, sighed, and rested his head on hers.

"You're getting married tonight," Tess said in his ear. "This should be the best day of your life. Don't let Dad or Mom or anyone take that away from you."

"You're right," he said, squeezing her back. "Absolutely right."

"Well, I'm the smartest of the four of us," she reminded him cheekily.

"God, that's so true." He smacked a kiss on her curly hair and pulled back to look at her. "Thank you. So much."

She reached up to hold his face in her hands and said, "I will always be here for you. You have Abby now, but that will never change. I've always got your back."

"For which I will be forever grateful."

Tess rubbed his scruffy jaw. "You're going to shave before the wedding, right?"

"Yes, ma'am."

"Okay, good."

He grinned but said quietly, "I didn't know I was doing that. The things you said." He huffed out a sigh and rubbed the back of his neck. "Jesus Christ, Tess."

"Lifelong, ingrained habits are very, very hard to break," she said. "A few steps forward, a few steps back. No damage done. Cut yourself some slack."

He nodded. "I'm a work in progress, I guess."

"We all are, Pierce. We all are. We stop growing and learning, we're dead in the water." She moved to sit down. "Now, let's get you fed before we get you married."

As Pierce sat, Dane and Julia approached the table. "Sorry we're late," Dane said as they all kissed one another's cheeks in greeting. "Did we miss anything?"

"Nah," Pierce said and reached for his water glass. "It's going to be a great day."

Chapter Six

Several months before, it had taken a long discussion and half a bottle of whiskey when Abby told her parents she wouldn't be getting married in a church. She'd sat them down and, despite their misgivings, got them to understand she wanted to be married out on the beach. Outside, by the ocean, with nothing above her but the sky.

Her dad had growled. Her mom had frowned. But, as always, they'd listened to her and ultimately come around to supporting her unequivocally.

"You better pray it doesn't rain," Jesse had said. "Or you'll wish you did it the traditional way, with a roof over your head. Marrying an untraditional guy, now this . . ." He sighed and shook his head, then wagged a finger at her in mock exasperation. "Whatever you want, that's how it'll be."

Abby had hugged her father tight. "You're still gonna walk me down the aisle, right?"

His grizzled expression had softened at that. He'd reached up, touched her cheek, and said with pride and deep affection, "You kidding? Been waiting to do that since the day you were born. No one on earth could stop me."

Now, as Abby stood in the resort, fully dressed and waiting,

she placed her hand in the crook of her father's arm and said,
"I'm so glad you're here with me, Dad."

He smiled down at her. "Nowhere else I'd be, sweetheart."
He straightened the jacket of his navy suit, then leaned in to
kiss her on the forehead. "I can't get over you. You look like
an angel. A princess. All those unearthly beautiful things.
Really."

Jesse McCord didn't give mushy compliments often. She
was moved. "Thank you." She drew a shaky breath and tried
to stay calm over the fluttering of her heart.

"Abby." Her father spoke quietly. "Listen. I, uh . . . just
wanna say, I know you two are going to be good. In your
marriage. Pierce is all right. I gave him a hard time at first,
sure. He deserved it."

Abby snorted out a giggle. "You were brutal."

"I'm a man with two daughters, that's my God-given
right," he said without apology. "But I've gotten to know
Pierce pretty well, and you were right. He's a good man. Got
his rough edges, but . . . hell, so do I." Jesse cleared his
throat. "I'd take you out of here right now if I thought you
needed me to. You know that, right?"

She blinked at him. "I don't need you to. I love him, Dad."

"I know. I said if I *thought* you needed me to. Just reminding you how I'll always, always have your back."

Her throat tightened a bit. "I know that, Dad. Thank you."

"You're fine. He loves you. From what I've seen, he probably loves you a little more than you love him, and that's a
good thing. He's good to you, and he's always gonna be good
to you. Besides, I'll kill him if he's not. So don't be nervous.
Enjoy everything today." He patted her hand on his forearm.
"I'm right here."

"Oh, Dad . . ." Tears stung her eyes and she swallowed
hard. "Don't you dare make me cry now."

"Well, then, don't cry, that's all."

She smiled through the tears. "Yes, sir. I love you so much."

"I love you too."

Marla, the resort employee who was their wedding coordinator, approached them with an excited smile. "Are you ready? Because we all are if you are."

Abby sniffed hard and nodded. "I'm ready."

"Let's do this, then . . ." Marla reached up for Abby's veil, lowering the front part over her face. "Want to help her with that, Dad?"

As Marla sprinted off to set things in motion, Jesse fixed the veil, making sure it was correctly in place. He gazed down at his daughter with something like wonder in his eyes. "You're the most beautiful bride I've ever seen," he said. "Well, except for your mother. Sorry, that stands."

"Thanks, Dad." She smiled as she gave his arm a squeeze, then reached over with her free hand to pick up her bridal bouquet. The white, yellow, and orange flowers were vibrant. "God. These are so gorgeous, but they're actually a little heavy!"

Jesse chuckled.

Marla moved to the glass doors and opened them. The wedding party was already out on the lawn, moving toward the beach.

"You got this," Jesse said, looking out before them.

Abby took a deep breath and looked out too. Excitement and exhilaration soared through her, lifting her heart. "Yes, I do."

As John Legend's "Stay with You" started to play over speakers aimed at the beach, the wedding party started their walk. They were brought to the edge of where the great lawn ended at the sand and made their way down the makeshift aisle, a boardwalk that stretched down the beach. Over 120 guests sat in white folding chairs on either side of the aisle, which was lined with white ribbons, glass jars with candles inside, and sunflowers hearty enough to withstand the soft breezes that blew off the ocean.

Pierce walked first, by himself, smiling a deeply contented smile. Striking in his light gray suit, white dress shirt, and gray striped tie, the wind gently ruffled his dark hair as he reached the standing canopy at the end of the aisle, mere feet from the ocean. He shook the hand of the wedding officiant, then turned to face the crowd. He flashed another smile and watched the wedding party come down the aisle.

Troy walked with Fiona, then Charles with Tess, then Dane with Allison. The men were handsome in their slate-gray suits and sky-blue ties, the women lovely in their sky-blue sheath dresses. Then came Dylan; Abby's nine-year-old nephew half-jogged down the aisle, a wide, excited smile on his adorable face, bringing warm laughs from the guests. Ava looked so pretty, older than her ten years. Her dark hair in a French braid and her slim frame in a dress resembling the bridesmaids', she was poised as could be as she let white and yellow flower petals flutter from her fingers. Lastly, Carolyn beamed as she proudly made her way down the aisle; the attractive mother of the bride was gorgeous in her sparkly ice-blue gown. Going off script, she went to Pierce and gave him a kiss on the cheek. Touched by the impulsive gesture, he hugged her quickly before she took her seat at the end of the front row.

An anticipatory hush fell over the crowd. John Legend's heartfelt, romantic song was perfect as it continued playing.

Pierce narrowed his eyes as they locked on his bride. A vision in white floating on the arm of her tall father, Abby's long, gauzy veil blew back in the breeze as they made their way from the grass to the sand and started down the aisle. As she got closer, and he could see her better, Pierce's breath caught. He knew she'd be a beautiful bride, but seeing her like this . . . she was extraordinary. She literally took his breath away.

His eyes traveled over her. Her silky blond hair, usually so
pin straight, had been curled at the ends, now barely touching
her bare shoulders. The sides of her hair had been pulled up,
tucked somewhere in that veil. Her strapless gown had a
curved top and was fitted down to her knee, where it softly
flared out into waves of gliding, billowing layers, down over
her feet and in the back, forming a train. Sunlight caught in
the fabric, making it shimmer and sparkle as she moved. She
was luminous. The whole look was elegant, classy, and time-
less, with a hint of sexy and a dash of sassy . . . just like
Abby herself. Pierce had never seen such perfection in his
life and she was walking down the aisle to *him*. Love overwhelmed him, rushing through his entire body.

He smiled so wide his cheeks started to hurt. She smiled
back, meeting his eyes as she got closer . . . and the world
fell away. All he saw was her. His woman, this wonderful gift
of a woman; his best friend, his lover, his partner, his rock.
His heart pounded with the depth of emotion that flowed
through him.

When she reached him, he stretched out his hand to her.
Her smile widened, and if he wasn't mistaken, her eyes were
glassy. Jesse took her hand from the crook of his elbow and
kissed the top of it before placing her hand in Pierce's. It was
the first time Pierce had ever seen her dad too choked up to
speak.

"I'll take good care of her," Pierce promised in a husky
whisper.

Jesse nodded and patted his shoulder. Then he kissed the
side of Abby's head and went to sit with her mother in the
front row. Fiona leaned in to take Abby's bouquet. Finally,
Abby turned to Pierce, and they clasped hands, intertwining
their fingers as they smiled at each other.

"You're absolutely stunning," Pierce whispered. "My
God, Abby. *Wow*."

Yup, she was tearing up. "Thank you," she whispered back.

"Let's do this." He grinned as he dropped a wink.

She nodded and smiled tremulously. "Yeah, let's."

While the guests enjoyed a lavish cocktail hour on the wide expanse of lawn behind the resort, the wedding party posed for photos on the beach. The sun's angle had shifted, just starting to deepen the blue of the sky. The ocean was a perfect backdrop as the photographer snapped a million pictures. At the end of the hour, Pierce announced, "I'm starving. And we need drinks. Time to celebrate!"

The wedding party all started to march back up the beach toward the resort. Abby grabbed Pierce's hand, stopping him. "Wait."

His brow furrowed as he looked down at her. "You okay?"

"I'm amazing," she said with a smile. "I just wanted a minute alone with you before we go to the reception."

Smiling back, he turned and pulled her into his arms. "That sounds perfect." He kissed her lips lightly. "You're perfect."

"I'm not," she said, even as she pressed herself closer into his embrace.

"You are. You're perfect for me." He kissed her again. "And I can't stop staring at you. You're off-the-charts beautiful, Abby. I'm the luckiest man alive."

Her smile deepened. "Thank you for that." She hugged him, resting her head on his shoulder. "The ceremony was perfect."

"I don't remember half of it," he admitted. "I just couldn't take my eyes off you."

She laughed. "Typical."

"I'm sure it was great," he went on with the joke. "I bet it was meaningful, right? Lots of nice things said?"

She pinched his ass and he yelped.

"I was there, baby," he assured her. "I was there. I've

rarely felt so present in my life. I just . . ." He tipped her chin up so they could look into each other's eyes. "I'm going to give you a good life. We're going to have everything. I promise."

"I'm going to give you a good life too," she said. "We're in this together."

They kissed tenderly, holding each other close as the waves crashed beyond.

"I love you," she said. "Husband."

He grinned. "I love you too, wife."

"We'd better get to the party," she murmured.

"I know." But he kissed her a few more times before taking her by the hand and bringing her along.

The reception was held in the spacious event room, with dangling crystal chandeliers and high glass walls that displayed panoramic views of the ocean and beach. Tiny white lights strewn everywhere and endless amounts of flowers added to the atmosphere, making it opulent. The DJ played all the best songs, magnificent food and endless drinks were served, and the guests talked and danced the evening away.

Midway through, Pierce sat at their dais as he watched Abby dance with her father. She'd chosen Stevie Wonder's "Isn't She Lovely" as their song, and if Pierce wasn't wrong, Jesse looked a little glassy-eyed as he twirled his daughter in his arms. The man was a grizzly bear, but when it came to his family, he was just a big mush. For a second, Pierce thought of his own father . . . having that traditional dance of the groom and his mother . . . then willfully batted the images away. He had his own family now. Abby.

"Hey there." Charles came up behind him and clapped him on the shoulder.

"Hey." Pierce rose to stand beside his oldest brother. He grabbed his half-empty beer and took another sip.

"She's stunning," Charles remarked, his eyes resting on Abby as she danced.

"I know." Pierce nodded and looked at her too. "She really is."

"She's . . . glowing. From the inside out." Charles quirked a grin. "I've rarely seen a more joyful bride. You did that, you know."

Pleased, Pierce could only grin back.

"You having a good time?" Charles asked.

"Hell yeah. You?"

"I am. You guys planned a beautiful wedding and a great party."

"Well, I only do a great party," Pierce joked. "Still got a rep to uphold."

They chuckled together. Then Charles said, "It's the first time we've been to a big party as the six of us." His gaze flicked over to his wife and went soft with adoration. "Lisette is enjoying herself. She's tired, of course, but she will be for a while—like a few years. So I'm glad she's here; she needed some fun."

"Glad you're all enjoying it." Pierce shot a glance over to the table where the entire Harrison clan sat. Lisette looked pretty in a royal purple dress, her dark hair pulled off her face in a slick ponytail that tumbled down her back. She did look relaxed, smiling leisurely, and Pierce was glad for her. Seated next to her, Tess had the baby in her arms, rocking her and cooing at her. Ava, Thomas, and Myles were eating and talking. Dane sat beside Julia, a knockout in emerald green. The woman didn't have it in her to be anything but eye-popping. They held hands on the tabletop as they talked with her son, Colin. Now almost twenty-four, he was a quiet, reserved, but friendly young man. Pierce liked him.

"That's a great group over there," he murmured.

"Who?" Charles followed his gaze. "You mean our family?"

Pierce nodded. Suddenly a lump formed in his throat, and

he swallowed it down. He cleared his throat and said, "If you'd told me two years ago that I'd be living on Long Island, getting married, and happy to be in the fold with my family, I'd've told you to stop smoking crack. I'd have laughed in your face."

Charles nodded slowly, considering. "Well, you were a hot mess when you came back here two years ago."

At that, Pierce barked out a laugh. "True. That's true. Thanks."

"Look how far you've come." Charles's voice wasn't needling but warm.

"I just did and it almost knocked me on my ass." Pierce sipped his beer to ease the tightness in his throat. "Growing up, I thought you and Dane didn't care about me. Only Tess. You guys were off doing your things. I hated you for that."

"I know," Charles said quietly, the remorse evident. "We were much older than you, but still . . . I'll always regret that period of time. I wish I could go back and—"

"I know. But that's all in the past. I'm not bringing it up to guilt you. I'm saying, look at everything now . . . look at that table. My whole family is here for me. And I *wanted* you all to be here. And I'm happy to be married. And it's just . . ." Pierce shook his head in wonder. "Funny how life works out, that's all."

"Indeed." Charles reached up to squeeze his brother's shoulder. "Listen . . . quick married life tip."

Pierce's brows shot up. "Really? Didn't you just get married in May?"

"Hey, wiseass, it's my second marriage. I know *some* things. Shut up and listen."

"I'm all ears."

"You've already started heading in that direction," Charles began, "but the fact is, you're likely going to spend more time with Abby and her family as time goes on. It's a natural progression. The wife usually dictates the social schedule and her family usually takes precedence. Especially when that family is as close as the McCords are."

Pierce nodded, listening.

"Luckily for you, they're really good people. I'm grateful to see they've taken you in as they have. It'll help make things even easier for you as a couple, especially when you have kids someday. But . . ." Charles rubbed his jaw as he chose his words. "You'll always have a place with the Harrisons too. Just don't forget that. No guilt here, no pressure—you come around when you can. But *do* come around, okay? We're here. We love you. Both you and your wife."

Pierce blinked. Charles wasn't usually an openly emotional man, but he had definitely softened since Lisette had entered his life. And though the brothers had grown closer over the past year or so, this was one of the most heartfelt declarations Charles had ever made to him. Pierce was so moved, he almost couldn't speak. "Thanks. I won't forget." He stared at his oldest brother. "Listen, I know you've been totally on guard behind the scenes . . . keeping Dad away from us and the wedding all these months. Maybe Mom too. This is me officially thanking you for that."

Charles shrugged, nonchalant. "My pleasure."

"No, seriously. It means a lot," Pierce said. "It's, uh . . . it's nice to have a powerful, protective big brother."

"You have two, actually," Charles reminded him.

"I know. Yeah. But *you* . . . *our* past has been . . . I just really appreciate it, man."

"You're very welcome." The side of Charles's mouth curved in an affectionate half grin. "I'll always have your back. And I know you have mine too."

They stood in silence for a few seconds. Then Pierce set his bottle down and threw his arms around Charles, clasping him in a hug. Charles was jolted for a second in shock but immediately embraced him, giving him a clap on the back for good measure.

* * *

As the resort employees wheeled the wedding cake away, Pierce kissed a last tiny drop of icing off Abby's lips. "Mmm. That was good."

"I guess we can finally sit down now," she said and turned to head back to their dais at the front of the glass-walled room.

"Um . . . wait. I have a better idea." He grasped her hand and led her across the dance floor, then out of the room altogether.

"Where are we going?" she asked.

"An idea got in my head," he said, "and now it's a moral imperative." He flashed a wicked smile that promised pure sin, then pulled her down the wide hallway.

"We are so not doing this." Abby giggled.

"We so are." He kept looking around, intent on his search.

"I never knew you had a wedding dress fantasy," she said.

"I never knew I did either 'til I saw you in that." He stopped and yanked her against him, kissing her hard and hot. His tongue plundered her mouth as his hands went around to squeeze her bottom. "I wanna push up that dress and drive myself into you," he whispered in her ear. He nipped the lobe, making her breath hitch. "I won't be satisfied until I watch you come apart, feel you shudder, hear you gasp my name while you're in this dress."

"You're dirty," she breathed, shivering as he licked the side of her neck.

"I wanna dirty you up *right now*," he said. "C'mon." He grabbed her hand again and led her down the corridor.

"We could just go up to our suite," she pointed out.

"Nah, not as fun," he said. "We need, like, quick and hot broom-closet sex."

"In the middle of our wedding day?"

"Hell yeah, on our wedding day!"

Both laughing, he stopped short in front of a door marked

"Supply Closet" and turned to her with a wide smile of victory. "The gods are with us," he declared and pushed the door open.

Inside, a couple was locked in a hot and heavy embrace against the wall. All four of them gasped at the same time. It was Troy and Fiona.

Abby's jaw dropped and her eyes flew wide. She barked out a laugh, then clapped her hand over her mouth.

"Oh my *God*," Fiona groaned, flushing bright red.

"Um, we're a little busy here," Troy growled. His ire was a bit less fearsome with his light brown hair tousled and Fiona's lipstick smeared on his lips.

Pierce gave a quick nod. "As you were." He shut the door quickly, then turned to look at his wife in surprise. They dissolved into laughter.

"I think that just killed the mood for me," Abby said as they walked away.

"I think I'm now more determined than ever," Pierce vowed.

When they returned to the reception eighteen minutes later, after a fast, hot romp in an empty coat room, Pierce and Abby were the very picture of a put-together bride and groom, not a hair out of place.

They walked around the room, hand in hand, chatting up every single guest who'd attended as they all ate their main course. They both made sure to keep straight faces as first Fiona reentered the room, then Troy a few minutes later. They gladly accepted the glasses of water Julia pushed into their hands, the hugs from their niece and nephews, the well-wishes of everyone they spoke with.

Toward the end of the evening, the sun outside dipped farther into the horizon, morphing the sky into a blend of blues, hot pink, and marmalade orange. Pierce took the microphone from the DJ, stopped the music, and asked for a moment. Standing across the room with her parents, Abby looked at him quizzically, with no idea what he was doing.

"Hi, everyone." Pierce flashed a ridiculously charming grin, the one that had grabbed Abby the very first time they met. Even now, it gave her heart the tiniest tug.

"I just wanted to thank you all for being here with us today," he said, his marine-blue eyes scanning the room as he spoke. "We're glad you were able to share this day with us. And we especially want to thank our families and the wedding party . . . you've been there for us, and Abby and I really do appreciate it." His gaze landed on her, and when it did, his smile turned warmer. "My beautiful Abby . . . my God, people, have you ever seen a more beautiful bride in your life? I know I haven't."

The crowd oohed and ahhed, and a few people applauded. Flattered, Abby felt herself blush but only smiled back at him, curious to hear what else he had to say.

"When Abby and I started dating, at first I messed it up. Badly. But I was smart enough to beg, and she gave me another chance. I thank God for that every day," Pierce murmured into the mic. He stared at her, talking directly to her now. "Abby, I've become a better man because you came into my life. I'm not overstating that." He smirked as he added, "Ask my family; they'll tell you. Some louder than others."

His siblings chuckled audibly.

He grinned at their response but continued to talk to her. "You're the best person I've ever met. You're smart and passionate and strong. You give so much to everyone. You've given me so much . . . strength and purpose and support. You're the home I always looked for. You're everything to me, baby. I love you so much."

Her eyes stung with tears and her breath caught. Never had she expected such an open declaration like this; it wasn't his style . . . but there he was, saying these things in front of everyone they knew. *I love you too*, she mouthed back.

He smiled, the corners of his eyes crinkling. He looked around the room and said, "So. The *second* time we were dating . . ." The crowd laughed. "I heard this song one night on the radio, after I dropped her back home. I started listening to the lyrics and it moved me so much I had to pull over. Because the words had described me, and my life before I met Abby, perfectly. It also described what I wanted for the future perfectly. It was, um . . . one of those epiphany moments, you know? I was just frozen, sitting in my car. Because I heard this song . . . and I imagined dancing with her to it at our wedding."

Abby lost it. Tears rolled out of her eyes, right down her face.

"So, Abby? I know it's not our official wedding song—we did that already—but will you please come have this one special dance with me?" Pierce held out a hand.

The crowd murmured, some people breaking into applause as Abby crossed the ballroom to go to him. She flung herself at him and held tight. His arms wrapped around her.

"I can't believe you," she sobbed.

"I know, I'm ruining your makeup." He pulled back to wipe her cheeks. "Sorry."

"I'll never forget this as long as I live," she whispered. She raised her hands to hold his face. "You're amazing. That was beautiful. I love you so much." She pressed her lips to his. As they kissed, the guests applauded, and the song Pierce had asked for started to play: "Forever in My Life" by Prince. He pulled her into his arms and pressed his cheek to hers; her arms slid around his waist and she closed her eyes.

As the quiet ballad played, Pierce and Abby danced in the center of the room. All eyes were on them, but it was as if they were the only ones there. They held each other close, swaying gently to the music, as Pierce sang every single word into her ear along with the song.

For those few minutes, a hush fell over the room, as if a spell had been cast. The song played and they danced and he whispered every word to her and Abby held him close. As her love for him battered her like a tidal wave, she clutched at him, holding on to him to keep her steady and upright.

When the song ended, the room broke into thunderous applause. He took her face in his hands. "See why that song means something to me? That was me, Abby. That was me until I found you."

She sniffled hard, and he kissed her lips gently.

"Remember that date we had," she said, her voice still quavering, "when you bought like two hundred dollars' worth of sushi and I said you might have gone a little over the top?"

He nodded.

"And you said, 'I excel at over the top. It's one of my special gifts,'" she quoted.

He grinned. "Sounds like me."

"Yup. Well, it's true. You've had a lot of those over-the-top moments," she said, sniffling again. "Proposing to me on top of a mountain in Sedona . . . surprising me with wanting to buy that wonderful house . . . making sure Fiona had your credit card so she could plan an extravagant bachelorette party at that spa for me. Those were pretty over-the-top things. Nice things. But all of that pales compared to this." She shook her head. "I don't think you'll ever be able to top this moment," she said. "This was the single most romantic thing you've ever said or done. I've never been so moved, so touched, in my entire life."

"Aww, babe." He lowered his head and kissed her, long and sweet. "I'll never stop trying to top it, though."

"Because you're so competitive," she said on a laugh.

"No. Because you're worth it."